THIS COULD NOT BE HAPPENING!

But it was. A spirit-Kal'enedral was manifesting before Tarma's and Kethry's astonished eyes, a spirit which was violating every precept to appear.

He seemed to be fighting against something; his form wavered in and out of visibility as he held out frantic, empty hands to her, and he seemed to be laboring to speak. Kethry saw with mage-sight the veil of sickly white power that was encasing the spirit like a filthy web, keeping him from full manifestation.

"There's—Goddess, there's a counterspell—" Kethry started out of her entrancement. "It's preventing *any* magic from entering this room! He can't manifest! I—I have to break it, or—"

"Don't!" Tarma hissed. "You break a counterspell and they'll *know* one of us is a mage!"

Tarma turned back to the spirit to see that he had given up the effort to speak—and she saw that his hands were moving. "Keth—his hands—"

As Kethry's eyes were again drawn to the wavering figure, Tarma read his message. *Death-danger*, she read, and *assassins. . . .*

OATHBREAKERS

BOOK II: VOWS AND HONOR

MERCEDES LACKEY

DAW BOOKS, INC.

DONALD A. WOLLHEIM, FOUNDER

375 Hudson Street, New York, NY 10014

ELIZABETH R. WOLLHEIM
SHEILA E. GILBERT
PUBLISHERS

DAW Book Collectors No. 768.

First Printing, January 1989

8   9   10   11   12   13   14

DAW TRADEMARK REGISTERED
U.S. PAT. OFF. AND FOREIGN COUNTRIES
—MARCA REGISTRADA
HECHO EN U.S.A.

PRINTED IN THE U.S.A.

Dedicated to:
Betsy, Don and Elsie

The *real* magic-makers

Thanks, folks.

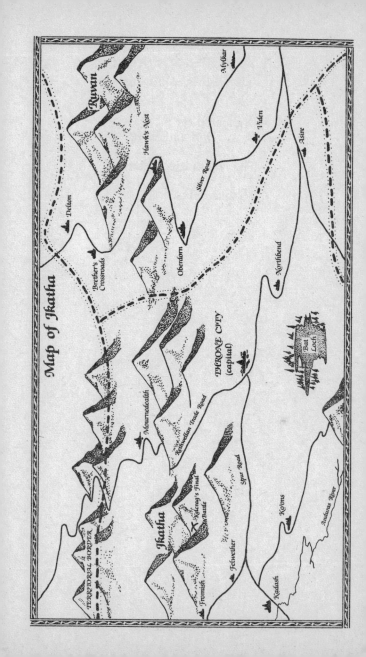

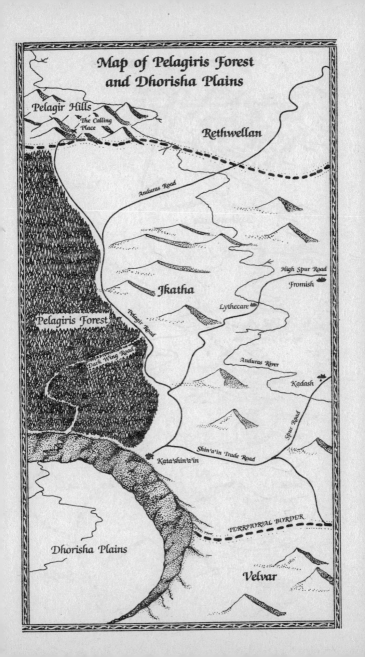

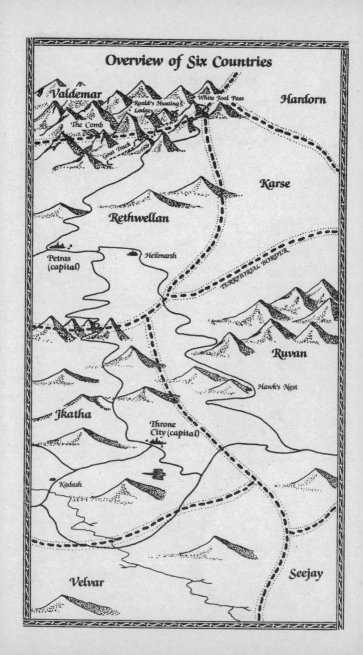

One

It was a dark and stormy night. . . .

:Pah!: Warrl said with disgust so thick Tarma could taste it. *:Must you even* think *in cliches?:*

Tarma took her bearings during another flash of lightning, tried and failed to make out Warrl's shaggy bulk against watery blackness, then thought back at him, *Well it* is, *damnit!*

Tarma shena Tale'sedrin, who was Shin'a'in nomad, Kal'enedral (or, to outClansmen, a "Swordsworn"), and most currently Scoutmaster for the mercenary company called "Idra's Sunhawks" was *not* particularly happy at this moment. She was sleet-drenched, cold and numb, and mired to her armpits; as was her companion, the lupine *kyree* Warrl. The Sunhawks' camp was black as the inside of a box at midnight, for all it was scarcely an hour past sunset. Her hair was plastered flat to her skull, and trickles of icy water kept running into her eyes. She couldn't even feel the ends of her fingers anymore. Her feet hurt, her joints ached, her nose felt so frozen it was like to fall off, and her teeth were chattering hard enough to splinter. She was not pleased, having to stumble around in the dark and freezing rain to find the tent she shared with her partner and oathbound sister, the White Winds sorceress, Kethry.

The camp was dark out of necessity; even in a downpour sheltered fires would normally burn in the firepits in front of each tent, or a slow-burning

11

torch would be staked out in the lee of every fourth, but that was impossible tonight. You simply couldn't keep a fire lit when the wind howled at you from directions that changed moment by moment, driving the rain before it; and torches under canvas were a danger even the most foolhardy would forgo. A few of the Sunhawks had lanterns or candles going in their tents; but the weather was foul enough that most preferred to go straight to sleep when not on duty. It was too plaguey cold and wet to be sociable. For heat, most stuck to the tiny charcoal braziers Idra had insisted they each pack at the beginning of this campaign. The Sunhawks had known their Captain too well to argue about (what had seemed at the time) a silly burden; now they were grateful for her foresight.

But with the rain coming down first in cascades, then in water*walls*, Tarma couldn't see the faint glow of candles or lanterns shining through the canvas walls that would have told her where the tents were. So she slogged her way through the camp mostly by memory and was herself grateful to Idra for insisting on an *orderly* camp, laid out neatly, in proper rows, and not the hugger-mugger arrangement some of the other merc officers were allowing. At least she wasn't tripping over tent ropes or falling into firepits.

:I can smell Keth and magic,: Warrl said into her mind. *:You should see the mage-light soon.:*

"Thanks, Furball," Tarma replied, a little more mollified; she knew he wouldn't *hear* her over the howl of the wind, but he'd read the words in her mind. She kept straining her eyes through the tempest for a sight of the witchlight Keth had promised to leave at the front—to distinguish their tent from the two hundred odd just like it.

They were practically on top of it before she saw the light, a blue glow outlining the door flap and brightening the fastenings. She wrestled with the balky rawhide ties (the cold made her fingers stiff) and it took so long to get them unfastened that she was swearing enough to warm the whole camp before she had the tent flaps open. Having Warrl pressed up against her like a sodden, unhappy cat did not help.

The wind practically threw Tarma into the tent, and half the sleet that was knifing down on their camp tried to come in with her. Warrl remained plastered against her side, not at all helpful, smelling in the pungent, penetrating way only a wet wolf can smell—even if Warrl only resembled a wolf superficially. The *kyree* was not averse to reminding Tarma several times a day (as, in fact, he was doing now) that they *could* have been curled up in a cozy inn if they hadn't signed on with this mercenary company.

She turned her back to the occupant of the tent as soon as she got past the tent flaps; she needed all her attention to get them laced shut against the perverse pull of the wind. "Gods of damnation!" she spat through stiff lips, "Why did I *ever* think this was a good idea?"

Kethry, only just now waking from a light doze, refrained from replying; she just waited until Tarma got the tent closed up again. Then she spoke three guttural words, activating the spell she'd set there before drowsing off—and a warm yellow glow raced around the tent walls, meeting and spreading upward until the canvas was bathed in mellow light and the temperature within suddenly rose to that of a balmy spring day. Tarma sighed and sagged a little.

"Let me take that," Kethry said then, unwinding herself from the thick wool blankets of her bedroll, rising, and pulling the woolen coat, stiff with ice, from Tarma's angular shoulders. "Get out of those soaked clothes."

The swordswoman shook water out of her short-cropped black hair, and only just prevented Warrl from trying the same maneuver.

"Don't you dare, you flea-bitten cur! Gods above and below, you'll soak every damned thing in the tent!"

Warrl hung his head and looked sheepish, and waited for his mindmate to throw an old thread-bare horse blanket over him. Tarma enveloped him in it, head to tail, held it in place while he shook himself, then used it to towel off his coarse gray-black fur.

"Glad to see you, Greeneyes," Tarma continued, stripping herself down to the skin, occasionally wincing as she moved. She rummaged in her pack, finding new underclothing, and finally pulling on dry breeches, thick leggings and shirt of a dark brown lambswool. "I thought you'd still be with your crew—"

Kethry gave an involuntary shudder of sympathy at the sight of her partner's nearly-emaciated frame. Tarma was always thin, but as this campaign had stretched on and on, she'd become nothing but whipcord over bone. She hadn't an ounce of flesh to spare; no wonder she complained of being cold so much! And the scars lacing her golden skin only gave a faint indication of the places where she'd taken deeper damage—places that would ache demonically in foul weather. Kethry gave her spell another little mental nudge, sending the temperature of the tent a notch upward.

I should have been doing this on a regular basis, she told herself guiltily. *Well—that's soon mended.*

"—so there's not much more I can do." The sweet-faced sorceress gathered strands of hair like sun-touched amber into both hands, twisting her curly mane into a knot at the back of her neck. The light from the shaded lantern which hung on the tent's crossbar, augmented by the light of the shielding spell, was strong enough that Tarma noted the dark circles under her cloudy green eyes. "Tresti is accomplishing more than I can at this point. You know my magic isn't really the Healing kind, and on top of that, right now we have more wounded men than women."

"And Need'll do a man about as much good as a stick of wood."

Kethry glanced at the plain shortsword slung on the tent's centerpole, and nodded. "To tell you the truth, lately she won't heal anybody but you or me of anything but *major* wounds, so she isn't really useful at all at this point. I wonder sometimes if maybe she's saving herself— Anyway, the last badly injured woman was your scout Mala this morning."

"We got her to you in time? Gods be thanked!" Tarma felt the harpwire-taut muscles of her shoulders go lax with relief. Mala had intercepted an arrow when the scouts had been surprised by an enemy ambush; Tarma had felt personally responsible, since she'd sent Warrl off in the opposite direction only moments before. The scout had been barely conscious by the time they'd pounded up to the Sunhawk camp.

"Only just; an arrow in the gut is not something even for a Master-Healer to trifle with, and all we have is a Journeyman."

"Teach me to steal eggs, why don't you? Tell me something I *don't* know," Tarma snapped, ice-blue eyes narrowed in irritation, harsh voice and craggy-featured scowl making her look more like a hawk than ever.

Oops. A little too near the bone, I think.

"Temper," Kethry cautioned; it had taken years of partnership for them to be able to say the right thing at the right time to each other, but these days they seldom fouled the relationship. "Whatever happened, you can't undo it; you'd tell me that if the case were reversed. And Mala's all right, so there's no permanent harm done."

"Gah—" Tarma shook her head again, then continued the shake right down to her bare feet, loosening all the muscles that had been tensed against cold and anger and frustration. "Sorry. My nerves have gone all to hell. Finish about Mala so I can tell the others."

"Nothing much to tell; I had Need unsheathed and in her hands when they brought her inside the camp. The arrow's out, the wound's purified and stitched and half-healed, or better. She'll be back dodging arrows—with a little more success, I hope!— in about a week. After that all I could do that was at all useful was to set up a *jesto-vath* around the infirmary tent—that's a shielding spell like the one I just put on ours. After that I was useless, so I came back here. It was bad enough out there I figured a *jesto-vath* on *our* tent was worth the energy expense, and I waited for you to get in before putting it in place so I wouldn't have to cut it. Can't have the Scoutmaster coming down with a fever." She smiled, and her wide green eyes sparkled with mischief. "Listen to you, though— two years ago, you wouldn't have touched a command position, and now you're fretting over your scouts exactly the way Idra fusses over the rest of us."

Tarma chuckled, feeling the tense muscles all over her body relaxing. "You know the saying."

"Only too well—'That was then, this is now; the moment is never the same twice.' "

"You're learning. Gods, having a mage as a partner is useful."

Tarma threw herself onto her bedroll, rolling over onto her back and putting her hands behind her head. She stared at the canvas of the tent roof, bright with yellow mage-light, and basked in the heat.

"I pity the rest of the Hawks, with nobody to weatherproof their tents, and nothing but an itty-bitty brazier to keep it warm. Unless they're twoing, in which case I wish them well."

"Me too," Kethry replied with a tired smile, sitting crosslegged on her own bedroll to fasten the knot of hair more securely, "though there's only a handful really twoing it. I rather suspect even the ones that aren't will bundle together for warmth, though, the way we used to when I wasn't capable of putting up a *jesto-vath*."

"You must be about Master-grade yourself by now, no?"

Tarma cracked her left eye open enough to see Kethry's face. The question obviously caught the mage by surprise.

"Uh—"

"Beyond it?"

"I—"

"Thought so." Tarma closed her eyes again in satisfaction. "This job should do it, then. Through Idra we'll have contacts right up into the Royal ranks. If we can't wangle the property, students and wherewithal for our schools after this, we'll never get it."

"We'd have had it before this if it hadn't been for that damned minstrel!" Now it was Kethry's turn to snap with irritation.

"*Must* you remind me?" Tarma groaned, burying her face in the crook of her arm. "Leslac, Leslac, if it weren't for Bardic immunity I'd have killed you five times over!"

"You'd have had to stand in line," Kethry countered with grim humor. "I'd have beat you to it. Bad enough that he sings songs about us, *worse* that he gets the salient points all bass-ackwards, but—"

"To give us the reputation that we're shining warriors of the Light is *too damned much!*"

They had discovered some four or five years ago that there was a particular Bard, one Leslac by

17

name, who was making a specialty of creating ballads about their exploits. That would have been all to the good, for it was certainly spreading their name and reputation far and wide—except that he was *also* leaving the impression that the pair of them were less interested in money than in Just Causes.

Leslac had stressed and overstressed their habit of succoring women in distress and avenging those who were past distress. So now anyone who had an ax to grind came looking for them—most particularly, women. And usually they came with empty pockets, or damned little in the way of payment to offer, while the paying jobs they would *rather* have taken had been trickling away to others—because those who might have offered those jobs couldn't believe they'd be interested in "mere money."

And to add true insult to injury, a good half of the time Kethry's geas-blade Need would force them into *taking* those worthless Just Causes. For Need's geas was, as written on her blade, "Woman's Need calls me/As Woman's Need made me./Her Need will I answer/As my maker bade me." By now Kethry was so soul-bonded to the sword that it would have taken a god to free her from it. Most of the time it was worth it; the blade imparted absolute weapons expertise to Kethry, and would Heal anything short of a death wound on any woman holding it. And after the debacle with the demon-godling Thalhkarsh, Need *had* seemed to quiet down in her demands, unless *directly* presented with a woman in dire trouble. But with all those Just Causes showing up, Need had been rapidly turning into something more than a bit expensive to be associated with, thanks to Leslac.

They'd been at their wits' ends, and finally had gone to another couple of mercenaries, old friends of theirs, Justin Twoblade and Ikan Dryvale, for advice. They hadn't really hoped the pair would have any notions, but they were the last resort.

And, somewhat to Tarma's surprise, they'd *had* advice.

It was the off-season for the Jewel Merchants' Guild, Justin and Ikan's employers; that meant no caravans. And *that* meant that the paired mercenary guards were cosily holed up in their privat quarters at the Broken Sword, with the winter months to while away. They certainly weren't stinting themselves; they had a pair of very decent rooms, the Broken Sword's excellent ale—and, as Tarma discovered when she tapped at their door, no lack of female companionship. But the current pair of bright-eyed lovelies was sent pouting away when straw-haired Ikan answered their knock and discovered just who it was that had chosen to descend upon himself and his partner.

One of the innkeeper's quick-footed offspring was summoned then, and sent off for food and ale—for neither Justin nor his shieldbrother would hear a word of serious talk until everyone was settled and comfortable at their hearth, meat and drink at their elbows. Justin and Ikan took their hospitality very seriously.

"I've figured this was coming," Justin had said, somewhat to Tarma's shock, "And not just because of that idiot songster. You two have very unique and specialized skills—not like me and Ikan. You've gotten about as far as you can as an independent pairing. Now me and Ikan, we had the opposite problem. We're just ordinary fighting types; a bit better than most, but that's all that distinguishes us. We had to join a company to *get* a reputation; then we could live off that reputation as a pair. But you—you've *got* a reputation that will get you high fees from the right mercenary company."

Tarma had shaken her head doubtfully at that, but Justin had fixed her with his mournful houndlike eyes, and she'd held her peace.

"You, Tarma," he'd continued, "need much wider experience, especially experience in commanding others—and only a company will give you that. Kethry, you need to exercise skills and spells you wouldn't use in a partnership, and to learn how to delegate if your school is ever going to be successful, and again, you'll learn that in a company."

"Long speech," Tarma had commented sardonically.

"Well, I've got one, too," Ikan had said, winking a guileless blue eye at her. "You also need exposure to highborns, so that they know your reputation *isn't* just minstrelsy and moonshine. You haven't a choice; you truly need to join a company, one with a reputation of their own, one good enough that the highborns come to *them* for their contract. Then, once you *are* ready to hang up your blades and start your schools, you'll have noble patrons and noble pupils panting in anticipation of your teaching—and two not-so-noble aging fighters panting in anticipation of easy teaching jobs."

Kethry had laughed at Ikan's comic half-bow in their direction. "I take it that you already have a company in mind?"

"Idra's Sunhawks," Justin had replied blandly.

"The *Sunhawks?* Warrior's Oath—you'd aim us bloody damned *high*, wouldn't you?" Tarma had been well taken aback. For all that they were composed of specialist-troops—skirmishers, horse-archers and trackers—the Sunhawks' repute was so high that kings and queens *had* been known to negotiate their contracts with Idra in person. "Good gods, I should bloody well think highborns negotiate with them; their leader's of the damned Royal House of Rethwellan! And just how are we supposed to get a hearing with Captain Idra?"

"Us," Ikan had replied, stabbing a thumb at his chest. "We're ex-Hawks; we started with her, and probably would still be with her, but Idra was going more and more over to horse-archers, and we were getting less useful, so we decided to light out on our own. But we left on good terms; if we recommend that she give you a hearing, Idra will take our word on it."

"And once she sees that you're what you claim to be, you'll be in, never fear." Justin had finished for him. "Shin'a'in Kal'enedral—gods, you'd fit in like a sword in a sheath, Hawkface. And you, Keth— Idra's always got use for another mage, 'specially one nearly Masterclass. The best she's got now is a couple of self-taught hedge-wizards. Add in Furball there—you'll be a combination she won't be able to resist."

So it had proved. With letters in their pouches from both Ikan and his partner (both could read and write, a rarity among highborn, much less mercenaries) they had headed for the Sunhawks' winter quarters, a tiny hill town called Hawksnest. The name was not an accident; the town owed its existence to the Sunhawks, who wintered there and kept their dependents there, those dependents that weren't permanent parts of the Company bivouac. Hawksnest was nestled in a mountain valley, sheltered from the worst of the mountaintop weather, and the fortified barracks complex of the Sunhawks stood between it and the valley entrance. When the Hawks rode out, a solid garrison *and* all the Hawks-in-training remained behind. Idra believed in creating an environment for her fighters in which the only worries they needed to have on campaign were associated *with* the campaign.

Signing with Idra was unlike signing with any other Company; most Hawks stayed with Idra for years—she had led the Company for nearly twenty years. She'd willingly renounced her position as third in line to the throne of Rethwellan twenty-five years earlier, preferring freedom over luxury.

She'd hired on with a mercenary company herself, then after five years of experience accompanied by her own steady rise within the ranks, had formed the Hawks.

Tarma had been impressed with the quarters and the town; the inhabitants were easy, cheerful and friendly—which spoke of good behavior on the part of the mercs. The Hawks' winter quarters were better than those of many standing armies, and Tarma had especially approved of the tall wooden palisade that stretched across the entrance to Hawksnest, a palisade guarded by *both* Hawks and townsmen. And the Hawks themselves—as rumor had painted them—were a tight and disciplined group; drilling even in the slack season, and showing no sign of winter-born softness.

Idra had sent for them herself after reading their letters; they found her in her office within the Hawks' barracks. She was a muscular, athletic looking woman, with the body of a born horsewoman, mouse-gray hair, a strong face that could have been used as the model for a heroic monument, and the direct and challenging gaze of the professional soldier.

"So," she'd said, when they took their seats across the scratched, worn table that served as her desk, "if I'm to trust Twoblade and Dryvale, it should be me begging *you* to sign on."

Kethry had blushed; Tarma had met that direct regard with an unwavering gaze of her own. "I'm Kal'enedral," Tarma said shortly. "If you know Shin'a'in, that should tell you something."

"Swordsworn, hmm?" The quick gray eyes took in Tarma's brown clothing. "Not on bloodfeud—"

"That was ended some time ago," Tarma told her, levelly. "*We* ended it, we two working together. That was how we met."

"Shin'a'in Kal'enedral and outClansman. Unlikely pairing—even given a common cause. So why are you still together?"

For answer they both turned up their right palms so that she could see the silver crescent-scars that decorated them. One eyebrow lifted, ever so slightly.

"Sa. *She'enedran*. That explains a bit. Seems I've heard of a pair like you."

"If it was in songs," Tarma winced, "let's just say the stories are true in the main, but false in the details. And the author constantly left out the fact that we've always done our proper planning before we ever took on the main event. Luck plays wondrous small part in what we do, if we've got any say in the matter. And besides all that—we're a lot more interested in making a living than being somebody's savior."

Idra had nodded; her expression had settled into something very like satisfaction. "One last question for each of you—what's your specialty, Shin'a'in—and what's your rank and school, mage?"

"Horseback skirmishing, as you probably figured, knowing me for Shin'a'in." Tarma had replied first. "I'm a damned good archer—probably as good as any you've got. I can fight afoot, but I'd rather not. We've both got battlesteeds, and I'm sure you know what *that* means. My secondary skill is tracking."

"I'm White Winds, Journeyman; I'd say I lack a year or two of being Masterclass." Kethry had given her answer hard on the heels of Tarma's. "One other thing I think Ikan and Justin may have forgotten—Tarma is mindmate to a *kyree*, and I've got a bespelled blade I'm soul-bonded to. It gives me weapons expertise, so I'm pretty good at keeping myself in one piece on a battlefield; that's damned useful in a fight, you won't have to spare anybody to look after me. And besides that, it will Heal most wounds for a woman—and that's any woman, not just me."

Idra had not missed the implication. "But not a man, eh? Peculiar, but—well, I'm no mage, can't fathom your ways. About half my force is female, so that would come in pretty useful, regardless. But White Winds—that's no Healing school."

"No, it's not," Kethry agreed, "I haven't the greater Healing magics, just a few of the lesser. But I've got the battle-magics, and the defensive magics. I'm not one to stand in the back of a fight, shriek, and look appalled—"

For the first time Idra smiled. "No, I would guess not, for all that you look better suited to a bower than a battlefield. About the *kyree*—we're talking Pelagir Hills changeling, here? Standard wolf-shape?"

"*Hai*—overall he's built like a predator cat, but he's got the coat and head of a wolf. Shoulder comes to about my waist, he runs like a Plains grasscat; no stamina for a long march, but he's used to riding pillion with me." Tarma's description made Idra nod, eyes narrowed in *definite* satisfaction. "He's got a certain ability at smelling out magic, and a certain immunity to it; given he's from the Pelagirs he might have other tricks, but he hasn't used them around me yet. Mindspeaks, too, mostly to me, but he could probably make himself heard to anyone with a touch of the Gift. Useful scout, even more useful as an infiltrator. But be aware that he eats a lot, and if he can't hunt, he'll be wanting fresh meat daily. That'll have to be part of any contract we sign."

"Well, from what my boys say, what I knew by reputation, and what you've told me, I don't think I need any more information. Only one thing I don't reckon—" Idra had said, broad brow creased with honest puzzlement. "If you don't mind my asking what's none of my business even if I *do* sign you, why's the *kyree* mindmate to the fighter and not the mage's familiar?"

Tarma groaned, then, and Kethry laughed. "Oh, Warrl has a mind of his own," the mage had answered, "I *had* been the one doing the calling, but he made the decision. He decided that I didn't need him, and Tarma did."

"So besides your formidable talents, I get three recruits, not two; three used to teamworking. No commander in her right mind would argue with that." Idra then stood up, and pushed papers across her desk to them. "Sign those, my friends, if you're still so minded, and you'll be Sunhawks before the ink dries."

So it had been. Now Tarma was subcommander of the scouts, and Keth was in charge of the motley crew concerned with Healing and magery—two hedge-mages, a field-surgeon and herbalist and his two apprentices, and a Healing Priest of Shayana. "Priestess" would have been a more accurate title, but the Shayana's devotees did not make any gender differences in their rankings, which ofttimes confused someone who expected one sex and got the opposite. Tresti was handfasted to Sewen, Idra's Second, a weathered, big-boned, former trooper; that sometimes caused Keth sleepless nights. She wondered what would happen if it was ever Sewen carried in through the door flap of the infirmary, but the possibility never seemed to bother Tresti.

Tarma and Kethry had fought in two intense campaigns, each lasting barely a season; this was their third, and it had been brutal from the start. But then, that was often the case with civil war and rebellion.

Ten moons ago, the King of Jkatha had died, declaring his Queen, Sursha, to be his successor and Regent for their three children. Eight moons ago Sursha's brother-in-law, Declin Lord Kelcrag, had made a bid for the throne with his own armed might.

Lord Kelcrag was initially successful in his attempt, actually driving Sursha and her allies out of the Throne City and into the provinces. But he could not eliminate them, and he had made the mistake of assuming that defeat meant that they would vanish.

Queen Sursha had talent and wisdom—the talent to attract both loyal and *capable* people to her cause, and the wisdom to know when to stand back and let *them* do what was needful, however distasteful that might be to her gentle sensibilities. That talent won half the kingdom to her side; that wisdom allowed her to pick an otherwise rough-hewn provincial noble, Havak Lord Leamount, as her General-In-Chief and led her to give *him* her full and open support even when his decisions were personally repugnant to her.

General Lord Leamount levied or begged troops from every source he could—and then hired specialists to fill in the skill gaps his levies didn't have.

And one of the first mercenary Captains he had approached was Idra. His troops were mostly foot, with a generous leavening of heavy horse—no skirmishers, no scouts, no light horse at all, other than his own personal levy of hill-clansmen. The hillmen were mounted on rugged little ponies; good in rough country but slow in open areas, and useless as strike-and-run skirmishers.

And by now Idra's troops were second to none, thanks in no small part to Tarma. The Shin'a'in had seen no reason why she could not benefit her presumptive clan's coffers, and her new comrades as well; she'd arranged for the Sunhawks to get first pick of the sale-horses of Tale'sedrin. These weren't battlesteeds, which were *never* let out of Shin'a'in hands, but they weren't culls either, which was what the Sunhawks had been seeing. And when the Hawks had snapped up every beast she offered, she arranged for four more clans to bring in their first-pick horses as well.

So now the Hawks were better mounted than

most nobles, on horses that could be counted as extra weapons in a close-in fight.

That fact was not lost on Lord Leamount, nor was he blind to Idra's canny grasp of strategy. Idra was made part of the High Command, and pretty much allowed to dictate *how* her Hawks were used.

As a result, although the fighting had been vicious, the Hawks were still at something like four-fifths strength; their ranks were nowhere near as decimated as they might have been under a commander who threw them recklessly at the enemy, rather than using them to their best advantage.

At Midsummer, Lord Leamount's combined forces had fallen on the Throne City and driven Lord Kelcrag out. Every move Kelcrag had made since then had been one of retreat. His retreat had been hard fought, and each acre of ground had been bitterly contested, but it had been an inexorable series of losses.

But now autumn was half over; he had made a break-and-run, and at this point everyone in Leamount's armies knew why. He was choosing to make a last stand on ground *he* had picked.

Both sides knew this next battle would *have* to bring the war to a conclusion. In winter it would be impossible to continue any kind of real fight—the best outcome would be stalemate as troops of both sides floundered through winter storms and prayed that ill-luck and hardship would keep from thinning their ranks *too* much. If Kelcrag retreated to his own lands, he'd come under siege, and ultimately lose if the besieging troops could be supplied and rotated. If he fled into exile, the Queen would have to mount an ever-present vigil against his return—an expensive proposition. She and Leamount had both wanted to invoke the Mercenary Code ritual of Oathbreaking and Outcasting on him—but while he *was* undeniably a rebel, he had actually broken no vows; nor could Sursha find the requisite triad for the full ceremony of priest, mage and honest man, all of whom *must* have suffered personal, irreparable harm at his hands as a result of violation of sworn oaths. So technically, he *could* have been seen by some to be the injured party.

And as for Kelcrag in such a situation, exile would mean impoverishment and hardship, circumstances he was not ready to face; further, it would bring the uncertainty of when or even *if* he could muster enough troops and allies to make a second try.

Kelcrag had chosen his ground with care, Tarma had to give him that. He had shale cliffs (impossible to scale) to his left, scrub forest and rough, broken ground to his right (keeping Leamount from charging from that direction); his troops were on the high ground, occupying a wide pass between the hills, with a gradual rising slope between the loyalists and his army—

It was as close to being an ideal situation for the rebels as Tarma could imagine. There was no way to come at him except straight on, and no way he could be flanked. And now the autumnal rains were beginning.

Of all of Idra's folks, only the scouts had been deployed, seeking (in vain) holes or weaknesses in Kelcrag's defenses. For the rest, it had been Set up camp, Dig in, and Wait. Wait for better weather, better information, better luck.

"Gah—" Tarma groaned again. "I hope Kelcrag's as miserable on his damned hill as we are down here. Anything out of the mages?"

"Mine, or in general?"

"Both."

"Mine have been too busy fending off nuisance-spells to bother with trying to see what's going on across the way. I've been setting up wards on the camp, protections on our commanders, and things like the *jesto-vath* on the Healer's tent. I haven't heard anything directly from Leamount's greater mages, but I've got some guesses."

"Which are?" Tarma stretched, then turned on her side.

"The Great Battle Magics were exhausted early on for *both* sides in this mess, and none of the mages have had time to regather power. That leaves the Lesser—which means they're dueling like a pair of tired but equally-matched bladesmen. Neither can see what the other is doing; neither can get anything through that's more than an annoyance. And neither wants to let down their guards and their shields enough to recharge in a power circle or open up enough to try one of the Greater Magics they might have left. So your people will be pretty much left alone except for physical, material attacks."

"Well, that's a blessing, any—"

"Scoutmaster?" came a plaintive call from outside the tent. "Be ye awake yet?"

"Who the bloody—" Tarma scrambled for the lacings of the door flaps as Kethry hastily cut the spell about the door with two slashes of her hands and a muttered word.

"Get in here, child, before you turn into an ice lump!" Tarma hauled the half-frozen scout into their tent; the girl's brown eyes went round at the sight of the spell energy in the tent walls, wide and no little frightened. She looked like what she was, a mountain peasant; short, stocky and brown, round of face and eye. But she could stick to the back of her horse like a burr on a sheep, she was shrewd and quick, and nobody's fool. She was one of the Hawks Tarma had been thinking of when she'd mentioned other ways of keeping warm; Kyra was shieldmated to Rild, a mountain of a man who somehow managed to sit a horse as lightly as thin Tarma.

"Keth, this is Kyra, she's one of the new ones. Replaced Pawell when he went down." Tarma pushed the girl down onto her bedroll and stripped the sodden black cloak from her shoulders, hanging it to dry beside her own coat. "Kyra, don't look so green; you've seen Keth in the Healer's tent; this is just a bit of magic so we sleep more comfortable. Keth's better than a brazier, and I don't have to worry about her tipping over in the night!"

The girl swallowed hard, but looked a little less frightened. "Beg pardon, but I ain't seen much magery."

"I should think not, out in these hills. Not much call for it, nor money to pay for it. So—spit it out; what brings you here, instead of curled up with that monster you call a shieldmate?"

The girl blushed brilliant red. "Na, Scoutmaster—"

"Don't 'na' me, my girl. I may not play the game anymore, but I know the rules—and before the Warrior put her Oath on me, I had my moments, though you children probably wouldn't think it to look at me, old stick that I am. Out with it—something gone wrong with the pairing?"

"Eh, no! Naught like that—I just been thinking. Couldn't get a look round before today; now seems I know this pass, like. Got kin a ways west, useta summer wi' 'em. Cousins. If I'm aright, 'bout a day's ride west o' here. And there was always this rumor, see, there was this path up their way—"

Tarma didn't bother to hide her excitement; she leaned forward on her elbows, feeling a growing internal certainty that what Kyra was about to reveal was vital.

"—there was this story abaht the path, d'ye ken? The wild ones, the ponies, they used it. At weanin' time we'd go for 'em t' harvest the foals, but some on 'em would allus get away—well, tales said they used that path, that it went all the way through t'other side. D'ye take my meaning?"

"Warrior Bright, you *bet* I do, my girl!" Tarma jumped lithely to her feet, and pulled Kyra up after her. "Keth?"

"Right." Kethry made the slashing motions again, and the magic parted from the door flaps. "Wait a hair—I don't want you two finding our answer and then catching your deaths."

Another pass of hands and a muttered verse sent water steaming up out of coat and cloak—when Tarma pulled both off the centerpole they were dry to the touch.

Tarma flashed her partner a grin. "Thanks, milady. If you get sleepy, leave the door open for me, hey?"

Kethry gave a most unladylike snort. "As if I could sleep after this bit of news! I haven't been working with you for this long not to see what you saw—"

"The end to the stalemate."

"You've said it. I'll be awake for hours on this one." Kethry settled herself with her blankets around her, then dismissed the magic altogether. The tent went dark and cold again, and Kethry relit her brazier with another muttered word. "I'll put that *jesto-vath* back up when you get back—and make it fast! Or I may die of nerves instead of freezing to death!"

Two

Back out into the cold and wet and dark they went, Kyra trailing along behind Tarma. She stayed right at Tarma's elbow, more a presence felt than anything seen, as Warrl, in mindtouch with Tarma, led both of them around washouts and the worst of the mud. Tarma's goal was the Captain's tent.

She knew full well it would be hours before Sewen and Idra saw *their* bedrolls; she'd given them the reports of her scouts just before fumbling her way to her own rest, and she knew they would still be trying to extract some bit of advantage out of the bleak word she'd left with them.

So Warrl led them to Idra's quarters; even in the storm-black *it* was the only tent *not* hard to find. Idra had her connections for some out-of-the-ordinary items, and after twenty years of leading the Hawks, there was no argument but that she had more than earned her little luxuries. There was a bright yellow mage-light shining like a miniature moon atop each of the poles that held up a canvas flap that served as a kind of sheltered porch for the sentry guarding the tent. Unlike Keth's dim little witchlight, these were bright enough to be seen for several feet even through the rain. If it had been reasonable weather, and if there had been any likelihood that the camp would be attacked, or that the commanders of the army would be sought out as targets, Idra's quarters would be indistinguishable from the rest of the Hawks'. But in weather like this—Idra felt that being able to *find* her, quickly, took precedence over her own personal safety.

Idra's tent was about the size of two of the bivouac tents. The door flap was fastened down, but Tarma could see the front half of the tent glowing from more mage-lights within, and the yellow light cast shadows of Idra and Sewen against the canvas as they bent over the map-table, just as she'd left them.

Warrl was already moving into the wavering glow of the mage-lights. He was a good couple of horse-lengths in front of them, which was far enough that the sentry under that bit of sheltering canvas couldn't see Kyra and Tarma to challenge them—at least not yet. No matter—and no matter that Warrl's black fur couldn't be seen in the rain even with the glow of the mage-lights on him. Warrl barked three times out of the storm, paused, then barked twice more. That was *his* password. Every man, woman, and noncombatant in the Hawks knew Warrl and Warrl's signal—and knew that where Warrl was, Tarma was following after.

So by the time Tarma and Kyra had slogged the last few feet to the tent, the sentry was standing at ease, the door flap was unlaced, and Sewen was ready to hold it open for them against the wind. His muddy gray eyes were worried as he watched the two of them ease by him. Tarma knew what he was thinking; at this hour, any caller probably meant more trouble.

"I trust this isn't a social call," Idra said dryly, as they squeezed themselves inside and stood, dripping and blinking, in the glow of her mage-lights. The mage-lights only made her plain leather armor and breeches look the more worn and mundane. "And I hope it isn't a disciplinary problem—"

Kyra's autumnal eyes were even rounder than before; Tarma suppressed a chuckle. Kyra hadn't seen the Captain except to sign with her, and was patently in awe of her. "Captain, this is my new scout, Kyra—"

"Replaced Pawell, didn't she?"

"Aye—to make it short, she thinks she knows a way to come in behind Kelcrag."

"Great good gods!" Idra half rose off of her tall stool, then sank down again, with a look as though she'd been startled out of a doze.

Well, that *certainly got their attention*, Tarma thought, watching both Idra and her Second go from weary and discouraged to alert in the time it took to say the words.

"C'mere, kid," Sewen rumbled. He took Kyra's wool-clad elbow with a hard and callused hand that looked fit to crush the bones of her arm, and which Tarma knew from experience could safely keep a day-old chick sheltered across a furlong of rough ground. He pulled her over to the table in the center of the tent. "Y'read maps, no? Good. Here's us. Here's him. Report—"

Kyra plainly forgot her awe and fear of magic, and the diffidence with which she had regarded her leaders, and became the professional scout beneath Sewen's prodding. The tall, bony Second was Idra's right hand and more—where her aristocratic bearing sometimes overawed her own people, particularly new recruits, Sewen was as plain as a clod of earth and awed no one. Not that anyone ever thought of insubordination around him; he was just as respected as Idra—it was just that he looked and sounded exactly like what he was; a common fighter who'd come up through the ranks on brains and ability. He still dressed, by preference, in the same boiled-leather armor and homespun he'd always worn, though he could more than afford the kind of expensive riveted brigandine and doeskin Idra and Tarma had chosen. He understood everything about the Hawks from the ground up—because he'd served the Hawks since Idra's fifth year of commanding them. Idra and Tarma just leaned over the map-table with him and let him handle the young scout.

"So—on the face of it, it bears checking. That's a task for the scouts," Idra said at last, when Kyra had finished her report. She braced both hands on the table and turned to her Scoutmaster. "Tarma, what's your plan?"

"That I take out Kyra and—hmm—Garth, Beaker and Jodi," Tarma replied after a moment of thought. "We leave before dawn tomorrow and see what we can see. If this trail still exists, we'll follow it in and find out if the locals are right. I'll have Beaker bring a pair of his birds; one to let you know if we find the trail at all, and one to tell you yea or nay on whether it's usable. That way you'll have full information for Lord Leamount without waiting for us to get back."

"Good." Idra nodded in satisfaction, as a bit of gray-brown hair escaped to get into her eyes. "Sewen?"

"What I'd do," Sewen affirmed, pushing away from the table and sitting back onto his stool. "Them birds don't like water, but that's likely to make 'em want their coops more, maybe fly a bit faster, hey? Don' wanta send a mage-message, or Kelcrag's magickers might track it."

"Uh-huh; that was my thought," Tarma agreed, nodding. "That, and the sad fact that other than Keth, *our* magickers might not be able to boost a mage-message that far."

"I need Keth here," Idra stated, "and none of Leamount's mages are fit enough to travel over that kind of territory."

Sewen emitted a bark of laughter, weathered face crinkling up for a moment. "Gah, that lot's as miserable as a buncha wet chickens in a leaky hennery right now. They don' know this weather, an' ev'ry time they gotta move from their tent, y'd think it was gonna be a trip t' th' end of th' earth!"

Idra looked thoughtful for a moment, and rubbed the side of her nose with her finger. "This isn't wizard weather, is it, do you suppose?"

Both Tarma and her scout shook their heads vigorously. "Na, Cap'n," Kyra said, cheerful light brightening her round face. "Na, is just a bit of a gentle fall storm. Y'should see a *bad* one, now—"

Idra's eyebrows shot upward; she straightened and looked seriously alarmed until Sewen's guffaw told her she'd been played for an ignorant flatlander.

"Seriously, no," Tarma seconded, "I asked Keth. She says the only sign of wizard weather would be if this *stopped*—that it's got too much weight behind it, whatever that means."

Sewen lifted his own eyebrow and supplied the answer. "She meant it's somethin' comin' in the proper season—got all the weight of time an' *what should be* behind it." He grinned at Tarma's loose jaw, showing teeth a horse could envy. "Useta study wizardry as a lad, hadn't 'nough Gift t' be more'n half a hedge-wizard, so gave't up."

"Good, then, we're all agreed." Idra straightened her shoulders, gave her head an unconscious toss to get that bit of her hair out of her face. "Tarma, see to it. Who will you put in to replace you tomorrow?"

"Tamar. Next to Garth and Jodi, he's my best, and he's come in from the skirmishers."

"Good. And tell him to tell the rest of your scouts not to give the enemy any slack tomorrow, but not to get in as close as they did today. I don't want them thinking we've maybe found something else to concentrate on, but I don't want any more gut-wounds, either."

It was dawn, or nearly, and the rain had slackened some. There was still lightning and growling thunder, but at least you could *see* through the murk, and it was finally possible to keep the shielded torches at the entrance to the guarded camp alight.

Tarma saw her scouts assembled beneath one of those torches as she rode up to the sentry. She felt like yawning, but wouldn't; she wouldn't be a bad example. *Cold, ye gods, I'm half-frozen and we haven't even gotten out of the camp yet,* she thought with resignation. *I haven't been warm since summer.*

:And then you were complaining about heat,: Warrl replied sardonically.

"I was not. That was Keth," she retorted. "I *like* the heat."

Warrl did not deign to reply.

Tarma was already feeling grateful for Kethry's parting gift, the water-repelling cape Keth had insisted on throwing over her coat. *It's not magic,* Keth had said, *I don't want a mage smelling you out. Just tight-woven, oiled silk, and bloody damned expensive. I swapped a* jesto-vath *on his tent to Gerrold for it, for as long as the rains last. I hope you don't mind the fact that it's looted goods—*

Not likely, she'd replied.

So today it was Keth looking out for and worrying about her. They seemed to take it turn and turn about these days, being mother-hen. Well, that was what being partners was all about.

:Took you long enough to come to that conclusion,: Warrl laughed. *:Now if you'd just start mother-henning me—:*

"You'd bite me, you fur-covered fiend."

:Oh, probably.:

"Ah—you're hopeless," Tarma chided him, smothering a grin. "Let's look serious here; this is business."

:Yes, oh mistress.:

Tarma bit back another retort. She never won in a contest of sharp tongues with the *kyree*. Instead of answering him, she pondered her choice of scouts again, and was satisfied, all things considered, that she'd picked the best ones for the job.

First, Garth: a tiny man, and dark, he looked like

a dwarfish shadow on his tall Shin'a'in gelding. He was one of Tarma's first choices for close-in night work, since his dusky skin made it unnecessary for him to smear ash on himself, but his most outstanding talents were that he could ride like a Shin'a'in and track like a hound. His one fault was that he couldn't hit a haystack with more than two arrows out of ten. He was walking his bay gelding back and forth between the two sentries at the sally-point, since his beast was the most nervous of the five that would be going out, and the thunder was making it lay its ears back and show the whites of its eyes.

Beaker: average was the word for Beaker; size, coloring, habits—average in everything except his nose—*that* raptor's bill rivaled Tarma's. His chestnut mare was as placid of disposition as Garth's beast was nervous, and Beaker's temperament matched his mare's. As Tarma rode up, they both appeared to be dozing, despite the cold rain coming down on their heads. Fastened to the cantle of Beaker's saddle were two cages, each the size of two fists put together, each holding a black bird with a green head. Beaker was a good tracker, almost as good as Garth, but *this* was his specialty; the training and deployment of his messenger birds.

Jodi: sleepy-eyed and deceptively quiet, this pale, ice-blonde child with evident aristocratic blood in her veins was their mapmaker. Besides that skill, she was a vicious knife fighter and as good with a bow as Garth was poor with one. She rode a gray mare with battlesteed blood in her; a beast impossible for anyone but her or Tarma to ride, who would only allow a select few to handle her. Jodi sat her as casually as some gentle palfrey—and with Jodi in her saddle, the mare acted like one. Her only fault was that she avoided situations where she would have to command the way she would have avoided fouled water.

And Kyra: peasant blood and peasant stock, she'd trained herself in tracking, bow and knife, and hard riding, intending to be something other than some stodgy farmer's stolid wife. When the war came grinding over her parents' fields and her family had fled for their lives, she'd stayed. She'd coolly sized up both sides and chosen Sursha's—then sized up the mercenary Companies attached to Sursha's army and decided which ones she wanted to approach.

She'd started first with the Hawks, though she hadn't really thought she'd get in—or so she had confessed to Tarma after being signed on. Little had she guessed that Scout Pawell had coughed out his life pinned to a tree three days earlier—and that the Hawks had been down by two scouts *before* that had happened. Tarma had interviewed her and sent her to Sewen, who'd sent her to Idra—who'd sent her back to Tarma with the curt order—"Try her. If she survives, hire her." Tarma had sent her on the same errand that had killed Pawell. *Kyra* had returned. Since Pawell had had no relatives, no leman and no shieldmate to claim his belongings, Tarma gave her Pawell's dun horse, Pawell's gear, and Pawell's tentmate. Kyra had quickly acquired something Pawell hadn't—tentmate had turned to shieldmate and lover.

The Scouts altogether approved, as Pawell had been standoffish and his replacement was anything but. The romance had amused and touched them. Kyra had begun to bloom under the approval, to think for herself, to make judgment calls. The Kyra that had joined them would never have come to Tarma with an old tale and a rumor; Kyra of "now" had experience enough to *know* how important that rumor could be, and enough guts to present the information herself. She was Tarma's personal pick to become a subcommander herself in a few years.

It was false dawn; one hour to real dawn, and

there was a hint that the sky was getting lighter.
No words were needed; they all knew what they
had to do. When Tarma rode gray Ironheart into
the waiting knot of Scouts and horses, those dismounted swung back up into their saddles. Tarma
didn't even slacken her pace; all five of them left
the camp in proper diamond formation, as if they'd
rehearsed the whole maneuver. Tarma had point
(since as commander she was the only one of the
five with all the current passwords), Garth tail,
Jodi right and Kyra left—Beaker and his precious
birds rode protected in the middle.

They rode along the back of the string of encampments; dark tents against slowly graying sky to
their right, scrub forest and hills stark black against
the sky to their left. The camps were totally dark,
since just about everyone had encountered the same
troubles as the Hawks had with lights and fires in
the pouring rain.

They were challenged almost as soon as they left
their own camp; a foot-sentry, sodden, but alert.
He belonged to Staferd's Cold-drakes; this was the
edge of *their* camp. Tarma nodded to herself with
satisfaction at his readiness, and gave him the
countersign.

Then came a heavy encampment of regular in-
fantry, whose sentry hailed Warrl, who was trotting at Ironheart's flank, by name, and called out:
"You're recognized, Sunhawks. Pass on." Tarma
felt a little twitchy about that one, but couldn't
fault him. You challenged those whom you didn't
recognize; you could let known quantities by. And
there were no *kyree* in Kelcrag's forces.

At the next encampment—Duke Greyhame's
levy—they were physically challenged; a fully-armed
youth with an arrogant sneer on his lips, mounted
on a heavy, wild-eyed warhorse. He blocked their
path until Tarma gave an elaborate countersign.
Even then, he wouldn't clear the path entirely. He

left only enough room for them to ride past in single file, unless they wanted to desert the firm ground and ride on the mushy banks. And he backed off with some show of reluctance, and much induced rearing and prancing of his gelding.

"Scoutmaster—"

Garth eased his horse alongside Tarma's and whispered angrily to her:

"I'd like to feed that little son of a bitch his own damned gauntlet!"

"Peace," Tarma said, "Let me handle this. Give me rear for long enough to teach him a lesson."

Garth passed the word; wry grins appeared and vanished in an instant, and the scout ranks opened and closed so that Beaker had point and Tarma had dropped back to tail. The scouts squeezed past the arrogant sentry, one by one, Tarma the last. She didn't move, only stared at him for a long moment, letting Ironheart feel her ground and set her feet.

Then she dropped her hands, and signaled the battlemare with her knees.

Black as a nightmare in the rain, the battlesteed reared up to her full height—and stayed there, as perfectly balanced as only a Shin'a'in trained warsteed could be. Another invisible command from Tarma, and she hopped forward on her hind hooves, forefeet lashing out at the stranger-gelding, who, not being the fool his rider was, cleared off the path and up onto the mucky shoulder. Then Ironheart settled to all four hooves again, but only for as long as it took to get past the arrogant sentry. As Tarma had figured he would, he spurred his beast down onto the path again as soon as they got by. Whatever he'd thought to do then didn't much matter. As soon as he was right behind them and just *out* of range of what was normally an attack move, Tarma gave her mare a final signal that sent her leaping into the air, lashing out with her rear hooves in a wicked kick as she reached the top of her arc. Had the boy *been* within range of those hooves, his face would have been smashed in. As it was (as Tarma had carefully calculated), the load of mud Ironheart had picked up flicked off her heels to splatter all over him, his fancy panoply, and his considerably cowed beast.

"Next time, boy," she called back over her shoulder, as her scouts snickered, "best *know* whose tail it is you plan to twist, and be prepared for consequences."

The edge of the camps was held by the freefighters—little clots of scum no good company would take into itself. They were one of the reasons each levy and company had its own set of sentries; politics was the other. Tarma didn't much understand politics—scum, she knew. It had been a band of this sort of flotsam that had wiped out her Clan.

But a sword was a sword, and Leamount was not above paying them so long as someone he trusted could keep an eye on them. *That, thank the Warrior, is not Idra's job,* Tarma thought to herself, wrinkling her nose at the stench of their huddle of makeshift shelters. Unwashed bodies, rotting canvas, garbage, privy pits right in the camp—the mix was hardly savory. Even the rain couldn't wash it out of the air. They rode past this lot (too sodden with drink or drug, or just too damn lazy to set one of their own to sentry duty) without a challenge, but with one hand on their knives and shortswords at all times. There'd been trouble with this lot before—and five were not too many for them to consider mobbing if they thought it worth their while.

Once out of the camps, they rearranged their order. Now it was Kyra who had point, and Tarma who took tail. This side of the mountains, danger would be coming at them from the rear—Kelcrag's scouts, sniffing around the edges of the Royalist army. All of them had taken care long ago to replace metal harness pieces with leather where they could, or even carved wood—anything that wouldn't shine and wouldn't clink. The metal they had to have was *not* brightwork; it was dulled and tarnished and left that way. Shin'a'in horses were trained to neck and knee, so all they needed was a soft halter with no bit. As for their own armor, or lack of it, their best protection would be speed on a mission like this—stay out of the way if you can, and never close for a fight unless you have no choice. So they saved themselves and their horses the few extra pounds, and dressed for the weather, not for battle. Tarma kept her short Shin'a'in horsebow strung and under her cape; if it came to a fight, she would buy the rest time to string theirs. Warrl ranged all over their backtrail, keeping in steady mindtouch with Tarma. He would buy them yet more advance warning, if there was going to be trouble.

But the trek west was quiet.

The storm gradually slackened to drizzle as the sky grew lighter; the landscape was dreary, even without the devastations of warfare all about them. The hills were dead and brown, and lifeless; the herds of sheep and gercattle that usually grazed them had gone to feed one or both armies. The scrub trees displayed black, leafless branches against the gray sky, and the silence around them intensified the impression that this area was utterly deserted. Wet, rotting leaves left their own signature on the breeze, a melancholy, bitter aroma more tasted than smelled, that lingered in the back of the throat. The track they followed was part rock, part yellow mud, a thick, claylike stuff that clung to hooves and squelched when it let go.

All five of them rode in that peculiar half-trance of the scout on his way *to* something; not looking for anything, not yet—not paying outward attention to surroundings—but should anything, however small, move—

A crow, flapping up to their right, got exactly the appropriate reaction; Tarma, ready-armed, had already sighted on him before he'd risen a foot. Jodi and Beaker had their hands on their bowcases and their eyes to left and right, wary for possible ambush. Garth had his sword out and was ready to back Tarma, and Kyra was checking the road ahead for more trouble.

They all laughed, shakily, when they realized what their "enemy" was.

"Don't think even Kelcrag's taken up with the corbies," Tarma said, shaking her head, and tucking her bow back under the oiled silk. "Still—*probably* he hasn't got anyone dedicated enough to go mucking around in this weather, but we can't count on it. Stay alert, children. At least until we get out of the war zone."

By midday they had done just that—there *were* herds on the distant hills, although the shepherds and herders quickly moved them out of sight when they saw the little band approaching. Tarma saw Garth nodding in sympathy, lips moving soundlessly in what she rather thought was a blessing. His people had been all but wiped out when some war had trampled them into *their* earth, somewhere down south.

Tarma knew everything there was to know about her "children"; she had made a point of getting drunk at least once with each of her scouts. It was damned useful to know what made them twitch. One of the reasons Garth was with Idra—he was so good a tracker he could have served with any company, or even as a pampered huntsman to royalty— was because she allowed no looting of the peasantry (nobles were another matter) and insisted on the Hawks paying in trade-silver and pure copper ingots for what they needed. Like Garth, all the Hawks tended to serve their lady-Captain for more than just coin.

By now they were all fairly well sodden except for Tarma, brown and black and gray cloaks all becoming a similar dark, indeterminant shade. Even Tarma was rather damp. Rain that was one scant point from being sleet still managed to get past her high collar to trickle down her neck, and muddy water from every puddle they splashed through had soaked through her breeches long ago. She was going numb with cold; the rest of them must be in worse case.

"Kyra," she called forward, "You in territory you know yet?"

The girl turned in her saddle, rain trickling down her nose. "Hmm—eh, I'd say so. Think this's Domery lands, they're kin of my kin—"

"I don't want to stretch anybody's hospitality or honesty, but we need to dry off a bit. There any herders' huts or caves or something around here? Something likely to be deserted this time of year?"

"I'll think on't."

A few soggy furlongs later—as Kyra scanned her memory and the land around them—

"Scoutmaster," she called back, " 'Bout three hills over there be a cave; used for lambin' and shearin' and never else. That do?"

"Room for all of us? I mean horses, too. No sense in shouting our presence by tethering them out, and plain cruel to make them endure more of this than we do."

Kyra's brow creased with thought. "If I don't misremember, aye. Be a squeeze, but aye."

Kyra had misremembered—but by *under*estimating the size of the cave. There was enough room at the back for all five horses to stand shoulder to shoulder, with enough space left over for one rider at a time to rub his beast down without getting trampled on. An overhanging shelf of limestone made it possible to build a fire at the front of the cave without all of them eating smoke. And there was wood stocked at the side, dry enough that there wasn't much of that smoke in the first place.

More to the point, where concealment was concerned, the rain dissipated what trickled past the blackened overhang.

"How much farther?" Tarma asked, chewing on a tasteless mouthful of trail-biscuit.

"Not much," Kyra replied. "We better be cuttin' overland from here if m' mem'ry be still good. Look you—"

She dipped a twig in muddy, black water and drew on a flat rock near the cave's entrance.

Tarma got down on her knees beside her and studied her crude map carefully. "One, maybe two candlemarks, depending, hmm?"

"Aye, depending." Kyra chewed on the other end of the twig for a moment. "We got to stick t' ridges—"

"What?" Beaker exclaimed. "For every gossip in the hills to see us?"

"Oh, bad to be seen, but worse to be bogged. Valleys, they go boggy this time of year, like. Stuff livin' in the bogs is bad for a beast's feet. Y' want yer laddy's hooves t' rot off 'fore we reach trail's end, y' ride the valleys."

"No middle way?" Tarma asked.

"Well. . . . We won't be goin' where there's likely many, an' most of those'd be my kin. They see me, they know what I was abaht, and they keep their tongues from clackin'."

"That'll have to do." Tarma got up from her knees, and dusted the gravel off the knees of her breeches—which were, she was happy to find, relatively dry. "All right, children, let's ride."

"I dunno—" Garth said dubiously, peering up

through the drizzle at what was little better than a worn track along the shale cliffside.

Tarma studied the trail and chewed at the corner of her lip. "Kyra," she said, finally, "your beast's the weakest of the lot. Give it a try. If she can make it, we all can."

"Aye," Kyra saluted, and turned her mare's head to the trail. She let the mare take her time and pick her own places to set her feet along the track. It seemed to take forever—

But eventually they could see that she was waving from the top.

"Send the first bird, Beaker," Tarma said, heading Ironheart after the way Kyra had followed. "We're going to see if this trail is a dead end or the answer to our prayers."

Twice before sunset they lost the track on broad expanses of bare rock, and spent precious time trying to pick it up again, all of them combing the ground thumblength by thumblength.

Sunset was fast approaching the second time they lost, then found the trail again. Tarma scanned the sky warily, trying to judge, with the handicap of lowering clouds, how much time they had before darkness fell. They obviously weren't going to make trail's end by sunset—so the choice was whether to camp here on this windswept slant of scoured stone, or to press on in the hope of coming up with something better and maybe instead find themselves spending the night on a ledge two handspans wide.

She finally decided to press on, allowing just enough time in reserve that they could double back if they had to.

The track led on through lichen and rubble: treacherous stuff, except where the wild ponies had pounded a thin line of solidity. Jodi was mapping as they went along, and marking their backtrail with carefully inconspicuous "cairns" composed of no more than three or four pebbles. The drizzle had stopped, at least, and the exertion that was warming them had driven most of the damp out of their clothing. The pony-track led down into a barren gulley—Tarma disliked that, and kept watching for water marks on the rocks they passed. If there was a cloudburst and this *happened* to be one of the local runoff sites, they could be hock-deep in tumbling rock and fast water in the time it took to blink.

But the gulley stayed dry, the track eased a bit—and then, like a gift from the gods, just before Tarma would have signaled a turnaround point, they came upon a possible campsite.

Sometime in the not-too-recent past, part of the hill above them had come sliding down, creating a horseshoe of boulders the size of a house. There would be shelter from the wind there, their fire would be out of sight of prying eyes—and it would be easy to defend from predators.

Garth eyed the site with the same interest Tarma was feeling. "No place to get out of the rain, if it decided to come down again," he observed, "and nothing much to burn but that scrub up there on the wall. We'd have us a pot of hot tea, but a cold camp."

"Huh. The choice is this or the flat back there," Tarma told them. "Me, I'd take this. Kyra? This is your land."

"Aye, I'd take this; we've slept wet afore," Kyra agreed. "This 'un isn't a runoff, an' don't look like any more of the hill is gonna slip while we're here. I'd say 'tis safe enough."

The others nodded.

"Let's get ourselves settled then, while there's light."

The rain began again before dawn and they were glad enough to be on the move and getting chilled muscles stretched and warmed. They lost the track once more, this time spending a frustrating hour searching for it—but that was the last of their hardships, for noon saw them emerging from the hills and onto the plains on the other side.

Tarma allowed herself a broad grin, as the rest whooped and pounded each other's backs.

"Send up that damned bird, Beaker; we just earned ourselves one *fat* bonus from Lord Leamount."

Returning was easier, though it was plain that nothing but a goat, a donkey, a mountain pony or a Shin'a'in-bred beast was ever going to make it up or down that trail without breaking a leg. Tarma reckoned it would take the full Company about one day to traverse the trail; that, plus half a day to get to their end and half to get into striking distance of Kelcrag's forces meant two days' traveling time, in total. Not bad, really; they'd had a setup that had taken almost a week, once. Knowing Idra as she did, Tarma had a pretty good idea of what the Captain's suggested strategy was going to be. And it would involve the Hawks and no one else. No bad thing, that; the Hawks could count on their own to know what to do.

The rain had finally let up as they broke back out into the herder's country; they were dead tired and ready to drop, but at least they weren't wet anymore. Tarma saw an outrider a few furlongs beyond the camp; he, she or it was waving a scarf in the Hawks' colors of brown and golden yellow. She waved back, and the outrider vanished below the line of a hill. They all relaxed at that; they were watched for, they need not guard their path—and there would almost certainly be food and drink waiting for them in the camp. That was exactly what they'd needed and hoped for.

They hadn't expected Idra and Sewen to be waiting for them at the entrance to the camp.

"Good work, children. Things are heating up.

Maps," Idra said curtly, and Jodi handed over the waterproof case with a half-salute and a tired grin. They were all achingly weary at this point; horses and humans alike were wobbly at the knees. Only Tarma and Ironheart were in any kind of shape, and Tarma wasn't too certain how much of Ironheart's apparent energy was bluff. Battlemares had a certain stubborn pride that sometimes made them as pigheaded about showing strain as—

:*Certain Kal'enedral,*: Warrl said in her head.

Shut up, she thought back at him, *you should talk about being pigheaded*—

"Good work. *Damned* fine work," Idra said, looking up from the maps and interrupting Tarma's train of thought. "Tarma, if you're up to a little more—"

"Captain." Tarma nodded, and sketched a salute.

"The rest of you—there's hot wine and hot food waiting in my tent, and a handful of Hawks to give your mounts the good rubdown and treat *they* deserve. Tarma, give Ironheart to Sewen and come with me. Warrl, too, if he wants. The rest of you get under shelter. We'll be seeing you all later—with news, I hope."

Tarma had been too fatigue-fogged to note where they were going, except that they were working their way deeply into the heart of the encampments. But after a while the size of the tents and the splendor of the banners outside of them began to penetrate her weariness.

What in the name—

:*On your best behavior, mindmate,*: Warrl said. For once his mindvoice sounded dead serious. :*This is the camp of the Lord Commander.*:

Before Tarma had a chance to react, Idra was ushering her past a pair of massive sentries and into the interior of a tent big enough to hold a half dozen of the Hawks' little two-man bivouacs.

Tarma blinked in the light and warmth, and felt her muscles going to jelly in the pleasant heat. Mage-lights everywhere, and a *jesto-vath* that made Kethry's look like a simple shieldspell.

Other than that, though, the tent was as plain as Idra's, divided, as hers was, into a front and back half. In the front half was a table, some chairs and document-boxes, a rack of wine bottles. The curtain dividing it was half open; on the other side Tarma could see what looked like a chest, some weapons and armor—and a plain camp cot, piled high with thick furs and equally thick blankets.

What I wouldn't give to climb into that right now, she was thinking, when her attention was pulled away by something more important.

"Leamount, you old warhorse, here's our miracle-maker," Idra was saying to a lean, grizzled man in half-armor standing by the map-table, but in the shadows, so that Tarma hadn't really noticed him at first. Tarma had seen Lord Leamount once or twice at a distance; she recognized him by his stance and his scarlet surcote with Sursha's rampant grasscat more than anything else, although once he turned in her direction she saw the two signature braids he wore in front of each ear, an affectation he'd picked up among his hillclans. "Lord Leamount, may I present Tarma shena Tale'sedrin—"

"Lo'teros, shas tella, Kal'enedral," he replied, much to Tarma's surprise; bowing, making a fist and placing it over his heart as he bowed.

"Ile se'var, Yatakar," she replied, returning his salute with intense curiosity and sharpened interest. *"Ge vede sa'kela Shin'a'in."*

"Only a smattering, I fear. I learned it mostly in self-defense—" He grinned, and Tarma found herself grinning back. "—to keep from getting culls pushed off on me by your fellow clansmen."

"Ah, well—come to me, and you'll get the kind of horses the Hawks mount."

"I'll do that. Idra has high praise for you, the *kyree*, and your *she'enedra*, Swordsworn," he said, meeting her intensely ice-blue eyes as few others had been able. "I could only wish I had a few more of your kind with us. So—the bird returned; that told us there *was* a path through. But what's the track like?"

Somehow Tarma wasn't overly surprised that he came directly to the point. "Bad," she said shortly, as Idra spread out Jodi's maps over the ones already on the table. "It'll be brutal. The only mounts that are going to be able to negotiate that terrain are the Hawks'. *Maybe* some of the ponies your mountain-clan scouts have could make it, but they'd be fair useless on the other side of those hills. No running ability, and on Kelcrag's side of the pass, that's what they'll need. Anything else would break a leg on that track, or break the path down past using."

"Terrain?"

"Big hills, baby mountains, doesn't much matter. Shale most of the way through, and sandstone. Bad footing."

"Huh." He chewed a corner of his mustache and brooded over Jodi's tracings. "That lets out plan one, then. Idra—seems it's going to be up to you."

"Hah—up to me, my rump! If you can't get old Shoveral to move his big fat arse in time, you'll get us slaughtered—"

Tarma glanced up out of the corner of her eye, alarmed at those words, only to see Idra grinning like Warrl with a particularly juicy bone.

"Shoveral knows damned well he's my hidden card; he'll move when he needs to—now, Swordsworn, how long do you reckon it will take all the Hawks to get from here—" His finger stabbed down at the location of their camp. "—to here?"

The second place he indicated was a spot about a candlemark's slow ride from the rear of Kelcrag's lines. As Tarma had figured—striking distance. "About two days, altogether."

"Huhn. Say you got to trail's start at dawn by riding half the night. Think you could get that lot of yours up over that trail, make trail's end by dark, camp cold for a bit of rest, then be within this strike distance by, say, midmorning?"

"No problem. Damn well better have the rest though. Horses'll need it or we won't be able to count on 'em."

"Idra, how do we keep the movement secret?"

Idra thought about that a while. "Loan me those hillclan levies and their bivouac; they're honest enough to guard our camp. We'll move out in groups of about twenty; you move in an equal number of the clansmen. Camp stays full to the naked eye—Kelcrag can't tell one merc from another, no more can his magickers. The people that could tell the difference between them and us won't be able to see what's going on."

"Hah!" He smacked his fist down into his palm. "Good; let me send for Shoveral. We'll plan this out with just the three of us—four, counting the Kal'enedral. Fewer that know, fewer can leak."

The Lord Commander sent one of his pages out after Lord Shoveral, then he and Idra began planning in earnest. From time to time he snapped out a question at Tarma; how far, how many, what about this or that—she answered as best she could, but she was tired, far more weary than she had guessed. She found her tongue feeling oddly clumsy, and she had to think hard about each word before she could get it out.

Finally Leamount and Idra began a low-voiced colloquy she didn't bother to listen to; she just hung on to the edge of the table and tried enforcing her alertness with Kal'enedral discipline exercises. They didn't work overly well; she was on her last wind, for certain.

Leamount caught Tarma's wavering attention. The maps on the table were beginning to go foggy to her eyes. "Swordsworn," he said, looking a little concerned, "you look half dead, but we may need you; what say you go bed down over there in the corner—" He nodded in the direction of his own cot. "If there's a point you need to clarify for us, we'll give you a shake." He raised his voice. "Jons—"

One of the two sentries poked his head in through the tent flap. "Sir?"

"Stir up my squire, would you? Have him find something for this starving warrior to eat and drink."

Tarma had stumbled to the other side of the tent and was already collapsing onto the cot, her weariness washing her under with a vengeance. The blankets felt as welcoming and warm as they looked, and she curled up in them without another thought, feeling Warrl heaving himself up to his usual position at her feet. As the tent and the voices faded, while the wave of exhaustion carried her into slumber, she heard Idra chuckling.

"You might as well not bother Jons," the Captain told Leamount, just before sleep shut Tarma's ears. "I don't think she cares."

Three

Kethry shifted her weight over her mount's shoulders, half-standing in her stirrups to ease Hellsbane's balance as the mare scrambled up the treacherous shale of another slope. They were slightly more than halfway across the hills; it was cold and damp and the lowering gray clouds looked close enough to touch, but at least it wasn't raining again. She wasn't too cold; under her wool cloak she wore her woolen sorceress' robe, the unornamented buff color showing her school was White Winds, and under *that*, woolen breeches, woolen leggings, and the leather armor Tarma had insisted she don. The only time she was uncomfortable was when the wind cut in behind the hood of the robe.

She was a member of the last party to leave the camp and make the crossing; they'd left their wounded to the care of Leamount's hillclansmen and his own personal Healer. Tresti, the Healer-Priest, had been in the second party to slip away from the camp, riding by the side of her beloved Sewen. Oreden and Jiles, the two hedge-mages, had gone two groups later; The herbalist Rethaire and his two young apprentices had left next. Kethry had stayed to the very last, her superior abilities at sensing mage-probes making her the logical choice to deflect any attempts at spying until the full exchange of personnel was complete.

She felt a little at a loss without her partner riding at her left. Tarma had preceded her more than half a day ago, leaving before midnight, as the guide with Idra and the first group. Of all the party that had made the first crossing, only Jodi had remained to ride with the tailguard group.

Jodi was somewhere behind them, checking on the backtrail. That was not as comforting to Kethry as it should have been. Kethry *knew* her fears were groundless, that the frail appearance of the scout belied a tough interior—but—

As if the thought had summoned her, a gray shadow slipped up upon Kethry's right, with so little noise it might have been a shadow in truth. Hellsbane had been joined by a second gray mare so similar in appearance that only an expert could have told that one was a Shin'a'in full-blood battle-steed and the other was not.

That lack of sound was one clue—there was mountain-pony in Lightfoot's background, somewhere. Jodi's beast moved as silently as a wild goat on this shifting surface, so quietly that the scout and her mount raised the hackles on anyone who didn't know them.

Jodi wore her habitual garb of gray leather; with her pale hair and pale eyes and ghost-gray horse, she looked unnervingly like an apparition of Lady Death herself, or some mist-spirit conjured out of the patches of fog that shrouded these hills, as fragile and insubstantial as a thing of shadow and air; and once again Kethry had a twinge of misgiving.

"Any sign of probing?" the scout asked in a neutral voice.

Kethry shook her head. "None. I think we may have gotten away with it."

Jodi sighed. "Don't count your coins before they're in the coffer. There's a reason why *we* are running tail, lady, and it's not just to do with magery, though that's a good share of it."

The scout cast a doubtful look at Kethry—and for the first time Kethry realized that the woman had serious qualms about *her* abilities to handle this mission, if it came to something other than a simple trek on treacherous ground.

Kethry didn't bother to hide an ironic grin.

Jodi noted it, and cocked her head to one side, moving easily with her horse. Her saddle was hardly more than a light pad of leather; it didn't even creak when she shifted, unconsciously echoing the movements of her mare. "Something funny, lady?"

"Very. I think we've been thinking exactly the same things—about each other."

Jodi's answering slow grin proved that Kethry hadn't been wrong. "Ha. And we should know better, shouldn't we? It's a pity we didn't know each other well enough to trust without thinking and worrying—especially since neither of us look like fighters. But we should have figured that Idra knows what she's doing; neither of us are hothouse plants —or we wouldn't be Hawks."

"Exactly. So—give me the reasons this particular lot is riding tail; maybe I can do something about preventing a problem."

"Right enough—one—" The scout freed her right hand from the reins to hold up a solemn finger. "—is the trail. Shale shifts, cracks. We're riding after all the rest, and we'll be making the last few furlongs in early evening gloom. This path has been getting some hard usage, more than it usually gets. If the trail is likely to give, it'll give under *us*. You'll notice we're all of us the best riders, and the ones with the best horses in the Hawks."

Kethry considered this, as Hellsbane topped the hill and picked her cautious way down the sloping trail. "Hmm-hmm. All right, can we halt at the next ridge? There's a very tiny bit of magery I can work that might help us out with that."

Jodi pursed her lips. "Is that wise?"

Kethry nodded, slowly. "It's a very low-level piece of earth-witchery; something even a shepherd wisewoman might well know. I don't think any of Kelcrag's mages is likely to take note of it—assuming they can even see it, and I doubt they will. It's witchery, not sorcery, and Kelcrag's magickers are all courtly mages, greater and lesser. *My* school is more eclectic; we use whatever comes to hand, and that can be damned useful—somebody looking for High Magick probably won't see Low, or think it's worth investigating. After all, what does Kelcrag need to fear from a peasant granny?"

Jodi considered that for a moment, her head held slightly to one side. "Tell me, why is it that Jiles and Oreden have gotten so much better since you've been with us?"

Kethry chuckled, but it was with a hint of sadness. It had been very hard to convince the hedge-wizards that their abilities did not match their dreams. "You want the truth? Their talents are all in line with Low Magick; earth-witchery, that sort of thing. I convinced them that there's *nothing* wrong with that, asked them which they'd rather ride, a good, steady trail-horse or *your* fire-eater. They aren't stupid; they saw right away what I was getting at." She set Hellsbane at the next slope, her hooves dislodging bits of shale and sending them clattering down behind them. "So now that they aren't trying to master spells they haven't the Talent to use properly, they're doing fine. Frankly, I would rather have them with us than two of those courtly mages. Water-finding is a lot more use than calling lightning, and the fire-making spell does us more good than the ability to light up a ballroom."

"You won't catch me arguing. So what's this magic of yours going to do?"

"Show me the weak spots in the trail. If there's something ready to give, I'll know about it before it goes."

"And?"

"I should be able to invoke a greater magic at that

point, and hold the pieces together long enough for us to get across."

"Won't *that* draw attention?"

"It would," Kethry replied slowly, "if I did what a court mage would do, and draw on powers outside myself—which causes ripples; no, I have just enough power of my own, and that's what I'll use. There won't be any stir on the other planes. . . ." *But it's going to cost me if I do things that way. Maybe high. Well, I'll handle that when the time comes.* "You said *one* reason we're riding tailmost—that implies there's more reasons."

"Two—we're tailguards in truth. We could find ourselves fighting hand to hand with Kelcrag's scouts or his mages. They haven't detected us that we know of, but there's no sense in assuming less than the worst."

"So long as they don't outnumber us—I'm not exactly as helpless in a fight as Tresti." She caught the cloud of uncertainty in Jodi's pale blue eyes, and said, surprised, "I thought everybody knew about this sword of mine."

"There's stories, but frankly, lady—"

"Keth. I, as Tarma would tell you, am no lady."

That brought a glimmer of smile. "Keth, then. Well, none of *us* have ever seen that blade do anything but heal."

"Need's better at causing wounds than curing them, at least in *my* hands," Kethry told her. "That's her gift to me; in a fight, she makes a mage the equal of any swordswoman born. If it comes to magic, though, she's pretty well useless for my purposes—it's to a fighter she gives magic immunity. But—I'll tell you what, I've got a notion. If it comes to battle by magery, I'll try and get her to you before I get involved in a duel arcane; she'll shield you from even a godling's magic. Tarma proved that, once. She may even be able to shield more than one, if you all crowd together."

There was a flash of interest at that, and a hint of relief. "Then I think I'll worry less about you. Well—there's a reason three that we're riding tail: if we find we've ridden straight into ambush at trail's end, we're the lot that's got the best chance of getting one of us back to tell Leamount."

"Gah. Grim reasons, all of them—can we stop here for a breath or two?"

They had just topped a ridge, with sufficient space between them and the next in line that a few moments spent halted wouldn't hamper his progress any. Jodi looked about her, grimaced, then nodded with reluctance. "A bit exposed to my mind, but—"

"This won't take long." Kethry gathered the threads of earth-magic, the subtlest and least detectable of all the mage-energies, and whispered a command along those particular threads that traced their path across the hills. There was an almost imperceptible shift in the energy flows, then the spell settled into place and became invisible even to the one who had set it. The difference was that Kethry was now at one with the path; she *felt* the path through the hills, from end to end, like a whisper of sand across the surface of her mental "skin." If the path was going to collapse, the backlash would alert her.

"Let's go—"

"That's all there is to it?" Jodi looked at her askance.

"Magery isn't all lightnings and thunders. The best magery is as subtle as a tripwire, and as hard to detect."

"Well." Jodi sent her mount picking a careful path down the hillside, and looked back at Kethry with an almost-smile. "I think I could get to appreciate magery."

Kethry grinned outright, remembering that Jodi's other specialty was subterfuge, infiltration, and assassination. "Take my word for it, the real difference between a Masterclass mage and an apprentice is not in the amount of power, it's in the usage. You've been over this trail already; what do you think—are we going to make trail's end by dark?."

Jodi narrowed her eyes, taking a moment. "No," she said finally, "I don't think so. That's when I'll take point, when it starts to get dark. And that's when we'll have to be most alert."

Kethry nodded, absently, and pulled her hood closer about her neck against a lick of wind. "If an attack comes, it's likely to be then. And the same goes for accident?"

"Aye."

It was growing dark, far faster than Kethry liked, and there was still no end to the trail in sight. But there had also been no sign that their movement was being followed—

Suddenly her nerves twanged like an ill-tuned harpstring. For one short, disorienting moment, she vibrated in backlash, for that heartbeat or two of time completely helpless to think or act. Then nearly fifteen years of training and practice took over, and without even being aware of it, she gathered mage-energy from the core of her very being and formed a net of it—a net to catch what was even now about to fall.

Just in time; up ahead in the darkness, she heard the slide of rock, a horse's fear-ridden shriek, and the harsh cry of a man seeing his own death looming in his face. She felt the energy-net sag, strain—then hold.

She clamped her knees around Hellsbane's barrel and dropped her reins, telling the horse mutely to "stand." The battlesteed obeyed, bracing all four hooves, far steadier than the rocks about her. Kethry firmed her concentration until it was adamantine, and closed her eyes against distraction. Since she could not see what she was doing, this would take every wisp of her attention—

Gently, this must be done as gently as handling a pennybird chick new-hatched. If she frightened the horse, and it writhed out of her energy-net—horse and rider would plummet to their doom.

She cupped her hands before her, echoing the form of the power-net, and contemplated it.

Broken lines of power showed her where the path had collapsed, and the positioning of her "net" told her without her seeing the trail ahead just where her captives were cradled.

"Keth—" Jodi's voice came from the darkness ahead, calm and steady; no sign of panic there. "We lost a very short section of the path; those of you behind us won't have any problem jumping the gap. The immediate problem is the rider that went over. It's Gerrold and Vetch; the horse is half over on his right side and Gerrold's pinned under him, but neither one of them is hurt and you caught both before they slid more than a few feet. Gerrold's got the beast barely calmed, but he's not struggling. Can you do anything more for them other than just holding them?"

Kethry eased her concentration just enough to answer. "If I get them righted, maybe raise them a bit, can he get Vetch back onto the path?"

"You can do that?"

"I can try—"

Hoof sounds going, then returning. Kethry "read" the lines of energy cradling the man and beast, slowly getting a picture of how they were lying by the shape of the energy-net.

"Gerrold's got Vetch gentled and behaving. He says if you take it slow—"

Kethry did not answer, needing all her focus on the task at hand. Slowly she moved her fingers; as she did she lessened the pressure on one side of the net, increased it on the other, until the shape within began to tilt upright. There was a lessening of tension within the net, as horse and rider lost fear; that helped.

Now, beneath the hooves of the trapped horse she firmed the net until it was as strong as the steadiest ground, taking away some of the mage-threads from the sides to do so. When nothing untoward occurred, she took more of those threads, using them to raise the level of that surface, slowly, carefully, so as not to startle the horse. One by one she rewove those threads, raising the platform thumblength by agonizing thumblength.

She was shaking and drenched with sweat by the time she got it high enough, and just about at the end of her strength. When a clatter of hooves on rock and an exultant shout told her that Gerrold had gotten his mount back onto safe ground, she had only enough energy left to cling to her saddle for the last few furlongs of the journey.

"Right now," Idra said quietly, stretched out along a hilltop next to Tarma, "The old war-horse should be giving them a good imitation of a *tired* old war-horse."

The hilltop gave them a fairly tolerable view for furlongs in any direction; they were just beyond the range of Kelcrag's sentries, and Kethry was shielding them in the way she had learned from the example of Moonsong k'Vala, the Tale'edras Adept from the Pelagiris Forest—making them seem a part of the landscape—to mage-sight, just a thicket of brinle-bushes. In the far distance was the pass; filling it was the dark blot of Kelcrag's forces.

At this moment—as he had for the last two days—Leamount was giving a convincing imitation of a commander truly interested in coming to an agreement with his enemy. Heralds had been coming and going hour by hour with offers and counter-offers—all of this false negotiation buying time for the Hawks to get into place.

"Well, it's now or never," Idra said finally, as she and Tarma abandoned their height and squirmed down their side of the hill to join her company. "Kethry?"

Kethry, on foot like all the rest, nodded and joined hands with her two mage-partners. "Shield your eyes," she warned them. "It'll go on a count of five."

Tarma and the rest of the Hawks averted their eyes and turned their horses' heads away as Kethry counted slowly. When Kethry reached five, there was a flare of light so bright that it shone redly through Tarma's eyelids even with her head turned. It was followed by a second flash, and then a third.

From a distance it would look like the lightning that flickered every day along the hillsides. But Leamount's mages were watching this particular spot for just that signal of three flickers of light, and testing for energy-auras to see if it was mage-light and not natural lightning. Now Leamount would break off his negotiations and resume his attacks on Kelcrag's army, concentrating on the eastern edge. That would seem reasonable: Kelcrag had stationed his foot there; they might be vulnerable to a charge of heavy cavalry. Leamount's own western flank was commanded by Lord Shoveral, whose standard was a badger and whose mode of battle matched his token; he was implacable in defense, but no one had yet seen him on the attack, so Kelcrag might well believe that he had no heart for it.

He was, one hoped, about to be surprised.

One also hoped, fervently, that Kelcrag's mages had *not* noticed that it was mage-light and not lightning that had flickered to their rear.

:*They've no reason to look for mage-light, mindmate,*: Warrl said soberly. :*Kelcrag's wizards are all courtly types. They very seldom think about* hiding *what they're doing, or trying to make it seem like something natural.*

To them, mage-light is something to illuminate a room with, not something to use for a signal. If they wish to pass messages, they make a sending.:

"I hope you're right, Furface," Tarma replied, mounting. "The more surprised they are, the more of us are going to survive this."

At Idra's signal, the Hawks moved into a disciplined canter; no point in trying too hard to stay undercover now.

They urged their mounts over hills covered only with scraggy bushes and dead, dry grass; they would have been hard put to find any cover if they'd needed it. But luck was with them.

They topped a final hilltop and only then encountered Kelcrag's few sentries. They were all afoot; the lead riders coldly picked them off with a few well-placed arrows before they could sound an alert. The sentries fell, either pierced with arrows or stumbling over their wounded comrades. And the fallen were trampled—for the Hawks' horses were war-trained, and a war-trained horse does not hesitate when given the signal to make certain of a fallen foe. That left no chance that Kelcrag could be warned.

Ahead of the riders, now stretching their canter into a gallop, was the baggage train.

Kethry and her two companions rode to the forefront for the moment. Each mage was haloed by one of Kethry's glowing mage-shields; a shield that blurred the edges of vision around a mage and his mount as well. It made Tarma's eyes ache to look at them, so she tried not to. The shields wouldn't deflect missiles, but not being able to look straight at your target made that target *damned* hard to hit.

The two hedge-wizards growled guttural phrases, made elaborate throwing motions—and smoking, flaming balls appeared in the air before their hands to fly at the wagons and supplies. Kethry simply locked her hands together and held them out in front of her—and each wagon or tent she stared at burst into hot blue flame seemingly of its own accord.

This was noisy; it was meant to be. The noncombatants with the baggage—drovers, cooks, personal servants, the odd whore—were screaming in fear and fleeing in all directions, adding to the noise. There didn't seem to be anyone with enough authority back here to get so much as a fire brigade organized.

The Hawks charged through the fires and the frightened, milling civilians, and headed straight for the rear of Kelcrag's lines. Now Kethry and the mages had dropped back until they rode—a bit more protected—in the midst of the Sunhawks. They would be needed now only if one of Kelcrag's mages happened to be stationed on this flank.

For the rest, it was time for bow work. Kelcrag's men—armored cavalry here, for the most part; nobles and retainers, and mostly young—were still trying to grasp the fact that they'd been hit from the rear.

The Hawks swerved just out of bowshot, riding their horses in a flanking move along the back of the lines. They didn't stop; that would make them stationary targets. They just began swirling in and out at the very edge of the enemy's range, as Tarma led the first sortie to engage.

About thirty of them peeled off from the main group, galloping forward with what must look to Kelcrag's men like utter recklessness. It wasn't; they stayed barely within their range as they shot into the enemy lines. This was what the Hawks were famous for, this horseback skirmishing. Most of them rode with reins in their teeth, a few, like Tarma and Jodi, dropped their reins altogether, relying entirely on their weight and knees to signal their mounts. Tarma loosed three arrows in the time it took most of the rest of her sortie group to launch one, her short horse-bow so much a part of her that she thought of nothing consciously but picking her targets. She was aware only of Ironheart's muscles laboring beneath her legs, of the shifting smoke that stung eyes and carried a burnt flavor into the back of her throat, of the sticky feel of sweat on her back, of a kind of exultation in her skill—and it was all over in heartbeats. Arrows away, the entire group wheeled and galloped to the rear of the Hawks, already nocking more missiles—for hard on their heels came a second group, a third—it made for a continuous rain of fire that was taking its toll even of heavily armored men—and as they rode, the Hawks jeered at their enemies, and shouted Idra's rallying call. The hail of arrows that fell on the enemy wounded more horses than men—a fact Tarma was sorry about—but the fire, the hail of arrows, and the catcalls inflamed their enemy's tempers in a way that nothing else could have done.

And, as Leamount and Idra had planned, the young, headstrong nobles let those tempers loose.

They broke ranks, leaders included, and charged their mocking foes. All they thought of now was to engage the retreating Hawks, forgetful of their orders, forgetful of everything but that this lot of commoners had pricked their vanity and was now getting away.

Now the Hawks scattered, breaking into a hundred little groups, their purpose accomplished.

Tarma managed to get to Kethry's side, and the two of them plowed their way back through the burning wreckage of the baggage train.

Iron-shod hooves pounding, their mounts raced as if they'd been harnessed side by side. Kethry clung grimly to the pommel of her saddle, as her partner could see out of the corner of her eye. She was not the horsewoman that the Shin'a'in was, she well knew it, and Hellsbane was galloping erratically; moving far too unpredictably for her to draw

Need. At this point she was well-nigh helpless; it would be up to Tarma and the battlemares to protect her.

An over-brave pikeman rose up out of the smoke before them, thinking to hook Tarma from her seat. She ducked beneath his pole arm, and Ironheart trampled him into the red-stained mud. Another footman made a try for Kethry, but Hellsbane snapped at him, crushed his shoulder in her strong teeth, shook him like a dog with a rag while he shrieked, then dropped him again. A rider who thought to intercept them had the trick Tarma and Ironheart had played on Duke Greyhame's sentry performed on him and his steed—only in deadly earnest. Ironheart reared, screaming challenge, and crow-hopped forward. The gelding the enemy rode backed in panic from the slashing hooves, and as they passed him, his rider's head was kicked in before they could get out of range.

The battlesteeds kited through the smoke and flames of the burning camp with no more fear of either than of the scrubby shrubbery. Three times Tarma turned in her saddle and let fly one of the lethal little arrows of the Shin'a'in—as those pursuing found to their grief, armor was of little use when an archer could find and target a helm-slit.

Then shouting began behind them; their pursuers pulled up, looked back—and began belatedly to return to their battleline. Too late—for Lord Shoveral had made his rare badger's charge—and had taken full advantage of the hole that the work of the Sunhawks had left in Kelcrag's lines. Kelcrag's forces were trapped between Shoveral and the shale cliffs, with nowhere to retreat.

Using her knees, Tarma signaled Ironheart to slow, and Hellsbane followed her stablemate's lead. Tarma couldn't make out much through the blowing smoke, but what she *could* see told her all she needed to know. Kelcrag's banner was down, and there was a milling mass of men—mostly wearing Leamount's scarlet surcoats—where it had once stood. All over the field, fighters in Kelcrag's blue were throwing down their weapons.

The civil war was over.

Kethry touched the tip of her index finger to a spot directly between the sweating fighter's eyebrows; he promptly shuddered once, his eyes rolled up into his head, and he sagged into the waiting arms of his shieldbrother.

"Lay him out there—that's right—" Rethaire directed the disposition of the now-slumbering Hawk. His partner eased him down slowly, stretching him out on his back on a horseblanket, with his wounded arm practically in the herbalist's lap. Rethaire nodded. "—good. Keth—"

Kethry blinked, coughed once, and shook her head a little. "Who's next?" she asked.

"Bluecoat."

Kethry stared askance at him. A Bluecoat? One of *Kelcrag's* people?

Rethaire frowned. "No, don't look at me that way, he's under Mercenary's Truce; he's all right or I wouldn't have let him in here. He's one of Devaril's Demons."

"Ah." The Demons had a good reputation among the companies, even if most of Devaril's meetings with Idra generally ended up as shouting matches. Too bad they'd been on opposite sides in this campaign.

Rethaire finished dusting the long, oozing slash in their companion's arm with blue-green powder, and began carefully sewing it up with silk thread. "Well, are you going to sit there all day?"

"Right, I'm on it," she replied, getting herself to her feet. "Who's with him?"

"My apprentice, Dee. The short one."

Kethry pushed sweat-soaked hair out of her eyes,

and tried once again to get it all confined in a tail while she glanced around the space outside the infirmary tent, looking for the green-clad, chubby figure of Rethaire's youngest apprentice. She resolutely shut out the sounds of pain and the smell of sickness and blood; she kept telling herself that this was not as bad as it could have been. The worst casualties were under cover of the tent; those out here were the ones that would be walking (or limping) back to their own quarters when they woke up from Rethaire's drugs or Kethry's spell. They were all just lucky that it was still only overcast and not raining. Sun would have baked them all into heatstroke. Rain . . . best not think about fever and pneumonia.

With no prospect of further combat, Kethry was no longer hoarding her magical energies, either personal or garnered from elsewhere, but the only useful spell she had when it came to healing wounds like these was the one that induced instant slumber. So that was *her* job; put the patients out, while Rethaire or his assistants sewed and splinted them back together again.

Poor Jiles and Oreden didn't even have *that* much to do; although as Low Magick practitioners they *did* have Healing abilities, they'd long since exhausted their powers, and now were acting as plain, nonmagical attendants to Tresti. That was what was bad about a late-fall campaign for them; with most of the land going into winter slumber, there was very little ambient energy for a user of Low Magick to pull on.

Tarma was out with Jodi and a few of Leamount's farriers, salvaging what horses they could, and killing the ones too far gone to save. And, sometimes, performing the same office for a human or two.

Kethry shuddered, and wiped the back of her hand across her damp forehead, frowning when she looked at it and saw how filthy it was.

Thank the gods that stuff of Rethaire's prevents infection, or we'd lose half the wounded. We've lost too many as it is. That last sortie had cost the Sunhawks dearly; they were down to two hundred. Fifty were dead, three times that were wounded. Virtually everyone had lost a friend; the uninjured were tending wounded companions.

But it could have been so much worse—so very much worse.

She finally spotted apprentice Dee, and picked her way through the prone and sleeping bodies to get to his side.

"Great good gods! Why is he out here?" she exclaimed, seeing the patient. He was half-propped on a saddle; stretched out before him was his wounded leg. Kethry nearly gagged at the sight of the blood-drenched leg of his breeches, the mangled muscles, and the tourniquet practically at his groin.

"Looks worse than it is, Keth." Dee didn't even look up. "More torn up than anything; didn't touch the big vein at all. He don't need Tresti, just you and me." His clever hands were busy cutting bits of the man's breeches away, while the mercenary bit his lip until it, too, bled; hoping to keep from crying out.

"What in hell got *you*, friend?" Kethry asked, kneeling down at the man's side. She had to have his attention, or the spell wouldn't work. The man was white under his sunburn, his black beard matted with dirt and sweat, the pupils of his eyes wide with pain.

"Some—shit!—big wolf. Had m' bow all trained on yer back, m'lady. Bastard come outa nowhere n' took out m'leg. Should'a known better'n t' sight on a Hawk; 'specially since I *knew* 'bout you havin' that beast."

Kethry started. "Warrl—Windborn, no wonder you look like hacked meat! Let me tell you, you're

71

lucky he didn't go for your throat! I hope you'll forgive me, but I—can't say I'm sorry—"

The man actually managed a bare hint of smile, and patted her knee with a bloody hand. "That's—gah!—war, m'lady. No offense." He clenched his other hand until the knuckles were white as Dee picked pieces of fabric out of his wounds.

Kethry sighed the three syllables that began the sleep-spell, and felt her hands begin to tingle with the gathering energy. Slow, though—*she* was coming to the end of her resources.

"But why did you come to us for help?"

"Don't trust them horse-leeches, they wanted t' take the leg off. I knew yer people'd save it. Them damn highborns, they got no notion what 'is leg means to a merc."

Kethry nodded, grimacing. Without his leg, this man would be out of a job—and likely starve to death.

"And th' Demons' ain't got no Healers nor magickers. Never saw th' need for 'em."

"Oh?" That was the root and branch of Devaril's constant arguments with Idra. "Well, now you know why we have them, don't you?" She still wasn't ready. Not *quite* yet; the level wasn't high enough. Until she could touch him, she had to keep his attention.

"Yeah, well—kinda reckon ol' Horseface's right, now. Neat trick y' pulled on us, settin' the camp afire wi' the magickers. An' havin' yer own Healers beats hell outa hopin' yer contract 'members he's s'pposed t' keep ye patched up. Specially when 'e's lost. Reckon we'll be lookin' fer recruits after we get mustered out." He grimaced again, and nodded to her. " 'F yer innerested, m'lady—well, th' offer's open. 'F not, well, pass th' word, eh?"

Kethry was a little amused at the certainty in his words. "You're so high up in the Demons, then, that you can speak for them?"

He bit off a curse of pain, and grinned feebly just as she reached for his forehead. "Should say. *I'm* Devaril."

Kethry was wrung with weariness, and her mage-energies were little more than flickers when Tarma came looking for her. She looked nearly transparent with exhaustion, ready to float away on an errant wind.

The swordswoman knelt down in the dust beside where Kethry was sitting; she was obviously still trying to muster up energies all but depleted.

"Keth—"

The mage looked up at her with a face streaked with dried blood—

Thank the Warrior, none of it hers.

"Lady Windborn. I think I hate war."

"Hai," Tarma agreed, grimly. Now that the battle-high had worn off, as always, she was sick and sickened. Such a damned waste—all for the sake of one fool too proud to be ruled by a woman. All that death, men, women, good beasts. Innocent civilians. "Hell of a way to make a living. Can you get loose?"

"If it isn't for magery. I'm tapped out."

"It isn't. Idra wants us in her tent."

Tarma rose stiffly and gave her hand to her partner, who frankly needed it to get to her feet. The camp was quiet, the quiet of utter exhaustion. Later would come the drinking bouts, the boasts, the counting of bonuses and loot. Now was just time to hurt, and to heal; to mourn the lost friends and help care for the injured; and to sleep, if one could. With the coming of dusk fires were being kindled, and torches. And, off in the distance, pyres. The Hawks, like most mercenary companies, burned their dead. Tarma had already done her share of funeral duty; she was not particularly unhappy to miss the next immolation.

Two of the Hawks not too flagged to stand watch

were acting sentry on Idra's tent. Tarma nodded to both of them, and pushed her way in past the flap, Kethry at her heels.

Idra inclined her head in their direction and indicated a pile of blankets with a wave of her hand. Sewen already occupied her cot, and Geoffrey, Tamas and Lethra, his serjeants, the equipment chest, the stool, and another pile of blankets respectively. The fourth serjeant, Bevis, was currently sleeping off one of Kethry's spells.

"Where's your *kyree*?" the Captain asked, as they lowered themselves down onto the pile.

"Sentry-go. He's about the only one of us fit for it, so he volunteered."

"Bless him. I got him a young pig—I figured he'd earned it, and I figured he'd like to get the taste of man out of his mouth."

Tarma grinned. "Sounds like he's been bitching at *you*, Captain, for a pig, he'd stand sentry all bloody night!"

"Have him see the cook when he's hungry." Idra took the remaining stool, lowering herself to it with a grimace of pain. Her horse had been shot out from under her, and she'd taken a fall that left her bruised from breast to ankle.

"Well." She surveyed them all, her most trusted assistants, wearing a troubled look. "I've—well, I've had some unsettling news. It's nothing to do with the campaign—" She cut short the obvious question hurriedly. "—no, in fact Geoffrey is sitting on our mustering-out pay. Leamount's been damned generous, above what he contracted for. No, this is personal. I'm going to have to part company with you for a while."

Tarma felt her jaw go slack; the others stared at their Captain with varying expressions of stunned amazement.

Sewen was the first to recover. "Idra—what'n th' hell is *that* supposed t'mean? Part company? Why?"

Idra sighed, and rubbed her neck with one sun-browned hand. "It's duty, of a sort. You all know where I'm from—well, my father just died, gods take his soul. He and I never did agree on much, but he had the grace to let me go my own way when it was obvious he'd never keep me hobbled at home except by force. Mother's been dead, oh, twenty-odd years. That means I've got two brothers in line for the throne, since I renounced any claim I had."

"Two?" Kethry was looking a bit more alert now, Tarma noticed. "I thought the law in Rethwellan was primogeniture."

"Sort of, sort of. That's where the problem is. Father favored my younger brother. So do the priests and about half the nobles. The merchants and the rest of the nobles favor following the law. My older brother—well, he may have the law behind him, but he was a wencher and a ne'er-do-well when I left, and I haven't heard he's improved. That sums up the problem. The Noble Houses are split right down the middle and there's only one way to break the deadlock."

"You?" Geoffrey asked.

She grimaced. "Aye. It's a duty I can't renounce—and damned if I like it. I thought I'd left politics behind the day I formed the Sunhawks. I'd have avoided it if I could, but the ministers' envoys went straight to Leamount; now there's no getting out of it. And in all honesty, there's a kind of duty to your people that goes with being born into a royal house; I pretty much owe it to them to see that they get the best leader, if I can. So I'm going back to look the both of my brothers over and cast my vote; I'll be leaving within the hour."

"But—!" The panic on Sewen's face was almost funny.

"Sewen, you're in charge," she continued implacably. "I expect this won't take long; I'll meet you all in winter quarters. As I said, we've been paid;

we only need to wait until our wounded are mobile before you head back there. Any questions?"

The weary resignation on her face told them all that she wasn't looking forward to this—and that she wouldn't welcome protests. What Idra wanted from her commanders was the assurance that they would take care of things for her in her absence as they had always done in her presence; with efficiency and dispatch.

It was the least they could give her.

They stood nearly as one, and gave her drillfield-perfect salutes.

"No questions, Captain," Sewen said for all of them. "We'll await you at Hawksnest, as ordered."

Four

Kethry was in trouble.

A glittering ball of blinding white hurtled straight for her eyes. Kethry ducked behind the ice-covered wall of the fortifications, then launched a missile of her own at the enemy, who was even now charging her fortress.

The leading warrior took her return volley squarely on the chest, and went down with a blood-freezing shriek of anguish.

"Tarma!" squealed the second of the enemy warriors, skidding to a stop in the snow beside the fallen Shin'a'in.

"No—onward, my brave ones!" Tarma declaimed. "I am done for—but you must regain our ancient homeland! You must fight on, and you must avenge me!" Then she writhed into a sitting position, clutched her snow-spattered tunic, pointed at the wall with an outflung arm, and pitched backward into the drift she'd used to break her fall.

The remaining fighters—all four of them—gathered their courage along with their snowballs and resumed their charge.

Kethry and her two fellow defenders drove them ruthlessly back with a steady, carefully coordinated barrage. "Stand fast, my friends," Kethry encouraged her forces, as the enemy gathered just outside their range for another charge. "Never shall we let the sacred palace of—of—Whatever-it-is fall into the hands of these barbarians!"

"Sacred, my horse's behind!" taunted Tarma, reclining at her ease in the snowbank, head propped up on one arm. "You soft city types have mush for brains; wouldn't know sacred if it walked up and bonked you with a blessing! That's *our* sacred ground you're cluttering up with your filthy city! My nomads are clear of eye and mind from all the healthy riding they do. *They* know sacred when they see it!"

"You're dead!" Kethry returned, laughing. "You can't talk if you're dead!"

"Oh, I wouldn't bet on that," Tarma replied, grinning widely.

"Well, it's not fair—" Kethry began, when one of Tarma's "nomads" launched into a speech of her own.

It was very impassioned, full of references to "our fallen leader, now with the stars," and "our duty to free our ancient homeland," and it was just a little confused, but it was a rather good speech for a twelve year old. It certainly got her fellow fighters' blood going. This time there was no stopping them; they stormed right over the walls of the snowfort and captured the flag, despite the best efforts of Kethry and her band of defenders. Kethry made a last stand on the heights next to the flag but to no avail; she was hit with three snowballs at once, and went down even more dramatically than Tarma.

The barbarians howled for joy, piled their other victims on top of Kethry, and did a victory dance around the bodies. When Tarma resurrected herself and came to join them, Kethry rose to *her* feet, protesting at the top of her lungs.

"No, you don't—dead is dead, woman!" Kethry had come up with one of her unthrown missiles in her hands; now she launched it from point-blank range and got the surprised Tarma right in the face with it.

The never-broken rule decreed loose snowballs

only. Tarma enforced that rule with a hand of iron, and Kethry would never even have thought of violating it. This was a game, and injuries had no part in it. So Tarma was unhurt, but now wore a white mask covering her from forehead to chin.

Only for a moment. "AAARRRG!" she howled, scraping the snow off her face, and springing at Kethry, fingers mimicking claws. "My disguise! You've ruined my disguise!"

"*Run!*" Kethry cried in mock fear, dodging. "It's—it's—"

"The great and terrible Snow Demon!" Tarma supplied, making a grab at the children, who screamed in excitement and fled. "I tricked you fools into fighting for me! Now I have *all* of you at my mercy, and the city as well! *AAAAARRRG!*"

It was only when a more implacable enemy—the children's mothers—came to fetch them away that the new game came to a halt.

"Thanks for minding them, Tarma," said one of the mothers, a former Hawk herself. She was collecting two little girls who looked—and were—the same age. Varny and her shieldmate Sania had met in the Sunhawks, and when an unlucky swordstroke had taken out Varny's left eye, they'd decided that since Varny was mustering-out anyway because of the injury, they might as well have the family they both wanted. Though how they'd managed to get pregnant almost simultaneously was a bit of a wonder. Somewhat to their disappointment, neither child was interested in following the sword. Varny's wanted to be a scrivener, and Sania's a Healer—and the latter, at least, was already showing some evidence of that Gift.

"No problem," Tarma replied, "You know I enjoy it. It's nice to be around children who don't take warfare seriously."

In point of fact, none of these children was being trained for fighting; all had indicated to their parents that they wished more peaceful occupations.

So their play-battles *were* play, and not more practice.

"Well, we still appreciate having an afternoon to ourselves, so I hope you don't ever get tired of them," one of the other mothers replied with a broad smile.

"Not a chance," Tarma told her. "I'll let you know next afternoon I've got free, and I'll kidnap them again."

"Bless you!" With that, and similar expressions of gratitude, the women and their weary offspring vanished into the streets of the snow-covered town.

"Whew." Tarma supported herself on the wall of the snowfort with both arms, and looked over at Kethry, panting. Her eyes were shining, and the grin she was still wearing reached and warmed them. "Gods, did *we* have that much energy at that age?"

"Damned if I remember. I'm just pleased I managed to keep up with them. Lady bless, I'd never have believed you could get this overheated in midwinter!"

"You had it easy. *I* was the one who had to keep leading the charges."

"So *that's* why you let me take you out so easily!" Kethry teased. "Shame on you, being in that poor a shape! You know, I rather liked that Snow Demon touch—I was a little uneasy with Jininan's rhetoric."

"Can't teach a child too early that there are folks that will use him. I just about had a foal when I found out there weren't any granny-stories up here on those lines. We Shin'a'in must have at least a dozen about the youngling who takes things on face value and gets eaten for his stupidity. Come to think of it, the Snow Demon is one of them. He ate about half a Clan before he was through."

"*Nasty* story!" Kethry helped Tarma beat some of the snow out of her clothing, and the powdery stuff sparkled in the late-afternoon sunlight as it drifted down. "Was there such a creature, really? And was that what it did?"

"There was. And it did. It showed up in an unusually cold winter one year—oh, about four generations ago. A Kal'enedral finally took it out—one of my teachers, to tell the truth. Mutual kill, very dramatic—also, he tells me, *damned* painful. I'll croak you the song sometime. Tonight, if you like."

Kethry raised an eyebrow in surprise. *That* meant Tarma was in an extraordinarily good mood. While time had brought a certain amount of healing to the ruined voice that had once been the pride of her Clan, Tarma's singing was still not something she paraded in public. Her voice was still harsh, and the tonalities were peculiar. She sometimes sounded to Kethry like someone who had been breathing smoke for forty-odd years. She was very sensitive about it and didn't offer to sing very often.

"What brought this on?" Kethry asked, as they crunched through the half-trampled snow, heading back to their double room in the Hawks' barracks. "You're seeming more than usually pleased with yourself."

Tarma grinned. "Partly this afternoon."

Kethry nodded, understanding. Tarma adored children—which often surprised the boots off their parents. More, she was very good with them. And children universally loved her and her never-ending patience with them. She would play with them, tell them stories, listen to their woes—if she hadn't been Kal'enedral, she'd have made an excellent mother. As it was, she was the willing child tender for any woman in Hawksnest who had ties to the company.

When she had time. Which, between drill and teaching duties, wasn't nearly as often as she liked. Somewhere in the back of her mind, Kethry was rather looking forward to the nebulous day when she and Tarma would retire to start their schools.

Because then, Tarma would have younglings of her *own*—by way of Kethry. More, she would have the children that would form the core of her resurrected Clan.

And bringing Tale'sedrin back to life would make Tarma happy enough that the smile she wore too seldom might become a permanent part of her expression.

"So—what's the other part?" Kethry asked, shaking herself out of her woolgathering when she nearly tripped on a clump of snow.

Tarma snickered, eyes narrowed against the snow-glare and the westering sunlight. Her tone and her expression were both malicious. "Leslac's cooling his heels in the jail as of last night."

"Oh, *really?*" Kethry was delighted. "What happened?"

"Let's wait till we get inside; it's a long story."

Since they were only a few steps from the entrance to their granite-walled barracks, Kethry was willing to wait. As officers, they *could* have taken more opulent quarters, but frankly, they didn't really want them. Tarma hardly had any need for privacy; Kethry had yet to find anyone in or out of the Hawks that she wanted to dally with on any regular basis. On the rare occasions where comradeship got physical, she was more than willing to rent a room in an inn overnight. So they shared the same kind of spartan quarters as the rest of the mercenaries; a plain double room on the first floor of the barracks. The walls were wood, paneled over the stone of the building, there were pegs for their weapons, and stands for their armor, a single wardrobe, two beds, one on each wall, and three chairs and a small table. That was about the extent of it. The only concession to their rank was a wood-fired stove: Tarma felt the winter cold too much otherwise. They had a few luxuries besides: thick fur coverlets and heavy wool blankets on the beds, some fine silver goblets, oil lamps and candles instead of rush-dips—but no few of the fighters had those, paid for out of their earnings. Both of them felt that since they worked as closely as they did with their underlings, there was no sense in having quarters that made subordinates uncomfortable. And, truth to tell, neither of them would truly have felt at ease in more opulent surroundings.

They pulled off their snow-caked garments and changed quickly, hanging the old on pegs by the stove to dry. Kethry noted as she pulled on a soft, comfortable brown robe and breeches, that Tarma had donned black, and frowned. It was true that Kal'enedral only wore dark, muted colors—but black was for ritual combat or bloodfeud.

Tarma didn't miss the frown, faint as it was. "Don't get your hackles up; it's all I've got left— everything else is at the launderers or wet. I'm not planning on calling anybody out—not even that damned off-key songster. Much as he deserves it— and much as I'd like to."

Warrl raised his head from the shadows of the corner he'd chosen for his own, with a contemptuous snort. The *kyree* liked the cold even less than Tarma, and spent much of his time in the warm corner by the stove curled up on a pad of old rugs.

:*You two have no taste. I happen to think Leslac is a fine musician, and a very talented one.*:

Tarma answered with a snort of her own. "All right then, *you* go warm his bed. I'm sure he'd appreciate it."

Warrl simply lowered his head back to his paws, and closed his glowing golden eyes with dignity.

"Tell, tell, tell!" Kethry urged, having as little love for the feckless Leslac as did her partner. She threw herself down into her own leather-padded hearthside chair, and leaned forward in her eagerness to hear.

"All right—here's what I was told—" Tarma lounged back in her chair, and put her feet up on the black iron footrest near the stove to warm them.

"Evidently his Bardship was singing *that* song in the Falcon last night."

That song was the cause for Tarma's latest grievance with the Bard. It seemed that Leslac, apparently out of willfulness or true ignorance, had not the least notion of what being Kal'enedral meant. He had decided that Tarma's celibacy was the result of her own will, not of the hand of her Goddess—

The fact was that, as Kal'enedral, Tarma was celibate because she had become, effectively, neuter. Kal'enedral *had* no sexual desire, and little sexual identity. There was a perfectly logical reason for this. Kal'enedral served first the Goddess of the South Wind, the Warrior, who was as sexless as the blade She bore—and they served next the Clans as a whole—and lastly they served their individual Clans. Being sexless allowed them to keep a certain cool perspective that kept them free of feuding and allowed them to act as interClan arbitrators and mediators. Every Shin'a'in knew the cost of becoming Kal'enedral. Some in every generation felt the price was worth it. Tarma certainly had—since she had the deaths of her entire Clan to avenge, and *only* Kal'enedral were permitted to swear to bloodfeud—and Kethry was mortally certain that having been gang-raped by the brigands that slaughtered her Clan had played no little part in the decision.

Leslac didn't believe this. He was certain—without bothering to check into Tarma's background or the customs of the Shin'a'in, so far as Kethry had been able to ascertain—that Tarma's vows were as simple as those of most other celibate orders, and as easily broken. He was convinced that she had taken those vows for some girlishly romantic reason; he had just recently written a song, in fact, that hinted—*very* broadly—that the "right man" could thaw the icy Shin'a'in. *That* was the gist of "that song."

And he evidently thought *he* was the right man. He'd certainly plagued them enough before they'd joined up with Idra, following behind them like a puppy that couldn't be discouraged.

He'd lost track of them for two years after they'd joined the Sunhawks and that had been a profound relief. But much to their disappointment, he'd found them again and tracked them to Hawksnest. There he had remained, singing in taverns to earn his keep—and occasionally rendering Tarma's nights sleepless by singing under her window.

"That song" was new; the first time Tarma had heard it was when they'd gotten back from the Surshan campaign. Kethry had needed to practically tie her down to keep her from killing the musician.

"That's not a wise place to sing that particular ballad," Kethry observed, "Seeing as that's where your scouts tend to spend their pay."

"*Hai*—but it wasn't my scouts that got him," Tarma chuckled, "which is why I'm surprised you hadn't heard. It was Tresti and Sewen."

"*What?*"

"It was lovely—or so I'm told. Tresti and Sewen sailed in just as he began the damned thing. Nobody's said—but it wouldn't amaze me much to find out that Sewen set the whole thing up, though according to my spies, Tresti's surprise looked real enough. *She* knows what Kal'enedral means. Hellfire, we're technically equals, if I wanted to claim the priestly aspects that go with the Goddess-bond. She *also* knows how you and I feel about the little warbling bastard. So she decided to have a very public and *very* priestly fit about blasphemy and sacrilegious mockery."

That was one of the few laws within Hawksnest; that *every* comrade's gods deserved respect. And to blaspheme *anyone's* gods, particularly those of a Sunhawk of notable standing, was an official offense, punishable by the town judge.

"She didn't!"

"She ruddy well did. That was *all* Sewen and my children had been waiting for. They called civil arrest on him and bundled him off to jail. And there he languishes for the next thirty days."

Kethry applauded, beaming. "That's thirty whole days we *won't* have to put up with his singing under our window!"

"And thirty whole days I can stroll into town for a drink without hiding my face!" Tarma looked *very* pleased with herself.

Warrl heaved a gigantic sigh.

"Look, Furface, if you like him so much, why don't you go keep him company?"

:*Tasteless barbarians*.:

Tarma's retort died unuttered, for at that moment there was a knock at their door.

"Come—" Kethry called, and the door opened to show one of the principals of Tarma's story. Sewen.

"Are you two busy?"

"Not particularly," Tarma replied, as Kethry rose from her chair to usher him in. "I was just telling Keth about your part in gagging our songbird."

"Can I have an hour or two?" Sewen was completely expressionless, which, to those that knew him, meant that something was worrying him, and badly.

"Sewen, you can have all of our time you need," Kethry said immediately, closing the door behind him. "What's the problem? Not Tresti, I hope."

"No, no—I—I have to talk to somebody, and I figured it had better be you two. I haven't heard anything from Idra in over a month."

"Bloody hell—" Tarma sat bolt upright, looking no little alarmed herself. "Pull up the spare chair, man, and give us the details." She got up, and began lighting the oil lamps standing about the room, then returned to her seat. Kethry broke out a bottle of wine and poured three generous goblets full before resuming her perch. She left the bottle on the table within easy reach, for she judged that this talk had a possibility of going on for a while.

Sewen pulled the spare chair over to the stove and collapsed into it, sitting slumped over, with his elbows on his knees and his hands loosely clasped around the goblet. "It's been a lot more than a month, really, more like two. I was getting a message about every two weeks before then—most of 'em bitching about one thing or another. Well, that was fine, that sounded like Idra. But then they started getting shorter, and—you know, how the Captain sounds when she's got her teeth on a secret?"

"*Hai.*" Tarma nodded. "Like every word had to wiggle around that secret to get out."

"Eyah, that's it. Hints was all I got, that things were more complicated than she thought. Then a message saying she'd made a vote, and would be coming home—then, right after, another saying she *wouldn't,* that she'd learned something important and had to do something—then nothing."

"*Sheka!*" Tarma spat. Kethry seconded the curse; this sounded very bad.

"It's been nothing, like I said, for about two months. Damnit, Idra knows I'd be worried after a message like that, and no matter what had happened, she'd find some way to let me know she was all right."

"*If* she could," Kethry said.

"So I'm figuring she can't. That she's either into something real deep, too deep to break cover for a message, or she's being prevented."

Kethry felt a tug on her soul-self from across the room. Need was hung on her pegs over there—

She let her inner self reach out to the blade. Sure enough, she was "calling," as she did when there were women in danger. It was very faint—but then, Idra was very far away.

"I don't dare let the rest of the Hawks know," Sewen was saying.

Tarma coughed. "You sure as hell don't. We've got enough hotheads among us that you'd likely get about a hundred charging over there, cutting right across Rethwellan and stirring up the gods only know what trouble. *Then* luck would probably have it that they'd break right in on whatever the Captain's up to and blow it all to hell."

"Sewen, she *is* in some sort of trouble. Need stirred up the moment you mentioned this; I don't think it's coincidence." Kethry shook her head a little in resignation. "If Need calls—it's got to be more than just a little difficulty. Need's muted down since she nearly got us both killed; I hardly even feel her on a battlefield, with women fighting and dying all around. I don't talk about her, much, but I think she's been changing. I think she's managed to become a little more capable of distinguishing *real* troubles that only Tarma and I can take care of. So—I think Idra requires help, I agree with you. All right, what do you want us to do? Track her down and see what's wrong? Just remember though, if we go—" She forced a smile. "—Tresti loses her baby-tender and you lose your Masterclass mage."

Sewen just looked relieved to the point of tears. "Look, I hate to roust you two out like this, and I know how Tarma feels about traveling in cold weather, but—you're the only two I'd feel safe about sending. Most of the kids are what you said, hotheads. The rest—'cept for Jodi, they're mostly like me, commonborn. Keth, you're highborn, you can deal with highborns, get stuff out of 'em I couldn't. And Tarma can give you two a reason for hauling up there."

"Which is what?"

"You know your people hauled in the fall lot of horses just before we got back from the last campaign. Well, since we weren't *here*, Ersala went ahead and bought the whole string, figuring she couldn't know how many mounts we'd lost, and figuring it would be no big job to resell the ones we didn't want. We've still got a nice string of about thirty nobody's bespoken, and I was going to go ahead and keep them here till spring, *then* sell 'em. Rethwellan don't see Shin'a'in-breds, much; those they do are crossbred to culls. I doubt they've seen purebloods, much less good purebloods."

"We play merchant princes, hmm?" Kethry asked, seeing the outlines of his plan. "It could work. With rare beasts like that, we'd be welcome in the palace itself."

"That's it. Once you *get* in, Keth, you can puff up your lineage and move around in the court, or something. You talk highborn, and you're sneaky, you could learn a lot—"

"While I see what the kitchen and stable talk is," Tarma interrupted him. "*Hai.* Good plan, 'specially if I make out like I don't know much of the lingo. I could pick up a lot that way."

"You aren't just doing this to ease your conscience, are you?" Kethry asked, knowing there would be others who would ask the same question. Sewen had been Idra's Second for years now—playing Second to a woman had let him in for a certain amount of twitting from his peers in other companies. Notwithstanding the fact that one quarter to one third of all mercenary fighters *were* female, female Company Captains were few, and of all of them, only Idra led a mixed-sex Company. And Idra had been showing no signs of retiring, nor had Sewen made any moves indicating that he was contemplating starting his own Company.

"I won't deny that I want the Hawks," he said, slowly. "But—*not like this.* I want the Company fair and square, either 'cause Idra goes down, or 'cause she hands 'em over to me. This—it's too damn iffy, that's what it is! It's eating at me. And what's worse, it's eating at me that Idra might be in something deep—"

"—and you *have* to do something to get her out of it, if you can."

"That's it, Keth. And it's for a *lot* of reasons. She's my friend, she's my Captain, she's the one who took me out of the ranks and taught me. I can' just sit here for a year, and then announce she' gone missing and I'm taking over. I *owe* her too damned much, even if she keeps tellin' me I don' owe her a thing! How can I act like nothin's wrong an' not try t' help her?"

"Sewen, if every merc had your ethics—" Tarma began.

He interrupted her with a nonlaugh. "If every merc had my ethics, there'd be a lot more work for freefighters. Face it, Swordsworn, I can *afford* to have ethics just because of what Idra built the Sunhawks into. So I'm not going to let those ethics —or her—down."

"This is an almighty cold trail you're sending us on," Kethry muttered. "By the time we get to Petras it'll be past Midsummer. What are you and the Hawks going to do in the meantime?"

"We're on two-year retainer from Sursha; we do spring and summer patrol under old Leamount around the Borders to keep any of her neighbors from getting bright ideas. Easy work. Idra set it up before she left. I can handle it *without* making myself Captain."

"All right, I've got some ideas. *Our* people can keep their lips laced over a secret; so you wait one week after we've left, then you tell them all what's happened and that we've been sent out under the ivy bush."

"Why?" Sewen asked bluntly.

"Mostly so rumors don't start. *Then* you and Ersala concoct some story about Idra coming back, but fevered. Tresti can tell you what kind of fever would need a two-year rest cure. That gives you a straw-Idra to leave behind while you take the Hawks out to patrol. The Hawks will know the *real* story— and tell them it might cost the Captain her life if they let it slip."

90

"You think it might," he said, soberly.

"I don't know what to think, so I have to cover every possibility."

"Huh." He thought about that for a long time, contemplating his wine. Finally he swallowed the last of it in a single gulp. "All right; I'll go with it. Now—should I replace you two?"

"I think you'd better," Tarma said. "I suggest promoting either Garth or Jodi. Garth is my preference; I don't think Jodi would be comfortable in a command position; she's avoided being in command too many times."

"I'll do a sending; there are White Winds sorcerers everywhere. You should be getting one or more up here within a couple of months." Kethry bit her lip a bit, trying to do a rough calculation on how far her sending would reach. "I can't promise that you'll get anything higher than a Journeymanclass, but you never know. I won't tell them more than that there's a position open with you—you can let whoever you hire in on the whole thing after you take them on. Remember, White Winds school has no edicts against using magic for fighting, and I'll make it plain in the sending that this is a position with a *merc company*. That it means killing as well as healing. That should keep the squeamish away. Have Tresti look them over first, then Oreden and Jiles. Tresti will be able to sense whether they'll fit in."

"I know; she checked you two out while Idra was waiting to interview you."

Kethry nodded wryly. "Figures; I can't imagine Idra leaving anything to chance. All right, does that pretty much take care of things?"

"I think so. . . ."

"Well, as cold as the trail is going to be, there is *no* sense in stirring up a lot of rumors by having us light out of here with our tails on fire," Tarma said bluntly. "We might just as well take our time about this, say our good-byes, get equipment put together— act like this was going to be an ordinary sort of errand we're running for you. Until we've been gone for about a week, you just make out like I'm running the string out to sell, and Keth's coming with me for company."

Sewen nodded. "That sounds good to me. I'll raid the coffers for you two. You'll be needing stuff to make you look good in the court, I expect." He rose and started for the door—then turned back, and awkwardly held out his arms.

"I—I don't know what I'd have done without you two," he said stiffly, his eyes bright with what Kethry suspected might be incipient tears. "You're more than shieldbrothers, you're friends—I—thanks—"

They both embraced him, trying to give him a little comfort. Kethry knew that Idra had been in that "more than shieldbrother" category, too—and that Sewen must be thinking what *she* was thinking—that the Captain's odds weren't very good right now.

"*Te'sorthene du'dera*, big man," Tarma murmured. "When we come across someone special, like you, like Tresti, like Idra—well, you help your friends, that's all I can say. That's what friends are there for, *her'y*?"

"If anybody can help her out, it'll be you two."

"We'll do our best. And you know, *you* can do *us* a favor—" Kethry almost smiled at the sudden inspiration.

"What? Anything you want."

"Leslac. I want you to teach him a lesson. I don't care what you do to him, just get him off Tarma's back."

The weather-beaten countenance went quiet with thought. "That's a pretty tall ord—wait a moment—" He began to smile, the first smile he'd worn since he walked in their door. "I think I've got it. 'Course, it all hinges on whether he's really as pig-ignorant about Shin'a'in as he seems to be."

"Go on—I think after that *damned* song we can count on *that* being true."

Sewen's arms tightened about both their shoulders as he looked down at them. "There's this sect of Spider-Priestesses down south; they sort of dress like Tarma—deal is, they *didn't* start out life as girls."

Tarma nearly choked with laughter. "You mean, convince the little bastard that I'm really a eunuched boy? Sewen, that's priceless!"

"I rather like that—" Kethry grinned. "—I rather *like* that."

"I'll get on it," he promised, giving them a last hug and closing the door to their room behind him.

Tarma went immediately to her armor-stand, surveying the brigandine for any sign of weakness or strain. Kethry put another log in the stove, then approached the wall where Need hung, reaching out to touch the blade with one finger.

Yes—the call's still there. And I can't tell anything, it's so faint—but it is Idra. The call gets perceptibly stronger when I think about her.

"Get anything?" Tarma asked quietly.

"Nothing definite, other than that Idra's in trouble. How long do you think it will take us to get to Petras?"

"With a string of thirty horses—about a month to cross the passes, then another two, maybe three. Like you said, it'll be Midsummer at the earliest."

Kethry sighed. "If I were an Adept, I could get us both there in an hour."

"But *not* the horses. And how would we explain ourselves? We'd make a lot more stir than we should if we did that."

"And stir is not what we want."

"Right." Tarma stood with a sigh, and stretched, then came back to her chair and flung herself down into it. "I seem to recall one contact we might well want to make. The Captain didn't talk about her past much, but she *did* mention somebody a time or two. The Court Archivist—" Her brows knitted in thought. "Javreck? Jervase? No—Jadrek, that's it. Jadrek. Seems like his father used to keep Idra and her older brother in tales; paid attention to them when nobody else had time for them. Jadrek was evidently a little copy of him. She'd mention him when something happened to bring one of those tales to her mind. And more imortant—" Tarma pointed a long finger at Kethry. "—she *also* never failed to preface those recollections by calling him 'the only completely honest man in the Court, just as his father was.' "

"That sounds promising."

"If he's still there. Seems to me she said something about him being at odds with her father and her younger brother when he took over the Archivist position. He did that pretty young, since he was younger than Idra or her brother, and she left the Court before she was twenty. She also said something about his being crippled, which could cut down on the amount he sees."

"Yes and no," Kethry replied, more than grateful for Tarma's remarkable memory. "People who are overlooked often see more that way. Need I tell you that I'm glad you have a mind like a trap?"

"What, shut?" Tarma jibed. "Now you *know* I've got a Singer's memory; if I'd forgotten *one* verse of any of the most obscure ballads, I'd have been laughed out of camp. Keth, you're worrying yourself, I can tell. You're wasting energy."

"I know, I know—"

"Take it one week at a time. Worry about getting us through the passes safely I'll get you the avalanche map tomorrow; she what you can scry out with it And speaking of snow, do you still want to hear that business about the Snow Demon?"

"Well . . . yes!" she replied, surprised. "But I hardly thought you'd be in the mood for it now."

"I'm jsut taking some of my own prescribed medicine." Tarma grinned crookedly, and went to fetch the battered little hand-drum she used on those rare occasions when she chanted—you couldn't call it singing anymore—one of the Shin'a'in history-songs. "Trying to remember all fifty-two verses will keep *me* from fretting into a sweat. And hoping," she looked down at her black sleeve, the black of vengeance-taking, "that this outfit doesn't turn out to be an omen."

Five

"**H**ai'vetha! Kele, kele, kele!"
Tarma wheeled Ironheart about on the
mare's heels in a piece of horsemanship that drew a
spattering of impromptu applause from those watching, and chivied the last of the tired horses into the
corral assigned to them by the master of the Petras
stock market. She controlled them with voice only—
not hand, nor whip. She didn't even call for any
encouraging nips at their heels from Warrl, another
fact which impressed the spectators no end.

They were already impressed by the horses. They
were not the kind of beasts that the inhabitants of
Petras were used to seeing. These were Shin'a'in
purebreds, and the only reason any of them had
been passed over by the Sunhawks was that they
were mostly saddlebreds, not trailbreds. The Shin'a'in
horses bred for trail work were a little rougher
looking, and a bit hardier than the saddlebreds, in
the main. There were always exceptions, like
Tarma's beloved Kessira, but the Shin'a'in kept the
exceptions for their own use and further breeding
—as Kessira was being bred, pampered queen mare
of the Tale'sedrin herds.

No, these horses were *not* what the inhabitants of
Petras were used to seeing in their beast-market.
Their heads, broad in the forehead, small in the
muzzle, and with large, doe-soft eyes were carried
high and proudly on their long, elegant necks; pride
showed in every line of them, despite their weariness. Their bodies were compact and muscular, the

95

hindquarters being a trifle higher than these people were accustomed to. Their legs were well-muscled and slim; they were no longer shaggy with winter growth as they had been when the trek started. Now their coats were silky despite the dust—and their manes and tails, the pride of a Shin'a'in mount, were flowing in the wind like many-colored waterfalls. And they moved like dancers, like birds on the wind, like music made visible.

In short, they were beautiful.

"Good enough to suit a king, eh, *she'enedra?*" Tarma asked in her own tongue, feeling rather proud of her charges.

"I should think—" Kethry began, when one of the onlookers, a man possessed of more than a little wealth, by the cut of his gray and green clothing, interrupted her.

"What *are* these beauties?" he asked, in tones that bordered on veneration. "Where on earth did they spring from? Valdemar? I'd heard Companions were magnificent, but I'd never heard of anyone other than Heralds owning them, and I'd never heard that Companions were anything but white."

"No, m'lord," Kethry replied, as Tarma privately wondered what on earth a Companion could be. "These are Shin'a'in purebred saddlemares and geldings from the Dhorisha Plains."

"Shin'a'in!" The man stepped back a pace. "Lord and Lady—how did you ever get Shin'a'in to part with them? I'd have thought they'd have shown you their sword-edge rather than their horses."

"Easily enough—I'm blood-sister to the handler, there. I thought to bring a string up here and try our luck."

"She's—Shin'a'in—?" The man gulped, and eased another footstep or two away, putting Kethry between himself and Tarma. Tarma wasn't certain whether to laugh or continue to look as if she didn't understand. The man acted like she was some kind of demon!

"Oh yes," Kethry answered, "and Kal'enedral." She must have noted his look of blank nonrecognition, because she added, "Swordsworn."

He turned completely white. "I—hope—excuse me, lady, but I trust she's—under control."

"Warrior's Oath, *she'enedra*, what in Hell have they heard about us?" Tarma kept to her own tongue, as per the plan, and was keeping her face utterly still and impassive, but she knew Kethry could hear the suppressed laughter in her voice.

"Probably that you eat raw meat for breakfast and raw babies for dinner," Kethry replied, and Tarma could see the struggle to keep *her* expression guileless in the laughter sparkling in her eyes.

"Pardon—but—what's she saying?" The man eyed Tarma as if he expected her to unsheathe her blade and behead him at any moment.

"That she noticed how much you admire the horses, and thanks you for the compliment of your attention."

Tarma took care to nod graciously at him, and he relaxed visibly. She then turned her attention back to the horses. The corral seemed sizable enough to hold them comfortably; she'd been a little worried about that. *Let's see—pump or well for the watering trough? And where would it be—ah!* She spotted a pump, after a bit of looking. *Good. One good thing about so-called civilization: pumps. Think maybe I might see if the Clans would agree to having a couple installed on the artesian wells. . . .*

"Stand," she told Ironheart. The battlemare obediently locked her legs in position; it would take an earthquake to move her now. Tarma unslung the sword from her back and looped the baldric over the pommel of the saddle. "Guard," she ordered. That blade was a sweet one, and had been dearly paid for in her own blood; she didn't intend to lose it. Ironheart would see that she didn't.

"You'd better tell your friend to stay clear of 'Heart or he'll lose a hand," she called to Kethry, then dismounted and vaulted over the fence into the stockade to water her other charges. That bit of bravado cost, too, but it was worth a bit of strain to put on a proper show. Tarma meant to leave these folks with their mouths gaping—for that meant that the highborns would hear of them that much sooner.

:*You're going to hurt in the morning*,: Warrl observed. Thus far, the crowd's attention had been so taken up with the horses that they hadn't paid much heed to him. He'd stayed in the shadow of Ironheart, who was so tall that he didn't stand out as the monster he truly was.

And—*she* couldn't tell, but he might well be exercising a bit of his own magic to look more like an ordinary herd dog. He'd hinted that he could do just that on the way here. Which was no bad idea.

Tarma felt the strain of the muscles she'd used, and privately agreed with his critical remark about hurting. For every scar she bore on her hide, there was twice the scar tissue under it, where it didn't show—but it certainly made itself felt. Particularly when she started showing off.

But they were drawing a bigger crowd by the moment; the onlookers murmured as the loose horses crowded around her, shoving their heads under her hands for a scratch, or lipping playfully at her hair. She laughed at them, pushed them out of the way, and got to the pump. As she began to fill the trough, they pushed in to get at the water, and she rebuked them with a single sharp "*Nes!*" They shied and danced a bit, then behaved themselves.

Tarma had been doing some serious training with them on the trail—knowing that once they were in Rethwellan she would *have* to be able to command them by voice, for if they spooked, she, Kethry, and Warrl would not be enough to keep them under control. Her ability to keep them in line seemed to impress their audience no end. She decided to go all out to impress them.

She picked out one of the herd mares she'd been

working with far more than the others, and called her. The chestnut mare pricked her ears, and came to the summons eagerly—she knew what this meant; first a trick from *her*, and then a treat was in store. Tarma ordered the others out of her way, then raised her hand high over her head. The mare stepped out away from her about fifteen paces, then as Tarma began to turn, followed her turn as if she was being lunged.

Except there was no lunging-rein on her.

At a command from Tarma she picked up to a trot, then a canter; after traveling all day, Tarma was *not* going to ask her to gallop. At a third command she stopped dead in her tracks. At the fourth, she reared—

The fifth command was "Come—" and meant a piece of dried apple and a good scratch behind the ears. She obeyed *that* one with eager promptitude.

The spectators, now thick on the fence, applauded. The horses flickered their ears nervously, but when nothing came of the noise, went back to watching Tarma, hoping for treats themselves.

Tarma was pleased—*more* than pleased. *Everything* was going according to the plan they'd mapped out. "Patience, children," she told the rest. "Dinner should be here soon."

Their ears flickered forward nearly as one at that welcome word, and they continued to watch her with expectation in their soft, sweet eyes.

And within moments, the beast-market attendants did appear, with the hay and sweet-feed Tarma had told Kethry to order—and more than that—

She saw carrots poking out of more than one pocket. Hmm. This was gratifying, if it was evidence of the fact that the attendants were taken with the looks of the string—but it *could* also be an attempt on the part of some other horsebreeder to poison her stock.

:*I'm checking, mindmate.*: the voice in her head told her.

"Keth, tell the younglings over there to hold *absolutely still*. I think they just want to treat the children, but Warrl's going to check for drugging, just in case."

Kethry called out the warning, and the attendants froze; the whole *crowd* froze when they saw Warrl's great gray body moving toward them. *Now* they could see just how huge he was—his shoulder came nearly to Tarma's waist—and how much like a wolf he looked. Tarma took advantage of the situation to vault the fence again, and begin relieving the attendants of their burdens. Warrl sniffed the feed over, then checked the youngsters themselves and the treats they'd brought.

:They're fine, mindmate,: Warrl told her, cheerfully. *:And about ready to soil themselves if I sneeze.:*

Tarma laughed, and patted the one next to her on the head as she took his bale of hay away from him. "They're all right, Keth. Um—tell them to wait until I've finished, then they can give the children their treats so long as they stay out of the corral. I don't want anybody in there; they get spooked, and it'll take half a day to calm them down again. And tell them we won't need any nightwatchers, that Warrl will be guarding them when I'm not here—that should prevent anybody even *thinking* about drugging them."

Warrl sprang over the fence with a single, graceful leap. The horses, of course, were so used to his presence that they totally ignored him, being far more interested in their dinner. With a fence between themselves and Warrl, the attendants calmed down a bit.

Tarma completed her task, and (with an inward wince) vaulted the fence a third time, to return to where Ironheart still stood, statue-firm.

"Rest," she said, and the battlemare unlocked her legs, and reached around to nuzzle at her rider's arm. The others were getting fed; she wanted *her* dinner.

"Hungry, *jel'enedra*?" Tarma murmured, letting her have the handful of sweet-feed she'd brought with her. "Patience, we'll be at the inn soon enough."

She cast a glance over at Kethry's companion. His eyes were taking up half of his head.

"Warrl, would you mind staying—"

:*If you send me a nice haunch of pig as soon as you get there.*:

"*And* a half-dozen marrowbones already cracked; you deserve it." She swung up into her saddle, and turned to Kethry, who was smiling broadly enough to split her face in two. "So much for the barbarian dog and pony show, *she'enedra*," she said, stifling a chuckle. "Tell these nice people they can go home, and let's find our inn, shall we?"

"So how barbarian do you want me to look?" Tarma asked her partner, as they strolled down the creaking wooden stairs of the inn to the dimly lit common room. "And what kind? The aloof desert princeling, the snarling beast-thing, what?"

"Better stick with the aloof desert princeling; we don't want these people afraid to have you near the Court," Kethry chuckled. Tarma was plainly enjoying herself, willing to act any part to the hilt. "Brood—that always looks impressive, and you've certainly got the face for it."

"Oh, have I now!" They were continuing to speak in Shin'a'in between themselves; it was better than a code. The likelihood of anyone knowing Tarma's tongue, here in a country where tales of Shin'a'in were obviously so outlandish that they *feared* the Swordsworn, was nil.

The common room went absolutely silent as they entered. Tarma stepped in first, looking around sharply, as if she expected enemies to emerge from beneath the tables. Finally she gave a quick nod as if to herself, stepped aside, and motioned Kethry to precede her. She kept a casual hand on the hilt of the larger of her daggers the entire time. She'd wanted to wear her sword, but Kethry had argued against the idea; now she was glad she'd won. If Tarma *had* worn anything larger than a dagger, she *might* well have caused a panicked exodus! As it was, the impression she left was a complicated one; that she was very dangerous and suspicious of everyone and everything, that she and Kethry were equal, but that she also considered herself in charge of Kethry's safety.

It was a masterful performance, carefully planned and choreographed to avoid a problem before it could come up. The people of the primary religious sect of Rethwellan took a dim view of same-sex lovers, and the partners were doing their best to make *that* notion, which was inevitably going to occur to *someone,* seem a total absurdity. This touch-me-not bodyguarding act Tarma was putting on was hopefully going to do just that—among other things.

They took a table with seats for two in a far corner. Tarma motioned for Kethry to take the seat actually *in* the corner, then took the outer seat so that *she* would stand (or rather, sit) between Kethry and The Rest Of The World, Kethry signaled the waiter while her partner turned her own chair so that the back was up against the wall, and finally sat down. Tarma continued to watch the room from that vantage, broodingly, while Kethry placed orders for both of them. Conversation started back up again once they were seated, but Kethry noted that it was a trifle uneasy, and most of the diners kept one eye on Tarma at all times.

"They think you're going to start a holy war any second, *she'enedra,*" Kethry said, finally.

"Good," her partner replied, folding her arms, leaning back against the wall beside their table, and continuing to watch the room with icy, hooded eyes. "I hope this act of mine gets us prompt service; I'm about to eat the candle."

"Now, now, I thought you were being princely."

"I am—but I'm a *hungry* prince."

At just that moment, a serving wench, shaking in her shoes, brought their orders. Tarma looked at the cutlery, sniffed disdainfully, and drew the smaller of her daggers, cutting neat bits with it and eating them off the point. After a look of her own at the state of the implements they'd been given, Kethry rather wished the part she was playing allowed her to do the same.

They were nearly finished when the innkeeper himself, sidling carefully *around* Tarma, came to stand obsequiously at Kethry's elbow. She allowed him to wait a moment before deigning to notice his presence. This was in keeping with the rest of the parts they were playing—

For although they had *arrived* in dusty, well-worn traveling leathers—Tarma's being all-too-plainly armor, Kethry's bearing no hint of her mage-status—they were now dressed in silks. Kethry wore a knee-length robe, of an exotic cut and a deep green, and breeches of a deeper green; Tarma wore Shin'a'in-style wrapped jacket, shirt, and breeches—in black. With them, she wore a black sweatband of matching silk confining her short-cropped hair, and a wrapped sash holding her two daggers of differing sizes, a black silk baldric for the sword that she had left in the room above, and black quilted silk boots. Her choice of outfitting had stirred uneasy feelings in Kethry, but Tarma had pointed out with irrefutable logic that if the Captain was to hear of two strangers in Petras, and have *that* outfit described to her, she would *know* who those strangers were. And she would know by the sable hue that Tarma was expecting her Captain to be in trouble—possibly in need of avenging.

Their clothing was clearly the most costly (and certainly the most outre) in the room, and this was (dubious eating utensils notwithstanding) *not* an inexpensive inn. They *wanted* their presence to be known and commented on; they *wanted* word to spread. Ideally it would spread to Idra, wherever she was; if not, to the ear of the King.

"My lady," the innkeeper said, in tones both frightened and fawning, tones that made Kethry long for their old friend Hadell of the Broken Sword, or plain, genial Oskar of the Bottomless Barrel. "My lady, there is a gentleman who wishes to speak with you."

"So?" she raised an elegant eyebrow. "On what subject?"

"He did not confide in me, my lady, but—he wears the livery of the King."

"Does he, then? Well, I'll hear him out—if you have somewhere a bit more—private—than this."

"Of a certainty, if my lady would follow—" He bowed, and groveled, and at length brought them to a small but comfortably appointed chamber, equipped with one table, four chairs, and a door that shut quite firmly. He bowed himself out; wine appeared, in cleaner vessels than they had been favored with before this, and finally, the visitor himself.

Kethry chose to receive him seated; Tarma stood, leaning against the wall with her arms folded, in the shadows at her right hand. Their visitor gave the Shin'a'in a fairly nervous glance before accosting Kethry.

"My lady," he said, bowing over her hand.

Kethry was having a hard time keeping from laughing herself sick. The right corner of Tarma's mouth kept twitching, sure sign that she was holding herself in only by the exertion of a formidable amount of willpower. This liveried fop was precisely the degree of lackey they had hoped to lure in; personal servant to the King, and probably a minor noble himself. He was languishing, and vapid, and quite thoroughly full of himself. His absurd court dress of pale yellow and green with the scarlet and gold badge of the King's Household on the right shoulder was exceedingly expensive as well as in appallingly bad taste. There was more than a little trace of a more careful toilette than Kethry *ever* bothered with in his appearance. His carefully pointed mouse-brown mustaches alone must have taken him an hour to tease into shape.

"My lord wishes to know the identity of two such—fascinating—strangers to our realm," he said, when he'd completed his oozing over Kethry's hand. "And what brings them here."

"I shall answer the second question first, my lord," Kethry replied, with just a hint of cool hauteur. "What brings us, is trade, purely and simply. But not just *any* trade, I do assure you; no, what we have are the mounts of princes, princes of the Shin'a'in—and we intend them to grace the stables of the princes of other realms. The horses we have brought are princes and princesses themselves—as I am certain you are aware."

"Word—*had* reached my noble lord that your beasts were extraordinary—"

"They are creatures whose like no one here has ever seen. It is only through my friendship with the noble Tarma shena Tale'sedrin, *the* Tale'sedrin of Tale'sedrin, that I was able to obtain them."

His glance lit again upon Tarma, who was still standing in the shadows behind Kethry. She moved forward into the light, inclined her head graciously at the sound of her name, and said in Shin'a'in, "I also happen to be the *only* Tale'sedrin other than you, but we won't go into that, will we?"

"My companion tells me she is pleased to make the acquaintance of so goodly a gentleman," Kethry said smoothly, as Tarma allowed the shadows to obscure her again. "As for myself, I am Kethryveris, scion of House Pheregul of Mournedealth, a House of ancient and honorable lineage."

From the blankness of his gaze, Kethry knew he'd never even heard of Mournedealth, much less her House—which, so far as she was concerned, was all to the good.

"A House of renown, indeed," he said, covering

his ignorance. "Then, let me now tender my lord's words. I come from King Raschar himself." He paused, to allow Kethry to voice the expected murmurs of amazement and gratification. "He heard of your wondrous beasts, and wishes to have his Master of Horse view them himself—more than view them, if what rumor says of them is even half the truth. And since you prove to be more than merely common merchants, he would like to tender you an invitation to extend your visit to Petras in his Court, that he may learn of you, and you of him."

"And you may end up in the bastard's bed, if he likes your looks," murmured Tarma from the darkness.

"Tell your lord that we are gratified—and that we shall await his Master of Horse with eagerness, and will be more than pleased to take advantage of the hospitality of his Court."

More smooth nonsense was exchanged, and finally the man bowed himself out.

They waited, holding their breaths, until they were certain he was out of earshot—then collapsed into each other's arms, helpless with stifled laughter.

"Goddess! 'Tale'sedrin of Tale'sedrin' indeed! That great booby didn't even know it was a clan name and not a title!" Tarma choked. "*Isda so'tre koth!* You know what my people say, don't you? 'Proud is the Clanchief. Prideful is the Clanchief of a two-member clan!' "

"Laid it on good and thick, didn't I?" Kethry replied, wiping tears out of her eyes. "Goddess bless, I didn't know I had that much manure in me!"

"Oh, you could have fertilized half a farm, 'm *la-*dy,' " Tarma gasped, imitating his obsequious bow. "Bright Star-Eyed! Here—" she handed Kethry one of the goblets and poured it full of wine, then took a second for herself. "We'd better get ourselves under control if we're going to get from here to our room without giving the game away."

"You're right," Kethry said, taking a long sip

and exerting control to sober herself. "There's more at stake than just this little game."

"*Hai'she'li*. This is just the tail of the beastie. We're going to have to get into its lair to see if it's a grasscat or a treehare—and if it's got Idra in its mouth."

"And I just realized something," Kethry told her, all thought of laughter gone. "We know the new King's name, but we don't know *which* of the brothers he is. And *that* could make a deal of difference."

"Indeed, *ves'tacha*," Tarma replied, her eyes gone brooding in truth. "In very deed."

At dawn Tarma relieved Warrl of his watch on the horses, and amused herself by first going through a few sword drills, then working them, much to the titillation of the gawkers. Toward noon, Kethry (who had been playing the aristo, rising late, and demanding breakfast in bed) put in her appearance. With her was a pale stranger, as expensively dressed as their visitor of the previous evening, but in *much* better taste. He, too, wore the badge of the King's Household on his right shoulder. By his walk Tarma would have known him for a horseman. By the clothing and the badge, she knew him for the Master of the King's Horse.

And by the appreciation in his eyes, Tarma knew him for a man who knew his business. She heaved a mental sigh of relief at that; she'd half feared he might turn out to be as big a booby as the courtier of the night before. It would have cut her to the heart to sell these lovelies to an ignoramus—but if she refused to sell, they'd lose their cover story.

She had been taking the horses out of the corral, one at a time, and working them in a smaller pen. Most of them she *did* work on a lunge—there were only a handful among the thirty she could work loose, the way she had the chestnut. She had a particularly skittish young buckskin gelding out when Kethry and her escort arrived, one she needed to devote most of her attention to. So after taking a few mental notes on the man, she went back to work.

He spent a long time looking over the herd as a whole, and all in complete silence.

:This is a good one, mindmate,: Warrl said, from his resting place under the horse trough. *:He smells of soap and leather, not perfume. And there's no fear in him, nor on him.:*

"Kathal, dester'edre," she told the buckskin, who kept wanting to break into a canter. "What else can you pick up from him?"

:Lots of horse-scent, and not a trace of horse-fear.:

"For'shava."

After a time the Master of Horse left his post at the corral, and took up a nearly identical stance at the fence of the pen where she was working the buckskin. She watched him out of the corner of her eye, appraisingly. He was older than she'd first thought. Medium height, dark eyes, dark hair, beard and mustache—his complexion would be very white if not for his suntan—muscles in his shoulders that made his tunic leather stretch when he moved. His sole vanity seemed to be a set of matching silver jewelry: fillet, torque, bracelets, all inset with a single moonstone apiece. He leaned comfortably on the fence, missing nothing she did. Finally, he spoke to Kethry, who was standing at his side, dressed for the day in a cleaner and far more expensive set of the leathers she'd worn to ride in yesterday. Sewen had not spared the Company coffers when it had come time to outfit them for their ruse.

"I understood that your companion was working the horses yesterday without a lunge. . . ."

"Only a few of the horses are schooled enough to work that way at the moment," Kehry said smoothly, "although eventually *all* of them could be trained so. Do you wish to see her work one of them now?"

"If you would both be so kind."

Kethry leaned over the fence. "You heard him, *she'enedra*; is Master Flutterby there ready to pause?"

The buckskin was obeying now, having tried to fret himself into a froth. Tarma halted him, then gave him a quick rubdown, and led him out. This time she called up a gentle dappled gelding—one she was rather glad hadn't been chosen by a Sunhawk. He was so good-natured—he really wasn't suited to a battlefield, but he was so earnest he'd have broken his heart or a leg trying to do what was asked of him.

She didn't even bother to take him into the pen; she worked him in the open, then mounted him bareback, and put him through a bit of easy dressage. When she slid off, the Horsemaster approached; she kept one hand on the dapple's neck and watched as he examined the animal almost exactly as she would have. The dapple, curious, craned his head around and whuffed the man's hair as he ran his hands gently down the horse's legs, rear, then front, then picked up a forefoot. At that, the man grinned —a most unexpected expression on so solemn a face—and held out his hand for the dapple to smell, then rubbed his nose, gently.

"Lady," he spoke directly to Tarma, though he must have been told she didn't speak the language—a courtesy as delicate as any she'd ever been given, "I would cheerfully sell the Palace to purchase these horses. For once, rumor has understated fact."

"I think he's rather well hooked, *she'enedra*," Kethry said, pretending to translate. "How is he as a horseman? Can you feel happy letting them go to his care?"

Tarma gave that slight bow of respect to him, and allowed a hint of a smile to cross her face. "I'm pleased, Warrl's pleased, and have a look at Dust, if you would."

The dapple's eyes were half-closed in pleasure as the Horsemaster continued to scratch under his loose halter.

"I think it's safe to say that they'll be in good hands. See if you can wangle a deal with him that will include me as a temporary trainer; that will give us another excuse to linger."

"My companion is gratified by your praise, my lord," Kethry said to him, "and impressed with your knowledge; she says she believes she could not find one to whose care she would be more willing to entrust her beasts."

Again, that unexpected smile. "Then, if you would care to return with me, I believe we can agree to something mutually pleasing. Since you will be selling into the King's household, there will be no merchant taxes. And I think—" He gave the dapple's forehead a last scratch. "—I think perhaps that I shall keep *this* one out of his Majesty's sight. I have my pick of the King's stables, but only after he has taken his choice. It is a pity a mount this intelligent is also so beautiful."

"Do you suppose you can come up with a distractor, Tarma?"

"*Do* I? I think so!" She led the dapple back into the pen, and walked into the center of the herd to bring out the one horse of the lot that was mostly show and little substance—a lovely gelding with a coat of gold, a mane and tail of molten silver, and without a jot of brains in that beautiful head. Fortunately, he was reasonably even of temper as well as being utterly gentle, or there'd have been no handling him.

He'd been included in the lot sent to the Sunhawks although if he'd had a bit less in the way of good looks he'd have been counted a cull. Tarma had gotten the notion that Idra might like a parade-mount, and had asked her people to be on the lookout for a truly impressive beast of good temper; for parade, brains didn't matter. You couldn't have told his beauty though, except by his lines and the way he carried himself. That was because he was filthy from rolling in the dust—which he *insisted* on doing when any opportunity presented itself.

Tarma went to work on him with brushes, as he

sighed and leaned into the strokes. He was dreadfully vain, and he loved being groomed. Tarma almost suspected him of dust-rolling on purpose, just so he'd get groomed more often. As the silver and gold began to emerge from under the dirt, the Horsemaster exclaimed in surprise. When Tarma was done, and paraded the horse before him, he smacked his fist into his palm in glee.

"By the gods! One look at *him* and his Majesty won't give a bean for the gray! I thank you, my ladies," he bowed slightly to both Kethry and her partner, "and let us conclude this business as quickly as may be! I won't be easy until these beauties are safely in the Royal Stables."

As he and Kethry returned the way they had come, Tarma turned the gold loose in the stockade—where he promptly went to his knees and wallowed in the dirt.

"You," she laughed at him, "are hopeless!"

By twilight they were installed, bag and baggage, in the Palace, in one of the suites reserved for minor foreign dignitaries.

It had all happened so fast that Tarma was still looking a little bemused. Kethry, who knew just how quickly high-ranking courtiers could get things accomplished when they wanted to exert themselves, had been a bit less surprised.

She and the Master of Horse had concluded their bargain in fairly short order—and to her satisfaction, it had been at *his* suggestion that Tarma was retained for continued training. No sooner had a price been settled on and a writ made out to a reputable goldsmith, than a stream of thirty grooms and stable hands had been sent to walk the horses from the corral at the stockyard to the Royal Stables, each horse to have its own handler. The Horsemaster was taking no chances on accident or injury.

When Kethry returned to the inn, there were

already three porters waiting for her orders, all in the Royal livery. They were none too sure of themselves; Tarma (still in her barbarian persona) had refused them entrance to the suite, and was guarding the door as much with her scowl as her drawn sword.

They allowed the porters to carry away most of their belongings, the ones that didn't matter, like some of that elaborate clothing. Tarma's armor and weaponry (including a few nasty little surprises she definitely did not want anyone to know about) Need, their trail gear, and the few physical supplies Kethry needed for her magecraft they brought themselves, in sealed saddlebags. They rode Hellsbane and Ironheart; Kethry had no intention of chancing accidents with a trained battlemare. "Accidents" involving a Shin'a'in warsteed generally ended up in broken bones—and *not* the horse's.

More obsequious servants met them once the mares were safely stabled, and again, Kethry made it plain to the stable crew that *only* Tarma was to handle their personal horses. To enforce that, they left Warrl with the mounts, provided with his own stall between the ones supplied to the two mares. One look at the *kyree* was all it took to convince the stablehands that they did *not* wish to rouse the beast's ire. That was where Tarma and Kethry left their *real* gear, the things they would truly need if they had to cut and run, and between Warrl and the horses, it would be worth a person's life to touch it.

But as they crossed the threshold of the Palace, a curious chill had settled over Kethry, a chill that had nothing to do with temperature. Her good humor and faint amusement had vanished. The Palace seemed built of secrets—dark secrets. Their mission suddenly took on an ominous feeling.

The suite, consisting of a private bathing room, two bedrooms, and an outer public room, all opulently furnished in dark wood and amber velvet, had been a good indication that their putative status was fairly high. The two personal servants assigned to them, in addition to the regular staff, had told them that they ranked somewhere in the "minor envoy" range. This was close to perfect: Kethry would be able to move about the Court fairly freely.

Now Tarma was immersed to her neck in a hot bath; Kethry had already had hers, and was dressing in her most impressive outfit, for there would be a formal reception for them in an hour.

Tarma did not look at all relaxed. Kethry didn't blame her; she'd been increasingly uneasy herself.

"There was no sign of Gray in the stables, and I looked for him," Tarma called abruptly from the bathing room. Gray was Idra's gelding; a palfrey, and not the Shin'a'in stallion she rode on campaign. "No sign of Hawk tack, either. It's like she's been long gone, or was never here at all."

Kethry heard splashing as her partner stood; and shortly thereafter the Shin'a'in emerged from the bathing room with a huge towel wrapped about herself. They'd turned down an offer of bath attendants; after one look at Tarma's arsenal, the attendants had seemed just as glad.

"If she's been here, we should find out about it tonight. Especially after the wine begins to flow. Do I look impressive, or seducible?" Kethry glided into Tarma's room, and turned so that her partner could survey her from all angles.

"Impressive," Tarma judged, vigorously toweling her hair.

"Good; I don't want to have to slap Royal fingers and get strung up for my pains."

Kethry's loose robes were of dark amber silk, about three shades darker than her hair, and high-necked, bound at the waist with a silk-and-gold cord. At her throat she wore a cabochon piece of amber the size of an egg; she had confined her hair into a severe knot, only allowing two decorous tendrils in front of her ears. The robes had full, scalloped-edged sleeves that were bound with gold thread. She looked beautiful, and incredibly dignified.

Tarma was dressing in a more elaborate version of her black silk outfit, this one piped at every seam and hem with silver; she had a silver mesh belt instead of a silk sash, and a silver fillet with black moonstone instead of a headband confining her midnight hair.

"You look fairly impressive, yourself."

"I don't like the feel of this place, I'll tell you that now," Tarma replied bluntly. "I've got my Kal'enedral chainmail on under my shirt, and I'm bloody well armed to the teeth. I'm going to stay that way until we're out of here."

Kethry rubbed her neck, nervously. "You, too?"

"Me, too."

"You know the drill—"

"You talk and mingle, I lurk behind you. If I hear anything interesting, I cough twice, and we get somewhere where we can discuss it."

All their good humor had vanished into the shadows of the Palace, and all that was left them was foreboding.

"I don't suppose that Need . . ."

"Not a hint. Just the same as back at Hawksnest. Which could mean about anything; most likely is that the Captain is out of the edge of her range."

"I hope you're right," Tarma sighed. "Well, shall we get on with it?"

Closing the door on the dubious shelter of their suite, they moved, side by side, deeper into the well of intrigue.

Six

Perfume, wine, and wire-tight nerves. Musk, hot wax, and dying flowers. The air in the Great Hall was so thick with scent that Tarma felt overpowered by all the warring odors. The butter-colored marble of the very walls and floor seemed warm rather than cool. Lighted candles were everywhere, from massed groupings of thin tapers to pillars as thick as Tarma's wrist. The pale polished marble reflected the light until the Great Hall glowed, fully as bright as daylight. The hundreds of jewels, the softly gleaming gold on brow and neck and arm, the winking golden bullion weighing down hems sparkled like a panoply of stars.

It was not precisely *noisy* here—but the murmuring of dozens, hundreds of conversations, the underlying current of the music of a score of minstrels, the sound of twenty pairs of feet weaving through an intricate dance—the combination added up to an effect as dizzying as the light, heat or scent.

Carved wooden doors along one wall opened up onto a courtyard garden, also illuminated for the evening—but by magic, not candles. But few moved to take advantage of the quiet and cool garden—not when the real power in this land was *here*.

If power had possessed a scent, it would have overwhelmed all the others in the hall. The scarlet-and-gold-clad man lounging on the gilded wooden throne at the far end of the Great Hall was young, younger than Tarma, but very obviously the sole agent of control here. No matter *what* they were doing, nearly everyone in this room kept one eye on him at all times; if he leaned forward the better to listen to one of the minstrels, all conversation hushed—if he nodded to a lady, peacock-bright gallants thronged about her. But if he smiled upon her, even her escort deserted her, not to return until their monarch's interest wandered elsewhere.

He was not particularly imposing, physically. Brown hair, brown eyes; medium build; long, lantern-jawed face with a hard mouth and eyebrows like ruler-drawn lines over his eyes—his was not the body of a warrior, but not the body of a weakling, either.

Then he looks at you, Tarma thought, *and you see the predator, the king of his territory, the strongest beast of the pack. And you want to crawl to him on your belly and present your throat in submission.*

:Unless,: the thin tendril of Warrl's mind-voice insinuated itself into her preoccupation, *:just unless you happen to be a pair of rogue bitches like yourself and your sister. You bow to your chosen packleader, and no one else. And you never grovel.:*

The brilliantly-bedecked courtiers weren't entirely certain how to treat Kethry and her black-clad shadow—probably because the King himself hadn't been all that certain. Wherever they walked, conversation faltered and died. There was veiled fright in the courtiers' eyes—*real* fright. Tarma wondered if she hadn't overdone her act a bit.

On the other hand, King Raschar had kept his hands off the sorceress. It *had* looked for a moment as if he was considering chancing her "protector's" wrath—but one look into Tarma's coldly impassive eyes, (eyes, she'd often been told, that marked her as a born killer) seemed to make him decide that it might not be worth it.

Tarma would have laid money down on the odds she knew exactly what he was thinking when he gave her that measuring look. He could well have reckoned that she might be barbarian enough to act if she took offense—and quick enough to do him harm before his guards could do anything about her. Maybe even quick enough to kill him.

:*The predator recognizes another of his kind.*:

Tarma nodded to herself. Warrl wasn't far wrong.

If this was highborn life, Tarma was just as glad she'd been born a Shin'a'in nomad. The candlelight that winked from exquisite jewels also reflected from hollow, hungry eyes; voices were shrill with artificial gaiety. There was no peace to be found here, and no real enjoyment. Just a never-ending round of competition, competition in which the smallest of gestures took on worlds of meaning, and in which they, as unknown elements, were a very disturbing pair of unexpected variables.

The only members of this gathering that seemed to be enjoying themselves in any way were a scant handful of folks, who, by the look of them, were not important enough to worry the power-players; a few courting couples, some elderly nobles and merchants—and a pair of men over in one corner, conversing quietly in the shadows, garbed so as to seem almost shadows themselves, who stood together with winecups in hand. They were well out of the swirl of the main action, ignored for the most part by the players of this frenetic game. When one of the two shifted, the one wearing the darkest clothing, Tarma caught a good look at the face and recognized him for the Horsemaster. He had donned that impassive mask he'd worn when he first looked the horses over, and he was dressed more for comfort than to impress. Like Tarma he was dressed mainly in black—in his case, with touches of scarlet. His only ornaments were the silver-and-moonstone pieces he'd worn earlier.

The other man was all in gray, and Tarma could not manage to catch a glimpse of his face. Whoever he was, Tarma was beginning to wish she was wit him and the Horsemaster. She was already tired the teeth of this reception.

Although Tarma usually enjoyed warmth, the ai in the Great Hall was stiflingly hot even to her. A she watched the men out of the corner of her eye they evidently decided the same, for they bega moving in the direction of one of the doors that le out into the gardens. As they began to walk, Tarm saw with a start that the second man limpe markedly.

"Keth, d'you see our friend from this afternoon? she said in a conversational tone. "Will you lay m odds that the fellow with him is that Archivist?"

"I don't think I'd care to; I believe that you' win." Kethry nodded to one of the suddenly-tongue tied courtiers as they passed, the very essence o gracious calm. The man nodded back, but his eye were fixed on Tarma. "Care for a breath of fresl air?"

"I thought you'd never ask."

They made their own way across the room, with out hurrying, and not directly—simply drifting grad ually as the ebb and flow of the crowd permitted They stopped once to accept fresh wine from servant, and again to exchange words with one o the few nobles (a frail, alert-eyed old woman swathe in white fur) who didn't seem terrified of them. I seemed to take forever, and was rather like tread ing the measures of an intricate dance. But eventu ally they reached the open door with its carving and panels of bronze, and escaped into the coo duskiness of the illuminated gardens.

Tarma had been prepared to fade into the shad ows and stalk until she found their quarry, but the two men were in plain sight beside one of the mage-light decorated fountains. They were clearly silhouetted against the sparkling, blue-glowing wa ters. The Archivist was seated on a white marble bench, holding his winecup in both hands: the Horsemaster stood beside him, leaning over to speak to him with one booted foot on the stone slab, his own cup dangling perilously from loose fingers.

The partners strolled unhurriedly to the fountain, pretending that Kethry was admiring it. The Horsemaster saw them approaching; as Tarma watched, his mouth tightened, and he made a little negating motion with his free hand to his companion as the two women came within earshot

But when they continued to close, he suddenly became resignedly affable. Placing his cup on the stone bench, he prepared to approach them.

"My Lady Kethryveris, I would not have recognized you," he said, leaving his associate's side, taking her hand in his, and bowing over it. "You surprise me; I would have thought you could not be more attractive than you were this afternoon. I trust the gathering pleases you?"

"A ... remarkable assemblage," Kethry replied, allowing a hint of irony to creep into her voice. "But I do not believe anyone introduced me to your friend—?"

"Then you must allow me to rectify the mistake at once." He led her around the bench, Tarma following silently as if she truly was Kethry's shadow, so that they faced the man seated there. The fountain pattered behind them, masking their conversation from anyone outside their immediate vicinity.

"Lady Kethryveris, may I present Jadrek, the Rethwellan Archivist."

For some reason Tarma liked this man even more than she had the Horsemaster, liked him immediately. The mage-light behind them lit his features clearly. He was a man of middle years, sandy hair going slightly to silver, his face was thin and ascetic and his forehead broad. His gray eyes held an echo of pain, and there were answering lines of pain about his generous mouth. That was an odd mouth; it looked as if it had been made expressly to smile, widely and often, but something had caused it to set in an expression of permanent cynicism. His gray tunic and breeches were of soft moleskin, and it almost seemed to Tarma that he wore them with the intent to fade into the background of wherever he might be.

This is a man the Clans would hold in high esteem —in the greatest of honor. There is wisdom in him, as well as learning. So why is he unregarded and ignored here? No matter what Idra said—I find it hard to understand people who do not honor wisdom when they see it.

"I am most pleased to make your acquaintance, Master Jadrek," Kethry said, softly and sweetly, as she gave him her hand. "I am more pleased because I had heard good things of you from Captain Idra."

Tarma felt for the hilts of her knives as inconspicuously as she could, as both men jerked as if they'd been shot. This had *not* been part of the plans she and Kethry had discussed earlier!

The Archivist recovered first. "Are you then something other than you seem, Lady Kethryveris, that you call the Lady Idra 'Captain'?"

Kethry smiled, as Tarma loosened the knife hidden in her sleeve and wished she could get at the one at the nape of her neck without giving herself away.

Damn—I can't get them both—Keth, what the hell are you doing?

"In no way," her partner replied smoothly. "I am all that I claim to be. I simply have not claimed all that I am. We hoped to find the lady here, but strangely enough, we've seen no sign of her."

Keth— Tarma thought, waiting for one or both of the men to make some kind of move, *—you bloody idiot! I hope you have a reason for this!*

The Horsemaster continued to stare in taut wariness, and Tarma had a suspicion that he, too, had a blade concealed somewhere about him. Maybe in his boot? The Archivist was eyeing them with suspicion, but also as if he was trying to recall something.

"You ... could be the chief mage of the Sunhawks. You seem to match the description," he said finally, then turned slightly to stare at Tarma. "And that would make *you* the ... Scoutmaster? Tindel, these may well be two of Idra's fighters; they certainly correspond with what I've been told."

The Horsemaster pondered them, and Tarma noted a very slight relaxation of his muscles. "Might be ... might be," he replied, "But there are ways to make certain. Why does Idra ride Gray rather than her warhorse when not in battle?" He spoke directly to Tarma, who gave up pretending not to understand him.

"Because Black enjoys using his teeth," she said, enjoying his start of shock at her harsh voice, "and if he can't take a piece out of anything else, he'll go for his rider's legs. She's tried kicking him from here to Valdemar for it, and still hasn't broken him of it. So she never rides him except in a fight. And if you know about Black, you'll also know that we almost lost him in the last campaign; he took a crossbow bolt and went down with Idra on his back, but he was just too damned mean to die. Now you tell me one; why won't she let me give her a Shin'a'in saddlebred to ride when she's not on Black?"

"Because she won't start negotiations with clients on a bad footing by being better-mounted than they are," the Archivist said quietly.

"*I* taught her that," the Horsemaster added. "I told her that the day she first rode out of here on her own, and wanted to take the best-looking horse in the stable. When she rode out, it was on a Karsite cob that had been rough-trained to fight; it was as ugly as a mud brick. When did she lose it?"

"Uh—long before we joined; I think when she

was in Randel's Raiders," Kethry replied to the lightning-quick question after a bit of thought.

"I think perhaps we have verified each other as genuine?" Tindel asked with a twisted smile. Jadrek continued to watch them; measuringly, and warily still.

"*Has* Idra been here?" Kethry countered.

"Yes; been, and gone again."

"Keth, we both know there's something going on around here that nobody's talking about." Tarma glanced at the two men, and Tindel nodded slightly. "If we don't want to raise questions we'd rather not answer, I think we'd better either rejoin the rest of the world, or drift around the garden, then retire.'

"Your instincts are correct; as strangers you're automatically under observation. It's safe enough to mention Idra, so long as you don't call her 'Captain,' " Tindel offered. "But I should warn you that we two are not entirely in good odor with His Majesty—Jadrek in particular. I might be in better case after tomorrow, when he sees those horses. Nevertheless it won't do *you* any good to be seen with us. I think you might do well to check with other information sources before you come to one of us again."

Tarma looked him squarely in the eyes, trying to read him. Every bit of experience she had told her he was telling the truth—and that now that the approach had been made, it would take a deal of courting before they would confide anything. She looked down at Jadrek; if eyes were the "windows of the soul" *his* had the storm shutters up. He had identified them; that didn't mean he trusted them. Finally she nodded. "We'll do that."

"Gods!" Tindel swore softly. "Of all the rabbit-brained—women!" He didn't pace, but by the clenching of his hand on his goblet, Jadrek knew that he badly wanted to. "If anybody had been close enough to hear her—"

"*If* they're what they say they are, they wouldn't have pulled this with anyone close enough to hear them," Jadrek retorted, closing his eyes and gritting his teeth as his left knee shot a spasm of pain up his leg. "On the other hand, *if* they aren't, they might well have wanted witnesses."

"If, if, if—Jadrek—" Tindel's face was stormy.

"I still haven't made up my mind about them," the Archivist interrupted his friend. "If they are Idra's friends, they're going about this intelligently. If they're Raschar's creatures, they're being very canny. They could be either. We haven't seen or heard of the pretty one so much as lighting a candle, but if she's really Idra's prime mage, she wouldn't. Char surely knows as much about the Hawks as we do, and having two women, one of them Shin'a'in Swordsworn, show up here after Idra's gone off into the unknown, must certainly have alerted *his* suspicions. If the other did something proving herself to be a mage, he wouldn't be suspicious anymore, he'd be certain."

"So what do we do?"

Jadrek smiled wearily at his only friend. "We do what we've been doing all along. We wait and watch. We see what *they* do. Then—maybe—we recruit them to our side."

Tindel snorted. "And meanwhile, Idra . . ."

"Idra is either perfectly safe—or beyond help. And in either case, nothing we do or don't do in the next few days is going to make any difference at all."

"Next time just stop my heart, why don't you?" Tarma asked crossly when they reached their suite. She shut the door tightly behind them and set her back against it, slumping weak-kneed at having safely attained their haven.

"I acted on a hunch. I'm sorry." Kethry paused for a fraction of a second, then headed for her bedroom, the soft soles of her shoes making scarcely a sound on the marble floor. Her partner followed staggering just slightly as she pushed off from the door.

"You *could* have gotten us killed," Tarma continued, following the mage into the gilded splendor of her bedroom. Kethry turned; Tarma took a good look at her partner's utterly still and sober expression, then sighed. "Na, forget I yelled. I'm a wool-brain. There were signs you were reading that I couldn't see, is that it?"

Kethry nodded, eyes dark with thought. "I can't even tell you exactly what it was," she said apologetically.

"Never mind," Tarma replied, reversing a chair to sit straddle-legged on it with her arms folded over the back and her head resting on her arms, forcing her tense shoulder muscles to relax. "It's like trail-reading for me; I don't even think about it anymore. First question; *can* you find other sources?"

"Maybe. Some of the older nobles, like that old lady who talked to us; the ones who weren't afraid of you. Most older courtiers love to talk, have seen *everything*, and nobody will listen to them. So—" Kethry shrugged, then glided over to the bed, slipping out of the amber robe and draping it over another chair that stood next to it. Fire and candle light glinted from her hair and softened the hard muscles of her body. "—I use a little kindness, risk being bored, and maybe learn a lot."

"I guess I'll stick to the original plan then; work the horses, play that I don't understand the local tongue, and keep my ears open." Tarma wasn't sure anymore that this was such a good plan, certainly not as certain as she had been when they first rode in. This place seemed full of invisible pitfalls.

"One other thing; there's more than a handful of mages around here, and I don't dare use my powers much. If I do, they'll know me for what I am. Some of them felt pretty strong, and *none* of them were in mage-robes."

"Is that a good sign, or a bad?"

"I don't know." Kethry unpinned her hair and shook it loose, then slipped on a wisp of shift—supplied by their host—and climbed into her bed. The mattress sighed under her weight, as she settled under the blankets in the middle: then she sat up, gazing forlornly at her partner. She looked like a child in the enormous expanse of featherbed—and she looked uncomfortable and unhappy as well.

Tarma knew that lost expression. This place was *far* too like the luxurious abode of Wethes Goldmarchant, the man to whom Kethry's brother had sold her when she was barely nubile.

Kethry plainly didn't want to be left alone in here. They also didn't dare share the bed without arousing very unwelcome gossip. But there was a third solution.

"I don't trust our host any farther than I could toss Ironheart," she said, standing up abruptly, and shoving the chair away with a grating across the stone floor. "And I'm bloody damned barbarian enough that *nothing* I do is going to surprise people, provided it's weird and warlike."

With that, she stalked into her bedroom, stripped the velvet coverlet, featherbed and downy blankets from the bedstead, and wrestled the lot into Kethry's room, cursing under her breath the whole time.

"Tarma! What—"

"I'm bedding down in here; at the foot of your bed so the servants don't gossip. They've been watching me bodyguard you all day, so this isn't going to be out of character."

She stripped to the skin, glad enough to be out of those over-fine garments, and pulled on a worn-out pair of breeches and another of those flimsy shifts, tossing her clothes on the chair next to Kethry's.

"But you don't have to make yourself miserable!"

Kethry protested feebly, her gratitude for Tarma's company overpowering her misgivings.

"Great good gods, this is a damn sight better than the tent." Tarma laughed, and laid her weapons, dagger and sword, both unsheathed, on the floor next to the mattress. "Besides, when the servants come in to wake us up, I'll rise with steel in hand. *That* ought to give 'em something to talk about and distract them from who *we* were associating with last night. And—"

"And?"

"Well, I don't entirely trust Raschar's good sense if his lust's involved; for all we know, he's got hidden passages in the walls that would let him in here when I'm not around. Hmm?"

"A good point," Kethry conceded with such relief that it was obvious to Tarma that she had been thinking something along the same lines. "Are you *sure* you'll be all right?"

Tarma tried her improvised bed, and found it better than she'd expected. "Best doss I've had in my life," she replied, wriggling luxuriously into the soft blankets, and grinning. "You'd better find out what happened to Idra pretty quick, *she'enedra*. Otherwise, I may not want to leave."

Kethry sighed, reached up for the sconce beside her, and blew out the candle, leaving the room in darkness.

The following day Tarma managed to frighten the maids half to death, rising from the pile of bedding on the floor with sword in hand at the first sound of anyone stirring. The younger of the two fainted dead away at the sight of her. The other squeaked and ran for the door. They didn't see *that* maid again, so Tarma figured she had refused to go back into their suite; defying any and all punishments. The other girl vanished as soon as Kethry revived her, and they didn't see *her* again, either, so she probably had done the same. The next servants to enter the suite were a pair of haglike old crones with faces fit to frighten fish out of water; they attended to the cleaning and picking up of the suite, and took themselves out again with an admirable efficiency and haste. That was more like what Tarma wanted out of servants; the giggly girls fussing about drove her to distraction at the best of times, and now—well, now she wasn't going to take anything or anyone at face value. Those giggly girls were probably spies—maybe more.

Kethry heaved a sigh or two of relief when they saw the last of the new set of servitors.

Hell, she's an old campaigner; she knows it, too. Gods, I hate this place.

After wolfing down some bread and fruit from the over-generous breakfast the second set of servants had brought, Tarma headed off to oversee the further training of the horses, concentrating on the gold and the dapple. The gold she wanted schooled enough that he wouldn't cause his rider any problems; the dapple she wanted trained to the limits of his understanding. She hoped *that* might sweeten the Horsemaster's attitude toward them.

She kept her ears open—and as she'd hoped, the stable folk were fairly free with their tongues while they thought she couldn't understand them. Besides several unflattering comments about her own looks, she managed to pick up that Idra had gone off rather abruptly, but that her disappearance had not been entirely unexpected. Her name was coupled on more than one occasion with the words "that wild-goose quest." She learned little more than that.

Of the other brother, Prince Stefansen, she learned a bit more. He'd run off on his brother's coronation day. And he'd done something worse than just run, according to rumor, though what it was, no one really seemed to know. Whatever, it had been enough

to goad the new king into declaring him an outlaw
If Raschar caught him, his head was forfeit.

And *that* was fair interesting indeed. And was
more than Tarma had expected to learn.

"That doesn't much surprise me, given what I've
heard," Kethry remarked that evening, when they
settled into their suite after another one of those
stifling evening gatherings. This one had been only
a little less formal than their reception. It seemed
this sort of thing took place *every* night—and
attendance was expected, even of visitors. "I'd
gathered something like that from Countess Lyris.
It was about the only useful thing to come out of
this evening."

"I think I may die of the boredom, provided the
perfume doesn't kill me off first," Tarma yawned.
She was sprawled on the floor of Kethry's room on
her featherbed (which the maids had not dared
move.) Her eyes were sleepy; her posture wasn't.
Kethry knew from years of partnering her that no
one and nothing would move inside or near the
suite without her knowing it. She was operating on
sentry reflexes, and it showed in a subtle tenseness
of her muscles.

"The perfume may; I don't think boredom is
going to be a problem," Kethry replied slowly. She
leaned back into the pillows heaped at the head of
the bed, and combed her hair while she spoke in
tones hardly louder than a whisper. The candlelight from the sconce in the headboard behind her
made a kind of amber aura around her head. "There
is one *hell* of a lot more going on here than meets
the eye. This is what I've gotten so far: when Idra
got here, she supported Raschar over Stefansen.
The whole idea was that Stefansen was going to be
allowed to exile himself off to one of the estates
and indulge himself in whatever way he wanted.
Presumably he was going to fade away into quiet

debauchery. Raschar was crowned—and suddenly Stefansen was gone, with a price on his head. Nobody knows where he went, but the best guess is north."

Tarma looked a good deal more alert at that, and leaned up against the bedside, propping her head on her hands. "Oh, really? And what came of the original plan? Especially if Stefansen had agreed to it?"

Kethry shrugged, and frowned. It was a puzzle, and one that left a prickle between her shoulderblades, as if someone were aiming a weapon for that spot. "No one seems to know. No one knows what it was Stefansen did to warrant a death sentence. But Raschar was—and *is*, still, according to one of my sources—very nervous about proving that he is the *rightful* claimant to the throne. There's a tale that the Royal Line used to have a sword in Raschar's grandfather's time that was able to choose the rightful heir—or the best king, the stories aren't very clear on the subject, at least not the ones I heard. It was stolen forty or fifty years ago. Idra apparently volunteered to see if she could find it for Raschar, the assumption being that the sword would pick *him*. They say he was very eager for her to find it—and at the moment everyone seems convinced that she took off to go looking for it."

Tarma shook her head, slowly. Her mouth was twisted a little in a skeptical frown. "That doesn't sound much like the Captain to me. Sure, she might well *say* she was going off looking for it, but to really *do* it? Personally? Alone? When the Hawks are waiting for her to join them and it's nearly fighting season? And why not rope in one of Raschar's tame mages to help smell out the magic? It's not likely."

"Not *bloody* likely," Kethry agreed. "I could see it as an excuse to get back to us, but not anything else."

"Have you made any moves at old Jadrek?"

Kethry sighed. Jadrek had been *exceptionally* hard to get at. For a lame man, he could vanish with remarkable dexterity. "I'm courting him, cautiously. He doesn't seem to trust anyone except Tindel. I did find out why neither Raschar nor his father cared for Jadrek or *his*. The hereditary Archivists of Rethwellan both suffered from an overdose of honesty."

"Let's not get abstruse, shall we?"

Kethry grinned. This part, at least, *did* have a certain ironic humor to it. "Both Jadrek and his father before him insisted on putting events in the Archives exactly as they happened, instead of tailoring them to suit the monarch's sensibilities."

"So what's to stop the King from having the Archives altered at his pleasure?"

"They can't," Kethry replied, still amused in spite of her feelings that they were both treading an invisible knife edge of danger. "The Archive books are bespelled. They *have* to be kept up to date, or and I quote, 'something nasty happens.' The Archives, once written in, are protected magically and can't be altered, and Raschar doesn't have a mage knowledgeable enough to break the spell. Once something is *in* the Archives, it's there forever."

Tarma choked on a laugh, and stuffed the back of her hand into her mouth to keep it from being overheard in the corridor outside. They had infrequent eavesdroppers out there. "Who was responsible for *this* little pickle?"

"One of the first Kings—predictably called 'the Honest'—he was also an Adept of the Leverand school, so he could easily enforce his honesty. I gather he wasn't terribly popular; I also gather that he didn't much care."

Tarma made a wry face. "Hair shirts and dry bread?"

"And weekly fasts—with the whole of his Court included. But this isn't getting *us* anywhere—"

Tarma nodded, and buried one hand in her short hair, leaning her head on it. "Too true. Ideas?"

Kethry sighed, and shook her head. "Not a one. You?"

To her mild surprise, Tarma nodded thoughtfully, biting her lip. "Maybe. Just maybe. But try the indirect approach first. My way is either going to earn us our information or scare the bird into cover so deep we'll never get him to fly."

"Him?"

Again Tarma nodded. "Uh-huh. Jadrek."

Three days later, with not much more information than they'd gotten in the first two days, Tarma decided it was time to try her plan.

It involved a fair amount of risk; although they planned to be as careful as they could, they were undoubtedly going to be seen at some point or other, since skulking about *would* raise suspicions. Tarma only hoped that no one would guess that their goal was Jadrek's rooms.

She waited for a long while with her ear pressed up against the edge of the door, listening to the sounds of servants and guests out in the hall. The hour following the mandatory evening gathering was a busy one; the nightlife of the Court of Rethwellan continued sometimes until dawn, and the hour of dismissal was followed by what Kethry called "the hour of scurrying" as nobles and notables found their own various entertainments.

Finally— "It's been quiet for a while now," Tarma said, when the last of the footsteps had faded and the last giggling servant departed. "I think this is a lull. Let's head out before we get another influx of dicers or something."

As usual, Kethry sailed through the door first, with Tarma her sinister shadow. There was no one in the gilded hallway, Tarma was pleased to note. In fact, at least half the polished bronze lamps were out, indicating that there would be no major entertainments tonight in this end of the Palace.

I hope Warrl's ready to come out of hiding, Tarma thought to herself, a little worriedly. *This whole notion of mine rests on him.*

:Must you think of me as if I couldn't hear you?: Warrl snapped in exasperation. *:Of course I'm ready. Just get the old savant's window open and I'll be in through it before you can blink.:*

Sorry, Tarma replied sheepishly. *I keep forgetting—damnit, Furface, I'm still not used to mind-talking with you! It's just not something Shin'a'in do.*

Warrl did not answer at once. *:I know,:* he said finally. *:And I shouldn't eavesdrop, but it's the mind-mate bond. I sometimes have to force myself not to listen to you. We've got so much in common; you're Kal'enedral and I'm neuter and we're both fighters. You know—there are times when I wonder if your Lady might not take me along with you in the end—I think I'd like that.:*

Tarma was astonished; so surprised that she stopped dead for a moment. *You—you would? Really?*

:Not if you start acting like a fool about it!: he snapped, jolting her back to sense. *:Great Horned Moon—will you keep your mind on your work?:*

To traverse the guests' section they wore clothing that suggested they might be paying a social call; but once they got into the plainer hallways of the quarters belonging to those who were not *quite* nobility, but not exactly servants—like the Archivist and the Master of Horse—they stepped into a granite-walled alcove long enough to strip off their outer garments to reveal their well-worn traveling leathers. In the dim light of the infrequent candles they looked enough like servants that Tarma hoped no one would look at them too carefully. They covered their hair with scarves, and folded their clothing into bulky bundles; they carried those bundles conspicuously, so that they were unlikely (Tarma hoped) to be levied into some task or other as extra hands.

The corridor had changed. Gone were the soft, heavy hangings, the frequent lanterns. The passage here was bare stone, polished granite, floor and wall, and the lighting was by cheap clay lanterns or cheaper tallow candles placed in holders along the walls at long intervals. It was chilly here, and damp, and the tallow candles smoked.

"Well, this explains one thing about that sour old bastard," Tarma muttered under her breath, while Kethry counted doors.

"Seven, eight—who? What?"

"Jadrek. Why he's such a meddlar-face. Man's obviously got bones as stiff as *I'm* going to have in a few years. Living in this section must make him as creaky as a pair of new boots."

"Ten—never thought of that. Remind me to stay on the right side of Royal displeasure. This should be it."

Kethry stopped at a wooden door set into the corridor wall, a door no different from any of the others, and knocked softly.

Tarma listened as hard as she could; heard limping footsteps; then the door creaked open a crack, showing a line of light at its edge—

She rammed her shoulder into it without giving Jadrek a chance to see who was on the other side of it, and shoved it open before the Archivist had time to react. Kethry was less than half a step behind her. They were inside and had the door shut tightly behind them before Jadrek had a chance to go from shock to outrage at their intrusion.

Tarma put her back to the rough wood of the door and braced herself against it; no half-cripple like Jadrek was going to be able to move her away from the door until she was good and ready. The rest was up to Kethry's silver tongue.

Jadrek glared, his whole attitude one of affronted

dignity, but did not call for help or gibber in help-less anger as Tarma had half expected. Instead every word he spoke was forceful, but deadly cold, controlled—and quiet.

"What, pray, is this supposed to mean?" The gray eyes were shadowed with considerable pain at the moment; Tarma hoped it was not because of something she'd done to him in getting the door open. "I have come to expect a certain amount of cavalier treatment, but not in my own quarters!"

"My lord—" Kethry began.

"I," he said bitterly, "am no one's lord. You may abandon that pretense."

Kethry sighed. "Jadrek, I humbly beg your par-don, but we were trying to find a way to speak with you without drawing undue attention. If you want us to leave this moment, we will—but dammitall, we are *trying* to find out what's become of our Captain, and you seem to be the only source of reliable information!"

He raised one eyebrow in surprise at her outspo-kenness, and looked at her steadily. "And you might well be the instrument of my execution for treason."

Tarma whistled softly through her teeth, causing both of their heads to swivel in her direction. "That bad, is it?"

His jaw tightened, but he did not answer.

"Believe or not, I've got an answer for you. Look, I would assume you are probably the most well-read man in this city; that's what the Captain seemed to think," Kethry continued. "Do you know what a *kyree* is?"

He nodded warily.

"Do you know what it means to be mindmated to one?"

"A little. I also know that they are reputedly incapable of lying mind-to-mind—"

At Kethry's hand signal, Tarma stood away from the door, crossed the room at a sprint and flung open the casement window that looked out over the stableyard. She had seen Jadrek at this window the night before, which was how she and Kethry had figured out which set of rooms was his. Warrl was ready, in the yard below; Tarma could see him bulking dark in the thin moonlight. Before Jadrek could react to Tarma's sudden movement, Warrl launched himself through the open window and landed lightly in the middle of the rather small room. It seemed that much smaller for his being there.

The *kyree* looked at Jadrek—seemed to look *through* him—his eyes glowing like topaz in the sun. Then he bowed his head once in respect to the Archivist, and mindspoke to all three of them.

:*I am Warrl. We are Captain Idra's friends; we want to help her, but we cannot if we do not know what has happened to her. Wise One, you are one of the few honest men in this place. Will you not help us?*:

Jadrek stared at the *kyree*, his jaw slack with astonishment. "But—but—"

:*You wonder how I can speak with you, and how I managed to remain concealed. I have certain small powers of magic,*: the *kyree* said, nearly grinning. :*You may have heard that the barbarian brought her herd dog with her. I chose to appear somewhat smaller than I am; the stablehands think me a rather large wolf-dog cross.*:

The Archivist reached for the back of a chair beside him to steady himself. He was pale, and there was marked confusion in his eyes. "I—please, ladies, sit down, or as a gentleman, I cannot—and I feel the need of something other than my legs to support me—"

There were only two chairs in the room; Tarma solved the problem of who was to take them by sinking cross-legged to the floor. Warrl curled behind her as a kind of backrest, which made the room look much less crowded. While Kethry took the second chair and Jadrek the one he had obviously (by the book on the table beside it) vacated at their knock, Tarma took a quick, assessing look around her.

There were old, threadbare hangings on most of the stone walls, probably put up in a rather futile attempt to ward off the damp chill. There was a small fire on the hearth to her right, probably for the same reason. Beside the hearth was a chair—or rather, a small bench with a back to it—with shabby brown cushions. This was the seat Jadrek had resumed, his own brown robes blending with the cushions. Beside this chair stood a table with a single lamp, a book that seemed to have been put down rather hastily, and a half-empty wineglass. Across from this was a second, identical seat. To Tarma's left stood a set of shelves, full of books, odd bits of rock and pieces of statuary, and things not readily identifiable in the poor light. At the sight of the books, Tarma felt a long-suppressed desire to get one of them in her hands; she hadn't had a good read in months, and her soul thirsted for the new knowledge contained within those dusty volumes.

In the wall with the bookcase was another door, presumably to Jadrek's bedchamber. In the wall directly opposite the one they had entered was the window.

Pretty barren place. This time Tarma was thinking directly at the *kyree.*

:He has less—far less—respect than he deserves,: Warrl said with some heat. *:This man has knowledge many would die for, and he is looked upon as some kind of fool!:*

"I . . . had rather be considered a fool," Jadrek said slowly.

The *kyree* raised his head off his paws sharply, and looked at the man in total astonishment. *:You hear me?:*

"Yes—wasn't I supposed to?"

Tarma and the *kyree* exchanged a measured glance, and did not answer him directly. "Why would you rather be considered a fool?" Tarma asked, after a moment of consideration.

"Because a fool hears a great deal—and a fool is not worth killing."

"I think," Kethry said, leaning forward, "you had better begin at the beginning."

Some hours later they had a full picture, and it was not a pleasant one.

"So the story is that Stefansen intended some unspecified harm to his brother, and when caught, fled. In actuality, Tindel and I overheard some things that made us think Raschar might be considering assuring that there would be no other male claimants to the throne and we warned Stefansen."

"Where did he go?" Kethry asked.

"I don't know; I don't want to know. The less I know, the less I can betray." His eyes had gone shadowy and full of secrets.

"Good point. All right, what then?"

"Have you had a good look around you?"

"Raschar's pretty free with his money," Tarma observed.

"Freer than you think; he supports most of the hangers-on here. He's also indulging in some expensive habits. *Tran* dust, it's said. Certainly some very expensive liquors, dainties, and ladies."

"Nice lad. Where's the money coming from?"

Jadrek sighed. "That's the main reason why I—and my father before me—are not in favor. King Destillion began taxing the peasantry and the merchant class *far* too heavily to my mind about twenty years ago; Raschar is continuing the tradition. About half of our peasants have been turned into serfs; more follow every year. Opposing *that* was a point Stefansen agreed with me on—and one of the reasons why Destillion intended to cut him out of the succession."

"But didn't?" Kethry asked.

Jadrek shook his head. "Not for lack of trying, but the priests kept him from doing so."

"Idra," Tarma reminded them.

"She saw what Raschar was doing, and began to think that despite Stefansen's habit of hopping into bed with anything that wiggled its hips at him, he might well have been a better choice after all. He certainly had more understanding of the peasantry and how the kingdom's strength depends on them." Jadrek almost managed a smile. "Granted, he spent a great deal of time with them, and pretty much with rowdies, but I'm not certain now that his experience with the rougher classes was a bad thing. Well, Idra wanted an excuse to go after him—I unearthed the old story of the Sword that Sings. Raschar has one chink in his armor; he's desperate to *prove* he's the rightful monarch. Idra took Raschar the old Archive books and got permission to look for the Sword. Then—she vanished."

The fire crackled while they absorbed this. "But she'd intended to go after Stefansen?" Kethry asked, finally.

Jadrek nodded. "It might well be that she decided to just go, before Raschar could change his mind—"

Tarma finished the sentence. "But you aren't entirely certain that something didn't happen to her. Or that something didn't happen right after she set out."

He nodded unhappily, twisting his hands together in his lap. "She would have said good-bye. We've been good friends for a long time. We used to exchange letters as often as her commissions permitted. I . . . saw the world through her eyes. . . ."

There was a flash of longing in his face, there for only a instant, then shuttered down. But it made Tarma wonder what it must be like, to have dreams of adventuring—and be confined to the body of a half-lame scholar.

She stood up, suddenly uncomfortable with the insight. The tiny room felt far, far too confining. "Jadrek, we'll talk with you more, later. Right now you've given us plenty to think on."

"You'll try and find out what's happened to her?" He started to stand, but Kethry gently pushed him back down into his chair as Tarma turned abruptly, not wanting to see any more of this man's pain. She turned the latch silently, cracked the door open and checked for watchers in the corridor beyond.

"Looks clear—" Kethry and Warrl slipped out ahead of her, and Tarma glanced back over her shoulder soberly. The Archivist was watching them from his chair, and there was a peculiar, painful mixture of hope and fear on his face. "Jadrek, that was why we came here in the first place. And be warned—if anything *has* happened to Idra, there might not be a town here once the Hawks find out about it."

And with that she followed her partner back into the corridor.

Seven

Jadrek tried to return to his book, but it was fairly obvious that he was going to be unable to concentrate on the page in front of him. He finally gave up and sat staring at the flickering shadows on the farther wall. His left shoulder ached abominably; it had been wrenched when the door had been jerked out of his hands. This would be a night for a double-dose of medicine, or he'd never get to sleep.

Sleep would not have come easily, anyway—not after this evening's conversation. Tindel had been after him for the past several days to talk to the women, but Jadrek had been reluctant and suspicious; now Tindel would probably refrain from saying "I told you so" only by a strong exercise of will.

What did decide me, anyway? he wondered, trying to find a comfortable position as he rubbed his aching shoulder, the dull throb interfering with his train of thought. *Was it the presence of the* kyree? *No, I don't think so; I think I had made up my mind before they brought him in. I think it was the pretty one that made up my mind—Kethry. She's honest in a way I don't think could be counterfeited. I can't read the Shin'a'in, but if you know what to look for, Kethry's an open book.*

He sighed. *And let's not be fooling ourselves; it's the first time in years that a pretty woman looked at you with anything but contempt, Jadrek. You're as susceptible to that as the next man. More. . . .*

He resolutely killed half-wisps of wistful might-be's and daydreams, and got up to find his medicines.

Tarma left Warrl watching the Archivist's door from the corridor, just in case. His positioning was not nearly as good as she'd have wished; in order to keep out of sight he'd had to lair-up in a table nook some distance away from Jadrek's rooms, and not in direct line of sight. Still, it would have to do. She had some serious misgivings about the Archivist's safety, especially if it should prove that he was being watched.

Creeping along the corridors with every sense alert was unnervingly like being back with the Hawks on a scouting mission. Kethry had hesitantly and reluctantly tendered the notion of using her powers to spy out the situation ahead of them; Tarma had vetoed the idea to her partner's obvious relief. If there was any kind of mage-talented spy keeping an eye on Jadrek, use of magic would not only put alerts on the Archivist but on *them* as well. Their own senses *must* be enough. But it was tense work; Tarma was sweating before they made it to the relative safety of the guesting section.

They slipped their more ornate outfits back on in the shelter of the same alcove where they'd doffed them, and continued on their way. Now was the likeliest time for them to be caught, but they got back to their rooms without a sign that they had been noticed—or so Tarma thought.

She was rather rudely disabused of that notion as soon as they opened the door to their suite.

Moonlight poured down through one of the windows in the right-hand wall of the outer room, making a silver puddle on a square of the pale marble floor. As Tarma closed the door and locked it, she caught movement in that moonlight out of the corner of her eye. She jerked her head around and pulled a dagger with the hand not still on the latch in the automatically defensive reaction to seeing motion where none should be. The moonlight shivered and wavered, sending erratic reflections across the room, and acting altogether unlike natural light.

Tarma snatched her other hand away from the latch, and whirled away from the door she had just locked. Her entire body tingled, from the crown of her head to the soles of her feet—with an energy she was intimately familiar with.

The *only* time she ever felt like this was when her teachers were about to manifest physically, for over the years she had grown as sensitive to the energies of the Star-Eyed as Kethry was to mage-energies. But the spirit-Kal'enedral, her teachers, *never* came to her when she was within four walls—and doubly never when she was in walls that were as alien to them as this palace was.

She sheathed her blade—little good it would do against magic and spirits—set sweating palms against the cool wood of the door. She stared dumbfounded at the evidence of all she'd been told being violated—the shadow and moonlight was hardening into a man-shaped figure; flowing before her eyes into the form of a Shin'a'in garbed and armed in black, and veiled. Only the Kal'enedral wore black and *only* the spirit-Kal'enedral went veiled—and here, where no one knew that, it was wildly unlikely that this could be an illusion, even if there were such a thing as a mage skilled enough to counterfeit the Warrior's powers well enough to fool a living Kal'enedral.

And there was another check—her partner, who had, over the years, seen Tarma's teachers manifesting at least a score of times. Beside her, Kethry stared and smothered a gasp with the back of her hand. Tarma didn't think it likely that any illusion could deceive the mage for long.

To top it all, this was not just any Shin'a'in, not just any spirit-Kal'enedral; for as the features became recognizable (what could be seen above his veil) Tarma knew him to be no less than the chief of all her teachers!

He seemed to be fighting against something; his form wavered in and out of visibility as he held out frantic, empty hands to her, and he seemed to be laboring to speak.

Kethry stared at the spirit-Kal'enedral in absolute shock. This—this *could not* be happening!

But it was, and there was no mistaking the flavor of the energy the spirit brought with him. This *was* a true *leshya'e Kal'enedral*, and he was violating every precept to manifest here and now, within sight of non-Shin'a'in. Which could only mean that he was sent directly by Tarma's own aspect of the four-faced Goddess, the Warrior.

Then she saw with mage-sight the veil of sickly white power that was encasing him like a filthy web, keeping him from full manifestation.

"There's—Goddess, there's a counterspell—" Kethry started out of her entrancement. "It's preventing *any* magic from entering this room! He can't manifest! I—I have to break it, or—"

"Don't!" Tarma hissed, catching her hands as she brought them up. "You break a counterspell and they'll *know* one of us is a mage!"

Kethry turned her head away, unable to bear the sight of the Kal'enedral struggling vainly against the evil power containing him. Tarma turned back to her teacher to see that he had given up the effort to speak—and she saw that his hands were moving, in the same Shin'a'in hand-signs she had taught Kethry and her scouts.

"Keth—his hands—"

As Kethry's eyes were again drawn to the *leshya'e's* figure, Tarma read his message.

Death-danger, she read, and *Assassins. Wise one.*

"Warrior! It's Jadrek—he's going to be killed!" She reached behind her for the door, certain that they were never going to make it to Judrek's rooms in time.

But Warrl had been watching her thoughts, probably alerted through the bond they shared to her agitation.

:Mindmate, I go!: rang through her head.

At the same moment, as if he had heard the *kyree's* reply the *leshya'e Kal'enedral* made a motion of triumph, and dissolved back into moonlight and shadow.

While Kethry was still staring at the place where the spirit had stood, Tarma was clawing the door open, all thought of subterfuge gone.

She headed down the corridor at a dead run, and she could hear Kethry right behind her; this time there would be no attempt at concealment.

Warrl's "voice" was sharp in her mind; angry, and tasting of battle-hunger. *:Mindmate—one comes. He smells of seeking death.:*

Keep him away from Jadrek!

There was no answer to that, as she put on a burst of speed down the corridor—at least not an answer in words. But there was a surge of great anger, a rage such as she had seldom sensed in the *kyree,* even under battle-fire.

Then Tarma had evidence of her own of how strong the mindmate bonding between herself and the *kyree* had become—because she began to get image-flashes carried on that rage. A man, or armed man, with a long, wicked dagger in his hand, standing outside Jadrek's door. The man turning to face Warrl even as Jadrek opened the door. Jadrek stepping back a pace with fear stark across his features, then turning and stumbling back into his room. The man ignoring him, meeting the threat of Warrl, unsheathing a sword to match the knife he carried.

Tarma felt the growl the *kyree* vented rumbling in her own throat as she ran. Felt him leap—

Now they were in the older section—running down Jadrek's corridor. Kethry was scarcely a step behind her as they skidded to a halt at Jadrek's open door.

There was blood everywhere—spilling out over the doorsill, splashed on the wall of the corridor. The *kyree* stood over a body sprawled half-in, half-out of the room, growling under his breath, his eyes literally glowing with rage. Warrl had taken care of the intruder less than seconds before their arrival, for the body at his feet was still twitching, and the *kyree's* mind was seething with aggression and the aftermath of the kill. His hackles were up, but he was unmarked; of the blood splashed so liberally everywhere, none of it seemed to be Warrl's.

"Goddess—" Tarma caught at the edge of the doorframe, and panted, her knees weak with relief that the *kyree* had gotten there in time.

"Jadrek!" Kethry snapped out of shock first; she slid past the slowly calming *kyree* into the room beyond. Tarma was right behind her, expecting to find the Archivist in a dead faint, or worse; hurt, or collapsed with shock.

She was amazed to find him still on his feet.

He had his back to the wall, standing next to the fireplace behind his chair, a dagger in one hand, a fireplace poker in the other. He was pale, and looked as if he was likely to be sick at any moment. But he also looked as if he was quite ready to protect himself as best he could, and was anything but immobilized with fear or shock.

For one moment he didn't seem to recognize them; then he shook his head a little, put the poker carefully down, sheathed the dagger at his belt, then groped for the back of his chair and pulled it toward himself, the legs grating on the stone. He all but fell into it.

"Jadrek—are you all right?" Tarma would have gone to his side, but Kethry was there before her.

Jadrek was trembling in every nerve and muscle as he collapsed into his chair. *Gods—one breath more—too close. Too close.*

Kethry took his wrist before he could wave her away and felt for his pulse.

He stared at her anxious face, so close to his own, and felt his heart skip for a reason other than fear. *Dammit, you fool, she's just worried that you're going to die on her before you can help her with the information they need!*

Then he thought, feeling a chill creep down his back; *Gods—I might. If Char has been a watcher on me all this time, it means he's suspected me of warning Stefan. And if that watcher chose to strike tonight only because I spoke to a pair of strangers—Archivist, your hours are numbered.*

Kethry checked Jadrek's heartbeat, fearing to find it fluttering erratically. To her intense relief, it was strong, though understandably racing.

"I—gods above—I think I will be all right," he managed, pressing his free hand to his forehead. "But I would be dead if not for your *kyree*."

"Who was that?" Kethry asked urgently. "Who—"

"That . . . was a member of the King's personal guard," he replied thickly. "Brightest Goddess—I knew I was under suspicion, but I never guessed it went this far! They must have had someone watching me."

"Watching to see who you talked to, no doubt," Tarma said grimly, her lips compressed into a thin line. "And the King must have left orders what was to happen to you if you talked to strangers. Hellfire and corruption!"

"Now I'm a liability, so far as Raschar is concerned." He was pale, and with more than shock, but there was determination in the set of his jaw as he looked to Tarma. "'Char has only one way of dealing with liabilities . . . as you've seen. Lord and Lady help me, I'm under a death sentence, without trial or hearing! I—I haven't got a chance unless I can escape. Woman, you've got to help me! If you want any more help with finding Idra, you've *got*—"

Kethry had angry words on her tongue, annoyed that he should think them such cowards, but Tarma beat her to them.

"What kind of gutless boobs do you think we are?" Tarma snapped. "Of *course* we'll help you! Dammit man, it was us coming to you that triggered this attack in the first place! Keth, clean up the mess. Go ahead and use magic, we're blown now, anyway."

Kethry nodded. "After the visitor, I should say so—even if there wasn't anyone 'watching,' he'll have left residue in the trap-spell."

"Did you pick up any 'eyes'?"

She let her mage-senses extend. "No . . . no. Not then, and not now. Evidently they haven't guessed *our* identity."

"Small piece of Warrior's fortune. Well, I'm getting rid of the body before somebody falls over it; it's likely this bastard was the only watcher, Archivist, or you'd have been caught out before this." She paused to think. "If I hide him, they may wait to check things out until *after* he was due to report. Hell, if they can't find him, they may wait a bit longer to see if he's gone following after one of Jadrek's visitors; that should buy us a couple more hours Jadrek, are there any empty rooms along here?"

"Most of them are empty," he said dully, holding his hands up before his eyes and watching them shake with a kind of morbid fascination "Nobody is quartered along here who isn't in disgrace; this is the oldest wing of the palace, and it's been poorly maintained and repaired but little."

"Gods, no wonder nobody came piling out to see what the ruckus was." Tarma's lip curled in disgust. "Bastard really gives you respect, doesn't he? Well, that's another piece of good luck we've had tonight."

And Tarma turned back to deal with the corpse as Kethry began mustering her energies for "clean-up."

147

*   *   *

Tarma bundled the body into its own cloak, giving Warrl mental congratulations over the relatively clean kill; the *kyree* had only torn the man's throat out. The man had been relatively small; she figured she could handle the corpse alone. She heaved the bundle over her shoulder with a grunt of effort, trusting to the thick cloak to absorb whatever blood remained to be spilled, and went out into the corridor, picking a room at random. The first one she chose didn't have its own fireplace, so she left that one—but the second did. It was a matter of moments and a good bit of joint-straining effort to stuff the carcass up the chimney; by the time she returned, a little judicious use of magic had cleaned up every trace of a struggle around Jadrek's quarters, and Kethry and the Archivist were in the little bedroom that lay beyond the closed door in his sitting room. The mage was helping Jadrek to make a pack of his belongings, and Jadrek was far calmer now than Tarma had dared to hope. Warrl was stretched across the doorway, still growling under his breath. He gave her a gentle warn-off as she sent him a thought; his blood-lust was up, and he didn't want her in his mind until he had quieted himself.

Jadrek had lit a half dozen candles and stuck them over every available surface. The bedroom was as sparse as the outer room had been, though smelling a little less of damp. There was just a wardrobe, a chest, and the bed.

"Jadrek, how well do you ride?" Tarma asked, taking over the bundle Kethry was making and freeing her to start a new one.

"Not well," he said shortly, folding packets of herbs into a cloth. "It's not my ability to ride, it's the pain. I used to ride very well; now I can't stand being in a saddle for more than an hour or so."

"And if we drugged you?"

He shrugged. "Drugged, aren't I likely to fall off? And you'd have to lead my beast, even if you tied me into the saddle; that would slow you considerably."

"Not if I put you on 'Heart. Or—better yet, Keth, you're light and you don't go armored. How about if I take all the packs and 'Bane carries double?"

Kethry examined the Archivist carefully. "It should be all right. Jadrek doesn't look like he weighs much. Put him up in front of me, and I can hold him on even if he's insensible."

The Archivist managed a quirk of one corner of his mouth. "Hardly the way I had hoped to begin my career of adventuring."

Tarma raised an eyebrow at him.

"You look surprised. Swordlady, I did a great deal of my studying in hopes of one day being able to aid some heroic quester. After all, what better help could a hero have than a loremaster? Then," he held out one hand and shoved the sleeve of his robe up so they could see the swollen wrists, "my body betrayed me and my dreams. So goes life."

Tarma winced in sympathy; her own bones ached in the cold these days, enough that rough camping left her stiff and limping these days for at least an hour after rising, or until she finished her warming exercises. She didn't like to think how much pain swollen joints meant.

"Have you any plan?" the Archivist continued. "Or are we just going to run for it?"

Tarma shook her head. "Don't you think it— Running off blindly is likely to run us right into a trap. We came out of the south, the Hawks are to the south and west—I'd bet the King's men'll expect us to run for familiar territory."

"So we go opposite?" Jadrek hazarded. "North? Then what?"

Tarma folded a shirt into a tight bundle and wedged it into the pack. "North is where Stefansen

went. North is where Idra likely went. No? So
we'll track them North, and hope to run into one or
both of them."

"I know where Stefansen intended to go," Jadrek
said slowly, "I *did* tell Idra before she went missing. But frankly it's some of the worst country to
travel in winter in all of Rethwellan."

"All the better to shake off pursuit. Cough it up,
man, where are we going?"

"Across the Comb and into Valdemar." He looked
seriously worried. "And winter storm season in the
Comb is deadly. If we're caught in an ice storm
without shelter, well, let me just say that we probably won't be a problem for Raschar anymore."

"This is almost too easy," Tarma muttered, surveying the empty court below Jadrek's window.
"Keth, is there anything you can't live without
back in the room?"

The mage pursed her lips thoughtfully, then shook
her head.

"Good, then we'll leave from here. Nobody's been
alerted yet, and evidently Jadrek's in poor enough
condition that nobody has even *considered* he might
slip out his window."

"With good reason, Swordlady," Jadrek replied,
coming to Tarma's side and looking down into the
court himself. "I can't imagine how I *could* climb
down."

"Alone, you couldn't; we'll help you," Kethry
told him. "I can actually make you about half your
real weight with magic, then we'll manage well
enough."

The Archivist looked down again, and shuddered,
but to his credit, did not protest.

They'd sent Warrl for a short coil of rope from
the stables; there were always lead-ropes and lunges
lying around, and any of those would be long enough.
He returned just as Kethry completed her spell—

casting; they tied one end around Jadrek's waist, then Kethry scrambled out of the window and down the wall to steady him from below as Tarma lowered him. Before they were finished, Tarma had a high respect for the man's courage; climbing down from the window put him in such pain that when they untied him they found he'd bitten his lip through to keep from crying out.

All their gear was still with the mares. When they'd left Hawksnest, they'd chosen to use a different kind of saddle than they normally chose, one meant for long rides and not pitched battles. Like the saddles Jodi preferred, these were little more than a pad with stirrups, although the pad extended out over the horse's rump. When Tarma carried Warrl pillion, he had a pad behind her battle-saddle to ride on; there was just enough room on the extended body of this saddle for him to do the same. So Kethry had no trouble fitting Jadrek in front of her, which was just as well—

Jadrek had mixed something with the last of his wine and gulped it down before attempting the window. He was fine, although still in pain, when they started saddling up. But by the time the mares were harnessed and all their gear was in place, he was fairly intoxicated and not at all steady.

They did manage to get him into the saddle, but it was obvious he wouldn't be staying there without Kethry's help.

Warrl? Tarma thought tentatively.

:*All is well, mindmate,*: came the reassuring reply. :*There is no one in sight, and I am distracting the gate guards. If you go swiftly, there will be no one to stop or question you.*:

"Let's move out now," she told her partner, "while Furface has the guards playing 'catch-me-if-you-can' with him."

Kethry nodded; they rode out of the palace grounds as quietly—they'd signaled the mares for silence, and now Hellsbane and Ironheart were moving as stealthily as only two Shin'a'in bred-and-trained warsteeds *could*. They managed to get ou unchallenged, and waited outside the palace fo Warrl to catch up with them, then put Ironhear and Hellsbane to as fast a pace as they dared, and by dawn were well clear of the city.

"Any sign of tracking?" Tarma asked her partner, reining Ironheart in beside her as they slowed to a brisk walk.

Kethry closed her eyes in concentration, extended a little tendril of energy along the road behind them, then shook her head. "My *guess* would be that they haven't missed the spy yet. But my guess would also be, that with all the mages I sensed in Raschar's court, they'll be sending at least one with each pursuit party."

"Anything you can do about that?"

"Some." She reformed that tendril of energy into a deception-web that *might* confuse their backtrail. "Listen, we need supplies; how about if I lay an illusion on you and 'Heart and you go buy us some at the next village we hit?"

"How about if you spell all three of us right now? Say—old woman and her daughter and son? Nobody knows Shin'a'in battlemares out here, and 'Heart and 'Bane are ugly enough to belong to peasants: you needn't spell them."

"Huh; not a bad thought. What about Warrl?"

:*I can seem much smaller if I need to.*:

Kethry started. "Furface, I *wish* you wouldn't just speak into my mind like that—you never used to!"

:*My pardon. I grow forgetful of courtesy. How does the Wise One?*:

Jadrek was three-quarters asleep, slumped forward in Kethry's hold, his head nodding to the rhythm of Hellsbane's hooves. Kethry touched his

eck below his ear lightly enough not to disturb
im. "All right; his pulse is strong."

:If you would have my advice?:

When the *kyree* tendered his opinion, it was worth
aving. "Go ahead."

*:Rouse him up and make him speak with you. He
vill do his body more harm by riding unconscious.:*

"On that subject," Tarma interrupted, "how long
:an you keep our illusions going? What kind of
shape are *you* in?"

Kethry shrugged. "I've been mostly resting my
powers so far. I can keep the spell up indefinitely.
Why?"

"Because I want to stay under roofs at night for
as long as we can. Rough camping is going to be
hard on our friend at best—be a helluva note to
save him from assassins and lose him to pneumonia."

Kethry nodded, thinking of how much pain the
Archivist was already in. "What kind of roofs?"

"In order of preference—out-of-the-way barns, the
occasional friendly farmer, and the cheapest inns
in town."

"Sound, I think. Pull up here, I might as well
cast this thing now, and I can't do it on a moving
horse."

"Here" was a grove of trees beside the road; they
got the horses off and allowed them to browse while
Kethry concentrated.

Warrl flung himself down into the dry grass, and
lay there, panting. He was not built for the long
chase. Before too very long, Tarma would have to
bring him up to ride pillion behind her for a rest.

Kethry got Jadrek leaning back against her, then
spread her hands wide, palms facing out. A shell of
faint, roseate light expanded from her hands outward, to contain them and their horses. Tarma could
see her lips moving silently in the words of the
spell. There was a tiny "pop" like a cork being

153

pulled from a bottle; then Tarma felt an all-too
familiar itching at the back of her eyes, and when
she looked down, she saw that she was wearing
man's garb of rough, brown homespun instead of
her Kal'enedral-styled black silks. So Keth was going
to disguise her as a young man; good, that should
help to throw off nonmage spies.

Jadrek was now an old, gray-haired woman with
a face like a wrinkled apple, and a body stooped
from years of hard work. Behind him, Kethry was a
chunky, fresh-faced peasant wench; brown-cheeked,
brown-haired and quite unremarkable.

"Huh," Tarma said. "This's a new one for *you.*
You look like you'd make some dirt-grubber a great
wife."

Kethry giggled. "Good hips. Breed like cow, strong
like bull, dumb like ox. Hitch to plow when horse
dies." As Tarma stifled a chuckle, she turned her
attention to her passenger. "Jadrek, wake up, there's
a good fellow." She shook his shoulder gently. "Open
your eyes slowly. I've put an illusion on us all and it
may make you dizzy at first."

"Huhnn. I . . . thought I heard you saying that. . . ."
The Archivist raised his head with care, and
opened eyes that looked a bit dazed. "Gods. What
am I?"

"A crippled-up old peasant woman. Warrl says
you'll do yourself more harm than good by riding
asleep; he wants you to talk to me."

"How . . . odd. I thought I heard him speaking in
my head again. I seem to remember him saying just
that. . . ."

The partners exchanged a startled look. Evidently
Jadrek had a mage-Gift no one had ever suspected,
for normally the only folk who heard Warrl's mind-
voice were those he *intended* to speak to. That Talent *might* be useful—if they all lived to reach the
Border.

"Let's get on with it," Tarma broke the silence

before it went on too long, and glanced at the rising sun to her right. "We need to get as far as we can before they figure out we've bolted back there."

They stopped at a good-sized village; there was a market going on, and Tarma rode in alone and bought the supplies they were going to need. By mercenary's custom, they'd kept all their cash with them in moneybelts that they never let out of their sight, so they weren't short of funds, at least. Tarma did well in her bargaining; better than she'd expected. Even more encouraging, no one gave her a second glance.

Poor Jadrek had not exaggerated the amount of pain he was going to be in. By nightfall his eyes were sunken deeply into their sockets and he looked more than half dead; but they found a barn, full of new-cut hay, dry and warm and softer than many beds Tarma had slept in. The dry warmth seemed to do Jadrek a lot of good; he was moving better the next morning, and didn't take nearly as much of his drugs as he had the day before.

And oddly enough, he seemed to get better as the trip progressed. Kethry was wearing Need at her side again, after having left the ensorcelled blade with her traveling gear in the stables. Tarma was just thanking her Goddess that they *hadn't* ever brought the blade into their quarters—no telling what would have happened had it met with the counterspell on their rooms. Of a certainty Raschar would have known from that moment that they were not what they seemed.

Fall weather struck with a vengeance on the sixth morning. They ended up riding all day through rain; Rethwellan's fall and early winter rains were notorious far and wide. Jadrek was alert and conversing quietly and animatedly with Kethry; he seemed in better shape, despite the cold rain, than he'd been back at the palace. Now Tarma wondered

—remembering the enigmatic words of Moonsong k'Vala, the Tale'edras Adept—if Need was working some of her magic on Jadrek because Kethry was concerned for him. It would be the first time in Tarma's knowledge that a *male* for whom Kethry cared had spent any length of time in physical contact with the mage while she was wearing the blade.

As for Kethry caring for him—they were certainly hitting it off fairly well. Tarma was growing used to the soft murmur of voices behind her as they talked for the endless hours of the day's ride. So maybe—just maybe—the sword was responding to that liking.

As the days passed: "Keth," she asked, when they'd halted for the night in the seventh of a succession of haybarns. "Do you remember what the Hawkbrother told you when we first met him—about Need?"

"You mean Moonsong, the Adept?" Kethry glanced over at Jadrek, but the witchlight she was creating showed the Archivist already rolled up in a nest of blankets and hay, and sound asleep. "He said a lot of things."

"*Hai*—but I'm thinking there's something that might be pertinent to Jadrek."

Kethry nodded, slowly. "About Need extending her powers to those I care for. Uh-huh; I've been wondering about that. Jadrek certainly seems to be in a lot less pain."

Tarma snuggled into the soft hay, sword and dagger within easy reach. Behind her, Warrl was keeping watch at the door, and Ironheart and Hellsbane were drowsing, having stuffed themselves with fresh hay. "He's not drugging himself as much, either. And . . ."

Kethry settled into her own bedroll and snuffed the witchlight.

"And he's not the bitter, suspicious man we met

at the Court," she said quietly in the darkness. "I think we're seeing the man Idra knew." Tarma heard the hay rustle a bit, then Kethry continued, very softly, "And I *like* that man, *she'enedra*. So much that I think your guess could be right."

"*Krethes, ves'tacha?*"

"Unadorned truth. I like him; he treats me as an intellectual equal, and that's rare, even among mages. That I'm his physical superior ... doesn't seem to bother him. It's just ... what I am. He'll never ride 'Bane the way I do, or swing a sword; I'll never be half the linguist he is, or beat him at chess."

"Sounds like—"

"Don't go matchmaking on me, woman!" Kethry softened the rebuke with a dry chuckle. "We've got enough on our plate with tracking Idra, the damned weather, and the mage we've got on our backtrail."

"So we *are* being followed."

"Nothing you can do about it; my hope is that when he hits the Comb he'll get discouraged and turn back."

Tarma nodded in the dark; this was Keth's province. She wouldn't do either of them any good by fretting about it. If it came to physical battle, *then* she'd be able to do some good.

And for whatever the reason, Jadrek was able to do with less of his drugs every day, and that was all to the good. They were making about as good a headway with him now as they would have been able to manage alone. And maybe ...

She fell asleep before she could finish the thought.

Now they were getting into the Comb, and as Jadrek had warned, the Comb was no place to be riding through with less than full control of one's senses.

The range of hills along the Northern border called the Comb was among some of the worst terrain Tarma had ever encountered. The hills them selves weren't all that high—but they were shee rock faces for the most part, with little more tha goat tracks leading through them, and not much i the way of vegetation, just occasional stands of wind warped trees, a bit of scrub brush, rank grasses and some moss and lichen—enough browse for th horses—barely, and Tarma was supplementing th browse with grain, just to be on the safe side.

It had been late spring, still winter in the moun tains where Hawksnest lay, when they'd headec down into Rethwellan. It had been early fall by th time they'd made it to the capital. It had been lat fall when they bolted. Now it was winter—the wors possible time to be traveling the Comb.

Now that they were in the hills the rains hac changed to sleet and snow, and there were n friendly farmers, and no inns to take shelter i when hostile weather made camping a grim pros pect. And they no longer had the luxury of pressing on; when a suitable campsite presented itself, they took it. If there wasn't anything suitable, they suffered.

They'd been three days with inadequate camps sleeping cold and wet, and waking the same. Kethry had dropped the illusions two days ago; there wasn' anybody to *see* them anymore. And when they were on easy stretches of trail, Tarma could see Kethry frowning with her eyes closed, and knew she wa doing *something* magical along the backtrail—which probably meant she needed to hoard every scrap o personal energy she could.

Jadrek, predictably, was in worst case. Tarma wasn't too far behind him in misery. And some times it seemed to her that their progress was mea sured in handspans, not furlongs. The only comfort was in knowing that their pursuers—if any—were not likely to be making any better progress.

Tarma looked up at the dead, gray sky and swore at the scent of snow on the wind.

Kethry urged Hellsbane up beside her partner when the trail they were following dropped into a hollow between two of the hills, and there was room enough to do so. The mage was bundled up in every warm garment she owned; on the saddle before her the Archivist was an equally shapeless bundle. He was nodding; only Kethry's arms clasped about him kept him in the saddle. He had had a very bad night, for they'd been forced to camp without any shelter, and he'd taken the full dosage of his drugs just so that he could mount this morning.

"Snow?" Kethry asked unhappily.

"*Hai*. Dammitall. How much more of this is *he* going to be able to take?"

"I don't know, *she'enedra*. I don't know how much more of this *I'm* going to be able to take. I'm about ready to fall off, myself."

Tarma scanned the terrain around her, hoping for someplace where they could get a sheltered fire going and *maybe* get warm again for the first time in four days. Nothing. Just crumbling hills, overhangs she dared not trust, and scrub. Not a tree, not a cave, not even a tumble of boulders to shelter in. And even as she watched, the first flakes of snow began.

She watched them, hoping to see them melting when they hit the ground—as so far, had always been the case. This time they didn't. "Oh hell*fire*. Keth, this stuff is going to stick, I'm afraid."

The mage sighed. "It would. I'd witch the weather, but I'd do more harm than good."

"I'd rather you conjured up a sheltered camp."

"I've tried," Kethry replied bleakly. "My energies are at absolute nadir. I spent everything I had getting that mage off our trail. I'd cast a *jesto-vath*, but I need some kind of wall and ceiling to make it work."

Tarma stifled a cough, hunched her shoulders against the cold wind, and sighed. "It's not like you

159

had any choice; no more than we do now. Let's get on. Maybe something will turn up."

But nothing did, and the flurries turned to a full-fledged snowstorm before they'd gone another furlong.

"We've got to get a rest," Tarma said, finally, as they gave the horses a breather at the top of a hill. "Jadrek, how are you doing?"

"Poorly," he replied, rousing himself. The tone of his voice was dull. "I need to take more of my medicines, and I dare not. If I fell asleep in this cold—"

"Right. Look—there's a bit of a corner down there." Tarma pointed through the curtaining snow to a cul-de-sac visible just off the main trail. "It might be sheltered enough to let us get a bit warmer. And the horses need more than a breather."

"I won't argue," Kethry replied. "I can feel 'Bane straining now."

Unspoken was the very real danger that was in all of their minds. It was obvious that the snow was falling more thickly with every candlemark; it was equally obvious that unless they found a *good* campsite they'd be in danger of death by exposure if they fell asleep. That meant pressing on through the night if they didn't find a secure site. This little rest might be the closest to sleep that they'd get tonight.

And when they got to the cul-de-sac, they found evidence of how real the danger was.

Huddled against the boulders of the back was what was left of a man.

Rags and bones, mostly. The carcass was decades old, at least. There were no marks of violence on him, except that done by scavengers, and from the way the bones lay Tarma judged he'd died of cold.

"Poor bastard," she said, picking up a sword in a half-rotten sheath, and turning it over, looking for some trace of ownership-marks. "Helluva way to die."

Kethry was tumbling stones down over the pitiful remains; Jadrek was doing his best to help. "Is there any *good* way to die?"

"In your own bed. In your own time. Here—can you make anything of this?"

Jadrek dug into his packs while the women were occupying themselves with the grisly remains they'd found. He was aching all over with pain, even through the haze of drugs. Worse, he was slowing them down.

But there was a solution, of sorts. They didn't need him now, and if the weather worsened, *his* presence—or absence—might mean the difference between life and death for the two partners.

So he was going to overdose. That would put him to sleep. If they *did* find shelter, there would be no harm done, and he would simply sleep the overdose off. But if they didn't—

If they didn't, the cold would kill him painlessly, and they'd be rid of an unwieldy burden. Without him they'd be able to take paths and chances they weren't taking now. Without him they could devote energy to saving themselves.

He swallowed the bitter herb pellets quickly, before they could catch him at it, and washed away the bitterness with a splash of icy water from his canteen. Then he pressed himself up against the sheltered side of Kethry's mount, trying to leech the heat from her body into his own.

Kethry took the sword from her partner, and turned it over. The sheath looked as if it had once had metal fittings; there were gaping sockets in the pommel and at the ends of the quillions of the sword that had undoubtedly once held gemstones. There was no evidence of either, now.

"Poor bastard. Might have been a merc, down on his luck," Tarma said. "That's when you know

161

you're hitting the downward slide—when you're
selling the decorations off your blade."

Kethry slid the sword a little out of the sheath; i
resisted, with a grating sound, although there wa
no sign of rust on the dull gray blade. Tarma leaned
over her shoulder, and scratched the exposed meta
with the point of her dagger, then snorted at the
shiny marks the steel left on the metal of the sword

"Well, *I* feel a little less sorry for him," Kethry
retorted. "*My* guess is that he was a thief. This
was some kind of dress blade, but the precious
metal and the stones have been stripped from it."

"Have to be a dress sword," the Shin'a'in said in
disgust. "Nobody in their right mind would depend
on *that* thing. It isn't steel or even crude-forged
iron. You're right, he must have been a thief—and
probably the pretties were stripped by somebody
that came across the body."

Tarma turned back to her inspection of her mare's
condition, and Kethry nodded, shoving the blade
back into its sheath. "You're right about this thing,"
she agreed. "Metal that soft wouldn't hold an edge
for five minutes. Damn thing is nearly useless. That
pretty much confirms it. The departed wasn't
dressed particularly well, I doubt he'd have much
use for a dress-sword." She started to stick the
thing point-down into the cairn they'd built—then
moved by some impulse she didn't quite understand, put it into her pack, instead.

There was something about that sword—something
buried below the seeming of its surface, something
that tasted of magic. And if there was magic involved, Kethry thought vaguely, it might be worth
saving to look into later.

Neither Tarma nor Jadrek noticed; Tarma was
checking Ironheart's feet, and Jadrek was pressed
up against Hellsbane's side with his eyes closed,
trying to absorb some of the mare's warmth into his
own body.

Tarma straightened up with a groan. "Well, people, I hate to say this, but—"

Kethry and Jadrek sighed simultaneously.

"I know," Kethry replied. "Time to go."

Darkness was falling swiftly, and the snow was coming down thicker than ever. They'd given up trying to find a campsite themselves; Tarma had sent Warrl out instead. That meant they had one less set of eyes to guard them, but Warrl was the only one who stood a chance of finding shelter for them.

Tarma was leading both horses; on a trail this uncertain, she wanted it to be *her* that stumbled or fell, not the mares. She was cold to the point of numbness, and every time Hellsbane tripped on the uneven ground, she could hear Jadrek catching his breath in pain, and Kethry murmuring encouragement to him.

Tarma was no longer thinking much beyond the next step, and all her hopes were centered on the *yree*. If they didn't find shelter by dawn, they'd be so weary that no amount of will could keep them from resting—and once resting, no amount of foreknowledge would keep them from falling asleep—

And they would die.

Tarma wondered how many ghosts haunted the Comb, fools or the desperate, lured into trying to thread the rocky hills and falling victim to no enemy but the murderous weather.

She half-listened to the wind wailing among the rocks above them. It sounded like voices. The voices of hungry ghosts, vengeful ghosts, jealous of the living. The kinds of ghosts that showed up in the songs of her people, now and again, who sought only to lure others to their deaths, so that they might have company.

How many fools—how many ghosts—

A white shape loomed up out of the dusk before

163

them, blocking the path. A vague, ivory rider on an ethereal silver horse, appearing suddenly and sound lessly out of the snow, like a pallid harbinger of cold death.

"Li'sa'eer!" Tarma croaked, and dropped the reins of both horses, pulling the sword slung at her back in the next instant, and wondering wildly if Goddess-blessed steel could harm a hungry ghost.

:Mindmate, no!:

Warrl jumped down from the hillside to her right to interpose his bulk between her and the spirit. *:Mindmate—this is help!:*

"Peace upon you, lady." The voice of the one astride the strange white beast was *not* that of a spirit; nor, when Tarma allowed a corner of herself to test the *feel* of him, was there any of the tingle she associated with magic. The man's voice was not hollow, as a spirit's normally sounded; it was warm, deep, and held a tinge of amusement. "Your four-footed friend came looking for aid, and we heard his calling. I did not mean to startle you."

Tarma's arms shook as she resheathed the blade. "Goddess bless—*warn* a body next time! You just about ate six thumbs of steel!"

"Again, your pardon, but we could not tell exactly where you were. Your presences seem rather ... blurred."

"Never mind that," Kethry interrupted from behind Tarma, her voice sharp. "Who are you? *What* are you? Why should we trust you?"

The man did not seem to be taken aback by her words. "You're wise not to take anything on appearance, lady. You don't know me—but I *do* know you; I've talked to your friend mind-to-mind, and I know who you are and what you wish. You can trust me on three counts." He and his horse moved in to stand nose to nose with Ironheart. Tarma saw with no little surprise that even in the fading light the beast's eyes were plainly a bright and startling *blue*. "Firstly—that you are no longer in Rethwellan; you crossed the Border some time back, and you are in Valdemar. The enemy on your backtrail will not be able to pass the Border, nor would I give you to him. Secondly, that the man you seek, Prince Stefansen, is Valdemar's most welcome guest, and I will be taking you to him as quickly as your tired beasts can manage. And thirdly, you can trust me because of my office."

"Look—we're tired, we *don't* know anything about your land, and our friend, who might, is not even half-conscious."

So *that* was what was making Keth's voice sound like she was walking on glass.

"I seem to be making a mess of this," the man replied ruefully. "I am Roald, one of the Heralds of Valdemar. And you may believe your large, hairy friend there, that any Herald is to be trusted."

:*They are, mindmate,*: Warrl confirmed. :*With more than life. There is no such creature as a treacherous Herald.*:

All right, Tarma thought, worn past exhaustion. *We've got no chance out here—and you've never been wrong before this, Furface.*

"Lead on, Herald Roald," she said aloud. And wearily hoped Warrl was right this time, too.

Eight

Tarma clasped her blue-gray pottery mug in both her hands and sniffed the spicy, rich aroma of the hot wine it contained a trifle warily. The stuff was too hot to drink; not that she minded. The heat of it had warmed the thick clay of the mug, and that, in turn, was warming her hands so that they no longer ached in each separate joint. And the heat gave her an excuse to be cautious about drinking it.

She blinked sleepily at the flames in the fireplace before her, trying to muster herself back up to full alertness. But she was feeling the heat seeping into her bones, and with the heat came relaxation. The fire cast dancing patterns of light and shadow up into the exposed rough-hewn beams of the square common room, and made the various trophies of horns and antlers hung on the polished wooden walls seem to move. *She* didn't want to stir, not at all, and that had the potential for danger.

She was wearing, bizarrely enough, some of Roald's spare clothing, all of her own too thoroughly soaked even to bother with. *A Kal'enedral in white—Warrior bless, now* that's *a strange thought.* Roald was the only one of them near to her size; off his horse he was scarcely more than a couple of thumblengths taller than Tarma, and was just as rangy-thin. He was exceedingly handsome in a rugged way, with a heavy shock of dark blond hair, a neat little beard, and eyes as blue as his horse's.

I thought I'd never be warm again. She settled a

166

ttle more down into her chair and the eiderdown
ley'd given her to wrap around herself, and blinked
t the *kyree* stretched out between her and the
ames. Warrl was fast asleep on the red-tiled hearth
t her feet, having bolted a meal of three rabbits
rst. *He trusts them. Especially Roald. Dare we?*

Her chair was set just to one side of the fireplace,
ractically on the hearthstone. Directly across from
er, Kethry was curled up in a second chair,
rrapped in eiderdown, looking small and unwontedly serious. She'd been summarily stripped of her
vet gear, the same as Tarma, but opted for one
f Lady Mertis' soft green wool gowns. Jadrek had
een spirited away as well, and regarbed in Ste-
ansen's warmest—heavy brown wool breeches and
unic and knitted shirt.

*If Roald hadn't come when he did—Star-Eyed, we
ame perilously close to losing him. If I'd known he'd
aken enough of that painkilling stuff to put him out
ike that—*

Jadrek was pacing the floor beside the two chairs
nd within the arc of heat and light cast by the fire.
Ie limped very badly—walking slowly, haltingly,
rying to shake the fog of his medicines from his
ead so that he could talk coherently again. He was
noving so stiffly that Tarma hurt just watching
im.

*I wonder; he knew we were in bad trouble when we
topped that last time. I wonder if he didn't dose him-
elf on purpose, figuring that we'd either find shelter
nd he'd be all right, or that we wouldn't, and while he
vas unconscious the cold would kill him painlessly and
et him out of our hair. That's something a Clansman
night do. Dammit—I like this man! And he has no
eservations about Stefansen and this Herald. But I do.
 must.*

Stefansen's wife, Mertis (*that* had come as a shock
o Jadrek, that Stefansen had actually wedded),
vas seated in another chair a bit farther removed

from the fire, nursing their month-old son. *I li[]
her, too. That's a sweet little one—why do I have [
distrust these people?*

Stefansen, who resembled Idra to a startlin[
degree, (except that on a man's face the feature[
that had been harsh for a woman were strong, an[
those that had been handsome were breathtaking[
was talking quietly with Roald, the two of the[
sitting on a pair of chairs they'd pulled up near t[
Mertis. A most domestic and harmonious scene, [
you could ignore the worry in everyone's eyes.

*Good thing we had Jadrek to vouch for us, or Stefanse[
might have left us to freeze, and be damned to h[
Herald friend. He did not like the fact that we'd com[
looking for him out of Rethwellan. He's still watchin[
me when he thinks I'm not paying any attention. We'r[
both like wary wolves at first meeting, neither one sur[
the other isn't going to bite.*

This turned out to be Roald's own hunting lodg[
which, since it was not exactly a *small* dwellin[
told Tarma that whatever else he was, the Heral[
was also a man of means. It was now the "humble[
abode of the Prince-in-exile, his bride of ten month[
and their infant son. Valdemar had given Stefanse[
the sanctuary he needed, but it was a secret sanctu
ary; the King and Queen of Valdemar dared no
compromise their country's safety, not with Reth
wellan sharing borders with both themselves an[
their hereditary enemy, Karse.

The wine was cool enough to drink now, an[
Tarma had decided she couldn't detect anythin[
dangerous in it. She sipped at it, letting it sooth[
her raw throat and ease the cold in the pit of he[
stomach. While she drank, she scrutinized Merti[
again over the edge of the mug.

Tarma watched the gentle woman rocking he[
son in her arms, studying her with the same car[
she'd have spent on the reconnoitering of an enem[
camp. Mertis was not homely, by any means, bu[

not a raving beauty, either. She had a sweet, soft face; frank brown eyes that seemed to demand truth of you; wavy, sable-brown hair. *Not* the kind of woman one would expect to captivate an experienced rake like Stefansen. Which meant there was more to her than showed on the surface.

Then again—Tarma hid a smile with her mug as she thought of the moment when Roald had brought them stumbling up to the door of the lodge. Mertis had been everywhere, easing Jadrek down from his grip on Kethry's saddle, helping him to stumble into the warm, brightly lit lodge, building up the fire with her own hands, issuing crisp, no-nonsense orders to her spouse, the Herald, and the two servants of the lodge, without regard for rank. That just *might* have been her secret—that she had been the only woman to treat Stefansen like a simple man, a person, and not throw herself at his feet, panting like a bitch in heat.

Or it might have been a half dozen other things, but *one* was a certainty; Tarma knew love well enough to recognize it when those two looked at each other. And never mind that Mertis was scarcely higher in birth than Kethry.

"Jadrek?" Stefansen called softly, catching Tarma's attention. "Have you walked yourself out yet? *I'd* rather you got a night's sleep, but Roald seems to think we need to talk *now!*"

"Not just you two—all of us, the mercenaries included," the Herald corrected. "We all have bits of information that need to be put together into a whole."

Stefansen is looking wary again. I'll warrant he didn't expect us to be included in this little talk. Ah well, duty calls. "Just for the record," Tarma said, unwinding herself from the eiderdown, "I'd tend to agree. And the sooner we get to it, the less likely one of us will forget some triviality that turns out to be be vital. My people say, 'plans, like eggs, are best at the freshest.'"

Kethry nodded, and got up long enough to turn her chair in a quarter-circle so that it faced the room rather than Tarma; Tarma did the same as the men pulled theirs closer, and Roald brought in a third chair for Jadrek. Mertis left hers where it was, but put the babe back in the cradle and leaned forward to catch every word.

Tarma watched the Prince, his spouse, and the Herald as covertly—but as intently—as she could. Warrl trusted them, and she'd never known the *kyree* to be wrong. He trusted them enough that he'd eaten without checking the food for tampering, and was now sleeping as soundly as if he hadn't a worry in the world. Still, there was a first time for everything, even for the *kyree* being deceived.

There's no sign of the Captain here, either. But that might not mean anything.

Jadrek spoke first, outlining what Raschar had been doing since Stefansen's abrupt departure. Tarma was surprised by the Prince's reactions; he showed a great deal more intelligence and thoughtfulness than rumor had given him credit for. He seemed deeply disturbed by the information that Raschar was continuing to tax the peasantry into serfdom. *He looks almost as if he's taking it personally—huh, for that matter, so does Mertis. And I don't think it's an act.*

Then Tarma and Kethry took up the thread, telling the little conclave what they'd observed in their week or so at the Court, and what they'd noted as they passed through the southern grainlands of Rethwellan.

The Prince asked more earnest questions of them, then, and seemed even more disturbed by the answers. He plainly did not like Kethry's report of the mages lurking in the Court—and the tale of the attack on Jadrek shocked him nearly white.

And that is not an act, Tarma decided. *He's more than shocked, he's angry. I wouldn't want to be Raschar and in front of him right now.*

And finally all three spoke of Idra—what Jadrek knew, and what the partners had heard before she'd vanished.

That changed the anger to doubt, and to apprehension. "If she headed here, she didn't arrive," Stefansen said, unhappily, the firelight flaring up in time to catch his expression of profound disturbance. "*Damn* it! Dree and I had our differences, not the least of which was that she voted for Char, but she's the one person in this world that I would *never* wish any harm on. Where in hell could she have gotten to if she didn't come here?"

Tarma wished at that moment that she could have Warrl's thought-reading abilities. The Prince *seemed* sincere, but it would have been so very easy for Idra to have met with an accident once she'd crossed into Valdemar, particularly if Stefansen hadn't known about her change of heart. He could be using his surprise and dismay at learning *that* to cover his guilt.

At the same time all her instincts were saying he was speaking only truth—

If only I knew!

She turned her attention to Roald. He seemed to be both holding himself apart from the rest, and yet at the same time vitally concerned about all of them. *Goddess—even us, and he just met us a few hours ago*, Tarma realized with a start. And there was a knowledge coming from somewhere near where her Goddess-bond was seated that told her that this Herald was, as Warrl put it, someone to be trusted with more than one's life. *If Stefansen murdered Idra, he'd know*, she thought slowly. *I don't know how, but somehow he'd know. And I bet he wouldn't be sharing hearth and home with him. I can't see him giving hearth-rights to a murderer of any kind, much less a kin-slayer. Now I wonder—how much of his worry is for us two, and how much is about us?*

After a long silence, Jadrek said: "This is not

171

something I ever expected to hear myself saying, but whatever has happened to Idra, I fear her fate is going to have to take second place to what is happening to the Kingdom." Jadrek turned to the Prince, slowly, and with evident pain. "Stefan, Raschar is a leech on the body of Rethwellan." Tarma could see his eyes now, and the open challenge in them. "You never retracted your oath to your people as Crown Champion. You still have the responsibility of the safety of the Kingdom. So what are you going to do about the situation?"

"Jadrek, you never were one to pull a blow, were you?" The Prince smiled thinly. "And you're still as blunt as ever you were. Well, let me put it out for us all to stare at. Do you think I should try to overthrow Char?"

"You *know* that's what I think," Jadrek replied, eyes glinting in the firelight. He looked alert and alive—and a candlemark ago Tarma would never have reckoned on his reviving so fast. "You'd be a thousand times better as a king than your brother, and I know that was the conclusion your sister came to after seeing him rule for six months."

"Roald?"

"You've matured. You've truly matured a great deal in the time you've been here," the Herald said thoughtfully. "I don't know if it was fatherhood, or my dubious example, but—you're not the witling rakehell you were, Stefan. The careless fool you were would have been a worse king than your brother, ultimately—but the man you are now could be a very good ruler."

Stefansen turned to Mertis, and stopped dead at a strange, hair-raising humming. Tarma felt the tingling of a power akin to the Warrior's along her spine; she glanced sharply at Kethry in startlement, only to see that the mage wore an equally surprised expression. The humming seemed to be coming from the heap of saddlepacks and weaponry they'd dumped just inside the door, after Mertis had extracted their soiled, soaked clothing for cleaning.

Stefansen rose as if in a dream, as the rest of them remained frozen in their seats. He walked slowly to the shadowed pile, reached down, and took something in his hands.

A long, narrow something.

Bits of enshrouding darkness began peeling from it, and light gleamed where the pieces had fallen away. The thing he held was a sword—not hers, not Kethry's—a sword in a half-decayed sheath—

As the last of the rotten sheath flaked off of it, Tarma could see from the shape of it that it was the dead man's sword that they'd found—and no longer the lifeless, dull gray thing it had been. In Stefansen's hands it was keening a wild song and glowing white-hot, lighting up the entire room.

Stefansen stood with it in both hands, as frozen for a moment as the rest of them were. Then he dropped it—and as it hit the wooden floor with a dull *thud*, the light died, and the song with it.

"Mother of the gods!" he exclaimed, staring at the blade at his feet. "What in hell is *that*?"

Jadrek shook his head. "This is just not to be believed—Idra pretends to go haring off after the Sword That Sings—then we just happen to stumble on it on a remote trail, and just *happen* to bring it with us—"

"Archivist, I hate to disagree," Tarma interrupted, "but it's not so much of a coincidence as you might think. Idra wanted an excuse to go north. If she'd wanted one to go south, I would bet you'd have found a different legend, but the Sword's legend says it was stolen and taken north, so that's the one you chose. There's only one real road through the Comb. No thief would take that, and no fugitive— well, that left this goat-track we followed. I *know* it's the closest path to the real road, and I'll bet it's one of the few that go all the way through. No great coincidence there. As for the coincidence of us finding the dead thief, and of Keth taking the sword—I'll bet he was found a good dozen times, or why were the goldwork and the gems gone from the sheath and the pommel? But nobody in their right mind would bother taking a blade that wouldn't cut butter. And we've been stopping in every likely sheltered spot, so it's small wonder that we ran across him and his booty. But I would be willing to stake Ironheart that no *mage* ever ran across the body. Mages can sense energies, even quiescent ones; right, Keth?"

"That's true," Kethry corroborated. "I knew there was *something* about it, but I didn't have the strength to spare to deal with it right then. So I did what most mages would do—I packed it up to look into it later, if there *was* a later. Besides, knowing how these mage-purposed things work, I would say that the sword might well have known where it was going. It could well have 'told' me to bring it here."

"And the sword, once it sensed you were wavering on making a bid for the throne, made itself known," Mertis concluded wryly.

"It appears," Stefansen said ruefully, "that *I* don't have any choice."

"No more than I did, my friend," Roald replied with a chuckle, and a smile. "No more than I did."

But Stefansen sagged, and his face took on an expression of despair. "This is utterly hopeless, you know," he said. "Just *how* am I supposed to get back the crown when my only allies are a baby, an outlander, three women, a—forgive me, Jadrek—half-crippled scholar, an outsized beast, and a sword that's likely to betray me by glowing and singing every time I touch it?"

"I really don't see why you're already giving up," Roald chided. "Thrones have been overturned with less. What do you really *need* for a successful rebellion?"

"For a start, you need someone who knows where each and every secret lies," Jadrek said, sitting up straighter, his eyes shining with enthusiasm. "Someone who knows which person can be bought and what his price is, which person can be blackmailed, and who will serve out of either love or duty. I haven't been sitting in the corners of the Court being ignored all these years without learning more than a few of those things."

"*We* could infiltrate the capital disguised," Kethry said, surprising her partner. "Magical disguises, if we have to. No one will know us then; Jadrek can tell me who are the ones he wants contacted; if we can get one of us into the Court itself, we could pass messages, arrange meetings. I *know* Tarma could go in as a man, with an absolute minimum of disguising, all physical."

So we've thrown in with this lot, have we, she'enedra? Is it the cause that attracts you, or the fact that it's Jadrek's cause? But, since Kethry had added herself to the little conspiracy, Tarma added her own thought, in spite of her better judgment. "Huh, yes—*if* we can figure something that would put me into the Court without suspicion."

"Challenge the current champion of the King's Guard to combat," Mertis put in, surprising Tarma considerably. "That's *anyone's* right if they want to get in the Guard. Free swords do it all the time, there's nothing out of the ordinary about it. If you do well, you've got a place; if you *beat* him, you automatically become head of the Guard. That would put you at Raschar's side every day. You couldn't get any closer to the heart of the Court than that."

Stefansen looked doubtfully at the lean swordswoman. "Challenge the champion? Has she got a chance?"

Still not sure you trust us, hmm, my lad? I can't say as I blame you. I'm still not entirely sure of you.

But Mertis smiled, and Tarma sensed that the

gentle-seeming lady had a good set of claws beneath her velvet. "If half the tales I've heard about the Shin'a'in Swordsworn are true, she'll have his place before he can blink. And right at Raschar's side is the place we could best use you, Swordlady."

It became evident to Tarma that guileless Mertis was no stranger to intrigue as the evening wore on, and the plan began to look more and more as if it had a strong chance of success. In fact, it was she who turned to Roald, and asked, bluntly, "And what is Valdemar prepared to grant us besides sanctuary?"

Roald blinked once, and replied as swiftly, "What will Valdemar get in return?"

"Alliance in perpetuity if we succeed," Stefansen said, "My word on that, and you know my word—"

"Is more than good."

"Thank you for that. You know very well that you could use an ally that shares a border with Karse. You also know we've stayed neutral in that fight, and you know *damned* well that Char would never change that policy. I will; I'll ally with you, unconditionally. More—I'll pledge Valdemar favor for favor should you ever choose to call it in. And I'll swear it on the Sword—*that* will bind every legal heir to the pledge for as long as the Sword is used to choose rulers."

Roald let out his breath, slowly, and raised his eyebrows. "Well, that's a lot more than I expected. But you know we don't dare do anything openly. So that means covert help . . ." His brow wrinkled in thought for a moment. "What about this—every rebellion needs finances, and arms. Those I think I can promise."

Kethry looked rather outraged; Tarma was just perplexed. Who exactly *was* this Herald?

Kethry took the question right out of her mouth.

"Just what power is *yours* that you can fulfill those promises?" Kethry asked with angry cynicism. "It's damned easy to promise things you know *you* won't have to supply just to get us off your backs and out of your kingdom!"

Stefansen looked as if Kethry had blasphemed the gods of his House. Mertis' jaw dropped.

I think Keth just put her foot in it, Tarma thought, seeing their shocked reaction to what seemed to be a logical question. *Something tells me that "herald" means more than "royal mouthpiece" around here—*

"He—Roald—is the heir to the throne of Valdemar," Mertis managed to stammer. "Your Highness, I am sorry—"

Tarma nearly lost her own jaw, and Kethry turned pale. Insulting a member of a Royal House like that had been known to end with a summary execution. "It's *I* who should beg pardon," Kethry said, shaken. "I—I've heard too many promises that weren't fulfilled lately, and I didn't want Jad—my friends, I mean, counting on something that wouldn't ever happen. Your Highness—"

"Oh, Bright Havens—" Roald interrupted her, looking profoundly embarrassed. " 'Highness,' my eye! How could I have been insulted by honesty? Besides, we aren't all that much sticklers about rank in the Heraldic Circle. Half the time I get worse insults than that! And how were *you* to know? You don't even know what a Herald of Valdemar *is*!" He shrugged, then grinned. "And *I* don't know what a Swordsworn is, so we're even! Look, the law of Valdemar is that every Monarch must also be a Herald; our Companions Choose us, rather like that musical sword of Stefan's. Both Father and Mother are Heralds, which makes them co-consorts, so until they seek the Havens—may that take decades! —I'm not all that important, and I act pretty much as any other Herald. The *only* difference is that I have a *few* more powers, like being able to make promises in the name of the throne to my friend, and know my parents will see that those promises are met. Now, about those arms—"

177

Tarma was profoundly troubled; Kethry had thrown herself in with these peole as if she had known them all her life, but it was the Shin'a'in's way to be rather more suspicious than her oath-sister—or at least more than Kethry was evidencing at the moment. She needed to think—alone, and undisturbed. And maybe ask for some advice.

She let the folds of the eiderdown fall to her sides, and stood up. Four sets of eyes gave her startled glances, Kethry's included.

"I need to clear my head," she said, shortly. "If you'll excuse me, I think I'd like to go outside for a little."

"In the *dark*? In a snowstorm?" Jadrek blurted, astounded. "Are you—" He subsided at a sharp look from Kethry.

"Swordlady," the Herald said quietly, but looking distinctly troubled, "you and the others are guests in my home; you are free to do whatever you wish. You willl find a number of cloaks hanging in the entry. And I am certain an old campaigner like you needs no admonitions to take care in a storm."

She followed the direction of his nod to the darkened end of the hall; past the door there, she found herself in an entryway lit by a single small lantern. As he had said, there were several cloaks hanging like the shadows of great wings from pegs near the outer door. She took the first one that came to her hand, one made of some kind of heavy, thick fur, and went out into the dark and cold.

Outside, the storm was dying; the snow was back to being a thin veil, and she could see the gleaming of the new moon faintly through the clouds. She was standing on some kind of sheltered, raised wooden porch; the snow had been swept from it, and there was an open clearing beyond it. She paced silently down the stairs and out into the untrampled snow, her footsteps making it creak underfoot, until she could no longer feel the lodge looming so

losely at her back. Trees and bushes made black
nd white hummocks in front of her and to both
ides; fitful moonlight on the snow and reflected
hrough the clouds gave just enough light to see by.
She felt unwatched, alone. This spot would do.
And, by sheer stroke of fortune, "south" lay directly before her.

She took three deep breaths of the icy, sharp-
edged air, and raised her head. Then, still with her
back to the building, she lifted her eyes to the
furtive glow of the moon, and throwing the cloak
back over her shoulders, spread her arms wide, her
hands palm upward.

She felt a little uncomfortable. This wasn't the
sort of thing she usually did. She was not accustomed to making use of the side of her that, as
Kal'enedral, was also priestess. But she needed answers from a source she *knew* she could trust. And
the *leshya'e Kal'enedral* would not be coming to her
here unless *she* called to *them*.

She fixed her gaze on that dimly gleaming spot
among the clouds; seeking, but not walking, the
Moonpaths. Within moments her trained will had
brought her into trance. In this exalted state, all
sensation of cold, of weariness, was gone. She was
no longer conscious of the passing of time, nor truly
of her body. And once she had found the place where
the Moonpaths began, she breathed the lesser of
the Warrior's true names. That murmur of meaning
on the Moonpaths should bring one of her teachers
in short order.

From out of the cold night before her came a
wind redolent of sun-scorched grasslands, of endless, baking days and nights of breathless heat. It
circled Tarma playfully, as the moonglow wavered
before her eyes. The night grew lighter; she tingled
from head to toe, as if lightning had taken the place
of her blood. She felt, rather than heard the arrival
of Someone, by the quickening of all life around
her, and the sudden surge of pure power.

179

She lowered her hands and her eyes, expecting to see one of Her Hands, the spirit-Kal'enedral that were the teachers of all living Kal'enedral—

—to see that the radiant figure before her, glowing faintly within a nimbus of soft light, appeared to be *leshya'e Kal'enedral*, but was unveiled—her body that of a young, almost sexless woman. A woman of the Shin'a'in, with golden skin, sharp features, and raven-black hair. A swordswoman garbed and armed from head to toe in unrelieved black—and whose eyes were the featureless darkness of a starry night sky, lacking pupil or iris.

The Star-Eyed Herself had answered to Tarma's calling, and was standing on the snow not five paces from her, a faint smile on Her lips at Tarma's start of surprise.

My beloved jel'enedra, do you value yourself so little that you think I would not come to your summons? Especially when you call upon Me so seldom? Her voice was as much inside Tarma's head as falling upon her ears, and it was so musical it went beyond song.

"Lady, I—" Tarma stammered.

Peace, Sword of My forging. I know that your failure to call upon Me is not out of fear, but out of love; and out of the will to rely upon your own strength as much as you may. That is as it should be, for I desire that My children grow strong and wise and adult, and not weakly dependent upon a strength outside their own. And that is doubly true of My Kal'enedral, who serve as My Eyes and My Hands.

Tarma gazed directly into those other-worldly eyes, into the deep and fathomless blackness flecked with tiny dancing diamond-points of light, and knew that she had been judged, and not found wanting.

"Bright Star—I need advice," she said, after a pause to collect her thoughts. "As You know my mind and heart, You know I cannot weigh these strangers. I want to help them, I want to trust them—but how much of that is because my oath-sister comes to *their* calling? How much do I deceive myself to please her?"

The warm wind stirred the black silk of Her hair as She turned those depthless eyes to gaze at some point beyond Tarma's shoulder for a moment. Then She smiled.

I think, jel'enedra, that your answer comes on its own feet, two and four.

Two feet could mean Kethry—but four? Warrl?

Snow crunched behind Tarma, but she did not remove her gaze from the Warrior's shining face. Only when the newcomers had arrived to stand shoulder to shoulder with her did she glance at them out of the tail of her eye.

And froze with shock.

On her right stood—or rather, knelt, since he fell immediately to one knee, and bowed his head—the Herald, Roald, his white cloak flaring behind him in Her wind like great wings of snow. On Tarma's left was the strange, blue-eyed horse.

Tarma felt her breath catch in her throat with surprise, but this was only to be the beginning of her astonishment. The horse continued to pace slowly forward, and as he did so, he almost seemed to blur and shimmer, much as Tarma's spirit-teachers sometimes did—as if he were, as they were, not entirely of *this* world. Then he stopped, and stood quietly when the Warrior laid Her hand gently upon his neck. He gleamed with all the soft radiance of the hidden moon, plainly surrounded by an aura of light that was dimmer, but not at all unlike Hers.

Rise, Chosen; it is not in Me to be pleased with subservience, She said to the Herald, who obeyed Her at once, rising to stand silently and worshipfully at Tarma's shoulder. *Vai datha—so, young princeling, your land forges white Swords that fit the same sheath as My black, eh?* She laughed, soundlessly, looking from Roald to Tarma and back again. *Such a pretty pair you make, like moon and cloud, day and night, bright and dark. How an artist would die for such a sight! Two such opposites—and yet so much the same!*

It was only then that Tarma saw that the white clothing she had been wearing had been transmuted to the Warrior's own ebony, as was proper for Kal'enedral.

And you, My gentle Child— She continued, caressing the white horse's shining neck, *—are leshya'e Kal'enedral of another sort, hmm? Like My Hands, and unlike. Perhaps to complete the set I should see if any of My Children would become as you. What think you, should there be sable Companions to match the silver?* The look the horse—no, Companion—bent upon Her was one of reproach. She laughed again. *Not? Well, it was but a thought. But this is well met, and well met again! This is a good land, yours. It deserves good servants, strong defenders—vigilant champions to guard it and hold it safe as My Hands hold Mine. Do we not all serve to drive back the Dark, each in his own fashion? So I cry—well met, Children of My Other Self!*

She turned that steady regard back to Tarma. *Are you answered, My cautious one?*

Tarma bowed her head briefly, filled with such relief that she was nearly dizzy with it. And filled as suddenly with an understanding of exactly what and who this Herald and his Companion were. "I am answered, Bright Star."

Then let white Sword and black serve as they are meant—to cleave the True Darkness, and not each other, as you each feared might befall.

There was another breath of hot wind, a surging of power that left Tarma's eyes dazzled, and She was gone.

The Herald closed his eyes briefly, and let out the breath he had been holding in a great sigh. As he horse returned to stand beside him, he opened is eyes again, and turned to face Tarma.

"Forgive me for doubting you, even a little," he aid, his voice and the hand he extended to her rembling slightly. "But I followed you out here ecause—"

"For the same reason I would have followed *you* ad our positions been reversed," Tarma interrupted, lasping the hand he stretched out. "I wasn't ex-ecting Her when I called, but I think I know now why She came. Both of us have had our doubts ettled, haven't we—brother?"

His hold on her hand was warm and steady, and is smile was unwavering and equally warm. "I hink, more than settled, sister."

She caught his other hand; they stood facing each ther with hands clasped in hands for a very long ime, savoring the moment. There was nothing even emotely sexual about what they shared in that imeless space; just the contentment and love of oul-sib meeting soul-sib, something akin to what arma had for Kethry—

—and, she realized, with all the knowledge that assed to her from her Goddess in her moment of enlightenment, what this Herald shared with his Companion. For it was no horse that stood beside Roald, and she wondered now how she could have ever thought that it was. *Another soul-sib. And—how dd—even the Heralds don't know exactly what their Companions are—*

It was Roald who finally sighed, and let the mo-ment pass. "I fear," he said, dropping her hands reluctantly, "that if we don't get back to the others oon, they'll think we've either frozen to death, or gotten lost."

"Or," Tarma laughed, giving his shoulders a quick embrace before pulling her cloak back around her-self, "murdered each other out here! By the way—" She stretched out her arm, showing him that the tunic she wore was still the black of a starless night. "—I wonder how we're going to explain what happened to the clothing I borrowed?"

He laughed, long and heartily. "Be damned if I know. Maybe they won't notice? Right—not likely. Oh well, I'll think of something. But you *owe* me, Swordlady; that *was* my second-best set of Whites before you witched it!"

Tarma joined his laughter, as snow crunched under their boots. "Come to the Dhorisha Plains when this is over, and I'll pay you in Shin'a'in horses and Shin'a'in gear! It will break their artistic hearts, but I *think* I can persuade some of my folk to make you a set of unadorned Kal'enedral *white* silks."

"Havens, lady, you tempt my wandering feet far too much to be denied! You have a bargain," he grinned, taking the porch steps two at a time and flinging open the door for her with a flourish. "I'll be at your tent flap someday when you least expect it, waiting to collect."

And, unlikely as it seemed, she somehow had the feeling that he would one day manage to do just that.

Nine

It was difficult, but by no means impossible, to pull energies from the sleeping earth in midwinter. All it took was the skill—and time and patience, and Kethry had those in abundance. And further, she had serious need of any mote of mage-energy she could harbor against the future, as well as any and all favors she could bank with the other-planar allies she had acquired in her years as a White Winds sorceress. She had not had much chance to stockpile either after the end of the Sunhawks' last commission, and the journey here had left her depleted down to her lowest ebb since she and Tarma had first met.

So *she* was not in the least averse to spending as much time in the hidden lodge with Stefansen and Mertis as the winter weather made necessary; she had a fair notion of the magnitude of the task awaiting them. She and Jadrek and Tarma might well be unequal to it—

In fact, she had come to the conclusion that they would need resources she did *not* have—yet.

On a lighter note, she was not at all displeased about being "forced" to spend so much time in Jadrek's company. Not in the least.

She was sitting cross-legged on the polished wooden floor next to the fireplace, slowly waking her body up after being in trance for most of the day. Jadrek was conversing earnestly with Roald, both of them in chairs placed where the fire could warm him, and she could study him through half-slitted eyes at her leisure.

Jadrek seemed so much happier these days—well, small wonder. Stefansen respected him, Mertis admired him, Tarma allowed him to carry her off to interrogate in private at almost any hour. She was willing to answer most of his questions about the "mysterious" (at least to the folk of Rethwellan) nomad Shin'a'in. Roald did him like courtesy about the equally "mysterious" Heralds of Valdemar. Both of them accorded him the deference due a serious scholar. Warrl practically worshiped at his feet (Jadrek's ability to "hear" the beast being in no wise abated), and he seemed to share Tarma's feeling of comradeship with the *kyree*. Being given the respect he was (in all sober truth) due had done wonders for his state of mind. As the days passed, the lines of bitterness around his mouth were easing into something more pleasant. He smiled, and often, and there was no shadow of cynicism in it; he laughed, and there was no hint of mockery.

Physically he was probably in less pain than he had been for years—which Kethry was quite sure *was* due to Need's Healing abilities. Need was exerting her magic for a *man* because he was important to Kethry. For Kethry had no doubt as to how *she* felt about the Archivist. If there was *ever* going to be one man for her, Jadrek was that man.

All the men I've known, she thought with a touch of wry humor, *and all the men I've been courted by—it boggles the mind. Mages, fighters—some of them damned good looking. Good lord, if you were to count Thalhkarsh, I've even been propositioned by a godling! And who is it that attracts me like no one else ever has? A scholar half again my age, who I could probably break in half if I put my mind to it, with no recourse to Need required.*

"... Like all those weirdling things out of the Pelagirs," Roald finished, "Except that this thing seems impossible to kill."

"The *Pelagirs*?" Jadrek exclaimed, perplexed. "But I thought you said this thing was seen north of Lake Evendim?"

"It was—right in the heart of the Pelagir Hills."

"Wait a moment," Jadrek said, rummaging in the pile of clutter under his chair, and hunting up a piece of scraped vellum and a bit of charcoal. "All right—here's the lake—your Pelagirs are where?"

"Up here." The Herald took the charcoal from him and sketched.

"Huh." Jadrek studied the sketch thoughtfully. "*We* have a range of hills we call the Pelagirs, too—here."

"Well! I will be dipped for a sheep—"

"Fairly obvious, now that we have the information, isn't it?" Jadrek said with a grin. "Your Pelagirs and ours are the same; except that your inland sea cuts off the tail of the range, leaving it isolated from the rest up in your northwest corner. And now that I know *that's* true, I think I know what your 'man-beast' is, assuming I've got the description right. Four arms, twice man-height, face like a boar and taloned hands? No sign of genitals, nipples or navel, and the color of clay?"

"That's it."

"It's a *krashak*, a mage-made construct. Virtually immortal and indestructible."

"You can name it; can you tell us how to get rid of it?" Roald pleaded.

"Oddly enough, yes; it's a funny thing, but High Magick seems curiously vulnerable to Earth Magick, and with all the mages hanging about Char I took to looking for spell-breakers. It will take courage, but if you can get in close to the thing without it seizing you, and throw a mixture of salt, moly and Lady's Star into its eyes and mouth, it will literally fall apart." He coughed, coloring a little with embarrassment. "I know it sounds like a peasant superstition, but it *does* work. I found a mage I

187

could trust, and asked him. Now I—I always carry some with me. . . ."

Roald only looked impressed. "Havens, how long did you have to look before you found *that* out?"

Jadrek flushed, this time with pleasure. "Well, I got the first hint of it from a translation of Grindel's *Discourses on Unnatural History."*

"The Orwind translation, or the Quenta?"

"The Orwind. . . ." Their voices sank again and Kethry lost the thread of their conversation. It didn't much matter; she was more interested in watching Jadrek in an unguarded mood. *Oh, that mind! I don't think anything ever escapes him. And, for all that he's been treated badly, he so enjoys people—such a vital spirit in that flawed body. He's so alive. And damn it, I—Windborn, he makes me so shameless that I feel like a cat in heat around him. I want to purr and cuddle up against him—gods, I am bloody well infatuated. If he so much as raised an eyebrow in invitation at me, I'd warm his bed in a minute!*

Unfortunately, he seemed blissfully unaware of that fact, so far as she could tell. Oh well. . . .

As for Tarma, from the moment she had reentered the hall arm in arm with Roald, Stefansen and Mertis accepted her without reservation. And that meant that Mertis was only too happy to let her play nursemaid to little Megrarthon whenever she wished. Which was most of the time.

And which was precisely what she was doing at this very moment.

She's as happy as Jadrek, Kethry mused. *For that matter, so is the babe. Just look at her—*

Tarma was cuddling the happily cooing child in her black-clad arms, her expression a soft and warm one that few besides Kethry had ever seen. The hands that had killed so often, and without remorse, were holding the little one as gently as if he were made of down and spun glass. The harsh voice that had frightened many an errant fighter into instant obedience was crooning a monotonous lullabye.

She'd be happiest surrounded by a dozen small ones, or two or three dozen. And they know it; children know it, somehow. I've never seen one run from her, not even in the midst of a house-to-house battle. More often than not, they run to her. And rightly; she'd die to protect a child. When this is over—when this is over, I swear we'll give this up. Win or lose, we'll refound her Clan for her, and to the nether hells with my school if that's what it takes. I'll spend the rest of my life as a hedge-wizard and Shin'a'in horsebreeder if I have to.

While she watched, Tarma put the now-slumbering child back in his cradle; rose, stretching like a cat, then began heading for the fire. The two men at hearthside turned at the soft sound of her footstep, and smiled as one. She saw the smiles, and returned their grins with a good-natured shake of her head.

"And what are you two smirking about?" she asked, clasping her hands behind her and detouring slightly to stroll over to them, her lithe, thin body seeming almost to move fluidly, bonelessly.

The rest has done her good, too. She's in better shape than she's been in months—years—

"Trying to imagine you as a man, Darksib," Roald teased, using the pet name he'd invented for her. "Put a youngling around you, and you'd give yourself away in a breath."

"Hah. I'm a better actor than that. But as to that," she paused before them, crossed her arms, and frowned a little, "you know, we really ought to be getting on with it. Raschar isn't sitting back, not likely. He's consolidating his power, you can bet on it. *We* had better be safely in place before he gets himself so ensconced on the throne that there'll be no dislodging him without an army."

Kethry felt the last of her muscles emerge into wakefulness, and began uncoiling from her position in the hearth-corner.

"The sleeper awakes," Roald noted.

"Not sleeper," she corrected, imitating Tarma's long stretch. "I've been listening while I was coming out of trance. And, loath though I am to leave, in agreement with Tarma. I'm at full power now; Tarma and Jadrek have recovered. It's time to go."

She half expected Jadrek to protest, but he, too, nodded. "If we don't go now," he opined, gravely, "Stefan won't have a kingdom to come back to. But I do have one excellent question—this plan of ours calls for Tarma to replace the champion, and you can bet that Char won't let a Shin'a'in within a spear's cast of him now. So to truly ensure her safety, that means a full magical disguise. With all the mages in the Court, how are you going to hide the fact that Tarma's bespelled? They won't let anyone with a smell of magic on him compete with the King's champion, you know."

Tarma raised an interrogative eyebrow at her. "The thought had occurred to me, too," she said. "Every trial-by-combat that *I've* ever seen has specifically forbidden any kind of magic taint, even lucky amulets."

"Well, I'll answer that in an hour," Kethry replied.

"Why in an hour?"

"Because that's how long it will take me to try a full Adept manifestation, and see if it succeeds or fails."

Kethry didn't want an audience, not for this. Not even Tarma. So she took one of the fur cloaks and went out into the snow-laden scrub forest until she found a little clearing that was far enough from the lodge that she couldn't see or sense the building or the people within it. The weather was beautiful; the air was utterly still, the sky a deepening blue, the sun beginning its downward journey into the west. There would be no better time than now.

A mage of the White Winds school was tested by

no one except himself, with a series of spells marking the rise in ability from Apprentice to Journeyman, from Journeyman to Master, and from Master to Adept. A mage could attempt these spells whenever he chose, and as many times as he chose. They would only *work* when he was truly ready. The series was constructed so that the power granted by each was used to fuel the spell for the next.

A little like priming a pump, I suppose; and if you don't have faith that you're ready, you can't bear to waste the power. I feel ready, Kethry decided. *Well—*

She initiated the Journeyman spell, gathering her own, strictly personal power about her like a cloak, and calling the Lesser Wind of Fire and Earth, the Stable Elements. It chose to come out of the south, always a good omen, and whirled about her three times, leaving more power than it took to call it. She fairly glowed with energy now, even to normal eyes.

Next—the Master Spell, and the Greater Wind of Air and Water, the Mutable Elements—the Mutables were much harder to control than the Stable Elements.

She raised her hands high over her head, and whispered the words of the spell as she formed the energy left by the first with her will into the mage-shapes called the Cup and the Mill—concentrating with all her soul—calling, but not coercing.

This time the wind came from all four directions and melded into a gentle whirlwind around her, a wind that sang and sparkled with unformed power. When it, too, had circled her three times, she was surrounded by a shell of light and force that shifted and changed moment by moment, opalescing with every color that the mind could conceive.

She drew a deep breath and launched herself fearlessly into the Spell of Adept Manifestation—calling the White Wind itself—the Wind of the Five Elements.

It required the uttermost of any mage that dared

it; she must take the power granted her by the first two spells and all of her own, and weave it into an intricate new shape with her will—and the power fought back, resisting the change to itself, twisting and twining in her mental "hands." Simultaneously, she must sing the words of the spell, controlling tone, tempo, and cadence to within a hairsbreadth of perfection. And she must keep her mind utterly empty of all other thought but the image of the form she strove to build. She dared not even allow a moment to contemplate failure, or fail she would. One mistake, and the power would vanish, escaping with the agility of a live thing.

She finished. She held her breath. There was one moment of utter quietude, as time and all time governed ceased—and she wondered.

Had she failed?

And then the White Wind came.

It fountained up out of the ground at her feet as she spread her arms wide, growing into a geyser of power and light and music that surrounded her and permeated her until all she could see and hear and feel was the light and the force. She felt the power fill her mind and give her soul great wings of fire—

It was sundown when she stepped back through the door; Tarma had plainly expected her to be exhausted, and was openly astonished to see that she wasn't.

"It worked," she said with quiet rapture, still held by the lingering exaltation—and just a little giddy with the intoxication of all that power flowing through her.

"It did?" Tarma asked, eyebrows arching toward her hairline, as Jadrek and Roald approached with avid curiosity plain on their faces.

"I'll prove it to you." Kethry cupped her hands together, concentrating on the space enclosed there. When the little wisp of roseate force she called into her hands had finished whirling and settled into a steady glow, she began whispering to it, telling it gently what she asked of it in the ancient language of the White Winds sorcerers.

While she chanted, Stefansen and Mertis joined the little group, surrounding Kethry on all sides. She just smiled and nodded, and continued whispering to her sorcerous "captive."

Then she let it go, with joy, as a child releases a butterfly, and no longer with the wrench of effort the illusion-spell used to cause her. She was an Adept now, and forces that she had been incapable of reaching were hers to command from this moment on. Not carelessly, no—and not casually—but never again, unless she *chose* to, would she need to exhaust her own strength to cast a spell. With such energies at her command, the illusion-spell was as easy as lighting a candle.

The faintly glowing globe floated toward Tarma, who watched it with eyes gone round in surprise. The Shin'a'in's eyes followed it, although the rest of her remained absolutely motionless, as the power-globe rose over her head.

Then it thinned into a faint, rosy mist, and settled over the swordswoman like a veil.

The veil clung to her for a moment, hiding everything but a vague shape within its glowing, cloudy interior. Then it was gone.

And where Tarma had been, there stood a young man, of no recognizable racial type. He had a harsh, stubborn, unshaven face, marked with two scars, one running from his right cheek to his chin, the other across his left cheek. His nose had been broken in several places, and had not healed straight at any time. His hair was dirty brown, shoulder-length, and curled; his eyes were muddy green. He was at least a handsbreadth taller than Tarma had been, and correspondingly broader in the shoulders. And that was a new thing indeed, for before this Kethry had never been able to change size or

general shape in her illusion spells. Even Tarma'
clothing had changed, from her Shin'a'in Kal'enedra
silks, to rough homespun and tattered leather. Th
only similarity between Tarma and this man wa
that both carried their swords slung across thei
backs.

"Bright *Havens*," breathed Roald. "How did yo
do that?"

Tarma studied her hands and arms, wonder i
her un-Tarmalike eyes. Tiny scars made a lace
work of white across the hands and as far up th
arms as could be seen beneath the homespun sleeves
They were broad, strong hands, and as dissimilar t
Tarma's fine-boned, long ones as could be imagined

Kethry smiled. "Magic," she said.

"And how do you keep Char's mages from seein
that magic?" Stephansen asked.

Kethry just smiled a little more. "What else
More magic. The spell only an Adept can control
the spell that makes magic undetectable and invisi
ble even to the best mage-sight."

Tarma was back to looking like herself again, an
feeling a good deal happier as a result, as the
rode out the next morning. Jadrek had his ow
horse now, a gentle palfrey that had belonged t
Mertis, a sweet-tempered bay gelding with a gait a
comfortable as any beast Tarma had ever encoun
tered. He also had some better medicines; mor
effective and far less dangerous than his old, cour
tesy of a Valdemaren Healer Roald brought to th
lodge himself after Jadrek had had a particularl
bad night.

Kethry had augmented the protection of his trav
eling cloak with another spell she had not been abl
to cast until she reached Adept level. Jadrek woul
ride warm now no matter what the weather.

Tarma had turned down Kethry's offer to do th
same for her; she wanted no spells on her tha
might betray her to a magic-sniffing mage if sh

needed to go scouting. But Roald had managed to round up enough cold-weather gear for all of them to keep them protected even without spellcasting. They were far better prepared this time for their journey as they rode away from the lodge on a clear, sparkling dawn just before Midwinter.

They felt—and to some extent, acted—like adolescents on holiday. If the weather turned sour, they simply put up their little tent, Kethry cast a *esto-vath* on it, and they whiled away the time talking. When the weather was fair, while they never completely dropped vigilance, they tended to rely mostly on Warrl's senses while they enjoyed the view and the company. Beneath their ease was the knowledge that this "holiday" would be coming to an end once they broke out of the Comb, and there was a definite edge of "cherish the moment while you have it" to their cheer.

An ice storm had descended on them, but you'd never have known it inside their little tent. Outside the wind howled—inside it was as warm as spring sunshine. This was a far cry from the misery of their earlier journey on this same path.

Jadrek was still not capable of sitting cross-legged on the tent floor the way the two women were doing, but they'd given him more than enough room to stretch out, and the bedrolls and packs to use as cushioning and props, and he was reasonably comfortable.

Better than I've been in ages, he thought wonderingly. *Better than—than since I took that fever as a child, and started having trouble with my poor bones afterward. That's been twenty, almost thirty years. . . .*

He watched his quest companions through slitted, sleepy eyes, marveling how close he had come to them in the space of a few short weeks. *Tarma—the strong arm, so utterly without a conscience when it comes to certain choices. Brave, Lady bless, braver than anyone I could have imagined. As honor-bound as anyone I know. The outside, so cold—the inside, so warm, so caring. I'm not surprised, really, that once she and Roald got the measure of each other, they hit it off so well that they began calling each other "Darksib" and "Brightsib." There's a great deal about her that is like the Heralds I've known.*

The *kyree* at Tarma's back sighed, and flicked his tail.

Warrl—if for no other reason than to have come to know something about his kind, I'd treasure this quest. If all kyree are like him, I don't wonder that they have little to do with humankind. There aren't many around like Tarma, and I can't imagine Warrl mindmating to anyone that didn't have her sense of honor and her profound compassion.

Kethry was unbraiding and combing out her amber hair; it caught the light of the *jesto-vath* on the tent walls and glowed with the warmth of a young sun. Jadrek felt his heart squeeze. *Keth, Kethry, Kethryveris—lady, lady, how is it you make me feel like a stripling again? And I have no hope, no right to feel this way about you. When this mad scheme of ours is over, some stalwart young warrior will come, and your eyes and heart will kindle, and he'll carry you off. And I'll never see you again. Why should you find a mind attractive enough to put up with a crippled, aging body? I'm half again your age—why is it that when we're talking you make me feel no age at all? Or every age? How is it that you challenge my mind as well as my heart? How did you make me come alive again?*

He stifled a sigh. *Enjoy it while it lasts, old man,* he told himself, trying not to be too bitter about it. *The end is coming all too soon.*

As it happened, the end came sooner than they had anticipated.

Kethry frowned, and broke off her teasing in mid-sentence.

"Keth?" Tarma asked, giving Ironheart the signal to slow.

"There's—oh Windborn! I thought I'd thrown that bastard off!" Kethry looked angry—and frightened. A gust of wind pulled her hood off and she didn't even bother to replace it.

"The mage," Tarma guessed, as Jadrek brought his horse up alongside theirs.

"The mage. He's better than I thought. He's waiting for us, right where the path breaks out of the hills."

"Ambush?"

Kethry frowned again, and closed her eyes, searching the site with mage-senses. "No," she said finally. "No, I don't think so. He's just—waiting. In the open. And he's got all his defenses up. He's challenging me."

Tarma swore. "And no way past him, as he probably *damn* well knows."

Kethry looked at her soberly, reining in Hellsbane. "*She'enedra*, you aren't going to like this—"

"Probably not; what if we charge him? You mages seem to have a problem with physical opposition to magical defenses."

"On that narrow path? He could take us all. And in no way are we going to be able to sneak past him, not with Jadrek. I'm going to have to challenge him to a duel arcane."

"*What?*"

"He's an Adept, I can tell that from here. If I issue Adept's challenge he'll *have* to answer it, or lose his status."

"And you've been Adept how long? He'll eat you for lunch!"

"Better he eats me alone than all of us. We can't just think of ourselves now, Stefan is depending on us. If—Tarma, he won't take me without a fight, and if I go down, it won't be alone. You can find another mage to disguise you. Once we get into

Rethwellan, *I* become the superfluous member of the party."

"You're *not* going down!" Tarma choked, as Jadrek tightened his mouth into a thin line.

"I don't plan on it," Kethry said wryly. "I'm just telling you what to do if it happens. Contract, my love."

Tarma's face went cold and expressionless; her heart stopped. "This is professional, right?" They lived by the mercenary code and would die by it, probably—and by that code, you didn't argue with the terms of the contract once you'd agreed to it.

Kethry nodded. "This is the job we've contracted for. We're not being paid in money—"

"But we've got to do our jobs." Tarma nodded. "You win. I stopped trying to keep you wrapped in wool a long time ago; I'm not going to start up again. Let's do it." And she kicked Ironheart into a canter, with Kethry, Warrl and Jadrek following behind.

I've got to do this, Kethry thought, countering her fear with determination. *If I don't, he'll kill them. I might escape, but I could never shield all four of us, not even at Adept level. I haven't tapped into enough of the shielding spells to know how, yet. But he doesn't know I'm Adept, and there aren't that many White Winds mages around. I might well be able to surprise him with a trick or two.*

She kicked Hellsbane and sent her galloping past Tarma, up the slope of the barren hill before them, knowing that *she* would have to reach the waiting magician first and issue her challenge before he caught sight of the others. Otherwise he would blast first, and ask questions after.

Her move took both Tarma and the mage by surprise, for she was able to top the rise and send up the challenge signal before either Tarma or her foe had a chance to react.

The mage waiting below her was one of the ones

she'd seen wandering about Raschar's court; a thin man, dark of hair and eye. He was clean-shaven, which made it all the easier to note his sardonic expression, and he wore his hair loose and shoulder length. *Now* he wore his mage-robes; whatever his school was, it was one Kethry didn't recognize. The robes were a dull red, and banded and embroidered in dark brown. Like hers, they were split front and back for ease in riding. The chestnut gelding he straddled appeared tired and drained, and stood quietly with head down as he sat with his reins loose.

"A challenge?" he called incredulously. "You'd challenge *me*? Why in the Names of the Seven should I even bother with you, girl?"

As answer, she called up her Adept Manifestation. From her body rose the misty golden form of a hawk, twenty feet tall, with fiery wings; a hawk that mantled at him and opened its beak in a silent screech of defiance. "I challenge you, Adept to Adept," she called coldly. "You will answer such a challenge; you have no choice."

He called up his Manifestation; a winged snake, with scales and wing membranes that glistened in shades of green and blue. Calling it was his formal answer to her formal challenge; now they were both bound to the duel. "You're a fool, you know that," he said matter-of-factly, dismounting, and letting his Manifestation fade away. "You can't have been an Adept for very long; I've been one for ten years. You can't hope to beat me."

By this time Tarma, Jadrek and Warrl had reached her on the crest of the hill. Kethry unbuckled Need, feeling strangely naked without the blade, and passed her to Tarma. "Hold her for me. Nothing's allowed in the circle but ourselves," she said, watching as the other mage took up a stand near the center of the tiny, barren, windswept valley and put up his half of the magical dome that would only be dispelled by the death or defeat of one of them. Then she allowed her Manifestation to dissipate, and leapt down from Hellsbane's saddle, striding purposefully to take her stand opposite him. "That remains to be seen," she answered him, locking all emotion down, and replying with absolute calm. "So—let it begin!"

With those words, the dome of mage-power sealed, leaving the others helpless witnesses outside.

For a long moment, the combatants stood, simply watching each other. Tarma took advantage of the lull to order Jadrek to station himself and Warrl on the dividing line between the two mages, and on the side of the dome opposite hers. "Warrl has some tricks—I expect you might, too," she said distantly, trying to think like a mage. "I don't trust this bastard not to cheat. Well, Keth won't either; I don't doubt she's expecting something. But if anything should happen—"

"I'll do what I can," Jadrek promised anxiously, taking out his little bag of herbs and salt from his pocket, then replacing it. "It—it isn't likely to be much, but—"

"Jadrek, I've seen a slung stone bring down a king." She frowned in thought. "We should split up; if something *does* go bad, you and Warrl go for Keth, *I'll* go for the mage. He can't know how Need works, he can't know that in my hands she protects from sorcery. *I'll* be safe from anything he can throw, and I'll keep him off your tail. Now, quick before they start to *do* anything—"

He limped to the opposite side of the dome; Tarma could see him dimly through the red energy-haze. Warrl crouched beside him, ready to spring in an instant.

Tarma unsheathed the bespelled sword called Need and took her own stance; blade point down in the earth, both of her hands resting on the pommel, feet slightly apart. She was ready.

Just in time, for within the dome of hazy red, the battle was joined in earnest.

From the body of the stranger came a man-sized version of his Manifestation, flying upward to the top of the dome; Kethry's met it halfway. Serpent struck at hawk and was deflected; hawk tried to seize serpent in its talons, but the serpent wriggled free, then the snake tried to wrap itself around the hawk's body and neck. The hawk struck with beak and talon; the serpent let go. Both buffeted each other with punishing wing-blows. The battle rained glowing scales, feathers, and droplets of fluid, all of which vanished before they touched the ground.

Both Manifestations froze for an instant, then plummeted groundward; hawk with eyes glazing and fang marks in its chest, serpent with one wing ripped from its body.

Both thinned to mist and were gone before either struck the ground. *Round one: a draw,* Tarma thought to herself, shifting her weight to relieve muscles that had tensed, and feeling a tiny pebble roll out from under her foot.

Within the dome appeared two smaller domes, each covering a mage. Then all the fury of all the lightning storms Tarma had ever witnessed rolled into one broke loose within the greater dome. Lightning struck again and again on the two shields, seeking weak spots; it crawled over the surface of the little domes or rolled itself into balls that circled the perimeters without finding entrance. And all in complete silence; that was the truly frightening and eerie part. Tarma's eyes were dazzled to the point of having trouble seeing when the lightning finally died to nothing, and the lesser domes vanished. As Tarma blinked away the spots interfering with her vision, she tried to assess the condition of both Kethry and her erstwhile rival. They both seemed equally tired.

Round two; another draw.

Kethry might have looked tired, but she also looked

slightly pleased. *Maybe a draw is good—Warrior bless, I hope so—*

Even more encouraging, the other mage looked slightly worried.

Kethry initiated the next round; throwing (literally) daggers of light at the red-robed sorcerer, daggers which he had to deflect, dodge, or absorb. He returned in kind, but he was not as good in this contest as Kethry; his blades tended to go awry. Hers never failed to reach their mark, and frequently hit.

Where they hit, they left real wounds, wounds that smoked and bled. The red mage managed to keep from being hit anywhere vital, but the daggers were taking a steady toll.

After being hit one too many times, he suddenly threw up his hands, and a wall of flame sprang up in front of him, a wall that devoured the daggers when they reached it.

The fire grew until it reached the top of the dome, cutting him off from Kethry. Arms of flame began to lick from the wall, reaching toward her.

Fighting fire with fire might not work, here, Keth, Tarma thought, biting her lip a little. *You could both end up scorched by your own powers—*

But Kethry chose not to fight with fire, but with air; a whirlwind, a man-high tornado of milky white sprang up in front of her, sucking in those reaching arms of flame. And every time it ate one of those arms, it grew a little larger. Finally, it reached nearly to the top of the dome—and it began to move on the red-robed mage and his fiery protective wall.

Star-Eyed! If it got bigger just by eating a couple of licks of flame, what'll it do when it hits the fire-mother?

Evidently the same thought occurred to the mage, for his eyes had gone white-rimmed with panic. He backed into the restraining wall of the protective dome, then began shouting and waving his hands wildly.

And a twice-man-sized *thing* rose from the barren earth behind Kethry.

No—oh no—that bastard, he had that thing hidden there; he's had this planned from the start! Tarma recognized the *krakash*, the mage-construct, from Jadrek's descriptions. She started to sprint for the edge of the dome, even knowing she wouldn't be able to pass it.

Kethry turned to meet it, first making frantic motions with her hands, then groping for a blade she did not have. The thing reached for her with the two upper arms, missing, but raking her from neck to knee with its outsized talons. She collapsed, clutching herself with pain; it seized her as she fell with the lower two of its four arms. It lifted her as she fought to get free—and broke her back across its knee, as a man would break a dry branch.

"No!"

Tarma heard her own voice, crying the word in anguish, but it didn't seem to belong to her.

The whirlwind died to a stirring of dust on the ground; the dome thinned to red mist, and vanished.

Tarma's mind and heart were paralyzed, but her body was not. She reacted to the disaster as she had planned, charging the mage at a dead run, while Jadrek sprinted fearlessly for the *thing*.

The startled wizard saw her coming, and threw blasts of pure energy at her—spheres of blinding ball-lightning which traveled unerringly toward her, hit, and did *nothing*, leaving not even a tingle behind as they dissipated. The mage had just enough time to realize that she was protected before she reached him.

While part of her sobbed with anguish, another part of her coolly calculated, and brought Need about in a shining, swift arc, as she allowed her momentum to carry her past him. She saw his eyes, filled with fear, saw his hands come up in a futile attempt to deflect the sword—then felt the shock

203

along the blade as she neatly beheaded him, a tiny trail of blood-droplets streaming behind the point of the sword as it finished its arc.

Before his body had hit the ground she whirled and made for Jadrek, cursing the fate that had placed mage and construct so many paces apart. The older man hadn't a chance.

As she ran, she could see that the Archivist had something in his hands. He ducked under the grasp of the horrid creature's upper two arms with an agility Tarma never dreamed to see in him. And with the courage she *had* known he possessed, came up in the thing's face, casting one handful of powder into its eyes and the second into its mouth.

The thing emitted a shriek that pierced Tarma's ears—

Then it crumbled into a heap of dry earth before she had made more than a dozen steps in its direction. As it disintegrated, it dropped Kethry into the brown dust like a broken, discarded boy.

Tarma flung herself down on her knees at Kethry's side, and tried to stop the blood running from the gashes the thing's talons had left. Uselessly—for Kethry was dying even as she and the Archivist knelt in the dust beside her.

Jadrek made a choking sound, and took Kethry into his arms, heedless of the blood and filth.

Tarma fumbled the hilt of Need into her hands, but it only slowed the inevitable. Need could not mend a shattered spine, nor could she Heal such ghastly wounds; all the blade could do was block the pain. It was only a matter of time—measured in moments—before the end.

"Well . . ." the mage whispered, as Jadrek supported her head and shoulders in his arms, silent tears pouring from his eyes, and sobs shaking his shoulders. "I . . . always figured . . . I'd never . . . die in bed."

Tarma clenched both of her hands around the limp ones on Need's hilt, fiercely willing the blade to do what she knew in her heart it could not. "*Damn* it, Keth—you *can't* just walk out on us this way! You *can't* just die on us! We—" she could not say more for the tears that choked her own throat.

"Keth—*please* don't; I'll do anything, take *my* life, only please don't die—" Jadrek choked out, frantically.

"Don't . . . have much choice . . ." Kethry breathed, her eyes glazing with shock, her life pumping out into the dust. "Be brave . . . *she'enedra* . . . finish the contract. Then go home . . . make Tale'sedrin live . . . without me."

"No!" Tarma cried, her eyes half-blind with tears. "*No!*" she wrenched her hands away, leaping to her feet. "It's *not* going to end this way! Not while I'm Kal'enedral! By the Warrior, I swear *NO!*"

Thrusting a blood-drenched fist at the sky, she summoned all the power that was hers as Kal'enedral, as priestess, as Swordsworn warrior—power she had never taken, never used. She flung back her head, and *screamed* a name into the uncaring, gray sky, a name that tore her throat even as her heart was torn.

The Warrior's Greater Name—

The harsh syllables of the Name echoed and reechoed, driving her several paces backward, then sending her to her knees in the dust. Then—silence. Silence as broodingly powerful as that in the eye of the hurricane. Tarma looked up, her heart cold within her. For a moment, nothing changed.

Then *everything* ceased; time *stopped*. The very tears on Jadrek's cheeks froze in their tracks. Sound died, the dust on the breeze hung suspended in little immobilized eddies.

Tarma alone could move; she got to her feet, and waited for Her—to learn what price *she* would be asked to pay for the gift of Kethry's life.

A single shaft of pure, white light lanced into the ground, practically at Tarma's feet, accompanied by an earsplitting shriek of tortured air. Tarma did *not* turn her eyes away, though the light nearly blinded her and left her able to see nothing but white mist for long moments. When the mist cleared from her vision, She was standing where the light had been, Her face utterly still and expressionless, Her eyes telling Tarma nothing.

They faced one another in silence for long moments, the Goddess and her votary. Then She spoke, Her voice still melodious; but this time, the music was a lament.

That you call My Name can mean only that you seek a life, jel'enedra, She said. *The giving of a life—not the taking.*

"As is my right as Kal'enedral," Tarma replied, quietly.

As is your right, She agreed. *As it is My right to ask a sacrifice of you for that life.*

Now Tarma bowed her head and closed her eyes upon her tears, for she could not bear to look upon that face, nor to see the shattered wreck that had been her dearest friend lying beyond. "Anything," she whispered around the anguish.

Your own life? The future of Tale'sedrin? Would you release Kethry from her vow if I demanded it and have Tale'sedrin become a Dead Clan?

"Anything." Tarma defiantly raised her head again, and spoke directly to those star-strewn eyes, pulling each of her words out of the pain that filled her heart. "Keth—she's worth more to me than anything. Ask anything of me; take my body, make me a cripple, take my life, even make Tale'sedrin a Dead Clan, it doesn't matter. Because without Kethry to share it, none of that has any meaning for me."

She was weeping now for the first time in years; mostly when she hurt, she just swallowed the tears and the pain, and forced herself to show an impassive face to the world. Not now. The tears scalded her cheeks like hot oil; she let them.

Do you, Kal'enedral, feel so deeply, then?

Tarma could only nod.

It—is well, came the surprising answer. *And what price your obedience?*

"I put no price on obedience, I will serve You faithfully, Lady, as I always have. Only let Kethry live, and let her thrive and perhaps find love—and most of all, be free. That's worth anything You could ask of me."

The Warrior regarded her thoughtfully for an eternity, measuring, weighing.

Then—She laughed—

And as Tarma stared in benumbed shock, She held out Her hands, palm outward, one palm facing Tarma, one Kethry. Bolts of blinding white light, like Kethry's daggers of power, leaped from Her hands to Tarma, and to the mage still cradled in Jadrek's arms.

Or, possibly, to the ensorcelled blade still clasped in the mage's hands.

Tarma did not have much chance to see which, for the dagger of light hit her full in the chest, and suddenly she couldn't hear, couldn't see, couldn't breathe. She felt as if a giant hand had picked her up, and was squeezing the life out of her. She was blind, deaf, dumb, and made of nothing but excruciating pain—

Only let Keth live—only let her live—and it's worth any price, any pain—

Then she was on her hands and knees, panting with an agony that had left her in the blink of an eye—half-sprawled in the cold dust of the valley.

While beside her, a white-faced Jadrek cradled a dazed, shocked—and completely Healed—Kethry. Only the tattered wreckage of her traveling leathers and the blood pooled beneath her showed that it had not all been some kind of nightmare.

As Tarma stared, still too numb to move, she could hear the jubilant voice of the Warrior singing in her mind.

It is well that you have opened your heart to the world again, My Sword. My Kal'enedral were meant to be without desire, not without feeling. Remember this always: to have something, sometimes you must be willing to lose it. Love must live free, jel'enedra. Love must ever live free.

Ten

Jadrek blinked, trying to force what he had just witnessed into some semblance of sense. He was mortally confused.

One moment, Kethry is dying; there is no chance anyone other than a god could survive her injuries. Then Tarma stands up and shrieks something in Shin'a'in—and—

Kethry stirred groggily in his arms; he flushed, released her, and helped her to sit up, trying *not* to stare at the flesh showing through the rents in her leather riding clothing—flesh that had been lacerated a moment ago.

"What . . . happened?" she asked weakly, eyes dazed.

"I don't really know," he confessed. And thinking: *Tarma was* here, *and now she's over* there *and I didn't see her move, I know I didn't! Am I going mad?*

Tarma got slowly to her feet, wavering like a drunk, and staggered over to them; she looked drained to exhaustion, her face was lined with pain and there were purplish circles beneath her eyes. It looked to Jadrek as if she was about to collapse at any moment.

For that matter, Keth looks the same, if not worse— what am I thinking? Anything is better than being a heartbeat away from death!

Tarma fell heavily to her knees beside them, scrubbing away the tears still marking her cheeks with the back of a dirty hand, and leaving dirt smudges behind. She reached out gently with the same hand, and patted Kethry's cheek. The hand she used was shaking, and with the other arm she was bracing herself upright. "It's all right," she sighed, her voice sounding raw and worn to a thread. "It's all right. I did something—and it worked. Don't ask what. Bright Star, I am tired to death!"

She collapsed into something vaguely like a sitting position right there in the dust beside them, head hanging; she leaned on both arms, breathing as heavily as if she had just run an endurance race.

Kethry tried to move, to get to her feet, and fell right back into Jadrek's willing embrace again. She held out *her* hand, and watched with an expression of confused fascination as it shook so hard she wouldn't have been able to hold a cup of water without losing half the contents.

"I feel awful—but—" she said, looking down at the shreds of her tunic with astonishment and utter bewilderment. "How did you—"

"I *said* don't ask," Tarma replied, interrupting her. "I can't talk about it. Later, maybe—not now. It—put me through more than I expected. Jadrek, my friend—"

"Yes?"

"I'm about as much use as a week-old kitten, and Keth's worse off than I am. I'm afraid that for once you're going to get to play man of muscle."

She looked aside at him, and managed to muster up a half grin. There wasn't much of it, and it was so tired it touched his heart with pity, but it was real, and that comforted him.

Whatever has happened, she knows exactly what she's doing, and it will be all right.

"Tell me what you want me to do," he said, trying to sound just as confident.

:*There's still myself,*: Warrl's dry voice echoed in their thoughts. :*I have no hands, but I can be of some help.*:

"Right you are, Furface. Oh gods," Tarma groaned as she got back up to her knees, and took Kethry's chin in her hand, tilting it up into the light. Jadrek could see that Kethry's pupils were dilated, and that she wasn't truly *seeing* anything. "What I thought—Keth, you're shocky. Fight it, love. Jadrek and Warrl are going to find some place for us to hole up for a while." Tarma transferred her hold to Kethry's shoulder and shook her gently. "Answer me, Keth."

"Gods—" Kethry replied, distantly. "And sleep?"

"As soon as we can. Fight, *she'enedra.*"

"I'll . . . try."

"Warrl, get the horses over here, would you? Jadrek, you're going to have to help Keth mount. She's got no more bones right now than a sponge." He started to protest, but she cut him off with a weary wave of her hand. "Not to worry; our ladies are battlemares and they know the drill. I'll get them to lie down, you watch what I do, then give Keth a hand, and steady her as they get up. No lifting, just balancing. *Hai?*"

"As long as I'm not going to have to fling her into the saddle," he replied, relieved, "I don't see any problem."

"Good man," she approved. "Next thing—Warrl will go looking for shelter; I want something more substantial than the tent around us tonight. You'll have to stay with us, keep Keth in her seat. *I'll* be all right, I've ridden semiconscious for miles when I've had to. When Warrl finds us a hole, you'll have to help us off, and do all the usual camp duties."

"No problem there, either; I'm a lot more trail wise than I was before this trip started." *Aye, and sounder in wind and limb, too.*

Warrl appeared, the reins of Jadrek's palfrey in his mouth, the two battlemares following without needing to be led. Jadrek watched as Tarma gave her Ironheart a command in Shin'a'in, and was astounded to see the mare carefully fold her long legs beneath her and sink to the dusty ground, positioning herself so that she was lying within an arm's length of the exhausted swordswoman. Tarma managed to clamber into the saddle, winding up kneeling with her legs straddling the mare's back. She gave another command, and the mare slowly lurched to her feet, unbalanced by the weight of the rider, but managing to compensate for it. Tarma glanced over at Jadrek. "Think you can deal with that?"

"I think so."

Tarma repeated her command to Hellsbane; the second mare did exactly as her herd-sister had. Jadrek helped Kethry into the same position Tarma had taken, feeling her shaking from head to toe every time she had to move. Tarma gave the second command, and the mare staggered erect, with Jadrek holding Kethry in the saddle the whole time.

Warrl flicked his tail, and Jadrek felt a wave of approval from the *kyree*. *:I go, packmates. You go on—it were best you removed yourselves from the scene of combat.:*

"Spies?" Jadrek asked aloud.

:Possible. Also things that feed on magic, and more ordinary carrion eaters. Shall we take the enemy beast?:

Tarma looked over her shoulder at the weary gelding, which was still where the mage had left it, off to one side of the trail. "I don't think so," she replied after a moment. "It's just short of foundering. Jadrek, could you strip it? Leave the harness, bring anything useful you find in the packs, then let the poor thing run free."

He did as she asked; once free of saddle and bridle the beast seemed to take a little more interest in life and moved off at a very slow walk, heading deeper into the hills. Warrl trotted down the trail, and vanished from sight once past the place where it exited the valley. Jadrek mounted his own palfrey with a grunt of effort, and rode it in close beside Kethry, so that he could steady her from the side.

"You ready, wise brother?" Tarma asked.

"I think so. And not feeling particularly wise."

"Take lead then; my eyes keep fogging. Ironheart knows to follow her sister."

They headed out of the little valley, and the trail became much easier; the hills now rolling rather than craggy, and covered with winter-killed grass. But after a few hundred feet it became obvious that their original plan wasn't going to work. Kethry kept drifting in and out of awareness, and sliding out of her saddle as she lost her hold on the world. Every time she started to fall, Jadrek had to rein in both Hellsbane and his palfrey to keep her from falling over. The gaits and sizes of the two horses just weren't evenly matched enough that he could keep her steady while riding.

He finally pulled up and dismounted, walking stiffly back toward the drooping Shin'a'in. Tarma jerked awake at the sound of his footsteps.

"What? Jadrek?" she said, shaking her head to clear it.

He looked measuringly at her; she looked awake enough to think. "If I tethered Vega's reins to the back of your saddle, would that bother 'Heart?" he asked.

"No, not 't all" Tarma replied, slurring her words a little. "She's led b'fore. Why?"

"Because this isn't going to work; I'm going to put the packs on Vega and ride double with Keth, the way you carried me up here, only with me keeping her on."

Tarma managed a tired chuckle. "Dunno why I didn' think of that. Too . . . blamed . . . tired. . . ."

She dozed off as Jadrek made the transfer of the packs, then put a long lead-rein on Vega's halter and fastened it to the back of Tarma's saddle. He approached Hellsbane with a certain amount of trepidation, but the mare gave him a long sniff, then allowed him to mount in front of Kethry with no interference—although with his stiff joints, swinging his leg over 'Bane's neck instead of her back wasn't something he wanted to repeat if he had any choice. He would have tried to get up behind Kethry, but he wasn't sure he could get her to shift forward enough, and he wasn't certain he'd be able to stick on the battlemare's back if she broke into anything other than a walk. So instead he brought both of Kethry's arms around his waist, and loosely tied her wrists together. She sighed and settled against his shoulder as comfortably as if it were a pillow in her own bed.

He rather enjoyed the feeling of her snuggled up against his back, truth be told.

He nudged Hellsbane into motion again, and they continued on down the trail. The sky stayed gray but showed no signs of breaking into rain or sleet, and there was no hint of a change in the weather on the sterile, dusty air. The horses kept to a sedate walk, Tarma half-slept, and Kethry was so limp he was certain she was completely asleep. It was a little frightening, being the only one of the group still completely functional. He wasn't used to having people rely on *him*. It was exciting, in an uneasy sort of way, but he wasn't sure that he liked that kind of excitement.

Warrl returned from time to time, always with the disappointing news that he hadn't found anything. Jadrek began to resign himself to either riding all night—and hoping that there wasn't going to be another storm—or trying to put up the tent by himself. But about an hour before sunset, the *kyree* came trotting back with word that he'd found a shepherd's hut, currently unused. Jadrek set Hellsbane to following him off the track, and Ironheart followed her without Tarma ever waking.

She did come to herself once they'd stopped, and she seemed a bit less groggy. She got herself dismounted without his help, got their bedrolls off Vega, and carried them inside with her. She actually managed to get their bedding set up while Jadrek slid the half-conscious mage off her horse, then assisted her to stagger inside, and laid her down on the bedding. With a bit of awkwardness at the unaccustomed tasks, he got the horses bedded down in a shed at the side of the little building.

By the time he'd finished, Kethry was sound asleep in her bedroll, and Tarma was crawling into her own. "Can't ... keep my eyes open ..." she apologized.

"Then don't try, I can do what's left." *I think,* he added mentally.

But his trail skills *had* improved; he managed to get a fire going in the firepit, thought about making supper, and decided against it, opting for some dried beef and trail biscuit instead. With the fire dimly illuminating their shelter, he made a quick inspection of the place, thinking: *It would be my luck to come upon a nest of hibernating snakes.*

But he found nothing untoward; in fact, it was a very well built shelter, with stone walls, a clean dirt floor, and a thatched roof. It was a pity it didn't have a real fireplace—a good half of the smoke from the fire was *not* finding the smokehole in the center of the roof, and his eyes were watering a bit—but it was clean, and dry, and now growing warm from the fire.

He watched the moving shadows cast by the fire onto the wall, chewed the leathery strip of jerky, and tried to sort himself out.

Warrl came in once to tell him that he'd hunted and eaten, and was going to stand guard outside; after that, he was alone.

What kind of a fool have I shown myself to be? he thought, still confused by the events of the last few hours. *Did anyone even notice?*

He watched Kethry as she slept, feeling both pleasure and pain in the watching. *How much did Tarma see? Gods above, I'm afraid I've gone and fallen in love, like a greensick fool. At my age I should bloody well know better.*

Still—given the state they'd all been in—

Tarma probably hadn't been in a condition to notice much of anything except her oathsister's plight.

And I would give a great deal to know how she managed to bring Kethry back from Death's own arms. Because she's as much as admitted it was all her doing. And I can only wonder what it cost her besides strength and energy—maybe that's why she didn't want to talk about it. Still and all, she really isn't acting as if it cost her nearly as much as if whatever had happened shook her down to her soul. I think perhaps she learned something she didn't expect to. Whatever it was—I think perhaps the outcome is going to be a good one. She almost seems warmer somehow. More open. Would she ever have put all her safety and Keth's in my hands before? I—I don't think so.

He stretched, taking pleasure in the feel of joints that weren't popping, and bones that didn't creak. He was sore from the unaccustomed work, but not unbearably so.

Although—Lady of Light, I've been working like a porter all afternoon, and not had so much as a twinge in the old bones! Now was that just because I was keyed up, or was it something else? Well, I'll know tomorrow. If I ache from head to toe, I'll know I was not privileged to be the recipient of a miracle!

And meanwhile—the fire needs feeding.

So he watched Kethry, huddled in his own blankets while he fed the fire, and waited for the morning.

Carter's Lane in the capital city of Petras was living up to its name, even this close to the time for the evening meal. The street was wide enough for four wagons moving two abreast in each direction, and all four lanes were occupied by various vehicles now. The steady rumbling of wheels on cobblestones did not drown out the equally steady hum of voices coming from all sides. Carter's Lane boasted several popular taverns and drinkshops, not the least popular of which was the Pig and Potion. This establishment not only had an excellent cook and an admirable brewmaster, but in addition offered various forms of accommodation—ranging from single cubbyholes (with bed) that rented by the hour, to rooms and suites of rooms available by the week or month.

It was from the window of one of the latter sorts of lodging that a most attractive young wench was leaning, her generous figure frequently taking the eyes of the cart drivers from their proper work. She was, in fact, the inadvertent cause of several tangles of traffic. She paid this no heed, no more than she did the equally persistent calls of admiration or inquiries as to her price. She was evidently watching for something—or someone.

And to the great disappointment of her admirers, she finally spotted what she watching for.

"Arton!" the brown-haired, laughing-eyed wench called from her second-floor window. "I've waited *days* for you, you ungrateful beast!"

"Now, Janna—" The scar-faced fighter who emerged from the crowd to stand on the narrow walkway beneath her looked to be fully capable of cutting his way out of any fracas—except, perhaps, this one.

"Don't you 'now, Janna,' *me*, you brute!" She vanished from the window only to emerge from a door beside it. The door let onto a balcony and the balcony gave onto a set of stairs that ran down the outside of the inn. Janna clattered down these stairs as fast as her feet could take her. "You leave me here *all alone*, and you *never* come to see me, and you *never* send me word, and—"

"Enough, enough!" the warrior begged, much to the amusement of the patrons of the inn. "Janna, I've been busy."

"Oh, *busy!* Indeed, I can guess how *busy!*" She confronted him with her eyes narrowed angrily, standing on the last two stairs so that her eyes were level with his. Her hands were on her hips, and she thrust her chin forward stubbornly, not at all ready to make peace.

"Give 'im a rest, lass," called another fighter lounging at an outside table, one wearing the same scarlet-and-gold livery as Arton. "King's nervy; keeps 'im on 'and most of th' time. 'E *'as* been busy."

"Oh, well then," the girl said, seeming a bit more mollified. "But you *could* have sent word."

"I'm here now, aren't I?" he grinned, with just a touch of arrogance. "And we ought to be making up for lost time, not wrangling in the street."

"Oh—*Oh!*" She squealed in surprise as he picked her up, threw her over his shoulder, and carried her up the stairs.

He pulled the door open; closed it behind him.

Silence.

One of the serving girls paused in her distribution of ale mugs, sighed, and made calf eyes at the closed door. "*Such* a man. Wisht I 'ad me one like 'im."

"Spring is aborning, and young love with it," intoned a street minstrel, hoping that the buxom server would take notice of *him*.

"Young *lust*, you mean, rhymester," laughed the second fighter. "Arton's no fool. That's a nice little piece he brought with him out of the country—and cheap at the price of a room, a bit of feeding, and a few gewgaws. One of these days I may go see if she's got a sister who wants to leave the cowflops for the city."

"*If* you can get any girl to look at your ugly face," sneered a third.

The mutter of good-natured wrangling carried as far as the second-floor room, where the young fighter had collapsed into a chair, groaning. The room's furnishings were simple; a bed, a table, a wardrobe and three chairs.

And an enormous wolflike creature on the hearth.

"Warrior's Oath, Keth—you *might* make yourself lighter next time!" the warrior groaned. "My poor back!"

"If I'd known you were going to play border-bridegroom, I'd have helped you out, you idiot!" the brown-haired girl retorted, closing the shutters of the room's single window, then snatching a second chair and plopping down into it. "Tarma, where the hell have you been these past few days? A note of three words does *not* suffice to keep me from having nervous prostrations."

:I told you she was all right,: the *kyree* sniffed. *:But you wouldn't believe me.:*

"Warrl's right, Keth. I figured that he'd tell you if anything was wrong, so I wasn't going to jeopardize my chances by doing something marginally out of character. And I've been busy, as I said," Tarma replied, rubbing her eyes. "Damn, can't you do something about the way these spells of yours make my eyes itch?"

"Sorry; not even an Adept can manage that."

Tarma sighed. "Char has gotten the wind up about something—maybe he's even getting some rumors about *our* work, who knows? Anyway, he's been keeping me with him day *and* night until I could find somebody he trusts as much as me to spell me out. How is the conspiracy business going?"

Kethry smiled, and ran her hands through her hair. "Better than we'd hoped, in a lot of ways. Jadrek will be giving me the signal as soon as he's done with his latest client, so why don't we save our news until we're all together?"

"Fine by me; I don't suppose you've got anything to eat around here?"

"Why? Don't they feed you at the palace?"

"Having gotten leave to go, I wasn't about to stick around and maybe get called back just so I could feed my face," Tarma retorted.

Kethry raised one eyebrow. "Char's *that* nervy?"

Tarma spotted half a loaf of bread and a chunk of cheese on the table behind Kethry and reached forward to seize both. "He's that nervy," she agreed, slicing bits off the cheese with her belt-knife and alternating those tidbits with hearty bites of bread. She would have said more, but a gentle tapping came from the wall. Kethry jumped up out of her chair and faced the wall, holding both palms at shoulder height and facing it. The wall itself blurred for a little, then the door that had been hidden by Kethry's illusion swam into view. Jadrek pushed it open and stepped into the room.

There had not been a door there when they'd taken these two rooms; Jadrek's suite opened only into the inn, and Kethry's had two doors, the exterior and one like Jadrek's, opening on the inn corridor. But what could be done by hands could also be done by magic, and within one day of Kethry's taking possession of this room, she had made, then concealed, the door in their common wall. It was a real door and not a magic portal, just in case Jadrek ever needed to make use of it when Kethry was not present, for Kethry had set the spell of concealment so that he controlled it on his side of the wall.

"And how does the Master Astrologer?" asked Tarma, genially.

"Better than when he was Master Archivist," Jadrek chuckled. "I think I shall have Stefan find a successor. Astrology is a more lucrative profession!"

"Why am I not surprised?" Tarma asked sardonically. "Gentle lies always cost more than the truth. I take it none of your 'clients' have recognized you?"

"It wouldn't be likely," he replied mildly, taking the third, unoccupied seat around the little table.

"Most of my 'clients' are merchants' wives. When would any of *them* have seen the Court Archivist?"

"Or, given your notable ability to fade into the background, noticed him if they'd seen him?" added Kethry. "All right—Tarma, love, you first."

"Right. Jadrek, I managed to deliver all but one of your messages; the one to Count Wulfres I left with Tindel. Wulfres wouldn't let me get near him; I can't much blame him, since I have been building quite a formidable reputation as Char's chief bully-boy."

"Is that why he trusts you?" Kethry asked.

"Partially. Don't worry, though. That reputation is actually doing me more good than harm. If anyone notices when I take somebody aside for a little chat, it doesn't do them any benefit to tell the King, because Char assumes I'm delivering threats!" She chuckled. "Keth, that Adept we took out was the only one Char had; the rest of his mages are Master and Journeyman class. So don't worry about this disguise continuing to hold."

Kethry heaved a sigh of profound relief. "Thank the gods for that. That *did* have me nervy. How are you getting on with Char? You said far better than we'd hoped—"

"That's a good summation; he *doesn't* trust any of his native Guards, and he doesn't trust his nobles. That leaves him with me, a couple of other landless mercs, and a handful of outland emissaries. Since I'm trying to give an imitation of a freefighter with a veneer of civilization and a range of interests slightly beyond 'food, fornication and fighting,' he seems to be gravitating more and more toward me."

"And needless to say, you're encouraging him."

:*Idra taught you well,*: Warrl commented. :*You encourage familiarity with the King while never going over the line of being social inferior. That takes a delicate touch I did not suspect you had, mindmate.*:

"Having you coaching me in my head hasn't hurt,

Furball. Thanks to you, I've never once been even remotely disrespectful; been pounding heads when some of the Guards go over the line, in fact. And as a result Char's slowly taking me as cup-companion as well as bodyguard."

"That's certainly *far* better than we hoped!" Jadrek exclaimed.

"Tarma, what about Idra?" Kethry asked, both elbows on the table, chin in her hands. She looked unwontedly sober.

Tarma sighed, and rubbed one temple. "Keth, we both know by now she's got to be dead."

Kethry nodded, reluctantly, as Jadrek bit his lip. "I just didn't want to be the one to say it," she replied sadly. "Need's pull just hasn't been strong enough for her to have still been alive."

:I, too, have suspected the same.:

Tarma sighed. "I think I realized it—I mean, really *believed* it—a couple of days after—" She stopped for a moment, and looked squarely at Jadrek. *He's an outClansman*—she thought, weighing him in her mind. —*but—why not? No reason why he shouldn't know; if Keth has her way, he won't be an outClansman for long.* "—after I called one of the *leshya'e* and got the Star-Eyed Warrior instead, that night in Valdemar. You know, the evening when Roald and I came back as best of friends? He saw Her, too—and She made it clear to both of us that we were all on the same side. D'you remember how She turned the set of his Whites I was wearing black?"

Kethry nodded slowly, then real enlightenment dawned. "Black . . . is for vengeance and blood feud. . . ."

"Right," Tarma nodded. "She could have left my clothing alone; She could have changed it to brown, if She was truly offended at me being out of Kal'enedral colors, which I think is rather unlikely. She doesn't get that petty. But She didn't leave the Whites white—and She'd already convinced me that

221

Roald and Stefansen were on the side of the righteous. She can be very subtle when She chooses, and She was trying to give me a subtle message, that I was back on blood-trail. So who would be the logical one for me to avenge—and who would be the logical target for vengeance?"

"Idra—and Char."

"Right and right again. My only questions *now* are—was it accident or premeditated, and how he did it." She tightened her jaw, and felt very nearly murderous at that moment. "And the closer I get to him, the likelier I am to find the answers to both."

She let the sentence hang for a long moment, then coughed slightly. "Jadrek? Your turn."

"I've been approached by three of those nobles you contacted for me, via their wives," he said, visibly shaken by Tarma's assertions—and yet, unsurprised by them, as if her words had only confirmed something he had known, but had not wished to acknowledge that he knew. "They were already planning some sort of action on their own, which, given their temperaments, was something I had thought fairly likely. In addition, I have been approached by those I did *not* expect—prelates of no less than five separate orders. It seems *they* had already spoken quietly with my chosen highborn—"

"And went on to you. Logical." Tarma nodded thoughtfully. "And what prompted *their* dissatisfaction?"

"Oh, a variety of causes—from the altruistic to the realistic." He wrinkled his brow in thought. "Mind you, I don't personally know as much about the clergy as I do the Court, but they seem to be appropriate responses given the personalities of those I spoke with and the philosophies of their orders."

"Huh. When we start to get *clergy* on our side. . . ." Tarma propped her feet up on the table, ignoring Kethry's frown of disapproval, and sat in thoughtful silence for a long time. "All right," she said, when the silence had begun to seem unbreakable, "It's time for some hard choices, friends. We're getting the support, and not only are we moving a bit ahead of schedule, but we're getting some unexpected help. So which of the plans are we going to follow?"

She tilted her head at Jadrek, who pursed his lips thoughtfully. "I'd rather not run a full-scale uprising, frankly," he said. "It's too unwieldy for this situation, I think; your commanders really have to be in the field for it to succeed. Tarma, you are the most militant of us, and we *need* you here—so that would leave me or Kethry."

"Not me," Kethry objected. "Fighters don't like following a mage, and I don't blame them. I'm no strategist, either."

"And I am neither fighter nor strategist," Jadrek replied.

"Stalemate," Tarma observed, flexing her shoulders to try and relax the tense muscles there. "Not that I don't agree with you both. Warrl?"

:*I, also. It is too easy to lose a civil war.*:

"All right, we're agreed that rousing the country-side is out, then?"

The other two nodded, slowly.

"Assassination."

:*That, I favor,*: Warrl replied, raising his head from his paws. :*It would be an easy thing for* me. *Wait until he is in the garden with a wench—over the wall—*: He snapped his jaws together suggestively. :*It would give me great pleasure, and I could easily be gone before alarm could be effective.*:

"Not clear-cut enough," Jadrek asserted. "There will always be those wanting to make a martyr out of Char. It's amazing how saintly a tyrant becomes after he's dead. We want Stefan *firmly* on the throne, or this country will be having as many problems as it already has, just different ones."

Warrl sighed, and put his head back down.

"Sorry, mindmate—I sympathize. That leaves the

small-scale uprising; here, in the city. Can we pull *that* off?"

"Maybe. By Midsummer we'll have the working people solidly behind us; those that aren't losing half their incomes to Char's taxes are losing half their incomes because the others have less to spend," Kethry said, nibbling at her thumbnail. "What I've been working with are the merchants, and they are vastly discontent with the way things are going. If there's an uprising, they will be on our side of the riot. The problem is that these are *not* people used to fighting."

"Maybe not, but I'll bet most of them have a few hired fighters each, either as guards for themselves, or for their goods," Tarma pointed out. "If there were some way that we could promise that their property would stay safe, I'll bet they'd turn those fighters over to us for—say—two days. Assuming that they are professional enough to fight together as a force instead of a gaggle of individuals."

"I'll work on that," Kethry replied.

"I suspect we'll have most of the clergy, too, by Midsummer," Jadrek offered. "And for many of the same reasons. And I know of at least two militant orders within the city walls. *Those* warriors *will* fight as a single unit."

"Good. What about the highborn? Don't they have retinues?"

Jadrek shook his head with regret. "No, not inside the city walls. That was one of Destillion's edicts; no noble can have more than four armed retainers when at Court. And *you* know the size of Char's guard force."

"He's got a small army, not even counting his personal guard," Tarma agreed ruefully. "Still— maybe I can come up with a notion. I might be able to work a bit of subversion in Char's forces, who knows? Let's stick with the local uprising plan. I think we're all agreed it's got the best chance of success."

She swung her feet down off the table, and noticed with surprise that the light coming through the closed shutters was red. "Damn! Sunset already? I've got to be getting back. Char's got another drunken orgy he's holding tonight, and wants his back safe."

Kethry mussed herself artistically, pulling one sleeve of her blouse so far down that a generous portion of breast was exposed. She stood up at the same moment as Tarma, followed her to the door, and let her out. For the benefit of anyone watching, they gave a well-acted imitation of a passionate farewell.

When Kethry finished locking the door behind Tarma, she turned to see that Jadrek was still sitting at the table, looking broodingly at a stain in the wood. She was not at all unhappy about that, because she had just about decided that certain other things were going to have to come to a head—one way or another.

"Still worried?" she asked, returning to her seat, and reaching out to touch her index finger to the wick of the candle standing in the middle of the table. It promptly ignited.

Jadrek had looked up as she had taken her chair, and watched her light the candle with rapt fascination. "I never get tired of seeing you do things like that," he said. "It's just—so—magical."

She laughed, and dispelled the illusion on herself. He relaxed visibly.

She raised an eyebrow, and he shrugged.

"I like you better this way," he confessed shyly. "The other—seems harder, somehow."

"Oh, she is; she's taking Arton for everything she can get," Kethry replied.

"To answer your question—yes, I'm still worried. But I also know that all three of us are doing the best that we can, so worrying isn't going to make a great deal of difference, one way or the other." He stood up, with visible reluctance. "I probably should leave you. . . ."

"Why?" Kethry asked, frankly. "Are you expecting anyone tonight?"

"Well, no, but—"

"Neither am I." She glanced at Warrl, who took the hint, padding through the still-open door between their rooms, shutting it behind him with a casual kick. Kethry moved closer to Jadrek before he could move away, not touching him but standing so near that their faces were within inches of each other.

"Jadrek, I want you to know that I find you very, very attractive."

His eyes registered his complete surprise as she deliberately held his gaze.

He licked his lips, nervously, and seemed utterly at a loss for anything to say.

"I also want you to know that I am *not* a virgin, and I'm perfectly capable of dealing with attentions that I don't welcome. You," she finished, "do not come under that category."

"I—you never stop surprising me. I hardly know what to say. . . ."

"Then don't say, do. Unless you don't find *me* attractive—"

Slowly he lifted one hand, and cupped it against her face. "Kethry—" he breathed, "Kethry, I find you very attractive. Almost unbearably attractive But I'm not a young man—"

She echoed his gesture, his cheek warm beneath her hand. "If I wanted a young man, there's a tavern full downstairs. It's *you* I admire, Jadrek the mind, the person. You're something special— something those pretty bodies downstairs aren't and probably never will be."

Very hesitantly, he leaned forward and kissed her. She returned the kiss as passionately as she dared, and suddenly he responded by embracing her and prolonging the kiss until she was breathless.

When they broke apart, his gray eyes were dark with confusion. "Kethry—"

"There are more comfortable places to be doing this," she said, very softly. "Over there, for one." She nodded at the curtained bed, half-hidden in the shadows.

He blushed. He blushed even harder when she led him there by the hand, and all but pushed him down onto it. "I—" he stammered, looking past her, "Kethry, I'm not—very experienced at this sort of—"

"You were doing just fine a moment ago," she interrupted him gently, then prevented further protests by embracing him and resuming the kiss where it had been left off.

He seemed to hesitate for a moment, then seemed to make up his mind all in an instant, and returned her embrace with a fervor that at least equaled her own. He pulled her down beside him; she did not resist in the least, that being exactly what she wanted from him.

For a very long time, all they did was kiss and exchange halting, hesitant caresses, almost like a pair of naive youngsters. But when she returned every tenderness with more of the same, he grew braver, daring to undo the lacings of her dress, daring to touch her with fingers that slowly grew bolder.

He frequently stopped what he was doing for long moments, just to look at her, his eyes full of wonder, as if this was something more magical for him than all the exercising of her powers as a sorceress. As if he couldn't believe that she was returning touch for touch and emotion for emotion. When he did that, she had to fight to keep back the tears of sympathy—the only way she *could* was to keep a little corner of her mind free to concentrate on the hatred she felt for the women who must have treated him with coldness or indifference, so that *this* experience was such an unexpected revelation for him.

He stroked her with hands so gentle that she could hardly credit it. He was by no means the best lover she'd ever had; he was, perhaps, a little clumsy, and as he had confessed, not at all practiced—but his gentleness made up for that, and more.

And besides, she rather figured that she had experience enough for both of them.

When they finally joined together, it was like nothing she'd ever dreamed of, for her heart was as involved in the act as her body.

"Kethry—" he whispered hoarsely as he started to sit up—whispering into the darkness, for the candle had long since burned out. She could hear the beginnings of an apology in his voice, and interrupted him.

"Don't you *dare*," she replied, reaching up for him and pulling him toward her so that his head rested on her shoulder. "Don't you *dare* spoil this with any of your nonsense about being old!"

"Then I—didn't make a fool of myself?" he asked shyly. "You don't want me to go?"

"You weren't making a fool of yourself any more than I was," she told him. "If showing how you feel is so very foolish. I don't think it is. And no, please, don't go. I *want* you to stay. I've had my fill of nights spent alone."

He sighed, and relaxed into her arms. "Kethry—I care for you, maybe more than I should."

She reached into the darkness, and brushed strands of damp hair from his forehead. "Don't think you're alone in caring more than you should." She let him take that in for a moment, then laughed, softly. "Or did you think I was only after you for your book collection?"

"Gods—Keth—" He who was usually so glib was

once again at a loss for words, then he joined in her laughter. "No—I didn't; *Tarma*, on the other hand—"

They held each other for another long moment, until he spoke again. "Kethry, what we've got ahead of us—"

"—makes *promises* foolish," she interrupted him. "We've already made all the promises either of us dare to for now. Let's just enjoy what times we have, and worry about staying alive, shall we?"

"That's probably wise," he replied, with a reluctance that made her heart race.

He raised himself on his elbow for a moment, and cupped her face in both hands, and kissed her— kissed her in a way that made his words about not making promises a lie.

And eventually he fell asleep with his head cradled on her shoulder.

Kethry held him, her heart full of song.

Oh Windborn, this is *the one,* she thought, before she joined him in slumber. *He's—he's like something I've always missed, and never known I missed it until now. But now—I could never be content with anyone but him.*

Not ever again.

Eleven

Kethry sighed, rose from her chair, and went once more to the window. She stood there restlessly, leaning on the sill, with her chin in her hand, watching the street below; a dark silhouette against the oranges and reds of a spectacular sunset.

More than a hint of weariness in that sigh, Jadrek thought sympathetically, rubbing his tired eyes. *Last night was yet another late night, with both of us too exhausted at the end of it to do anything other than sleep. Tonight looks to be the same. There's never a moment to spare for simple things like food and sleep, much less anything else. I want to tell her how I feel—that I—I love her. But there never seems to be any time, much less the right time.*

He studied the way she was holding herself, the sagging shoulders, the way she kept turning her head a little to ease the stiffness he knew was in her neck because he had loosened those muscles for her far too many times of late. His own neck felt as stiff, and he felt echoes of those same aches in his own shoulders. *Gods. We're both tired, mentally and physically. She's spent more hours cajoling stubborn suspicious merchants than I care to think about; I've spent almost the same number of hours dancing around the touchy sensibilities of priests and highborn. Not the way I would have chosen to spend our time, and both of us return from meetings so—completely drained. Conspiracy is for the young. Combining it with a love affair is insanity!*

230

Warrl gave an amused snort from where he lay curled on his chosen spot on the hearth. *:You manage well enough, wise one,:* the rough voice in Jadrek's mind said.

That is solely, I suspect, because our opportunities have numbered far less than our wishes, Jadrek thought at him, feeeling a little more revived just by the casual contact with the *kyree's* lively mind. *I fear that even the supposed wisdom of accumulated years fails to keep my desire from outstripping my capabilities. The only difference between my youth and my age is that now I am not ashamed to admit the fact.*

The *kyree* snorted contemptuously again, but Jadrek ignored him and continued. *Furthermore, I shudder to think what Tarma is likely to say about this liaison when she learns of it.*

:You know less about her than you think,: was the *kyree's* enigmatic reply. Suddenly the great beast raised his head, and stared in the direction of the palace. *:A message—:*

"What?" Jadrek asked aloud, as Kethry turned to look sharply at the lupine creature.

:Tarma sends her regrets, but Char requires her presence, and she seems to think that the tran-dust he intends to abuse this evening might make him talkative. Needless to say, she does not intend to miss her opportunity.: The *kyree* turned warm and glowing eyes on the Archivist. *:She asks me to come to the table at dark, so that she can return here afterward without worrying about spies on her backtrail. I would suggest, given your earlier plaint about not having any time to yourselves, that you might take advantage of the occasion that has been presented to you . . . unless you have other plans.:*

Jadrek nearly choked on a laugh at Kethry's indignant blush.

"I think we can find some way of filling in the time," he said aloud, as she glared at both of them.

*   *   *

231

The hour grew late; the candle burned down to a stub, and Kethry replaced it—and still no sign of Tarma. Jadrek regretted—more than once—that his ability to communicate with Warrl was sharply limited by distance.

Kethry suddenly dropped the candle end she was about to discard, and her whole body tensed.

"What?" Jadrek asked, anxiously, wondering if she had sensed some sort of occult probing in their direction.

"It's—anger," she replied, distantly. "Terrible, terrible *anger*. I've never felt anything like this in her before."

"Her? Her who?" She didn't answer him, and he said, a little more sharply. "*Who*, Keth? Keth?"

She shook her head as if to clear it, and resumed her seat at the table, but he could see that her hands were trembling before she clasped them in front of her on the table to conceal the fact.

"Keth?" he repeated gently, but insistently.

"It's—it's the *she'enedran* bond between us," she said at last. "We each can feel things the other does, sometimes. Jadrek, she's in a killing rage; she's just barely keeping herself under control! And I *can't* tell why."

She looked up at him, and he could see fear, the mirror to his own, in her eyes. "I've never felt anything like this out of her; she's usually so controlled, even when I'm ready to spit nails. It has to be something Char said or did—but what could bring *her* to the brink like this? There's enough rage resonating down the bond that I'm half prepared to go kill something!"

"I don't know," he said slowly. "And I'm almost afraid to find out."

They stared at each other helplessly, until finally he reached out and laid his hand over her clenched ones, offering what little comfort he had to give.

After that, it was just the deadly waiting.

Finally, after both of them had fretted themselves into a state of nervous exhaustion, they heard Warrl's nails clicking on the wooden steps outside. Tarma's presence was revealed only by the creaking of the two trick boards, one in the fifth step, one in the eighth—otherwise she never made a sound. Kethry jumped to her feet, ran to the door and flung it open.

Tarma/Arton stood in the light streaming from the door, so very still that for a moment Jadrek wasn't entirely certain she was breathing. She remained in the doorway for a long, long moment, her face utterly expressionless—except for the eyes, which burned with a rage so fierce Kethry stepped back an involuntary pace or two.

Warrl came up from behind her and nudged Tarma's hand with his nose; only then did she seem to realize where she was, and walk slowly inside, stopping only when she came to the table.

She did not take a seat as she usually did; she continued to stand, half-shrouded in shadows, and looked from Jadrek to Kethry and back again. Finally she spoke.

"I've found out what happened to Idra."

". . . so once Char had downed a full bottle of brandy to enhance the *tran*, he'd gotten himself into a mood where he was talkative, but wasn't really thinking about what he was saying."

Kethry tensed, feeling Tarma's anger burning within *her*, a half-mad fire at the pit of her stomach.

Tarma spoke in a tonelessly deadly voice, still refusing to seat herself. "Alcohol and *tran* have that effect in combination—connecting the mind to the mouth without letting the intellect have any say in what comes out. And as I'd been hoping, his suspicious nature kept him from wanting to confide in any of his courtiers. And there was good old Arton, so sympathetic, so reliable, always dependable. So

233

he threw his rump-kissers out, and began telling
me how everybody abused him, everybody turned
on him. Especially his sister."

She shifted her weight a little; the floorboard
creaked beneath her, and Kethry could feel the
anger rising up her spine. *Channel that*—she told
herself, locking her will into Adept's discipline.
*There's enough pure rage here to burn half the city
down, if you channel it. Use the anger*—don't let it
use you!

With that invocation of familiar discipline came
a certain amount of relief; the fires were partially
contained, harvested against future need. It wasn't
perfect; she was still trembling with emotion, but
at least the energy wasn't being all wasted.

And there will be future need—

"Then he told me about how his sister had first
supported him, then betrayed him. How he had
known from the first that the hunt for the lost
sword had been nothing more than a ruse to get her
across the border and into contact with Stefan. He
carried on about that for long enough to just about
put me to sleep; what an ungrateful, cold bitch she
was, how she deserved the worst fate anyone could
imagine. He was pretty well convinced she was
she'chorne, too, and you know how they feel about
that here—I had just about figured that was all I
was going to get out of him, when suddenly he
stopped raving."

Kethry felt a prickle of fear when the bond of
she'enedran between herself and Tarma transmitted
another surge of the incredibly cold rage her
oathsister was feeling. *I've never known anyone who
could sustain that kind of emotion for this long without
berserking.* Had Tarma been anything other than
Kal'enedral—someone, or several someones, would be
long dead by now, hacked into many small pieces. . . .

" 'I *fixed* her,' he said 'I fixed her properly. I
planned it all so beautifully, too. I had Zaras bespell

one of his apprentices to look like me, and sent the apprentice off with the rest of the Court on a three-day hunt. Then Zaras and I waited for the bitch in the stables; I distracted her, he hit her from behind with a spell, and when she woke up, her body belonged to Zaras. He had her saddle up and ride out just as if it were any other day, but this time her destination was *my* choice. We took her to the old tower on the edge of Hielmarsh; it's deserted, and the rumors I had spread about hauntings keep the clods away.' "

From there, what Tarma told them horrified even Kethry, inured to the brutality of warfare as she was. And she, of the three of them, had been the least close to the Captain; Tarma's own internal torment was only too plain to her oathsister, who was continuing to share in it—and Jadrek's expression could not be described.

Idra's torture and "punishment" had begun with the expedient most commonly used to break a woman—multiple rape. Rape in which her own brother had been the foremost participant. Char's methods and means when that failed became more exotic. Jadrek excused himself halfway through the toneless recitation to be audibly sick. When he returned, pale, shaking and sweating with reaction, Tarma had nearly finished. Kethry's stomach was churning and her throat was choked with silent weeping.

"His own *sister*—" Kethry shuddered, her eyes burning and blurring with her tears. "No matter *how* much he hated her, she was still his *sister!*"

Tarma came closer, looming over the table like a dark angel. She took the dagger from her belt, and held it out into the light of the table-candle. She held it stiffly, point down, in a fist clenched so tightly on the hilt that her knuckles were white.

"Oathbreaker, I name him," Tarma said, softly, but with all the feeling that she had not given vent

235

to behind the words of the ages-old ritual of Outcasting. "Oathbreaker he, and all who stand by him. Oathbreaker once—by the promises made to kin, then shattered. Oathbreaker twice—by the violation of king-oath to liegeman. Oathbreaker three times—Oathbreaker a *thousand* times—by the violation of every kin-bond known and by the shedding of shared blood."

"Oathbreaker, I name him," Kethry echoed, rising to place her cold hand over Tarma's, taking up the thread of the seldom-used passage from the Mercenaries' Code. She choked out her words around a knot of black anger and bleak mourning, both so thick and dark that she could barely manage to speak the ritual coherently through the chaos of her emotions. She was still channeling, but now she was channeling the emotion through the words of the ritual. Emotion *was* power; that was what made a death-curse so potent, even in the mouth of an untutored peasant. This may well once have *been* a spell—and it was capable of becoming one again. She knew that even though she was no priest, channeling *that* much emotion-energy through it had the potential of making the Outcasting into something more than "mere ritual."

"Oathbreaker I do name him, mage to thy priest. Oathbreaker once—" she choked, hardly able to get the words out, "by the violation of sacred bonds. Oathbreaker twice—by the perversion of power granted him for the common weal to his own ends. Oathbreaker three times—by the invocation of pain and death for pleasure."

Somewhat to her surprise, she saw Jadrek stand, place his trembling, damp hand atop hers, and take up the ritual. She had never guessed that he knew it. "Oathbreaker, I name him, and all who support him," he said, though his voice shook. "Oathbreaker I do name him, who am the common man of good will, making the third for Outcasting. Oathbreaker once—by the lies of his tongue. Oathbreaker twice —by the perversion of his heart. Oathbreaker three times—by the giving of his soul willingly to darkness."

Tarma slammed the dagger they all had been holding into the wood of the table with such force that it sank halfway to the hilt. "Oathbreaker is his name;" she snarled. "All oaths to him are null. Let every man's hand be against him; let the gods turn their faces from him; let his darkness rot him from within until he be called to a just accounting. *And may the gods grant that* mine *be the hand!*"

She brought herself back under control with an effort that was visible, and turned a face toward them that was no longer impassive, but was just as tear-streaked as Kethry's own. "This is the end of it: he couldn't break her. She was too tough for him, right up to the last. He didn't get one word out of her, not one—and in the end, when he thought his bullyboys had her restrained, she managed to break free long enough to grab a knife and kill herself with it."

The fire-and-candle light flared up long enough to show that the murderous rage was still burning in her, but still under control. "I damn near killed him myself, then and there. Warrl managed to keep me from painting the room with his blood. It would have been suicide, and while it would have left the throne free for Stefan, I'd have left at least two friends behind who would have been rather unhappy that I'd gone and gotten myself killed by the rest of Char's Guard."

" 'Unhappy' is understating the case," Jadrek replied gently, slowly resuming his seat. "But yes—at least two. Good friend—sister—please sit." Kethry could see tears still glinting in his eyes—but she could also see that he was thinking *past* his grief; something she and Tarma couldn't quite manage yet.

As Tarma lowered herself stiffly into her accustomed chair, he continued. "Our plans have been plagued by the inability to bring a force of trained fighters whose loyalty is unswervingly ours into the city. Now I ask you, who served under Idra—*what would her Sunhawks think to hear this?*"

"Gods!" Kethry brought her fist to her mouth, and bit her knuckles hard enough to break the skin. "They'd want revenge, just like us—and *not* just them, but every man or woman who *ever* served as a Hawk!"

Jadrek nodded. "In short—an army. *Our* army. One that won't swerve from their goal for any reason, or be stopped by anything short of the death of every last one of them."

Now, for a brief time, they fought their battle with pen and paper. Messages, coded, in obscure dialects, or (rarely) in plain tradespeech left the city every day that there was someone that they judged was trustworthy enough to carry them. Tarma, from her position as trusted insider, was able to tell them that the few messages that were intercepted baffled Char's adherents, and were dismissed out of hand as merchant-clan warring. The rest went south and east, following the trade roads, to find the men and women who wore (or had once worn) the symbol of the Sunhawk.

The answers that returned were not of paper and ink, but flesh and blood—and of deadly anger.

The last time Justin Twoblade and his partner had entered Petras, it had been with a feeling of pleasant anticipation. Petras had been the turnaround point for the caravan they'd been guarding, and it was well known for its wines and its wenches. He'd had quite a lively time of it, that season in Petras.

Now he entered the city a second time, again as a

caravan guard. Three things differed: he would not be leaving, at least not with the traders he was guarding; his partner was not Ikan Dryvale—

And his mood was not pleasant.

He and his partner parted company with the caravan as soon as their clients had selected a hostelry, taking their pay with them in the form of the square silver coins that served as common currency among the traders of most of this part of the world. Then, looking in no way different than any other mustered-out guards, they collected their small store of belongings, loaded them on their horses, and headed for a district with a more modest selection of inns.

And if they seemed rather heavily armed and armored, well, they *had* been escorting jewel traders; it was only good sense to arm heavily when one escorted such tempting targets.

"What was the name of that inn we're looking for?" Justin asked his new partner, his voice pitched only just loud enough to be heard over the street noise. "I didn't quite catch it from the contact."

"The Fountain of Beer," Kyra replied, just as quietly, her eyes flicking from side to side in a way that told Justin she was watching everything about her without making any great show of doing so.

"I suspect that's it ahead of us." His hands were full; reins of his horse in the left, pack in the right, so he pointed with his chin. The sign did indeed sport a violently yellow fountain that was apparently spouting vast quantities of foam.

"If you'll take care of the lodgings, I'll take care of the stableman," Kyra offered. "We've both got tokens; one of us should hit on a contact if we try both."

"Good," Justin replied shortly; they paused just at the inn gate and made an exchange of packs and reins. Kyra went on into the stableyard with their horses, as he sought the innkeeper behind his bar.

Justin bargained heatedly for several minutes, arriving at a fee of two silver for stabling, room and meals for both; but there was a third coin with the two square ones he handed the innkeeper—a small, round, bronze coin, bearing the image of a rampant hawk on one side and the sun-in-glory on the other. It was, in fact, the smallest denomination of coin used in Hawksnest—used *only* in Hawksnest, and almost never seen outside of the town.

The innkeeper neither commented on the coin, nor returned it—but he *did* ask "*Justice* Twoblade?" when registering them on his rolls.

"Justice" was one of the half-dozen recognition words that had come with Justin's message.

"Justin," the fighter corrected him. "Justin of the Hawk."

That was the appropriate answer. The man nodded, and replied "Right. *Justice.*"

Justin also nodded, then stood at the bar and nursed a small beer while he waited for Kyra to return. The potboy showed them to a small, plain room on the ground floor at the back of the inn.

"Stableman's one contact for certain sure," Kyra told him as soon as the boy had left. "He wished me 'justice,' I gave 'im m'name as Kyra Brighthawk, and then 'e tol' me t' wait fer a visitor."

"Innkeeper's another, gave me the same word. Always provided we aren't in a trap." Justin raised one laconic eyebrow at Kyra's headshake. "My child, you don't grow to be an *old* fighter without learning to be suspicious of your own grandmother. I would suggest to you that we follow 'enemy territory' rules."

Kyra shrugged. "You been the leader; I'll live with whatever ye guess we should be doin'."

Justin felt of the bed, found it satisfactory, and stretched his lanky body on it at full length. "It is a wise child that obeys its elders," he said sententiously, then quirked one corner of his mouth. "It is also a child that *may* live to *become* an elder."

Kyra shrugged good-naturedly.

A few moments later, the boy returned with a surprisingly good dinner for two, which he left. Justin examined it with great care, by smell and by cautious taste.

"Evidently we aren't supposed to leave," Justin guessed, "And if this stuff has been tampered with, I can't tell it."

Kyra followed his careful inspection of the food with one of her own. "Nor me, an' my grandy was a wisewoman. I don' know about you, friend, but I could eat raw snake."

"Likewise. My lady?" Justin dug a healthy portion out of the meat pie they'd been served, and handed it to her solemnly.

She accepted it just as solemnly. It might have been noted, had there been anyone else present, that neither partook of anything the other had already tried. If any of the food *had* been 'tampered with,' it would likely be only one or two dishes. If that were the case—*one* of them would still be in shape to deal with the consequences.

When, after an hour, nothing untoward happened to either of them, Justin grinned a little sheepishly. "Well—"

"Don't apologize," Kyra told him. "I tell ye, I druther eat a cold dinner than find m'self wakin' up lookin' at the wrong end'f somebody's knife."

They demolished the rest of the food in fairly short order—then began another interminable wait. After a candlemark of pacing, Kyra finally dug a long branch of silvery derthenwood out of her pack, as well as a tiny knife with a blade hardly bigger than a pen nib. She sat down on the floor next to the bed and began the slow process of turning the branch into a carved chain. Justin watched her from half-closed eyes, fascinated in spite of himself by the delicate work. The chain had only a few links to it when the wait began; when it ended, there was scarcely a fingerlength of branch remaining.

241

Then, without warning, a portion of the wall blurred and Kethry stepped through it.

Kethry just held out her arms, welcoming both of them into an embrace which included tears from all three of them.

"Gods, Keth—" Justin finally pulled away, reluctantly. "It has been so damned *hard* keeping this all inside."

"I know; none better—Windborn, I cannot tell you how glad I am to see *you* two! You're the first to come; may the Lady forgive me, but there were times I wondered if this was going to work."

"Oh, it's working all right; better than you could guess." He wiped his eyes and nose on the napkin from their tray and locked his emotions down. "All right, lady-mage, we need information, not waterfalls."

"First—tell me how you got here so fast."

"We weren't *about* t' let anybody beat us here," Kyra replied. "Not after that message. Sewen sent me on ahead t' tell ye that Queen Sursha give us leave t' deal with this soon's we get some of her new army units in t' replace us. The rest of the Hawks'll be here in 'bout a month."

"Ikan's out rounding up all the former Hawks we can track down," Justin continued. "We'll be trickling in the same as the Hawks will—no more than two or three at a time, and disguised. One of the merchant houses is going to let some of us use their colors; Ikan took the liberty of taking your name in vain to old Grumio. We have the support of Sursha's Bards, and half a dozen holy orders. We'll be everything from wandering entertainers to caravan guards. You've got a plan, I take it?"

"Tarma has; she's worked it out with a couple of highborn we can trust," Kethry told him. "All I really know about is my part of it, but generally we're hoping to accomplish the whole thing with a minimum of bloodshed."

"Specific blood," Kyra replied, with a smoldering anger Justin shared.

"*Oh*, yes. One of the lot we've already taken out—Raschar's Adept. But the others—" Kethry allowed her own anger to show. "—Tarma's identified every person that had a hand in the deed. And they *will* answer to us."

Justin nodded, slowly. "What about arms? There's going to be at least half of us without much, given the disguises."

"Being smuggled in to us from an outside source, so that Char won't be alerted that something's up by activity in forges and smithies. We're getting everything Tarma could think of; bows, arrows with war-points, various kinds of throwing knives, grapnels, climbing spikes, pikes, swords—the last is the hardest, that, and armor, but we're hoping most of you will manage to bring your own. Do either of you have a guess how many there might be that we can count on?"

"Six hundred at an absolute minimum," Justin said with grim satisfaction. "That's four hundred Hawks and the two hundred that either retired to Hawksnest or that Ikan knows for a fact he can get hold of and will want in."

"Gods—that's better than I'd hoped," Kethry said weakly. "There're four hundred regular troops here, about a hundred and fifty assorted militia, and fifty personal guards belonging to Char. There're some other assorted fighters, but Tarma tells me they won't count for much; there're Char's adherents, and their private guards, but we don't know but that they won't turn their coats or hide if things look chancy. That means we'll be going pretty much one-on-one; all the professionals starting the fight even."

"Even with his mages?" Justin asked dubiously.

Kethry raised her chin, her eyes glinting like emerald ice in the light from the window beside her. "He hasn't a mage that can come close to me in ability, and I have more power at my disposal than any of them could hope for."

"Where are you getting *that* kind of power?" Justin asked in surprise. "I mean—you're alone—"

"You—and the Hawks. Your anger. I can't begin to tell you how strong a force I've already tapped off just you two; when I start to think about *six hundred* Hawks, it makes *my* head reel. It's the kind of power a mage sees perhaps once in a lifetime, and if I weren't an Adept I'd never be able to touch it, much less control it."

"You're *Adept* class now?" Justin said incredulously. "Great good gods—no wonder you aren't worried!"

"Not with power like that at my disposal. I can channel all that anger, harvest it, and save it for the hour of striking. *We're* the attackers, this time. I can set up as many spells as it takes as far in advance as I need to, spells specifically designed to take out each mage; and wait until the moment of attack to trigger them. I'm assuming only half of those will work. The rest will probably be deflected. But the mages will be off-balance, and I can take them out one at a time. I know how mages think— when they're under magical attack they tend to ignore anything mundane, and they seldom or never work together. White Winds is one of the few schools that teaches working in concert. I think we can plan that they will be concentrating on *me* and not on anything nonmagical. And that they won't even think to band together against me."

Justin nodded, satisfied. "Sounds like you people have a pretty good notion of what you're about. Now comes the hard part."

"Uh-huh," Kethry nodded. "Waiting."

Singly, or by twos and threes, the Hawks came, just as Justin had told Kethry they would. Each of hem arrived in some disguise, some seeming utterly harmless—a peasant farmer here, a party of minstrels there, a couple of merchant apprentices. Day by day they trickled into Petras, and no one seemed to notice that they never left it again. Each went to one of the dozen inns whose masters had bought into the conspiracy, carrying with them a small bronze coin and a handful of recognition words. Each was met by Kethry, or by one of the other "official greeters"—Justin, Kyra or Ikan, who had arrived within days of the first two.

From there, things got far more complicated than even most of these professional mercenaries were used to.

Beaker coughed, scratched his head, and turned his weary donkey in to what passed for a stableman at the Wheat Sheaf inn. The stableman here was, like most of the clients, of farm stock; and probably had never even seen a warhorse up close, much less handled one. Beaker's dusty donkey was far more in his line of expertise. The "stable" was a packed-earth enclosure with a watering trough and a pile of hay currently being shared by three other mangy little donkeys and a brace of oxen. Beaker had serious second and third thoughts about *this* being the contact point for a rebel force, but the instructions had said the Wheat Sheaf and specified the stableman as the contact.

"Ye wanta watch that one," Beaker drawled, handing the wizened peasant the rough rope of the donkey's halter with one hand, and four coins with the other—three copper pennies and one bronze Hawkpiece. "She'll take *revenge* if she even thinks ye're gonna lay hand to 'er."

"Oh, aye, I know th' type," the fellow replied, grinning, and proving that a good half of his teeth had gone with his lost youth. "Ol' girl like this, she hold a grudge till *judgment* day, eh?" He pocketed all four coins without a comment.

Well, that was the proper sign and counter. Beaker felt some of his misgivings slide away, and ambled on into the dark cave of the rough-brick inn.

Like most of its ilk, it had two floors, each one large room. The upper would have pallets for sleeping; the lower had a huge fireplace at one end where a stout middle-aged woman was tending an enormous pot and a roast of some kind. It was filled with clumsy benches and trestle tables now, but after the inn shut down for the night, those that could not afford a pallet upstairs would be granted leave to sleep on table, bench, or floor beneath for half the price of a pallet. Opposite the fireplace was the "bar"; a stack of beer kegs and a rack of mugs, presided over by the innkeeper.

Beaker debated looking prosperous, when his stomach growled and made the decision for him. He paid the innkeeper for a mug of beer, a bowl of soup and a slice of roast; the man took his money, gave him his drink and a slice of not-too-stale bread. Beaker slid his pack off his back, rummaged his own bowl and spoon out of it, then shrugged it back on before weaving his way through the tables to the monarch of the "kitchen."

Rather to his surprise—the inn staff of places like this one were rather notorious for being surly—the woman gave him a broad smile along with a full bowl, and put a reasonably generous slice of meat on his bread. Juggling all three carefully, he took a seat as near to the door as possible, and sat down to eat.

The food was another pleasant surprise; fresh and tasty and stomach-filling. And the inn was cool after the heat and dust of the road. The beer was doing a respectable job of washing the grit out of his throat. Beaker was about halfway through his meal when her heard someone come up behind him.

"How's the food t'day, sojer?"

Beaker grinned and turned in his seat. "Kyra, when are you gonna get rid of that damn accent?"

"When cows fly, prob'ly. Makes me fit in here, though." She straddled the bench beside him, a mug and bowl of her own in hand. "Eat here ev'ry chance I get. Ma Kemak, she sure can cook. Pa Kemak don' water the beer, neither. Finish that up, boy. We gotta get you off th' street soon's we can." She set him a good example by nearly inhaling her soup.

From the inn Kyra led Beaker on a rambling stroll designed to shake off or bore any pursuit, bringing him at last to the stableyard entrance of a wealthy merchant. A murmured word with the chief stableman got them inside; from there they slipped in the servant's door and climbed a winding staircase to the attic of the house. Normally a room like this was crowded with the accumulated junk of several generations, now it was barren except for a line of pallets. There were only two windows—both shuttered—but there was enough light that Beaker could recognize most of those sprawled about the room.

"Beat you, Birdbrain," Garth mocked from a corner; looking around, Beaker could see that a good half of the pallets were occupied—and that evidently, he was the last of Tarma's scout troop to arrive.

"Well, hell, if they'd given me somethin' besides a half-dead dwarf donkey t' *get* here on—"

"No excuse," Jodi admonished. "Tresti and I were Shayana mendicants; we came here on our own two feet."

"Beaker, what have you got in the way of arms?" asked someone off on the opposite side of the room; peering through the attic gloom, Beaker could make out that the speaker was a skirmisher he knew vaguely, a Hawk called Vasely.

"One short knife, and my sword," he replied. "And I've got my brigandine under this shirt."

"Get over here and pick out what you want, then. Take whatever you think you can use, we aren't short of anything but swords and body-armor."

Beaker crossed the attic, picking his way among the pallets, and sorted through the piles of arms. Shortly thereafter he was being caught up on the developments by his fellow scouts.

He learned that they hid their faces by day, slipping out only at night to meet in the ballrooms and stableyards of the great lords who had also joined the conspiracy. There they would hear whatever news there was to hear, and practice their skills.

Each night, as the Hawks gathered to spar, Kethry would siphon off the incredibly dangerous energy of their anger and hate. Dangerous, because the energy generated by negative emotions was hard to control—and attracted some very undesirable otherplanar creatures. But it was a potent force, and one Kethry was not going to let go unused. She channeled what she accumulated each night into the dozen trap-spells she was building, one for each of Char's mages. She was beginning to think that she might well be able to carry this off—for despite her brave words to Justin, she had no idea if what she planned was going to work, nor how well. She was just too new at being Adept to be certain exactly what her capabilities were.

"I wish you'd tell me what you're going to do," Jadrek said plaintively. He'd been watching her as she traced through the last of the parchment diagrams, laying in the power she had acquired that night. There were times his patience astounded her still. . . .

"I didn't realize you'd want to know," she replied, sealing the new layer of power in place, and looking up at him with surprise as she finished. "Come around here behind me and have a look, then."

He rose, moved to her right shoulder, and bent over the table with his expression sharp with curiosity. "Well, you *know* I'm not a mage, but I *do* know some of the mage-books—and Keth, what you've been doing doesn't even look remotely familiar."

"You know what a trap-spell is. That's this part." She leaned over the parchment and pointed out the six tiny diagrams encircling the last mage's Name, as he looked over her shoulder with acute interest she could feel without even seeing his face.

"That's just the part that's like a trigger on a physical trap, right?"

"Exactly, except that what will activate the trigger *won't* be something the mage does, but something *I* do—a kind of a mental twist to release the rest of it."

He examined the elaborately inscribed sheet with care, leaning on the back of Kethry's chair, and not touching the page. "That looks familiar enough from my reading—but what's all the rest of this?"

"That's something new, something I put together. There's a mind-magic technique called a 'mirror-egg' that Roald told me about," she said, sitting back. He responded to her movement by beginning to massage her neck as she talked. "It involves surrounding someone with an egg-shaped shield that is absolutely reflective on the inside. It's something you do, he told me, when you've got a projective that refuses to lock his mind-Gift down, or is using it harmfully. Everything he projects after that gets flung straight back into his face—Roald says it's a pretty effective way of teaching someone when admonishment fails."

"I would think so," Jadrek agreed.

"Ah—" his gentle hands hit a particularly tense spot, and Kethry fell silent until he'd gotten the muscles looser. "I thought about it, and it occurred to me that there was no reason why the same kind of thing couldn't be applied to magical energy. So I found a spell to make a mirrored shield, and another to shape a shield into an egg shape, and combined them. That's this bit." She traced the twisted patterns with her finger above the diagram. "When Jiles got here, he agreed to let me throw one on him as a test."

"It worked?"

"Better than either of us had guessed. Scared him white. You see, with most other trap-spells if you have the patience to work your way through it, you can find the keypoint and get yourself loose by cutting it. Not this one—because everything you do reflects back at you. There're only two ways to break this one—from the outside, or to build up such pressure *inside* that the spell can't contain it."

Jadrek pondered that in silence for a moment, while Kethry let her head sag and reveled in the relaxation his hands were leaving in their wake.

"What's to keep the mages from building up that kind of pressure?" he asked at last.

"Nothing—*if* they can. But if they try—and they don't figure out that they're going to have to shield themselves within the shield—they'll fry themselves before they free themselves."

Jadrek spoke slowly, and very quietly. "That—is *not* a nice spell. . .."

"These aren't nice people," Kethry replied, recalling all the soul-searching she'd done before deciding that this *was* the thing to do. "Frankly, if I could call lightnings down on all of them, I would, and take the guilt on my soul. I agree, it isn't a thing one should use lightly, and just before I trigger the traps, I intend to burn the papers. I won't need them any more at that point, and I'd rather that the knowledge didn't get into too many hands just yet."

"And later? How do you keep someone else from finding out how you did it? What if—"

"Gods—Jadrek, love, once a thing's been thought of—it gets out, no matter what. So once this is all over with, I'm going to arrange for the information to be sent to every mage school I know of, and spread it as far and wide as I can."

"What?" Jadrek asked, so aghast that he stopped massaging.

"You can't stop knowledge; you shouldn't try. If you do, half the time it's the wrong people that get it first. So I'm doing the best thing you *can* do with something like this—making sure *everybody* knows about it. That way, if it's used, it will be recognized. Mages trapped inside one of these eggs will realize what's happened and get outside help before they hurt themselves, ones outside will know the counter."

"Oh," he said, resuming what he'd broken off. There was silence for a while as he plainly pondered what she'd said.

One more thing to love about him. He doesn't always agree with me, but he hears me out, and he thinks about what I've said before making up his own mind.

"Huh," he said, when she'd begun to drowse a little under his gentle ministrations. "I guess you're right; if you can't guarantee that something harmful stays out of the wrong hands—"

"And I can't; there's no way."

"Then see that all the right hands get it."

"And that they get the antidote. I don't know that this is all that moral, Jadrek, I only know that the alternative—taking the chance that someone like Zaras figures out what I did *first*—is less moral." She sighed. "I never thought that becoming an Adept would bring all these moral predicaments with it."

He kissed the top of her head. "Keth, power brings with it the need to make moral judgments; history proves that. You have no choice but to make those decisions."

She sighed again, and reached up to lay one of her hands across his where it rested on her shoulder. "I just hope that I always have someone around to keep reminding me when something I'm thinking about doing 'isn't nice.' I may still *do* it—but I'd better have good reasons for doing so."

He squeezed her shoulder, gently. "Don't worry. As long as I'm around, you will."

That's what I hoped you'd say, she thought to herself closing her eyes and leaning back. *That is exactly what I hoped you'd say.*

Twelve

"Tarma—"

Tarma looked up from the maps spread before her to see Jadrek nudging his way into the knot of fighters she was tutoring. She'd had ample time to learn every twist and turn of the maze within the Palace, and she was endeavoring to make sure every person of the secret army knew every corridor and storeroom before the planned coup. She felt a twinge of excitement when she saw that Jadrek's expression was at once tense and anticipatory.

She excused herself and turned her pupils over to Jodi. "What is it?" she asked him quietly, not wanting to raise hopes that might be dashed in the next moment. "You look like you've swallowed a live fish, and you're not certain if you're enjoying the experience."

He raised an eyebrow. "You aren't far wrong; that's about how my stomach is feeling. Stefan's in Petras."

"Warrior's Oath!" She bared her teeth in a feral grin as those nearby glanced at her in startlement. Although they had been planning for this very moment, suddenly *she* felt rather as though the fish was wriggling about in *her* stomach.

"When? How long ago did you make contact? Where is he now?"

"About three candlemarks ago, and he's with Keth at the inn; it seemed the safest place for him."

"All right—this is it. He's here, we're ready. Let

me get Sewen and Ikan, and I'll meet you at Kethry's." She turned on her heel and began making her way across the crowded, dimly lit ballroom. She kept sight of Jadrek as he slipped back out the door, and she noticed that he was slump-shouldered and limping slightly.

Poor devil, he looks like warmed-over death. All this is giving me energy, but it's sapping his. Keth, too. Talk all day, plot all night, spellcast when you aren't plotting—

:Chase one another around the bedroom when you aren't spellcasting—: Warrl broke into her thoughts.

Still at it, are they? Tarma thought at him. *Well, if the liaison has survived this much stress for this long, Keth's right about him being The One. Good. I'd welcome Jadrek as Clanbrother with no reservations. He's the closest thing I've seen since Keth to a Shin'a'in.*

:And he has more sense than both of you put together. You know, he still thinks you don't know about the love affair,: Warrl chuckled. *:Keth hasn't enlightened him. I can't read her as easily as I can him, what with all her mage-shields, so I don't know why she hasn't told him that you knew about it from the first. She might assume he knows you know—or she might be waiting to see how he handles the situation.:*

I suspect the latter, given Keth's devious mind. Hmm. If anyone would know about Jadrek's condition, you would; you're practically in his pocket most of the day. He was limping—how's he doing, physically?

:Extremely well; his bones only bother him when he's very tired, like tonight, or very chilled. Need knows how Kethry worries about him, so Need takes very good care of him.:

Good enough to make the Palace assault with us? We need his knowledge.

:I would judge so. He'll have every fighter of the Hawks watching out for him, after all.:

Hai. He'll probably come out better than the rest of us will. Well—back to business.

She had reached Sewen and Ikan by the end of that mental conversation, which had all taken place in the space of a few heartbeats. They looked up at her approach, and knowing her as well as they did, she reckoned they would have no trouble reading the news in her eyes.

"Time, is it?" Sewen straightened, and rolled up the map they'd been working with.

She nodded. "He's here." No need to say *who* "he" was—not when all they lacked for the past several days to put the plan into motion had been Stefansen's physical presence. "Keth's room. Ready?"

Both nodded; Ikan signaled Justin, who came to take his place, Sewen did the same with the scout Mala. Within moments the three of them, darkly cloaked and moving like shadows through the ill-lit streets, were on their way to Kethry's room.

Warrl, as always, told the others of their approach; Kethry was at the door before they set foot on the staircase, and held it open just enough that they could slip inside.

Jadrek was already there, seated at the table; beside him, looking somehow far more princely than Tarma had remembered, was Stefansen.

It was Stefansen the ruler who rose to greet them; to clasp the hands and shoulders of both Ikan and Sewen with that same ease and frank equality Idra had always shown, and thank them for their presence and help with a sincerity that none of them doubted. The meeting was, in some ways, rather unnerving for Sewen and Ikan; Tarma knew how much like his sister Stefansen looked, but the others hadn't been warned. And in the soft light from their candles the resemblance was even stronger. Tarma could almost hear their thoughts—shock, a touch of chill at the back of the neck—

Then they shook themselves into sense.

Kethry gestured, bringing three more chairs into abrupt existence, as Jadrek unrolled the first of a series of maps on the table. All six of them seated themselves almost simultaneously; Stefansen cleared his throat, and the odd note in the sound caught Tarma's attention—and by the way the other two looked up at him in startlement, Sewen's and Ikan's as well.

"Jadrek has kept me appraised of what's been going on," he said, with a kind of awkward hesitation that he had not displayed before. "So I *know* the reason all you Sunhawks are here. I don't—I don't deal well with emotion, it's hard for me to say things that I feel. But I just want you to know that I—understand. I have half a dozen reasons for wanting to roast Char over a slow fire, and that one is at the top of the list. But I think all of you have a prior claim on his hide. I was never as close to Idra as even the lowliest of her Hawks. So—if it's possible—when this is over, he's yours."

Sewen's eyes lit at those words. "The Hawks thank you for that, Highness—an' I'll tell you true, they'll fight all the better for the knowing of the promise."

"It only seemed fair. . . ." He looked straight into Tarma's eyes, as if asking whether this had been the wise choice. She nodded slightly, and he looked easier.

"Very well, gentlemen, ladies—" he said after a moment of silence. "All the pieces are on the game board. Shall we begin?"

It was Midsummer's Night, and folk in carnival garb thronged the streets. Among the mob of wildly costumed maskers, who would notice six hundred-odd more celebrants?

Who would notice masks on a night of masking? Who would note six hundred-odd sets of phony weaponry among so many thousand tawdry pieces of junk like them? Who would take alarm from another merchant or peasant playing at warrior?

Except that beneath the cheap gilding and pasted-on glass jewels, beneath the paper and the tinsel, the arms and armor of *this* lot was very real.

This was the night of all nights that the rebels had hoped to be able to use—in part because of the ability to move freely, and in part because of one aspect in particular of the Midsummer's Night celebrations of Rethwellan. Though the folk of Petras were mostly long since severed from any direct ties to the farms that formed a good third of Rethwellan's wealth, Midsummer's Night was *still* the night which ensured the fertility of the land. There would be reveling in the streets right up until the stroke of midnight—but *at* midnight, the streets would be deserted. Every man and woman in Petras would be doing his or her level best to prove to the Goddess in Her aspect as Lover that the people of Rethwellan still worshiped Her in all the appropriate ways. *This* Midsummer's Night they would be trying especially hard, because over the past three months the priests of the city had been doing *their* best to encourage exactly that behavior tonight. Some of them had even unbent themselves enough to admit that—on *this one night*—perhaps it didn't altogether worry Her if your partner did not happen to be your lawfully wedded spouse. And that if one felt guilty after being infected with Her sacred desires and fulfilling same—well, for a case of indulgence after Midsummer's Night, penances would be few and light, and forgiveness easily obtained.

For all but six hundred-odd, who would not be fulfilling Her desires as Lover, but as Avenger.

Tarma picked her way through the thinning crowds, still wearing her guise of Arton. It was that guise that was going to give the Hawks the entry to the Palace grounds. From all directions, she knew, the Hawks were converging on the Palace; she would be one of the last to arrive. Kethry was already in place, waiting to spring her trap-spells. If they didn't work, she would be in a position to guide Hawks to the mages to deal with them physically while she kept them occupied magically. If they *did* work, she would be a most welcome addition to their arsenal.

And just in case Char somehow slipped through their fingers—*Warrl?*

:Here, mindmate.:

Got the horses in place?

Warrl's duty was to work with Horsemaster Tindel; the fastest of the Shin'a'in-bred mounts she'd sold Char the year before were to be saddled and kept at the ready, in a cul-de-sac just outside the Palace gate, with Warrl and Tindel guarding them. If Char got away from them, Tarma and the best riders among the Hawks would be hot on his heels—

:Saddled, bridled, and ready to ride.:

:Good. Let's hope we don't have to use them.

:Devoutly.:

Tarma approached one of the side gates, that gave out onto a delivery area. Tonight the gate stood open for the convenience of servants, and the courtyard beyond was dark and deserted. And there was Kethry—still in *her* own disguise, and looking angry enough to bite a board in two. Tarma altered her walk, swaying a little, as if drunk. She was carrying what looked like a jug loosely in her right hand. As it happened, it *wasn't* a jug; it was her sword, magicked with another illusion.

Kethry spotted her; Tarma put a little more of a stagger into her step.

"*There* you are, you *beast!* And drunk as a pig!" she shrilled, to the amusement of the two gate guards.

"J-janna?" Tarma slurred uncertainly, coming to a halt just before the gate.

"Of course it's Janna, you brute! You asked me to meet you here, you sot! I've been waiting for *hours!*"

"Don't you believe her, Arton," snickered the right-hand gate guard. "She ain't been here more'n half a candlemark—an' she showed up with a big blond lad on one arm, too. Reckon she's been playin' more'n one game tonight, eh?"

"You—damned—slut!" Tarma snarled, feigning that she had suddenly gone fighting-drunk. She advanced on Kethry, brandishing the jug. Kethry backed up until she was just inside the gate itself, giving every evidence of genuine and absolute fear. "I'm gonna beat you bloody, you fornicating little bitch!"

Kethry whirled, and threw herself on the left-hand guard, begging his protection, distracting both guards for the crucial moment that it took Tarma to get within arm's length of the right-hand guard.

Then Tarma pivoted, and took her guard out with the pommel of her sword, just as Kethry executed a neat right cross to the point of her target's chin. Both went down without a sound. Within heartbeats the Hawks were swarming the gate—as two of their number, already bespelled into looking like the two guards they were replacing, dragged the bodies into the gatehouse, trussed and gagged them, and took up their stations. The fighters filled the courtyard on the other side, hidden in the dark shadow of the Palace, waiting for Tarma and Kethry to make the next moves.

Kethry stood in frozen immobility for a single moment; sensitized to stirrings of energies by her own status as Kal'enedral, Tarma actually *felt* her spring her trap-spells.

"Well?"

Kethry's eyes met hers with incredulous shock. "They're holding—all of them!"

"Lady with us, then, and let's hope they keep holding. New body, Keth."

"Right," the mage answered, and Tarma waited impatiently as the figure of "Janna" blurred, became a rosy mist, and the mist solidified into a new guise—a very ordinary looking female fighter in the scarlet-and-gold livery of Char's personal guard.

"All right, Hawks," Tarma said, in a low, but carrying voice. "This is it—form up on your leaders—"

She marched up to the unlocked delivery door, Kethry beside her, and pushed it open. The half-drunk guard beyond blinked at her without alarm, and bemusedly; he was one of Char's own personal guards and Tarma (in her guise of Arton) had ordered him to stand duty tonight on this door for a reason. He was one of the men that had participated in the rape and torture of Idra.

She swung once, without a qualm, cutting him down before he had a chance to do more than blink at her. Her only regret was that she had not been able to grant him the lingering death she felt he deserved. She and Kethry hastily dragged his body out of the way; then she waved to the waiting shadows in the court behind her.

And the Sunhawks poured through the door, a flood of vengeance in human shape, a flood which split into many smaller streams—and all of them were deadly.

"No luck," Tarma said flatly, as her group met (as planned) with Stefan's, just outside the corridor leading to the rooms assigned to the unattached ladies of the court. "He wasn't in his quarters, and he wasn't with the mages."

"Nor with any of his current mistresses," Stefansen reported. "That leaves the throne room."

Their combined group, which included Jadrek (who had accompanied Stefan) and both the other Sunhawk mages, now numbered some fifty strong. The new force surged down the pristine white marble of the Great Hall to their goal of the throne room, all of them caught up in battle-fever. The Hawks had met with opposition from Char's fighters, some of it fierce. The bodies lying in pools of spreading scarlet on the snowy marble of the hall were not all wearing Char's livery. Sewen had been hurt, and Ikan. Garth was dead, and more than fifty others Tarma had known only vaguely. But the Hawks had triumphed, even in the pitched battle with the seasoned troupers of Char's army, and all but a handful of those who had murdered their Captain were now making their atonements to her in person.

But among that handful—and the only one as yet uncaught—was Raschar.

Those in the lead shouted as they reached their goal—the great bronze double doors of the throne room—first in triumph, and then in anger, as they attempted to force those doors open. The sculptured doors to the throne room were locked, from the inside.

Justin and Beaker and a half dozen more battered at them—futilely—as the rest came up. Their efforts did not even make the glittering doors tremble.

"Don't bother," Stefansen shouted over the noise, "Those damned doors are a handspan thick. We'll have to try to get in from the garden."

"No we won't," Kethry snarled, audible in her rage even over the frustrated efforts of those still trying to batter their way in. *"Stand back!"*

She raised her hands high over her head, her face a mask of fury, and Tarma felt the surge of power that could only mean she had summoned some of that terrible anger-energy she had channeled away but not used in the trap-spells. This was the best purpose for such energies, Tarma knew—anything destructive would do—

Kethry called out three piercing words, and a bolt of something very like scarlet lightning lanced from her hands to the meeting point of the double doors. There was a smell of hot metal and scorched air, and a crash that shook every ornament in the hall to the floor. The fighters around her cringed and protected their ears from the thunder-shock; the doors rocked, but did not open.

"Fight it down, girl," Tarma cautioned her, and Kethry visibly wrestled her own temper into control; if she lost to it, she had warned Tarma, she would be prey to the stored anger.

Kethry closed her eyes, took three deep breaths, then faced the obstacle again. "Oh no," she told the doors and the spell that was on them, "you don't stop *me* that easily!"

Again she called the lightning, and a third time— and on the fourth, the doors burst off their hinges, and fell inward with a crash that shook the floor, cracked the marble of the walls of the Great Hall, and rained debris down on all their heads from the ceiling. None of which they particularly noticed, as they stormed into the throne room—

To find it empty.

Jadrek cursed, with a command of invective that astounded Kethry, and pointed to where a scarlet and gold tapestry behind the throne flapped in a current of air. "The tunnel—it was walled off years ago—"

"Figures that the little bastard would have it opened up," Stefan spat. "Think, man—where does it come out?"

Jadrek closed his eyes and clenched both hands at his temples, as Kethry tried to will confidence and calm into him. "If the records I studied are right—*and* I remember them right," he said finally, "it exits in the old temple of Ursa, outside the city walls."

Tarma and her chosen riders had already spur around and were sprinting for the door, and Kethry was right behind them. Because she had already laid most of the spell on them, it was child's play to invoke the guises she'd set for just this eventuality— even while pelting down the hall as fast as her legs could carry her. They were exceedingly simple illusions, anyway—not faces, but livery, the scarle and gold livery of Char's personal guards, exactly as the guise *she* wore was garbed.

They didn't have far to run; and Hawks now held the main gate and had forced it open, so there was nothing to bar the path to their allies. As they pounded into the torch-lit court behind the main gate, a dozen Shin'a'in-bred horses, driven by Warrl, and led by Tindel, galloped past that portal. Their iron-shod hooves drew sparks from the stones of the paving, and they tossed their heads as they ran, plainly fresh and eager for an all-out run.

Which was exactly what they were going to get.

As the horses swirled past the Palace door, the Hawks ran to meet them, not bothering to give Tindel the time to bring them to a halt. Instead they mounted on the run, as Tarma had taught them. Even Kethry, the worst rider of all, managed somehow, grabbing pommel and cantle and getting herself in the saddle of the still-cantering gelding she'd singled out without really thinking about what she was doing.

"Where?" Tindel shouted, over the pounding of hooves as they thundered out the gates again, leaving a panting Warrl to collapse behind them. This was no race for *him* and he knew it.

"Temple of Ursa—" Tarma yelled in reply, and Tindel cut anything else she was about to say off with a wave of his hand.

"I know a quicker way," he bellowed.

He urged his gray into the fore, and led them in a mad stampede down crazy, twisting alleys Kethry had never seen before, a good half of which were just packed dirt. Festival gewgaws and dying flowers were pounded to powder as they careened through; once a tiny hawker's cart—thankfully unattended—was knocked over and kicked aside; reduced to splinters as it hit a wall. Kethry's nose was filled with the stench of back-alley middens and trampled garbage; she was splashed with stale water and other liquids best left nameless. Her eyes were dazzled by sudden torchlight that alternated with the abyssal dark valleys between buildings. She got only vague impressions of walls flying past, half-seen openings as they dashed by cross streets; and the pounding of hooves surrounding her throbbed like the pounding of the power at her fingertips.

Then, a startled shout, a wall that loomed high against the stars, and an invisible wall of cooler air and absolute blackness that they plunged through—still without a pause—

Then they were outside the city walls, continuing the insane gallop along the road that led to a handful of old, mostly deserted temples, and beyond that, to Hielmarsh.

The moon was full; it was nearly as bright as day, without a single cloud to obscure the light. The fields and trees before them were washed with silver, and the horses, able now to see where they were going, increased their pace.

Kethry urged her beast up to the front of the herd, until she rode just behind Tarma and Tindel. She gripped her horse with aching knees and tried to see up the road. The temple couldn't be far—not if it was to be reached by a tunnel.

It wasn't. The white marble of a building that could only be the temple in question stood out clearly against the dark shadows of the trees behind it—at this pace, hardly more than a breath or two away.

Just as they came within shouting distance of the temple, moonlight reflecting from a cloud of dust on the road ahead of them told them without words that Char had already started the next stage of his flight. This road led almost directly to Hielmarsh, Kethry knew. He was heading for his little stronghold, or perhaps the mazes of the marsh. There would be *no* pulling him out of there.

But Hielmarsh was hours away, and that dust cloud a few furlongs at most. And *their* horses were Shin'a'in, not much exhausted by the race they'd run so far, scarcely sweating, and still on their first wind.

The little party ahead of them knew they were coming, though, they had to; they had to hear the rolling thunder of two dozen pairs of hooves. They also had to know there was no escaping—

But the Hawks didn't want a pitched battle if they could help it.

The dust was settling, which meant the quarry had turned at bay. Kethry saw Tarma give the signal to pull up as they came within sight of Char and his men. The knot of fighters ahead of them huddled together on the moon-drenched road, swords glinting silver as they held them at ready. Kethry and the rest of the Hawks obeyed their leader, and slowed their horses to a walk.

The King's party numbered almost forty—putting the Hawks at a two-to-one disadvantage if they fought. Tarma's contingency plan, as Kethry knew, called for no such fight. That was the reason for the magical disguises.

"Majesty!" Tarma called, knowing Char would see the Arton he trusted. "Your brother's stormed and taken the Palace; he's holding the city against you. I got what men I could and tried to guess which way you'd be heading."

Raschar dug his spurs into his gelding's sides and rode straight to his "faithful retainer." "Arton!" he cried, panic straining his voice, "Hellfire, I heard you'd gone down at the gates! I have never been so glad to see anybody in my life!"

As he pulled up beside Tarma, Kethry could see his skin was pale and he was sweating, and his eyes were hardly more than black holes in his head.

"Rein in, Majesty; I've got you some help. Here—" she called up at the mixed group of guards and common soldiers still milling about uncertainly up ahead. "—you lot! Get back to the temple! Split yourselves up, I don't much care how. Half of you head back down to hold the road for as long as you can, the rest of you lay a false trail off to Lasleric. Come on, move it out, we haven't got all night!"

There hadn't been a single officer among them, and the mixed contingent was obviously only too happy to find someone willing to issue orders that made *sense*—unlike the frantic babbling of their King.

They obeyed Tarma without a murmur, sending their nervous beasts around the clot of Hawks blocking the road. Within moments they were out of sight, returning back toward the temple and beyond.

Tarma waited until they were completely out of sight before giving Kethry a significant *look.*

Kethry nodded, and dropped the spell of illusion she'd been holding on their company.

Char stared, his jaw sagging, as what appeared to be his guard was revealed as something else entirely.

Then he paled, his face going whiter than the moonlight, as he recognized Tindel, Tarma and Kethry.

"What—" He started to stutter, then drew himself up and took on a kind of nervous dignity. "Just what is this supposed to mean? Who are you? What do you want?"

"You probably haven't heard of us before, your Majesty," Tarma drawled, as two of the Hawks closed in on the King from the rear, coming up on either side. "We're just a common mercenary troop. We go by the name of 'Idra's Sunhawks.' "

When she spoke the name, he choked, and rowled his horse savagely. Too late; the Hawks were already within grabbing distance of his reins. He tried to throw himself to the ground, but other hands caught him, and held him in his saddle until he could be tied there.

"Should take us about three candlemarks to get him back—" Tindel began.

A growl from the ranked fighters behind Tarma interrupted him, and he stopped, looking startled.

"Stefan promised him to us, my friend," Tarma said quietly. "He goes back only when we're finished with him."

"But—"

"We called the Oathbreaking on him," Kethry pointed out. "He's ours by the code, no matter how you look at it."

Tindel looked from face to stubbornly set face, and shrugged. "Well, what do we do with him?"

"Huh. Hadn't thought that far—" Tarma began.

"*I* had," Kethry said, firmly.

There was still a vast reservoir of anger-energy for her to draw on, and while the coercion of innocent spirits was strictly forbidden a White Winds sorceress, the opening of the gates of the other-world to a ghost that had a debt to collect was *not*.

And Idra most certainly had a long, bitter debt owed to her.

"We called Oathbreaking on him—that's a spell, partner. I do believe we ought to see that spell completed."

Tarma looked at her askance; so did the rest of the Hawks. Char, gagged, made choking sounds. "How do you propose to do that? And just what does it mean to see it completed?"

Kethry shifted in her saddle, keeping Char under the tail of her eye. "It only takes the priestess and the mage to complete the spell, and I know how. Jadrek found the rest of it in some of the old histories. As for what it does—it brings all the broken oaths home to roost."

"Does that mean what I *think* it does?"

Kethry nodded, and Tarma smiled, a bloodthirsty grin that sent a chill even up her partner's backbone.

"All right—where?"

"The temple back there will do, I think; all we need is a bit of sanctified ground."

With Char's horse between them, they led the mystified mercenaries toward the white shape of the temple on their backtrail. It was, fortunately, deserted. Kethry did not especially want any witnesses to this besides the principals.

The temple was in a state of extreme disrepair; walls half fallen and crumbling, the pavement beneath their horse's hooves cracked and uneven. Tarma began to look dubious as they penetrated deeper into the complex.

"Are we far enough in, do you think? I don't want to chance one of the horses falling, and maybe breaking a leg if there's any help for it."

"This will do," Kethry judged, reining in her mount, and swinging a little stiffly out of the saddle.

The rest dismounted as well, with several of them swarming the King's mount to pull him roughly to the ground. The horses, eased of their burdens, sighed and stamped a little, pawing at the weathered stone.

"Now what?" Tarma asked.

"Tindel—you and Beaker and Jodi stand here; you three hold Char." She indicated a spot on the pavement in the center of a roughly circular area that was relatively free from debris. "Tarma, you stand South, I'll stand North. The rest of you form a circle with us as the ends."

The Hawks obeyed, still mystified, but willing to trust the judgment of the mage they'd worked so closely with for three years.

"All right—Tarma, just—be Kal'enedral. That's all you need to do. And hold in mind what this bastard has done to our sister and Captain."

"That won't be hard," came the icy voice from across the circle.

Kethry took a deep breath and brought stillness within herself, for everything depended now on creating a channel from herself for the anger of the others. If she let it affect her—it would consume her.

When she thought she was ready, she took a second deep breath, raised her arms, and began.

"Oathbreaker, he stands judged; Oathbreaker to priestess, Oathbreaker to mage, Oathbreaker to true man of his people. Oathbreaker, we found him; Oathbreaker in soul, Oathbreaker in power, Oathbreaker in duty. Oathbreaker, we brought him; Oathbreaker in thought, Oathbreaker in word, Oathbreaker in deed. Oathbreaker, he stands, judged, and condemned—"

She called upon the power she had not yet exhausted, and the rising power within the circle.

"Let the wall of Strength stand between this place and the world—"

As the barrier had been built between herself and the dark mage for the magic duel, so a similar barrier sprang up now; one pole beginning from where she stood, the other from where Tarma was poised. This wall was of a colorless, milky white; it glowed only faintly.

"Let the Pillars of Wisdom stand between this world and the next—"

Mist swirled up out of the ground, just in front of Char and his captors. Kethry could see his eyes bulging in fear, for the mist held a light of its own that augmented the moonlight. The mist formed itself into a column, which then split slowly into two. The two columns moved slowly apart, then solidified into glowing pillars.

"Let the Gate of Judgment open—"

More mist, this time of a strange, bluish cast, billowed in the space between the two Pillars. Kethry felt the energy coursing through her; it was a very strange, almost unnerving feeling. She could see why even an Adept rarely performed this spell more than once in a lifetime—it wasn't just the *amount* of power needed, it was that the mage became only the vessel for the power. It, in a very real sense, was controlling *her*. She spoke aloud the final Word of Opening, then called with thought alone to the mist-shape within the Pillars, and fed it all the last of the Hawks united anger in a great burst of unleashed power.

The mist swirled, billowed—grew dark, then bright, then dark again. It glowed from within, the color a strange silver-blue. Then the mist condensed around the glow, forming a suggestion of a long road, a road under sunlight—and out of the center of the glowing cloud rode Idra.

Char gave a strangled cry, and fell to his knees before the rider. But for the moment she was not looking at *him*.

She was colorless as moonlight, and as solidly real as any of Tarma's *leshya'e-Kal'enedral*. When Kethry had decided to open the Gate, she had faced this moment of seeing Idra's face with a tinge of fear, wondering what she would see there. She feared no longer. The long, lingering gazes Idra bestowed upon each of her "children" were warm, and full of peace. This was no spirit suffering torment—

But the face she turned upon her brother was full of something colder than hate, and more implacable than anger.

"Hello, Char," she said, her voice echoing as from across a vast canyon. "You have a very great deal to answer for."

Tarma led two dozen bone-weary Hawks back into Petras that morning; they made no attempt to conceal themselves, and word that they were coming—and word of what they carried—preceeded them. The streets of Petras cleared before their horses ever set hoof upon them, and they rode through a town that might well have been emptied by some mysterious plague. But eyes were watching them behind closed curtains and sealed shutters; eyes that they could feel on the backs of their necks. There was fear echoing along with the sounds of hoofbeats along those streets. Fear of what the Hawks had done; fear of what else they might do—

By the time they rode in through the gates of the Palace, a nervous crowd had assembled in the court, and Stefansen was waiting on the stairs.

The Hawks pulled up in a semicircle before the new King, still silent but for the sound of their horses' hooves. As the last of the horses moved into place, the last whisper coming from the crowd died, leaving only frightened, ponderous silence, a silence that could almost be weighed and measured.

There was a bloodstained bundle lashed on the back of Raschar's horse, a bundle that Tindel and Tarma removed, carried to the new King's feet, and dropped there without ceremony.

The folds of what had been Char's cloak fell open, revealing what the cloak contained. Stefan, though he had visibly steeled himself, turned pale. There was just about enough left of Raschar to be recognizable.

"This man was sworn Oathbreaker and Outcast," Tarma said harshly, tonelessly. "And he was so sworn by the *full* rites, by a priest, a mage, and an upright man of his own people, all of whom he had wronged, all of whom had suffered irreparable loss at his hands. We claim Mercenary's Justice on him, by the rights of that swearing; we executed that Justice upon him. Who would deny us that right?"

There was only appalled silence from the crowd.

"I confirm it," Stefansen said into the silence, his voice firm, and filling the courtyard. "For not only have I heard from a trusted witness the words of his own mouth, confessing that he dishonored, tortured and slew his own sister, the Lady Idra, Captain of the Sunhawks and Princess of the blood, but I have had the same tale from the servants of his household that we questioned last night. Hear then the tale of Raschar the Oathbreaker."

Tarma stood wearily through the recitation, not really hearing it, although the murmurs and gasps from the crowd behind her told her that Stefan was giving the whole story in all its grimmest details. The mood of the people was shifting to their side, moment by moment.

And now that the whole thing was over, all she wanted to do was rest. The energy that had sustained her all this time was gone.

"Are there *any*," she heard Stefansen cry at last, his voice beaking a little, "who would deny that true justice has been dispensed this day?"

The thunderous *NO!* that followed his question satisfied even Tarma.

Quite a little family party, Tarma thought wryly, surveying the motley individuals draped in various postures of relaxation around the shabby-comfortable library of Stefansen's private suite.

:*Enjoy it while you can,*: Warrl laughed in her mind, :*It won't be too often that you can throw cherry-stones at both a King and a Crown Prince when they tease you.*:

It was only Roald, and he was asking for it—

Stefansen had been officially crowned two days ago, and Roald had arrived as Valdemar's official representative, complete with silver coronet on his blond head—*and* with a full entourage, as well. The time between the night of the rebellion and the day of the coronation had been so hectic that no one had had a chance to hear the full story of the rebellion from either Tarma, Kethry or Jadrek. So Stefansen had decreed today that he was having a secret Council session, had all but kidnapped his chosen party and locked all of them away. Included in the party were himself and Merits; and he had taken care that there was a great deal of food and drink and comfortable seats for all. And once everyone was settled in, he had demanded *all* the tales in their proper order.

The entire "Council" was mostly Sunhawks or ex-Hawks; Sewen and Tresti; Justin and Ikan; Kyra, Beaker and Jodi. Tarma herself, and Kethry, of course. Then the "outsiders"—Tindel, Jadrek, and Roald.

It had taken a long time to get through the whole story—and when Kyra had finished the last of the tales, telling in her matter-of-fact way how Idra had ridden out of the cloud of mist and moonlight, you could have heard a mouse sneeze.

"What I don't understand is how you Hawks took that so calmly," Tindel was saying. "I was as petrified as Char, I swear—but you—it was like she was—real."

"Lad," Beaker said in a kindly tone (to a man at least a decade or two his senior!), "We've ridden with Idra through things you can't imagine; she's stood by us through fear and flood and Hellfire itself. How could we have been afraid of her? She was only dead. It's the *living* we fear."

"And rightly," Justin rumbled into the somber silence that followed Beaker's words. "And speaking of the living, you will never guess who sauntered in two days ago, Shin'a'in."

Tarma shook her head, baffled. She'd been spending most of her free time sleeping.

"Your *dear* friend Leslac."

"Oh *no!*" she choked. "Justin, if I've ever done you any favors, *keep him away from me!*"

"Leslac?" Roald said curiously. "Minstrel, isn't he? Dark hair, swarthy, thin? Popular with women?"

"That's him," groaned Tarma, hiding her face in her hands.

"What's it worth to you," he asked, leaning forward, and wearing a slyly humorous expression, "to get him packed off to Valdemar? Permanently?"

"Choice of Tale'sedrin's herds," she said quickly, "Three mares and a stallion, and anything but battlesteeds."

"Four mares, and one of them sworn to be in-foal."

"Done, done, done!" she replied, waving her hands frantically.

"Stefan, old friend," Roald said, turning to the King, "Is it worth an in-foal Shin'a'in mare to force a swordpoint marriage by royal decree on one motheaten Bard?" Roald's face was sober, but his eyes danced with laughter.

"For that, I'd force a swordpoint marriage on Tindel!" Stefansen chuckled. "Who's the lucky lady?"

"Countess Reine. She's actually a rather sweet old biddy, unlike her harridan sister, who is—thank the gods!—no longer with us. I'm rather fond of her, for all that she hasn't the sense of a new-hatched chick." Roald shook his head, and sighed. "A few years back, her sister went mad during a storm and killed herself. Or so it's said, and nobody wants to find out otherwise. I'm supposed to be keeping an eye on her, to keep her out of trouble."

"How delightful."

"Oh, it isn't too bad; she just has this ability to attract men who want to prey on her sensibilities. They are, of course, all of honorable intent."

"Of course," said Stefan, solemnly.

"Well, Leslac seems to be another of the same sort. It's common knowledge in my entourage that the poor dear is absolutely head over heels with him. *And* his music. He, naturally, has been languishing at her feet, accepting her presents, and swearing undying love when no one else is around, I don't doubt. I can see it coming now; he figures that when I find out, I'll confront him—he'll vow he isn't worthy of her, being lowborn and all, I'll agree, and he'll get paid off. But *I* actually have no objection to lowborn-highborn marriages; I expect Reine's family will be only too happy to see the end f the stream of vultures that's been preying on er, and I can see a way of doing two friends a avor here. I'm certain that the threat of royal displeasure if he makes Reine unhappy will keep the wandering fancy in line once I get him back with ne."

"I," Tarma said fervently, "will be your devoted slave for the rest of your life. Both of you."

Stefan shook his head at her. "I owe you too much, Tarma, and if this will really make you happy—"

"It will! Trust me, it will!"

"Consider it ordered, Roald. Now I have a question for you two fellow-conspirators over there. What can *I* do for *you*?"

"If you're serious—" Kethry began.

"Totally. Anything short of being crowned; unless the Sword sings for you, even I can't manage that. Titles? Lands? Wealth—I can't quite supply; Char made too many inroads in the Treasury, but—"

"For years we have wanted to found a joint school," Kethry said, slowly. " 'Want' is actually too mild a word. By the edicts of my own mage school, now that I'm an Adept I just about *have* to start a branch of the White Winds school. What we need, really, is a place with a big enough building to house our students and teachers, and enough lands to support it. But that kind of property isn't easily come by."

"Because it's usually in the hands of nobles or clergy. I'm disappointed," Stefan said with a grin, "I thought you'd want something *hard*. One of Char's hereditary holdings was a fine estate down in the south, near the border—a large manorhouse, a village of its own, and an able staff to maintain it. It is, by the by, where I was supposed to end my days in debauchery. It has an indoor riding arena attached to the stable because Char hated to ride when it rained, it has a truly amazing library; why it even has a *professional* salle, because the original

275

builder was a notable fighter. Is that just about what you're looking for?''

Tarma had felt her jaw dropping with every word until, when Stefan glanced over at her with a sly smile and a broad wink, she was unable to get her voice to work.

Kethry answered for her. "Windborn—gods, *yes*. I—Stefan, would you *really* give it to us?''

"Well, since the property of traitors becomes property of the crown, and since *I* have some very unpleasant memories of the place—Lady Bright, I'm only too pleased that you want it! Just pay your taxes promptly, that's all I ask!''

Tarma tried to thank him, but her voice still wouldn't work. Kethry made up for her—leaping out of her chair and giving the King a most disrespectful hug and kiss, both of which he seemed to enjoy immensely.

"Furthermore, I'll be sending my offspring of both sexes to you for training," he continued. "If nothing else, I want them to have the discipline of a good swordmaster, something I didn't have. Maybe that will keep them from being the kind of brat I was. This will probably scandalize my nobles—''

"Oh, it will, lover," Mertis laughed, "But I agree with the notion. It will do the children good.''

"Then my nobles will have to live with being scandalized. Now, I want the rest of you to decide what you'd like," he said when Kethry had resumed her seat, but not her calm. "Because I'm going to do my best by all of you. But right now I fear I *do* have a Council session, and there are a lot of unpleasant messes Char left behind him that need attending to.''

Stefan rose, and gave his hand to Mertis, and the two exited gracefully from the library. The rest clustered around Tarma and her partner, congratulating them—

All but Jadrek, who had inexplicably vanished.

*   *   *

The partners made their weary way to their rooms. It had been a long day, but for Tarma, a very happy one

But Kethry was preoccupied—and a little disturbed, Tarma could sense it without any special effort.

"Keth?" she asked, finally, "What's stuck in your craw?"

"'It's a Jadrek. He hasn't said anything or come near me since the night of the rebellion." She turned troubled and unhappy eyes on her partner. "I don't know why; I *thought* he loved me—I *know* I love him. And this afternoon—just disappearing like that—"

"Well, we're official now. He's reverting to courtly manners. You don't go sneaking around to a lady's room; you treat her with respect."

"Courtly manners be hanged!" Kethry snapped. "Dammit Tarma, we'll be gone soon! Doesn't he care? If he doesn't say something—"

"Then you'll hit him over the head and carry him off, like the uncivlized barbarian mercenary I know you are. And I'll help."

Kethry started laughing at that. "I hate to tell you this, but that's exactly what I've been contemplating."

"Go make wish-lists of things you think you'll be needing for this new school of ours," Tarma advised her. "That should keep your mind occupied. I have the feeling this is going to sort itself out before long."

She parted company with her *she'enedra* at Kethry's door. They had rooms inside the royal complex now, not in the visitors area. Stefansen was treating them as *very* honored guests.

She knew she wasn't alone the moment she closed the door behind her. She also knew who it was—*without* Warrl's helpful hint of : *It's Jadrek. I let him in. He wants to talk:*

"Tarma—"

"Hello, Jadrek," she said calmly, lighting a candle beside the door before turning around to face him. "We haven't been seeing a lot of you; we've missed you."

"I've been thinking," he said awkwardly. "I—"

She crossed her arms, and waited for him to continue. He straightened his back and lifted his chin. "Tarma shena Tale'sedrin," he said, with all the earnest solemnity of a high priest, "Have I your permission to pay my court to your oathsister?"

She raised an eyebrow. "Can you give me a good reason why I should?"

Her question wilted him. He sat down abruptly, obviously struggling for words. "I—Tarma, I *love* her, I really do. I love her too much to just play with her, I want something formal binding us, something—in keeping with her honor. She's lovely, you know that as well as I do, but it isn't just her exterior I care for, it's her *mind*. She challenges me, like nobody I've ever known before. We're equals—I want to be her partner, not—not a—I don't know, I want to have something like Mertis and Stefan have, and I *know* we'll give each other that! I want to help you with your schools, too. I think it's a wonderful dream and I want to make it real, and work alongside of both of you to make it more than a dream."

"We're something more than partners, she and I," Tarma reminded him. "There's certain things between us that will affect any children Kethry may have."

"I took the liberty of asking Warrl about that," he said, blushing. "I don't have any problem with—children. With them being raised Tale'sedrin. Everything I know about the Shin'a'in, everything I've learned in working with you—I would be very, very proud if you considered my blood good enough to flow into the Clans. Tarma, this is probably going to sound stupid, but I've come to—love—you. You've done so much *for* me, more than you guess. What I *really* want is that what we've built with the three of us in the last few months should endure—the friendship, the love, the partnership. I never had that before—and I'd do anything right now to prevent losing either of you."

Tarma looked into his pleading eyes—and much to his evident shock *and* delight, she took both his hands, pulled him up out of his chair into her arms, hugged him just short of breaking his ribs, and planted a kiss squarely in the middle of his forehead before letting him go again.

"Well, outClan *brother*," she laughed, "while I can't speak for the lady, I would suggest you trot next door and ask her for her hand yourself—because I *do* know that if you don't, you're going to find yourself trussed hand and foot and lying over Hellsbane's rump like so much baggage. You see, *we* happen to be barbarians, and we *will* do anything to prevent losing *you. He shala?*"

His mouth worked for a moment, as he stared at her, his eyes brightening with what Tarma suspected were tears of joy. Then he took her face in both his hands, kissed *her,* and ran out her door as if joy had put wings on his back.

"Better get Stefan to pick your successor," she called after him. "Because we're going to keep you *much* too busy to putter about in his Archives."

And so they did.

Appendix One

Dictionary of Shin'a'in Terms

PRONUNCIATION:

' : glottal stop, a pause, but not quite as long a pause as between two words
ai: as in air
ay: long "a" as in way
ah: soft "a" as in ah
ee: long "e" as in feet
ear: as in fear
e: as in fend
i: long "i" as in violent
oh: long "o" as in moat
oo: as in boot

corthu: (cohr-thoo)—one being
dester'edre: (destair ay-dhray)—wind(born) sibling
dhon: (dthohn)—very much
du'dera: (doo dearah)—(I) give (you) comfort
for'shava: (fohr shahvah)—very, very good
get'ke: (get kay)—(could you) explain
gestena: (gestaynah)—thank you
hai: (hi)—yes
hai shala: (hi shahlah)—do you understand?
hai'she'li: (hi she lee)—surprised "yes," literally "yes, I swear!"
hai'vetha: (hi vethah)—yes, (be) running
her'y: (hear ee)—(is this not) the truth
isda: (eesdah)—have you (ever) seen (such)
jel'enedra: (jel enaydrah)—little sister

jel'sutho'edrin: (jel soothoh aydthrin)—"forever younger siblings," usually refers to horses

jostumal: (johstoomahl)—enemy, literally, "one desiring (your) blood"

kadessa: (kahdessah)—rodent of the Dhorisha Plains

Kal'enedral: (kahl enaydhrahl)—Her sword-brothers or Her swordchildren

Kal'enel: (kahl enel)—the Warrior aspect of the four-faced Goddess, literally, "Sword of the Stars." Also called Enelve'astre (Star-Eyed) and Da'gretha (Warrior).

kathal: (kahthahl)—go gently

kele: (kaylay)—(go) onward

kestra: (kestrah)—a casual friend

krethes: (kraythes)—speculation

kulath: (koolahht)—go find

leshya'e: (layshee-ah ee)—spirit; *not* a vengeful, earthbound ghost, but a helpful spirit

Liha'irden: (leehah eardhren)—deer-footed

li'ha'eer: (lee hah eeahr)—exclamation, literally, "by the gods"

li'sa'eer: (lee sah eeahr)—exclamation of extreme surprise, literally "by the highest gods!"

nes: (nes)—bad

nos: (nohs)—it is

pretera: (praytearah)—grasscat

sadullos: (sahdoolohs)—safer

se: (sy)—is/are

she'chorne: (shay chornah)—homosexual; does not have negative connotations among the Shin'a'in.

she'enedra: (shay enaydrah)—sister by blood-oathing

sheka: (shaykah)—horse droppings

shena: (shaynah)—of the Clan, literally 'of the brotherhood'

shesti: (shestee)—nonsense

Shin'a'in: (shin ay in)—the people of the plains

so'trekoth: (soh traykoth)—fool who will believe anything, literally, "gape-mouthed hatchling"

staven: (stahven)—water

Tale'edras: (tahle aydhrahs)—Hawkbrothers, a race who may or may not be related to the Shin'a'in, living in the Pelagiris Forest

Tale'sedrin: (tahle saydhrin)—children of the hawk

te'sorthene: (tay sohrthayne)—heart-friend, spirit-friend

Vai datha: (vi dahthah)—expression of resignation or agreement, literally "there are many ways."

var'athanda: (vahr ahthahndah)—to be forgetful of

ves'tacha: (ves tahchah)—beloved one

vysaka: (visahkah)—the spiritual bond between the Kal'enedral and the Warrior; its presence can actually be detected by an Adept, another Kalenedral, and the Kal'enedral him/herself. It is this bond which creates the "shielding" that makes Kal'enedral celibate/neuter and somewhat immune to magic.

vyusher: (vi-ooshear)—wolf

yai: (yi)—two

yuthi'so'coro: (yoothee soh cohr-oh)—road courtesy; the rules Shin'a'in follow when traveling on a public road.

Appendix Two

Songs and Poems

SUFFER THE CHILDREN
(Tarma: *Oathbreakers*)

These are the hands that wield a sword
With trained and practiced skill;
These are the hands, and this the mind,
Both honed and backed by will.
Death is my partner, blood my trade,
And war my passion wild—
But these are the hands that also ache
To hold a tiny child.

CH: Suffer, they suffer, the children,
      When I see them, gods, how my heart breaks!
      It is ever and always the children
      Who will pay for their parents' mistakes.

Somehow they know that I'm a friend—
I see it in their eyes,
Somehow they sense a kindly heart—
So young, so very wise.
Mine are the hands that maim and kill—
But children never care.
They only know my hands are strong
And comfort is found there.

Little enough that I can do
To shield the young from pain—
Not while their parents fight and die
For land, or goods, or gain.
All I can do is give them love—
All I can do is strive
To teach them enough of my poor skill
To help them stay alive.

OATHBREAKERS

CH: Cursed Oathbreakers, your honor's in pawn
   And worthless the vows you have made—
   Justice shall see you where others have gone,
   Delivered to those you betrayed!

These are the signs of a mage that's forsworn—
The True Gifts gone dead in his hand,
Magic corrupted and discipline torn,
Shifting heart like shifting sand;
Swift to allow any passion to run,
Given to hatred and rage.
Give him wide berth and his company shun—
For darkness devours the Dark Mage.

These are the signs of a traitor in war—
Wealth from no visible source,
Shunning old comrades he welcomed before,
Holding to no steady course.
If you uncover the one who'd betray,
Heed not his words nor his pen.
Give him no second chance—drive him away—
False once will prove false again.

These are the signs of the treacherous priest—
Pleasure in anyone's pain,
Abuse or degrading of man or of beast,
Duty as second to gain,
Preaching belief but with none of his own,
Twisting all that he controls.
Fear him and never face him all alone,
He corrupts innocent souls.

These are the signs of the king honor-broke—
Pride coming first over all,
Treading the backs and the necks of his folk
That he alone might stand tall,
Giving himself to desires that are base,
Tyrannous, cunning, and cruel.
Bring him down—set someone else in his place.
Such men are not fit to rule.

ADVICE TO YOUNG MAGICIANS
(Kethry)

The firebird knows your anger
And the firebird feels your fear,
For your passions will attract her
And your feelings draw her near.
But the negative emotions
Only make her flame and fly.
You must rule your heart, magician,
Or by her bright wings you die.

Now the cold-drake lives in silence
And he feeds on dark despair
Where the shadows fall the bleakest
You will find the cold-drake there.
For he seeks to chill your spirit
And to lure you down to death.
Learn to rule your soul, magician,
Ere you dare the cold-drake's breath.

And the griffon is a proud beast
He's the master of the sky.
And no one forgets the sight
Who has seen the griffon fly.
But his will is formed in magic
And not mortal flesh and bone
And if you would rule the griffon
You must first control your own.

The *kyree* is a creature
With a soul both old and wise

You must never think to fool him
For he sees through all disguise.
If you seek to call a *kyree*
All your secrets he shall plumb—
So be certain you are worthy
Or the *kyree*—will not come.

For your own heart you must conquer
If the firebird you would call
You must know the dark within you
Ere you seek the cold-drake's hall
Here is better rede, magician
Than those books upon your shelf—
If you seek to master others
You must master first yourself.

OATHBOUND

(*The Oathbound*, Tarma & Kethry)

CH: Bonds of blood and bonds of steel
Bonds of god-fire and of need,
Bonds that only we two feel
Bonds of word and bonds of deed,
Bonds we took—and knew the cost
Bonds we swore without mistake
Bonds that give more than we lost,
Bonds that grant more than they take.

Tarma:

Kal'enedral, Sword-Sworn, I,
To my Star-Eyed Goddess bound,
With my pledge would vengeance buy
But far more than vengeance found.
Now with steel and iron will
Serve my Lady and my Clan
All my pleasure in my skill—
Nevermore with any man.

Kethry:

Bound am I by my own will
Never to misuse my power—
Never to pervert my skill
To the pleasures of an hour.
With this blade that I now wear
Came another bond indeed—
While her arcane gifts I share
I am bound to woman's Need.

Tarma:

And by blood-oath we are bound
Held by more than mortal bands
For the vow we swore was crowned
By god-fires upon our hands.

Kethry:

You are more than shield-sib now
We are bound, and yet are free
So I make one final vow—
That your Clan shall live through me.

ADVICE TO WOULD-BE HEROES
(Tarma)

So you want to go earning your keep with your
    sword
And you think it cannot be too hard—
And you dream of becoming a hero or lord
With your praises sung out by some bard.
Well now, let me then venture to give you advice
And when all of my lecture is done
We will see if my words have not made you
    think twice
About whether adventuring's "fun!"

Now before you seek shelter or food for yourself
Go seek first for those things for your beast
For he is worth far more than praises or pelf
Though a fool thinks to value him least.
If you've ever a moment at leisure to spare
Then devote it, as if to your god,
To his grooming, and practice, and weapons-repair
And to seeing you both are well-shod.

Eat you lightly and sparingly—never full-fed—
For a full belly founders your mind.
Ah, but sleep when you can—it is better than
    bread—
For on night-watch no rest will you find.
Do not boast of your skill, for there's always one
    more
Who would prove he is better than you.
Treat swordladies like sisters, and not like a whore
Or your wenching days, child, will be few.

When you look for a captain, then look for the man

Who thinks first of his men and their beasts,
And who listens to scouts, and has more than
   one plan,
And heeds not overmuch to the priests.
And if you become captain, when choosing your
   men
Do not look at the "heroes" at all.
For a hero dies young—rather choose yourself ten
Or a dozen whose pride's not so tall.

Now your Swordmaster's god—whosoever he be—
When he stands there before you to teach
And don't argue or whine, think to mock foolishly
Or you'll soon be consulting a leech!
Now most booty is taken by generals and kings
And there's little that's left for the low
So it's best that you learn skills, or work at odd
   things
To keep food in your mouth as you go.

And last, if you should chance to reach equal my
   years
You must find you a new kind of trade
For the plea that you're still spry will fall on
   deaf ears—
There's no work for old swords, I'm afraid.
Now if all that I've told you has not changed
   your mind
Then I'll teach you as best as I can.
For you're stubborn, like me, and like me of the
   kind
Becomes one *fine* swords-woman or -man!

THE PRICE OF COMMAND
(Captain Idra)

This is the price of commanding—
That you always stand alone,
Letting no one near
To see the fear
That's behind the mask you've grown.
This is the price of commanding.

This is the price of commanding—
That you watch your dearest die,
Sending women and men
To fight again,
And you never tell them why.
This is the price of commanding.

This is the price of commanding,
That mistakes are signed in red—
And that *you* won't pay
But others may,
And your best may wind up dead.
This is the price of commanding.

This is the price of commanding—
All the deaths that haunt your sleep.
And you hope they forgive
And so you live
With your memories buried deep.
This is the price of commanding.

This is the price of commanding—
That if you won't, others will.
So you take your post,
Mindful of each ghost—
You've a debt to them to fill.
This is the price of commanding.

THE ARCHIVIST
(Jadrek)

I sit amid the dusty books. The dust invades my
  very soul.
It coats my heart with weariness and chokes it
  with despair.
My life lies beached and withered on a lonely,
  bleak, uncharted shoal.
There are no kindred spirits here to understand,
  or care.

When I was young, how often I would feed my
  hungry mind with tales
And sought the fellowship in books I did not
  find in kin.
For one does not seek friends when every over-
  ture to others fails
So all the company I craved I built from dreams
  within.

Those dreams—from all my books of lore I plucked
  the wonders one by one
And waited for the day that I was certain was to
  come
When some new hero would appear whose quest
  had only now begun
With desperate need of lore and wisdom I alone
  could plumb.

And then, ah then, I'd ride away to join with
  legend and with song.
The trusted friend of heroes, figured in their
  words and deeds.

Until that day, among the books I'd dwell—but
have dwelt too long
And like the books I sit alone, a relic no one
needs.

I grow too old, I grow too old, my aching bones
have made me lame
And if my futile dream came true, I could not
live it now.
The time is past, long past, when I could ride
the wings of fleeting fame
The dream is dead beneath the dust, as 'neath
the dust I bow.

So, unregarded and alone I tend these fragment
of the past
Poor fool who bartered life and soul on dreams
and useless lore.
And as I watch despair and bitterness enclose
my heart at last
Within my soul's dark night I cry out, "Is there
nothing more?"

LIZARD DREAMS
(Kethry: *Oathbound*)

Most folk avoid the Pelagir Hills, where ancient
    wars and battles
Were fought with magic, not with steel, for land
    and gold and chattels.
Most folk avoid the forest dark for magics still
    surround it
And change the creatures living there and all
    that dwell around it.
Within a tree upon a hill that glowed at night
    with magic
There lived a lizard named Gervase whose life
    was rather tragic.
His heart was brave, his mind was wise. He
    longed to be a wizard.
But who would ever think to teach their magic
    to a lizard?

So poor Gervase would sit and dream, or sigh as
    sadly rueing
That fate kept him forever barred from good he
    could be doing.
That he had wit and mind and will it cannot be
    debated
He also had the kindest heart that ever gods
    created.
One day as Gervase sighed and dreamed all in
    the forest sunning
He heard a noise of horse and hound and sounds
    of two feet running.
A human stumbled to his glade, a human worn
    and weary

Dressed in a shredded wizard's robe, his eyes
    past hope and dreary.

The magic of his birthplace gave Gervase the
    gift of speaking.
He hesitated not at all—ran to the wizard,
    squeaking,
"Hide human, hide! Hide in my tree!" he danced
    and pointed madly.
The wizard stared, the wizard gasped, then hid
    himself right gladly.
Gervase at once lay in the sun until the hunt
    came by him
Then like a simple lizard now he fled as they
    came nigh him.
And glowered in the hollow tree and hissed when
    they came near him
And bit a few dogs' noses so they'd yelp and leap
    and fear him.

"Thrice damn that wizard!" snarled his foe. "He's
    slipped our hunters neatly.
The hounds have surely been misled. They've
    lost the trail completely."
He whipped the the dogs off of the tree and sent
    them homeward running
And never once suspected it was all Gervase's
    cunning.
The wizard out of hiding crept. "Thrice blessing
    I accord you!
And is there somehow any way I can at all re-
    ward you?"
"I want to be a man like you!" Gervase replied
    unthinking.
"A wizard—or a man?" replied the mage who
    stared, unblinking.

"For I can only grant you one, the form of man,
    or power.
What will you choose? Choose wisely, I must
    leave within the hour."

Gervase in silence sat and thought, his mind in
  turmoil churning.
And first the one choice thinking on, then to the
  other turning.
Yes, he could have the power he craved, the
  magic of a wizard
But who'd believe that power lived inside a lowly
  lizard?
Or he could have the form of man, but what
  could he do in it?
And all the good he craved to do—how then
  could he begin it?

Within the Councils of the Wise there sits a
  welcome stranger
His word is sought by high and low if there is
  need or danger.
He gives his aid to all who ask, who need one to
  defend them
And every helpless creature knows he lives but
  to befriend them.
And though his form is very strange compared
  to those beside him
The mages care not for the form, but for the
  mind inside him.
For though he's small, and brightly scaled, they
  do not see a lizard.
He's called by all, both great and small, "Gervase,
  the Noble Wizard."
He's known by all, both great and small, Gervase
  the Lizard Wizard!

LOVERS UNTRUE
(Tarma: "Swordsworn")

"I shall love you till I die!"
Talasar and Dera cry.
He swears "On my life I vow
Only death could part us now!"
She says "You are life and breath
Nothing severs us but Death!"
Lightly taken, lightly spoke,
Easy vows are easy broke.

"Come and ride awhile with me,"
Talasar says to Varee,
"Look, the moon is rising high,
Countless stars bestrew the sky.
Come, or all the hours are flown
It's no night to lie alone."
This the one who lately cried
That he'd love until he died.

"Kevin, do you think me fair?"
Dera smiles, shakes back her hair.
"I have long admired you—
Come, the night is young and new
And the wind is growing cold—
I would see if you are bold—"
Is this she who vowed till death
Talasar was life and breath?

Comes the dawn—beneath a tree
Talasar lies with Varee.
But look—who should now draw near—

Dera and her Kevin-dear
He sees her—and she sees him—
Oh confusion! Silence grim!
Till he sighs, and shakes his head—(pregnant
  pause)
"Well, I guess we must be dead!"

THE LESLAC VERSION
(Leslac and Tarma)

Leslac: The warrior and the sorceress rode into
      Viden-town
      For they had heard of evil there and
      meant to bring it down
      An overlord with iron hand who ruled his
      folk with fear—

Tarma: Bartender, shut that minstrel up and
      bring another beer.

L: The warrior and the sorceress went search-
    ing high and low

T: That isn't true, I tell you, and I think that I
    should know!

L: They meant to find the tyrant who'd betrayed
    his people's trust
    And bring the monster's power and pride to
    tumble in the dust.

L: They searched through all the town to find
    and bring him to defeat.

T: Like Hell! What we were looking for was wine
    and bread and meat!

L: They found him in the tavern and they chal-
    lenged him to fight.

T: We found him holding up the bar, drunk as
    a pig, that night.

L: The tyrant laughed and mocked at them, with
    vile words and base.

T: He tripped on Warrl's tail, then took excep-
    tion to my face.

L: The warrior was too wise for him; his blade
    clove only air!

T: He swung, I ducked, he lunged—and then he
   tripped over a chair.

L: With but a single blow the warrior brought
   him to his doom!

T: About that time he turned around—I got him
   with a broom.

L: And in a breath the deed was done! The
   tyrant-lord lay dead!

T: I didn't *mean* for him to hit the fire iron with
   his head!

L: The wife that he had kept shut up they
   freed and set on high
   And Viden-town beneath her hand content-
   edly did lie.

T: I went to find his next-of-kin and to the girl
   confess—
   "Your husband wasn't much before, but now
   he's rather less—"

T: "He was a drunken sot, and I'll be better
   off," she said.
   "And while I can't admit it, I'm not sorry
   that he's dead.
   So here's a little something—but you'd best
   be on your way—
   I'll claim it was an accident if you'll just
   leave today."

L: In triumph out of Viden-town the partners
   rode again
   To find another tyrant and to clean him
   from his den—
   The scourge of evil and the answer to a desperate prayer!"

T: Don't you believe a word of it—I *know*, 'cause
   I was there!

WIND'S FOUR QUARTERS
(Tarma: "Swordsworn")

CH: Wind's four quarters, air and fire
Earth and water, hear my desire
Grant my plea who stands alone—
Maiden, Warrior, Mother and Crone.

Eastern wind blow clear, blow clean,
Cleanse my body of its pain,
Cleanse my mind of what I've seen,
Cleanse my honor of its stain.
Maid whose love has never ceased
Bring me healing from the East.

Southern wind blow hot, blow hard,
Fan my courage to a flame,
Southern wind be guide and guard,
Add your bravery to my name.
Let my will and yours be twinned,
Warrior of the Southern wind.

Western wind, stark, blow strong,
Grant me arm and mind of steel
On a road both hard and long.
Mother, hear me where I kneel.
Let no weakness on my quest
Hinder me, wind of the West.

Northern wind blow cruel, blow cold,
Sheathe my aching heart in ice,

Armor 'round my soul enfold.
Crone I need not call you twice.
To my foes bring the cold of death!
Chill me, North wind's frozen breath.

THE SWORDLADY, OR:
"THAT SONG"
(Leslac)

Swordlady, valiant, no matter the foe,
Into the battle you fearlessly go—
Boldly you ride out beyond map and chart—
Why are you frightened to open your heart?

Swordlady, lady of consummate skill,
Lady of prowess, of strength and of will,
Swordlady, lady of cold ice and steel,
Why will you never admit that you feel?

Swordlady, mistress of all arts of war,
Wise in the ways of all strategic lore,
You fear no creature below or above,
Why do you shrink from the soft touch of love?

Swordlady, brave to endure wounds and pain,
Plunging through lightning, through thunder and
    rain,
Flinching from nothing, so high is your pride,
Why then pretend you hold nothing inside?

Swordlady, somewhere within you is hid
A creature of feeling that no vow can rid,
A woman—a girl, with a heart soft and warm,
No matter the brutal deeds that you perform.

Swordlady, somewhere inside of you deep,
Cowers the maiden that you think asleep,
Frozen within you, in ice shrouded womb
That you can only pretend is a tomb.

Swordlady, all of the vows you have made

Can never make your heart die as you've bade.
Swordlady, after the winter comes spring;
One day your heart will awaken and sing.

Swordlady, one day there must come a man
Who shall lift from you this self-imposed ban,
Thawing the ice that's enshrouded your soul,
On that day swordlady, you shall be whole.

SHIN'A'IN WARSONG

(The old tradition holds that the Shin'a'in—now forty-odd Clans in all—originally came from four: the Tale'sedrin (Children of the Hawk), the Liha'-irden (Deer-sibs), the Vuysher'edras (Brothers of the Wolves), and the Pretera'sedrin (the Children of the Grasscats). Hence the monumental seriousness of the threat of declaring Tale'sedrin a dead Clan in *Oathbound*.)

Gold the dawn-sun spreads his wings—
Follow where the East-wind sings,
Brothers, sisters, side by side,
To defend our home we ride!

Eyes of Hawks the borders see—
Watchers, guard it carefully
Let no stranger pass it by—
Children of the Hawk, now fly!

CH: Maiden, Warrior, Mother, Crone,
     Help us keep this land our own.
     Rover, Guardian, Hunter, Guide,
     With us now forever ride.

Speed of deer, oh grant to these—
Swift to warn of enemies,
Fleeter far than any foe—
Deer-child, to the border go!

Cunning as the Wolf-pack now,
To no overlord we bow!

Lest some lord our freedom blight,
Brothers of the Wolves, we fight!

Brave, the great Cat guards his lair,
Teeth to rend and claws to tear.
Lead the battle, first to last,
Children of the Cat, hold fast!

Hawk and Cat, and Wolf and Deer,
Keep the plains now safe from fear,
Brothers, sisters, side by side,
To defend our home, we ride!

SHIN'A'IN SONG
OF THE SEASONS

(Although Tarma seldom mentioned the fact, her
people have a four-aspected male deity to compliment the female. This song gives Him equal time
with Her.)

The East wind is calling, so come ride away,
Come follow the Rover into the new day,
Come follow the Maiden, the Dark Moon, with
    me,
The new year's beginning, come ride out and see.

Come follow the Rover out onto the plains,
Come greet the new life under sweet, singing
    rains,
Come follow the Maiden beneath vernal showers,
For where her feet passed you will find fra-
    grant flowers.

The South wind, oh hear it, we ride to the call
We follow the Guardian, the Lord of us all,
We follow the Warrior, the strong to defend,
The New Moon to fighters is ever a friend.

With summer comes fighting, with summer, our
    foes;
And how we must thwart them the Guardian
    knows.
The Warrior will give them no path but retreat,
The Warrior and Guardian will bring their defeat.

Come follow the West wind, the wind of the
    fall,

The Mother will cast her cloak over us all.
Come follow the Hunter out onto the plain,
Return to the Clan with the prey we have slain.

For now comes the autumn, the time of the
  West,
The season of Full Moon, of harvest, then rest.
So take from Her hands all the fruits of the
  fields,
And thank Him for all that the autumn-hunt
  yields.

The North wind, the cold wind, the wind of the
  snow,
Tells us, it is time winter pastures to go.
The Guide knows the path, and the Crone shows
  us how—
The Old Moon, and time for returning is now.

And if, with the winter, should come the last
  breath,
And riding, we ride out of life into death,
The Wise One, the Old Moon, will ease our last
  load,
The Guide will be waiting to show the new road.

THREES

(Leslac)

Deep into the stony hills, miles from keep or
  hold
A troupe of guards comes riding with a lady and
  her gold—
Riding in the center shrouded in her cloak of fur,
Companioned by a maiden and a toothless, aged
  cur.
Three things see no end, a flower blighted ere it
  bloomed,
A message that was wasted, and a journey that
  is doomed.

One among the guardsmen has a shifting, rest-
  less eye,
And as they ride he scans the hills that rise
  against the sky.
He wears both sword and bracelet worth more
  than he can afford,
And hidden in his baggage is a heavy, secret
  hoard.
Of three things be wary, of a feather on a cat,
The shepherd eating mutton and the guardsman
  that is fat.

From ambush, bandits screaming charge the
  packtrain and its prize,
And all but four within the train are taken by
  surprise,
And all but four are cut down as a woodsman
  fells a log,

The guardsman, and the lady, and the maiden,
   and the dog,
Three things know a secret—first, the lady in a
   dream,
The dog that barks no warning and the maid who
   does not scream.

Then off the lady pulls her cloak, in armor she
   is clad,
Her sword is out and ready, and her eyes are
   fierce and glad.
The maiden gestures briefly and the dog's a cur
   no more—
A wolf, sword-maid and sorceress now face the
   bandit corps!
Three things never anger or you will not live for
   long,
A wolf with cubs, a man with power and a woman's sense of wrong.

The bandits growl a challenge and the lady only
   grins,
The sorceress bows mockingly, and then the fight
   begins!
When it ends there are but four left standing
   from that horde
The witch, the wolf, the traitor, and the woman
   with the sword!
Three things never trust in, the maiden sworn
   as "pure,"
The vows a king has given and the ambush that
   is "sure."

They strip the traitor naked and they whip him
   on his way
Into the barren hillsides like the folks he used
   to slay.
They take a thorough vengeance for the women
   he cut down

And then they mount their horses and they journey back to town.
Three things trust and cherish well, the horse
on which you ride,
The beast that guards and watches and the sister at your side!

For further information on these songs, send a
stamped, self-addressed envelope to:

FIREBIRD ARTS AND MUSIC
(formerly Off-Centaur Publications)
PO Box 424
El Cerrito, CA 94530

Mercedes Lackey

The Novels of Valdemar

DAW

A note from the publishers concerning:

QUEEN'S OWN

You are invited to join "Queen's Own," an organization o
readers and fans of the works of Mercedes (Misty) Lackey
This appreciation society has a worldwide membership of al
ages. Nominal dues are charged.

"Queen's Own" publishes a newsletter 9 times a yea
providing information about Mercedes Lackey's upcomin
books, tapes, convention appearances, and more. A networ
of pen friends is also available for those who wish to shar
their enjoyment of her work.

For more information, please send a business-size SAS
(self-addressed stamped envelope) to:

"Queen's Own"
P.O. Box 132
Shiloh, NJ 08353

*(This notice is inserted gratis as a service to readers. DA
Books is in no way connected with this organization profe
sionally or commercially.)*